cutting
teeth

cutting teeth

Julia Fierro

St. Martin's Press ⚏ New York

CUTTING TEETH. Copyright © 2014 by Julia Fierro. All rights reserved. Printed in the United States of America. For information, address St. Martin's Press, 175 Fifth Avenue, New York, N.Y. 10010.

www.stmartins.com

Designed by Steven Seighman

Library of Congress Cataloging-in-Publication Data

Fierro, Julia.
    Cutting teeth : a novel / Julia Fierro.
        pages cm
      ISBN 978-1-250-04202-6 (hardcover)
      ISBN 978-1-4668-3922-9 (e-book)
  I. Title.
    PS3606.I368C88 2014
    813'.6—dc23
                        2014008040

St. Martin's Press books may be purchased for educational, business, or promotional use. For information on bulk purchases, please contact Macmillan Corporate and Premium Sales Department at 1-800-221-7945, extension 5442, or write specialmarkets@macmillan.com.

First Edition: May 2014

10 9 8 7 6 5 4 3 2 1

For
Justin,
my everything

and

Luca and Cecilia,
who taught me to love
and be loved

contents

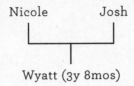

Nicole   Josh

Wyatt (3y 8mos)

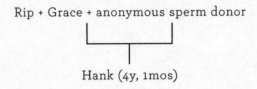

Rip + Grace + anonymous sperm donor

Hank (4y, 1mos)

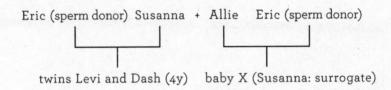

Eric (sperm donor) Susanna + Allie   Eric (sperm donor)

twins Levi and Dash (4y)   baby X (Susanna: surrogate)

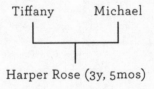

Tiffany   Michael

Harper Rose (3y, 5mos)

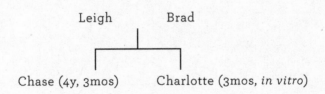

Leigh   Brad

Chase (4y, 3mos)   Charlotte (3mos, *in vitro*)

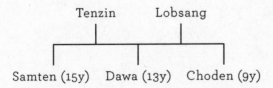

Tenzin   Lobsang

Samten (15y) Dawa (13y) Choden (9y)

Parents are the bones on which children cut their teeth.

—PETER USTINOV

Prologue

Thursday

red alert

Nicole

The playground was half-empty, as it is most late-summer Thursdays in the Brooklyn neighborhoods where the young professionals live. Those who summer, who go in with one or two couples and rent a cottage on Fire Island or out East. Those who eat organic and buy green and practice hot yoga and are in treatment and who name their children, without a second thought, after Greek goddesses and dead poets.

Nicole pushed her almost-four-year-old son Wyatt on the swings, his cries of *more more more* fading, then rising as he swayed back and forth. Dusk was settling, the smoky veil that had hinted at danger for as long as Nicole could remember. The gloaming. The word still made her think of restless spirits and mistrustful things, the ghoulish witches in the dark woods of her childhood.

The sun ricocheted off the sunglasses of the mother standing next to her, the spinning spokes of the tricycles, the side doors of the cars squeezed up and down the block, and Nicole shielded her eyes with her hand. The fumes from the ice-cream truck idling on the corner scratched at her throat.

The little girl in the next swing coughed, and Nicole steeled herself. The child had a wet phlegmy cough, after all, not a dry raspy cough, which is what the Centers for Disease Control had listed as symptoms. Warning signs.

Relax, Nicole thought. It's just a summer cold.

"Honey," the girl's mother said. "How do we cough?"

The little girl lifted her arm to her face and coughed in the direction of her elbow, all the while looking up at her mother, seeking her approval.

The mother smiled at Nicole with an apologetic shrug, and Nicole knew she was expected to commiserate.

She shook her head knowingly and pointed to Wyatt, still clad in his white karate uniform.

"I tell this guy the same thing. Every day."

The woman smiled, relieved. "They make you so paranoid, you know? All those hand-washing ads."

She was pretty, this fellow mother, and Nicole wished she had smoothed a little product into her own humidity-frizzed hair before leaving the house. Maybe some mascara to widen her tired eyes. As she gave Wyatt's swing a big push, she felt the extra weight in her thighs jiggle.

She tried to swing Wyatt away from the little girl who continued to cough, a cough so productive Nicole thought she could see the miniscule drops of saliva flying toward Wyatt's gaping mouth.

"Higher, higher, Mommy," he yelled. "Up in the sky. I'm an airplane. I'm a superhero. I'm a pterodactyl. The fastest pterodactyl in the world. Watch what I do!"

"Oh-kay," she said with a big exhale between syllables, "we have to go now."

She gripped the chain of the swing and stopped him too abruptly. Wyatt nearly flew out of the seat.

"I'm sorry, sweetie," she laughed. "Mommy's so silly."

"I don't want to go. I want to stay." His lower lip displayed a clownish quiver.

"I'm sorry. I really am. But we have to go, Mister."

Nicole was sorry. Sorry she was ruining his afternoon and, perhaps, she thought with a growing panic, ruining his life by visiting the park because she was certain the little girl was very ill, certain that within a few hours, the girl would be shivering with fever in bed, a nasal swab sample on its way to the hospital lab. Because isn't that what they said online, on the news, and in the handouts that had been given out at Wyatt's preschool? That it hit fast and hard? That you woke with a sore throat in the morning and by nightfall had a high fever, cough, chills, vomiting? She knew the incubation rate, the statistics, the symptoms, and the percentage of children—healthy children, robust children (like her Wyatt)—who had died. At first, Nicole had tried to avoid the news. She had even considered, at her husband Josh's prodding, disabling the wireless, shutting off the cable, but reminders were practically everywhere. In CNN's top headlines and most popular online searches. The death toll, the latest CDC reports. The public-service commercials with that ridiculous rhyme, *Know what to do about the flu.* She had googled "flu" and "swine flu" and "h1n1" so many times that the little ads that popped up in the margins of her e-mail were all for antibacterial hand soaps and flu remedies. *How to stay healthy. Ten ways to keep you and your family safe.*

Then, after so many months spent fearing the flu, Nicole had spotted, just the night before, the paranoid chatter on urbanmama.com, the online mommy message board she browsed regularly. Post after post by mothers fretting over rumors that some computers were predicting the world might end? Josh had laughed at her that morning when she told him, then laughed again when she had tried to explain what a Web bot was, all of which she had learned via Wikipedia. Web bots were superpower computers that scanned the Internet for patterns, and many of their predictions—9/11, the market crash, Oklahoma City, bird flu—had come true. Josh had muttered something about overeducated women with too much time on their hands, ignoring her pleas for him to *just google it*!

Thank God they'd be away that weekend. What luck that she'd scheduled the playgroup's Labor Day weekend trip to her parents' house out on Long Island. When she had first read about the rumor that morning, what the moms on urbanmama.com were calling a potential "catastrophic event," implying that it might take place that very weekend (Saturday night, to be exact), she had thought about canceling the playgroup's three-day vacation out East. But it had been such a hassle to find a weekend that worked for all five parents in the Friday afternoon playgroup, *and* their significant others. The e-mailing and texting, scheduling and rescheduling had gone on for weeks until they had found a weekend when they were all free. Nicole knew that if she canceled, she'd ruffle many a feather. A few of the parents had even arranged to take off work the next day. She could already hear Tiffany, with her sanctimonious tone, "It's just so cruel to disappoint the children, Nic. Don't you think?"

Wyatt's hands, white-knuckled, gripped the swing's chains.

Nicole leaned over him and whispered, her lips close to his flushed cheek, "You want a treat?"

She tucked her fingers into the sweat-damp curls at the back of his neck. Sweet little boy sweat that smelled of apple juice and cut grass. She inhaled, wishing she could stop time and bottle the smell—bottle Wyatt even—because one day it would all be over. Wyatt would be a harsh-smelling hard-angled man. She and Josh would be old. Dead.

A plane passed overhead. A whoosh that built and built until it seemed to Nicole that a great big hand had unzipped the sky, and she looked around to see if anyone else had heard it, had felt it, as a warning of some kind. A prelude to disaster. There were a few mothers looking up, shielding their eyes with freshly manicured hands. Was it too low? Nicole wanted to ask; did they think it was suspicious? The engines were awfully loud, weren't they? She snapped the rubber band on her wrist, an assignment from her therapist, pulling it farther away each time, the sting growing with each release. *Nothing bad is happening, nothing bad is happening.* She looked again at the sky to watch, to wait for the sign that all was clear, that it was just her ever-faulty interpretation she had, even as a child, doubted.

She was about to turn to the sick child's mother, to ask, *Did you feel that,* when something changed. What exactly, she couldn't say, but it was there, an offness that reminded Nicole of the light right before an eclipse, an other-worldly light, and she kept asking herself *What is it? What is it? What is happening?* She lunged for the chains of Wyatt's swing, jerking him up and out so fast his foot caught in the seat and he fell to the ground, his plump fingers splayed in the dirt. *This is it, this is it.* The panic buzzed in her chest, and there was a sudden adjustment in her vision, like she could see through goddamned walls.

It was only the pink chemical blush of the overhead streetlamps coming on. A child behind her yelled *pretty, lights,* and Nicole heard comfort in the little girl's voice. She, too, wanted to be fearless.

She pressed Wyatt's face to her chest, hiding that silent openmouthed wail, the precursor to great gulping cries. She shushed him, whispering, "Sorry, baby, sorry."

Nicole let out a shuddering sigh as Wyatt's screams arrived. Yes, she thought, what a relief it would be to go away that weekend. Even if there was just a tiny chance those silly end-of-the-world predictions might come true. At least her little boy would not be in the city when it happened.

URBANMAMA.COM A Community and Forum for Parents

Welcome to UrbanMama, an anonymous forum where you can interact in sincere and open-minded conversation with other parents.

Speak your mind and share your thoughts about parenting, family life, marriage, relationships, and everything that makes you an urbanmama!

Sign up now!   Already a member, log in!

Web bots predict a catastrophic event on September 4
Posted 9/1/2010   8:43pm

(18 replies)

—what is web bots? 8:43pm

—they're predicting something for THIS Saturday? creepy. 8:46pm

   —for real? 8:48pm

   —on Labor Day Weekend? Bummer. 8:48pm

—Here is a link: www.webbotpredictions.com   8:49pm

   —shit. really really wish I hadn't read that. 8:55pm

   —this is freaking me out. 9:30pm

—you're all egging each other on into hysteria. chill the fuck out. 9:33pm

—things do not feel right to me. 10:28pm

   —me too. my hubby is making fun of me, but I can't help it. I am scared. 10:31pm

   —put on your tinfoil hat, sister. 10:34pm

—can someone summarize the impending crisis, please?
10:46pm

>—RE: summary (from the site) "The sort of agony, grief,
>and pain felt in the six days following 9/11 will be felt
>for five and a half months" 10:48pm

—Where do you find this shit? 10:52pm

—yeesh. wtf is this? 10:58pm

—scary 11:04pm

—who/what are the web bots? 11:09pm

—is it safe in NYC? should we evacuate? 11:11pm

The last post, at 11:11 P.M., had been Nicole's.

As a child, at elementary-school sleepovers, she and her girlfriends had made a wish when the clock struck 11:11, as if the synchronicity was unique to them, a sign fortune was on their side. For each and every wish: at 11:11, at the side of a fountain with a handful of coins in her sweaty little hand, and with the sharp intake of breath before extinguishing her birthday candles, she said the same wish. More of a plea. *Dear God, please keep me safe. Please don't let anyone or anything bad hurt me.*

She still whispered the words every night before bed. When Wyatt was born almost four years earlier, the *me* had turned into *us*.

But when Nicole had read about the Web bot prediction the night before, and the rumor that something truly terrible would happen, there had been nothing she could tell herself (*nothing bad is happening, nothing bad is happening*) to calm her instinct to flee.

She'd been visiting urbanmama.com; reading, posting a few comments, as was her nightly ritual, to see what the mommies' hot topics were that day (to circumcise or *not* to circumcise, breast vs. the bottle, time-out vs. talk-it-out), and to check if there was news of (*fingers crossed!*) openings in that year's highly coveted Pre-K at the local public school.

Wyatt and Josh were forgotten, but for the whistling of their snores. After midnight, it felt to Nicole as if an enchantment had fallen over the city. The screech of the bus banished, the car horns muted, even the trucks rumbling over the Brooklyn-Queens Expressway subdued into a soft tremor under her feet. She knew she should go to bed, that she'd wake tired and irritable, but in this newish mommy life, the sacrifice of sleep for a few hours of still and silent solitude was worth the exhaustion.

As a child growing up in the outer suburbs, on a wooded road without streetlamps, Nicole had feared the night. Loathed the open-ended *what-ifs* darkness invited. Her phobia had worsened over the years until she grew to fear even the darkness of a familiar room, the fumbling for the light switch that seemed to ridicule her vulnerability.

Now, the night was her refuge.

The day was for doing. For organizing and reorganizing. For finagling. For dealing with Wyatt's tantrums and his resistance to eating vegetables, to dressing himself, to wiping his own butt. The negotiations. *Yes, you can play with Mommy's tweezers if you promise to take your nap. Sure, you can cover yourself in Band-Aids, as long as you eat your broccoli.*

Daytime had expectations of Nicole. She had to drop Wyatt off at preschool (two hours of respite, just enough time to take a shower and clean the apartment), usher him to karate, toddler tom-tom drumming class, and playdates. Each interaction felt fraught with the possibility of conflict—with other mothers, between Wyatt and other children, and, of course, with Wyatt himself. Although Nicole knew that life with one healthy (knock on wood) child was a relatively easy one (what about those Orthodox women she saw on the train, seven children in tow?), it often felt as if even the most simple tasks were a test to prove to herself that she was a good mother after all.

By the end of the long day, when Josh finally returned from work, she heard a tone in her voice (he was always complaining about her tone)—a pathetic desperation. As if she were an impoverished third-world mother with a disease-riddled baby. As if she had to roam the streets begging and whoring herself to put food in her children's bloated bellies. As if she, a privileged American housewife, had just narrowly escaped disaster. Which was, she thought, exactly who she was, and exactly how she felt.

When they returned home from the playground—Wyatt still pouting after his fall from the swing, "Mommy, you hurt me," he said—Nicole was already longing for the night. But the late-summer, late-afternoon light was still strong as it streamed through their windows. Josh would not be home for another three hours.

They performed the routine stripping of clothes, both she and Wyatt down to their underwear (you never knew where a pair of bedbugs might lurk these days). She heated up a vacuum-packed roast from Trader Joe's and lip-synced to an entire Raffi album, which made Wyatt laugh and finally stop complaining about his boo-boo and the tear in his karate pants.

Nicole had sworn to herself she wouldn't go online, she wouldn't google "Web bot end-of-world prediction," she wouldn't reread the warnings on urbanmama.com.

Then she was logging on, posting a few benign questions about alternative preschools in her neighborhood (*best Montessori in Cobble Hill? thx!*), switching pediatricians (*Dr. Zimmerman's office smells like puke!*), and a request for advice on a good handheld vacuum. Then she found herself tapping the refresh button on her laptop, waiting, waiting for someone to respond to her new post titled *end-of-world stuff serious??* And, in what she hoped would read as a self-deprecating tone, *neurotic mama freaked about world ending this weekend.*

Sure enough there were mocking responses, like, *get a grip, sister* and *oh, God, it's alarmist mom* (she could hear the eye roll in that one) and the scathing *quick, run to the supermarket and stock up, you stupid cunt,* but there were also those who responded with a fear too suggestive of her own—*oh, shit, maybe I should go to my mom's in Jersey* and *first swine flu, now this?* The sound of fear in another anonymous mother's voice was enough for Nicole's mind to grab and roll and knead until she could see the future clearly. The emptied supermarkets. The looters. The disease. The end.

She felt like a fool when she thought of it—*the end of days*. Like she was some right-wing evangelical. Or one of those people who believed the Mayan prediction that the world would end in 2012. But talk of *the end* was everywhere. Armageddon. Apocalypse. By flood. By tsunami. By flaming asteroid. Shortage of water and food was inevitable, claimed even the most rational voices on NPR—the only news (at Josh's firm suggestion) Nicole allowed herself. Despite her news purge, she caught the headlines on the stand in front of the convenience store and watched snippets of the primetime news while on line at the pizzeria. The ads plastered across the subway walls announced new apocalyptic movies—via plague, zombies, earthquake, fire and/or ice. Novels set in dystopian landscapes lined the shelves of bookstores. Autism rates were skyrocketing, the ozone depleting, and you couldn't eat a tuna sandwich because of the mercury. The world was a mess, and people were terrified; there was no denying it.

Despite her outward nonchalance (she had friends who actually called her laid-back), after Wyatt was born, when all she had at stake multiplied exponentially, she had come to see that terrible things—the witches and boogeymen of her childhood nightmares—could, and did, happen during the day. An airplane, once a benign sight, could slice open the world on a perfect blue morning. A pair of psychopaths could take a high school hostage as the lunch bell rang. You, yes *you*, could receive mail coated in white dust. You could be pushed into the path of the A train by God knows what kind of mentally deranged person. And what about that woman on the West Side who was walking her dog—electrocuted when she stepped on a seemingly innocent manhole cover?

Measles in Park Slope. Mumps in Midwood. And the bees were disappearing.

Years ago, in college, the dying bees had been the talk at parties while a blunt was passed, discussed with irreverence unique to youth. Now, years later, Nicole couldn't stop worrying about the bees. Among other things.

It would be safer out on Long Island, wouldn't it? She knew the idea of fleeing the city was ridiculous. Because of a computer's prediction? So she revised. *It would be good to get away.* Yes, that was better. It was the Labor Day holiday, after all. Best to take advantage of the beach house while her parents were in Florida. To get a break from the end-of-summer heat that rose from beneath the sidewalks, sending cockroaches skittering to the surface after sunset. To squeeze in one last beach weekend before summer officially fled. And, she added, the playgroup would be so grateful.

For three years, Nicole, three other new moms, and one stay-at-home dad, had rotated hosting Friday afternoon play dates. Complete with wine and cheese for the parents, and goldfish crackers and juice boxes for the babies, now babies no more, all between three and four years old. The children had grown up together, taking first steps and uttering first words in each other's company. She owed it to them, Nicole thought, to follow through on her promise of a weekend at the beach.

Nicole found her iPhone and tapped out a text:

Hey! Hope to see y'all on the Gold Coast tomorrow! Forecast: sunny days & breezy nights. We have a baby pool, floaties, & sand toys for kiddies!
Bring sweaters for bonfire on beach! Mojitos await you . . .
xxxooo Nic

She then sent it to the whole playgroup: to Leigh (mommy to Chase and Charlotte), Rip (daddy to Hank), and Susanna (mommy to twins Dash and Levi). Even, after some thought, to Tiffany (mommy to Harper), who was a bit high maintenance and always in some kind of disagreement with one or another of the playgroup parents.

Nicole set Wyatt's dinner (carefully cut pork cubes and steamed broccoli) in front of him and paused the episode of *Blue's Clues,* breaking his iPad-induced trance.

"Don't forget to take bites," she sang. "Or I'll have to turn off the show."

"Okay," Wyatt said as he stared at the iPad screen, waiting for the man who dressed like a boy to reappear.

"Mommy's going to the bathroom. 'Kay?"

She locked herself in the bathroom, rolled a towel, and tucked it at the bottom of the door.

Fan on.

Window open.

She heard Wyatt on the other side of the wall, singing along with the man-boy on TV, trilling enthusiastically of the joys of brushing your teeth. *Make them sparkle! Make them shine!*

She steadied the glass pipe (purchased at Lollapalooza almost twenty years ago) on the sink and slipped the small purple plastic box—her weed-delivery guy's signature—from the rolled-up socks she kept hidden in a box of tampons under the sink.

Opening the plastic purple box was part of her ritual. The smell, both sweet and sour, reminded her of the scent of good old clean dirt under a child's nails on a midsummer afternoon.

She caught her reflection in the mirror. The bud was lifted to her nose, the red hairs glimmering as if coated with fine sugar. She would have laughed if she had been someone else, watching a grown woman prepare to get stoned with such ceremony. A mom. A thirty-five-year-old woman hiding in her bathroom.

She stuffed the pipe's bowl with fluffy green buds, and before she lit up, she found the device, an invention reclaimed from her college days, which had taken her just a few minutes to re-create. The cardboard tube from a paper-towel roll, a scented dryer sheet taped over one end.

The first pull. The glass stem clicking against her teeth. The heat scratching at the back of her throat. The fullness of her lungs. The sense of safety was immediate, as if her body were saying, "Okay, now. There it is, Nicole. Oh. Kay."

Nicole blew the smoke through the cardboard tube, and the bathroom smelled of fresh laundry.

They were tiny puffs. *Little sips, really,* she reassured herself. And what did it matter, when those tiny puffs chased away the worry that bullied her each day. She imagined the smoke's curled fingers kneading her shoulders, her neck, her jaw, her brain, delivering the calm she needed but without the drab side effects that came with the Zoloft she'd started taking soon after Wyatt was born.

She had been so nervous to call the dealer's pager number—a gift from her hairstylist. Nicole had held on to the Post-it note until, finally, three months ago, after she had stopped the Zoloft, the anxiety returning, flooding her system like a virus, she had made the call. Her fingers had fumbled when she opened the door for the delivery guy with his knapsack of purple plastic boxes, each packed with a cluster of dewy buds.

Five more pulls, each followed by a spritz from the fig-scented ambiance mist her acupuncturist had recommended. Five was her lucky number. It made her think of one person surrounded by two on each side. Protected.

Nicole was relaxed now. It felt as if the sharp edges of life had blurred, softened, been capped with those plastic triangles she had suctioned to the corners of the coffee table after Wyatt was born. Just to be safe.

With the premium red-haired marijuana ($85 a quarter ounce), Nicole felt *okay*. Like she could handle anything. In those few hours of weed-cushioned calm, she had started to think that maybe she could finish the novel she'd been working on for six years, maybe she could be a better mother, a better wife, and maybe, just maybe, she could stay off her meds. Josh had been insistent she stay on the Zoloft, despite her attempts at explaining how sluggish, how blah it made her feel. She hadn't told him when she'd stopped taking it.

In life before Wyatt and Zoloft, her favorite conversational adjectives had been "amazing" and "exquisite." After Wyatt was born, when she'd fallen into what their pediatrician called the baby blues (she'd wanted to stab him every time he used the phrase), and accepted his prescription for Zoloft, she felt flat, like she'd been transformed into one of the one-dimensional stock characters she lectured against in the undergrad Creative Writing 101 classes she taught twice a week at City College. Where were her highs and lows, the dips and valleys that made life so varied, so interesting? Where was her material?

Writing was impossible. Even reading anything more challenging than a mediocre thriller felt intolerable. Why read when she could sit in front of the television in the few hours between when Wyatt fell asleep and when exhaustion defeated her?

The Z made everything feel so *whatever*, she had told her psychiatrist, Dr. Greenbaum, who claimed (with a condescending chuckle) that this middle zone was healthy. He suggested she experiment with lowering the Z, five milligrams at a time, to find a happy medium between anxious and sedated. But the lowering of the dose was like a drug in itself. With every five-milligram drop, Nicole could feel the lifting of her spirits (and she wasn't one to use a cliché lightly).

Four months ago, in the height of the swine-flu panic, she had quit therapy. Without calling, without e-mailing. She deleted the messages Dr. Greenbaum left on her phone without listening to them, an action that gave her a deliciously empowering thrill. She was free of having to listen to her unlikable self in therapy as she recited the dreadful *what-ifs* circling her mind. *What if Wyatt's sore throat was the first symptom of h1n1? What if terrorists bombed Josh's subway train? What if the lump in her neck was cancer?*

She was down to only twenty-five milligrams of Z per day when her thoughts returned. Brilliant thoughts, genius even! A crystal-clear memory (her first kiss), a fantasy (her next novel idea), an observation (oh, how many people there are yearning their way through life).

Hello! Where have you been? Her thoughts hadn't disappeared; they had been trapped under the mellowing blanket of Z. Under Wyatt's whining, under the tinny songs his toys played over and over, under her own voice that was always prodding Wyatt. *Use your words, honey. Use your words.*

She decided she was through with medication, and despite the rocky months that followed, Josh's complaints she was irritable, erratic, unstable—all those words starting with negative prefixes—she had stayed strong.

With a little help from the monthly delivery of purple plastic boxes.

*   *   *

The first text was from Susanna, mom to twins, who the parents in the play-group called (with affection, of course) the lesbian mommy. Cheerful and rosy-cheeked, Susanna, Nicole thought, would've made a perfect soccer mom in another life, despite the fact that Allie, Susanna's partner and some kind of vi-sual artist, was Susanna's opposite—pale, dangerously thin. Black turtlenecks. Black skinny jeans. Allie reminded Nicole of the goth kids who had moved like zombies through the corridors of her high school.

Susanna:

We'll be there. Two newly hitched mommies and two little monsters arriving round 5!

Nicole:

congrats!!! glad Allie finally made an honest woman of you. ;) see you tom!

Her phone buzzed with two more texts.

First Leigh, the playgroup's resident debutante. A blue-blooded blonde, whose slim frame looked chic draped in just about anything. Cheap Old Navy, white jeans, horizontal stripes, even pastels—on Leigh everything looked de-signer. There was something a bit Grace Kelly-esque about Leigh, Nicole had always thought. Maybe if Grace Kelly were constipated.

Leigh:

Thank you, Nicole. Looking forward.

Rip, the playgroup's only dad came next:

woo-hoo! we'll bring the tequila. body shots!!

Nicole knew Rip was sure to show up in his uniform of frayed cargo shorts and faded tee. His straw fedora crushed over unruly brown curls. Rip's hipster dad-look was cute. Carefully assembled to look as if it were *not* carefully assembled. But just when Nicole thought she saw a glimpse of something attractive in Rip, he ruined it with an overeager comment, like calling himself a feminist too often and with too much gusto. Or a careless mistake, like arriving sockless at playgroup (there was a strict no-shoe rule at all their homes) so they had to stare at his hairy toe knuckles all afternoon.

Last, came a text from Tiffany. Sultry and unpredictable, Tiffany was the wild card in the playgroup. She knew how to work her perfectly placed curves and rusty Aphrodite-length hair.

Tiffany:

oh sweetie. the serenity of the beach sounds divine. you are SO good to us.

* * *

Night had arrived at last. The ten to fifteen minutes before Josh arrived was Nicole's favorite time, and although she knew it was wrong, this was when she loved Wyatt most, knowing that the day—and her shift—would soon end.

She missed him already, she thought, as she hovered over her little boy. His eyes were frozen to the iPad while Lightning McQueen raced across the screen.

"I like it when you are still," she whispered as she knelt next to him, close enough to see his chest lift, his belly fill, with each breath, "That's a Pablo Neruda poem. I gave it to a boy in college. The first boy I ever loved."

She felt awkward, as if performing, but continued, "He broke my heart."

She leaned forward, her nose and lips an inch from Wyatt's cheek. It was a game she played to see how close she could get before he pushed her away. Her boy looked down his nose at her, his eyes nearly crossed, and said, "You're a pretty girl, Mommy."

He knew this always made her smile, and she knew he was hoping she'd say yes to more TV.

"Mmm," she said. "You always smell good after your bath. Like a milkshake."

"One more show, Mommy? Please?"

"Sure. Just one more before Daddy gets home."

She stroked his cheek. As soft as a kitten's ear.

"Mama's going to take care of you, pumpkin. She's never going to let anyone, or anything hurt you. Promise."

"Okay, Mommy," he said, nudging her away. "Can I watch *Spider-Man*?"

Part 1

Friday

babe in the wood

Allie

Allie called the playgroup Mommy Camp. This had made Susanna laugh at first, when they were new mothers juggling the fussy twin boys Susanna had birthed, when their clothes, the urban artist's uniform of all black, showed every spot of spit-up and streak of snot. But lately, Allie's jokes sounded, even to Allie, like the jabs of an outsider. Instead of life feeling like *us vs. them,* it felt like *Allie vs. Susanna.*

They had been driving for over an hour, Levi and Dash asleep in the backseat, when the map on Allie's phone directed them off the main road. Susanna drove onto a causeway flanked by the wind-whipped waves of the Long Island Sound. The narrow road was dotted with trees; their branches stripped white, gnarled by the salt wind.

"You didn't say the beach house was this far," Allie said, as the sun bounced off the water, assaulting her eyes. She sank into the passenger seat and pulled the hood of her black sweatshirt over her head.

She had been up most of the night color-correcting a cover photo she'd shot for a Danish magazine. She was behind on the deadline after their three-day trip (with the boys, Susanna had insisted), to Massachusetts, where they'd been married at the Northampton town hall. Then Levi, the more demanding of their boys, had woken at four this morning, shuffling into their room, his thick honey-dusted hair spilling into his eyes. He had begged to join Susanna and Allie in their bed, and Susanna had relented. Not for the first time, Allie had thought about how Susanna coddled the twin who looked most like her. Susanna and Levi looked as if they belonged on a Swiss mountaintop, herding goats. Yodeling. Dash, the more diminutive twin, took after Allie, or at least after Eric, their beloved sperm donor and good friend whose appearance had matched Allie's brother. Straight brown hair. Skin so pale you could see the green veins that crisscrossed his temples.

"Oh," Susanna gushed, "it's amazing. Should we stop? Look, we can pull over right there and look at the water."

"Wait. The boys." Allie sprang forward. "They'll wake if we stop."

When the boys had simultaneously fallen asleep in Queens after thirty minutes of gridlock, it had felt like a gift from who-knows-who-or-what. Allie was an atheist, like most of the artists, filmmakers, and designers who made up her and Susanna's elite New York City circle. Still, she thought, they should wring every drop from the blessing.

"Please," Allie pleaded softly, "sweetheart. Let's keep going. I have to pee, and my head is killing me."

Silently, Susanna accelerated, the eight-month-sized globe of her belly bumping the steering wheel. Allie could see, in the tightness under Susanna's jaw, that she had, once again, said the wrong thing.

"Maybe the pregnant woman carrying your baby is the one who has to pee," Susanna said. With the quick-fire anger of a woman in her last term, Allie thought.

"I'm sorry," Allie said. "That was selfish."

She couldn't help adding, "It's not a competition, you know." She knew that this, in Susanna's mind, negated the apology, but Susanna's tone irked her, the "you-owe-me-big-time" tone Susanna used more and more as she neared the end of her pregnancy.

Our pregnancy, Allie thought, correcting herself, though she preferred to call the pregnancy "the egg swap." She found levity worked best when describing their situation to her childless friends, all immersed in a world of unscheduled and unbridled creation, and who she bumped into at the few SoHo gallery shows she could get to these days.

Susanna, my partner, is carrying my egg, fertilized with the sperm of our twins' father, aka, our homo best friend. Ba dum bump! Like a punch line.

Some of these friends, like Allie, had been Susanna's teachers years ago when she was a student at the Parsons School of Design, and they relished in teasing Allie. *You knocked up your student, did ya?* This made Allie smile and remember that other Susanna—Susie, she'd corrected Allie (Professor Strong) on that first day of class over a decade ago, her high ponytail swinging.

The sleek European station wagon (Susanna had wanted a minivan of all things, but Allie had prevailed) wound around the curved road. The sun flickered through the canopy of trees, some already splashed with autumn gold, and Allie imagined herself in her studio, painting, mixing colors until she found a match for the green-gold that unfurled like silk streamers above. Hot coffee. Lou Reed. Guilt-free smokes. But the fantasy dissipated as Susanna began to talk about her new business, a rental stroller franchise, Babes-on-the-Go!™.

When Allie had first heard the name of the franchise, she'd responded with another instance of zero self-control.

"You realize, hon," she'd said, "some yuppie folk might confuse this stroller company with a traveling stripper show. You know? Babes-on-the-Go?"

She had yanked her gray tee up (she'd been braless since college, since coming out) and jiggled her small breasts.

Susanna had said, "not funny," but when Allie repeated the joke (sans flashing) at a dinner with their art friends, Susanna had laughed the loudest.

Since Babes-on-the-Go! had entered their lives, Allie was expected to watch Dash and Levi on weekends while Susanna descended into the co-op building basement now overrun with the monstrous double strollers and stacks of car seats Susanna rented to desperate Brooklyn parents. Susanna spent hours down there, repairing tires, adjusting alignment, and scrubbing the child travel systems, which is how Allie had heard Susanna describe them when on the phone with a rental customer. Allie was left in charge (Susanna's favorite phrase these days), and when the boys' play inevitably turned to roughhousing, she put on a movie. Something a tad too mature, like *Spider-Man* or *Iron Man*, guaranteed to keep them subdued in terror. When Allie heard the creak of the stairs, she quickly turned off the TV and gave the boys a double wink before Susanna rose from the basement—her hair curled with sweat, her hands kneading her lower back, her newly popped belly jutting forth. Allie was pretty sure most part-time parents, like herself, used the secret-TV trick when their parenting partners had their backs turned.

They drove by the entrance to a lush overgrown park—Caumsett State Historic Park, the sign read. They were way out in the middle of nowhere, Allie thought, and she'd be screwed if there were crap wireless at the beach house.

Her agent was shopping her next book of photography around, the deadline for the Danish cover was in just a few hours, and there was also the panel she was hosting at the upcoming Parsons School of Design Fall Symposium.

"Did I tell you I found a Phil and Ted double stroller?" Susanna said, with an excitement that jolted Allie.

"That's great," Allie said, feigning enthusiasm.

Her phone buzzed. Speak of the devil. A message from her agent. A gig shooting female comedians for a magazine layout. *Hot,* she typed back.

"It's not just great. It's really great," Susanna said, and although Allie could hear the growing annoyance in Susanna's voice, she continued to text. $?

"You think you could stop that and listen to me?" Susanna asked. "Please? Remember the promise you made? Email-checking, texting, tweeting. Limited this weekend. Okay?"

"Sorry. It's a work thing," Allie said, stuffing the phone into the back pocket of her skinny black Rag & Bone jeans.

"You'll get cancer if you keep carrying that phone on your body," Susanna said. "Didn't you read that article I forwarded you? This isn't just me. This is *science* talking."

Allie tossed her phone onto the dashboard, where it slid with a clatter against the windshield. Both women sucked in their breath, shooting glances at the boys in the back. Their collective fear made them smile.

"What pussies we are," Allie whispered.

She reached over and squeezed Susanna's hand. Susanna's face had grown fuller each week and now, with the scheduled C-section only a month away, she looked younger. Her nose was dotted with summer freckles like an apple-cheeked farm girl, and for a moment, with the backdrop of the leaves and overgrown grass on the side of the road, Allie felt a humming desire. She imagined a girlish Susanna (without the belly bump) stretched out on dewy grass, Susanna's hips bucking against Allie's face. She was about to dip her fingers under Susanna's thin cotton maternity skirt when Susanna spoke.

"We need the extra Babes-on-the-Go money," Susanna said. "For your adoption fees."

Allie sighed. "I know."

Susanna was always reminding her that Allie would have to adopt the baby once it was born. As if what Susanna really wanted to say was, *Sure, it's your egg, but it's still my baby.*

"And so you can take off work," Susanna added, and Allie felt Susanna waiting for a response.

She wasn't going to talk about *that* again. She couldn't take more than two weeks off, and that was final.

She pulled her hand out of Susanna's.

"Your hands are like mini freaking heat pads," she said.

A pregnant woman's body temperature rises ten degrees above normal, she remembered. Just one of the pregnancy facts Susanna shared daily.

"I know you think the stroller business is duller than dull," Susanna said.

"You're not dull," Allie said, sighing.

"I didn't say *I* was dull," Susanna said.

Allie thought she heard a small indignant *huh*. As in, *so that's what you think of me.*

"I'm glad you have something to do besides take care of the boys," Allie said, eager to shift the mood. "Maybe you can save the stroller rental money and get more babysitting hours. And then," she paused, daring herself, "you can get back to your art."

Susanna sighed. "The boys are my art for now. I have the rest of my life to be selfish."

Allie felt Susanna's eyes leave the road and flash to her face.

"Plus," Susanna said, now more sweetly, "I don't think there's enough room for two artists in this family."

Allie stared ahead. She wasn't going to give Susanna's passive-aggressive BS a reaction.

Susanna leaned over the steering wheel and looked up at the sky, a perfect blue corridor running between the trees.

"But it *is* so beautiful here. I mean, really," she said. "Don't you think?"

And for a moment, as she let the sunglasses slip down her nose, Allie could forget Susanna's question was a test, and she could see the beauty. The restless white-tipped waves tossing driftwood—a bleached-out black-and-white photograph waiting for Allie's capture. The tree canopy shimmering like aged bronze. The sky that cerulean blue paint they had brought back from Venice in their life before children. The sunlight that yellow from Sedona, hand-mixed by a tired old Navajo woman. Places they wouldn't visit again for years, not until the boys had grown, not until the care of this new baby—*my* baby, she reminded herself—had become manageable. The thought of the dirty-diaper, runny-nose, tantrum-filled delay, the unreachable future freedom, suddenly exhausted her.

"We could move here," Susanna said.

Allie knew it had taken courage for Susanna to say this because if there was one disagreement they had worn to death, it was the city vs. the 'burbs debate.

"The city is close enough," Susanna continued. "I looked it up online. There's a direct train. Forty-five minutes to Penn Station."

"It *is* pretty," Allie tried, too tired to get into it, to recite her usual lines. "Maybe someday."

"We don't want to wait until the boys are too old. They might get used to the city. Levi cries when he sees a mosquito!" Susanna laughed, and it clanged false to Allie.

"Levi cries about everything." Allie knew she had said it too loudly because Susanna threw a glance over her shoulder.

"You need to be more thoughtful," Susanna said. "He could've heard you."

Allie often forgot that the boys had grown old enough to listen, to learn, to repeat, to have their feelings hurt. No longer impulsive cavemanlike toddlers immune to threat or negotiation. Susanna had lectured Allie on how, sometimes, honest can be too honest.

"What was your favorite thing about yesterday?" Allie asked.

"Nice topic change," Susanna teased. "You think I don't know you by now?" But she smiled when she said it and reached over and squeezed Allie's hand, bringing Allie's fingers to her bow-shaped lips.

Levi had the same lips, Allie thought. Both Susanna's and Levi's bottom lip quivered when they cried. The day before at the courthouse in Massachusetts, when the judge had declared them legally wed, Susanna's lip had seemed to tremble, then she had thrown her arms around Allie's neck, her abundant belly pressing into Allie's diaphragm. For a moment, Allie hadn't been able to breathe. Then she'd been swaddled in that sweet scent that was Susanna's alone, that Allie had loved for nearly twelve years. Like a newly flowering almond tree.

Usually iffy about public affection, Allie had reminded herself all day. *Hold Susanna's hand.* After the courthouse, at the bohemian-chic restaurant where they'd brunched with Eric, who the boys called Daddy and who had traveled to Northampton for the ceremony, and the boys in the matching seersucker suits Susanna had picked out (Allie had lobbied for blazers and skinny jeans). *Kiss her. Tell her you love her.* Allie hated that she had to remind herself to do these things, but, as she had told Susanna many times, it was who she was. It was how Allie's people were made. On holidays, Susanna's family greeted each other with kisses on the lips. Allie's father had never and, it seemed, *could* never, tell Allie or her brother he loved them. As kids, they had taunted him, repeating, "I love you, Dad! I love you, Dad!" until he had shouted at them to *cut it out.*

"Okay, I'll go first," Allie said with a deep sigh, as if she was clearing the air. "My favorite part was how hot you looked in your fancy schmancy Diane Von Furstenburg maternity dress."

Susanna smiled, and Allie thought she saw a release in Susanna's grip on the steering wheel.

"Thanks for wearing the corsage," Susanna said. "I know you didn't want to."

Eric, a lover of all things beautiful, who threw elaborate dinner parties and whose Chelsea studio apartment was never without a vase or two of fresh flowers, had surprised them with a bouquet of white calla lilies for Susanna. And a single white lily corsage for Allie.

"For you, baby?" Allie said. "I'll stick a flower in my lapel."

She slid her hand over Susanna's belly—her fingers, the nails gnawed, looked child-sized against the cloth-draped orb.

"How's our baby girl?" Allie asked.

"Oh, don't start that again," Susanna said and shook her head slowly, as if Allie was a disobedient child who should know better.

"I know," Allie said, "and *you* know, you want a girl too."

"I truly don't care. As long as it's healthy."

It had been Susanna's idea to keep the sex of the baby a surprise, and that was fine, Allie thought, but Susanna's feigned indifference toward the penis vs. vagina preference sounded a bit holier-than-thou to Allie.

"Lace-trimmed socks," Allie cooed as if teasing one of the twins. "Pink bows in ponytails. And those ruffly underwear you see sticking out from under their little dresses. What do you call those things?"

"Bloomers?" Susanna laughed, and Allie was relieved to see her easy smile.

Then Susanna let out a wet-sounding belch and winced.

"You okay? Need to pull over?" Allie asked.

"I'm fine," Susanna said through a slow exhale.

She sniffed furiously at her wrist, the inside of which, Allie knew, Susanna dabbed with lavender-scented oil. To combat yet another side effect of the pregnancy, what Susanna called her superhuman sense of smell.

"Are you going to puke?"

"I'm fine," Susanna stuttered as she breathed through her nose, her wrist tucked under her nostrils. "Just don't." She paused to inhale. "Don't talk."

Allie knew she should say something. A few gentle words to help Susanna's pulsing blood pressure drop, to make the reflux settle back down in Susanna's gut. Couldn't Allie pretend—for Susanna's sake, for the baby's sake—that they *would* buy the four-bedroom Cape, the one Susanna searched for in the real-estate listings every weekend, they *would* plant a kitchen garden, fence in a big yard for the boys, renovate the little cottage in back. *Voila!* An art studio for the two women to share. Maybe they'd even adopt a dog. Hadn't Dash been asking for a pet?

No, Allie couldn't pretend. Despite Susanna's deep breathing and the defeated hunch of her back—the back Allie had painted and photographed and even copied in clay when it was pure muscle and bone, when the taut tendons in Susanna's neck had defined all that was beauty and art and youth and sex and love.

She knew she had the power to make Susanna happy, maybe even beautiful again, but Allie couldn't help feeling her own anger. That they weren't at a bed-and-breakfast out on the Cape, just the two of them on a naked honeymoon. Emptied oyster shells and chocolate-candy-bar wrappers on the bedside table. The windows cracked to let in the salt-crisped air. Or showering together after uninterrupted sex, the kind of sex where you didn't whisper a moan, you didn't freeze midstroke and look at the bedroom door, waiting for it to burst open, a sleepy boy whining that he had to pee. They certainly could have left the boys with Eric. He had even offered to take them back to NYC for the night, for a *Dadurday*, Eric taking the boys to a café for brunch the next day, somewhere he was sure to bump into his friends, many ex-lovers, many hoping to be, and show off his progeny.

But *no*, the day before, Susanna had reminded Allie of the invite for a weekend out East, something from one of the "mommies" in Susanna's playgroup. They had bickered—Allie demanding Susanna cancel (*They were getting married, for fucksake*), and Susanna calling Allie out on what they both knew

was bullshit, reminding Allie that she hadn't cared about getting married anyway. An hour spent snapping at each other as they got the boys ready for bed—
until Susanna burst into pregnant-woman-pitched tears, promising Allie
(between sobs) that they'd get away soon and have a real honeymoon. Allie had
been the one to apologize—again—the defeated opponent of every bout they'd
had since the twins were born.

The woman hosting the weekend had gotten hold of Allie's cell number,
and Allie's and Susanna's phones had dinged simultaneously with the arrival
of every exclamation-point-laden, smiley-face-emoticon-punctuated response
from the moms in the playgroup, and the one dad who wrote, with what she
hoped was irony,

woo-hoo! we'll bring the tequila. body shots!!

Here they were, Allie thought, moving closer and closer to a destination
where the talk would be of what viruses had recently ravaged the children's immune systems, of the preschool drama that never ceased to bring a sparkle of
urgency to Susanna's eye, and the minutiae of day-to-day child-rearing that
made Allie feel as if life were running out. That by the time they woke from the
monotonous half slumber of parenthood, they'd be old, probably get cancer or
something, have just a little time left to be Allie and Susanna, to live the life
they had shared before.

Susanna pointed toward the glove compartment.

"Get me one of those candy bars, Al?"

Allie couldn't stop herself.

She said, "I thought Dr. Patka told you no sweets. That chocolate made
heartburn worse?"

"*What* did you just say?"

Allie shrank back, the way she had as a girl each time her father confronted
her after she'd been caught in a lie or gotten detention (again) for doodling in
her textbook. He had used the same words when she tried to lie her way out of
punishment, usually a few licks on her bare legs with his belt. *What did you just
say?* As he bent to peer in her eyes.

"You know," Allie said, "that you have to be careful of what you eat?"

"Do you want me to puke?" Susanna asked quietly.

"No."

"Then give me the goddamn Snickers bar."

* * *

The sea cottage was shabby, bordering on decrepit: piles of junk near the front door, along with a tangle of driftwood and half a buoy. Allie practiced her smile as Susanna rang the doorbell.

"Lay-dies," sang the woman who answered the door, clad in a white tube top that showed off her bronzed skin.

Tiffany, thought Allie. The oversexed, self-righteous mommy Susanna always crabbed about.

"It's so exciting to have you here!" Tiffany said.

The woman, Allie thought, might as well have said, *Well lookee here, if it isn't those darn lesbians? How interesting!*

Awkward introductions followed—and reintroductions; one could never remember whom you had or hadn't met in the hazy, sleep-deprived early parenting years. There was Michael, Tiffany's baby daddy, a greasy-haired hipster dude. Then Nicole, whose parents owned the beach house; Rip, the sole daddy in the playgroup—springy with nervous energy—and finally Rip's wife, Grace, a boxy Asian woman, whose firm handshake made Allie wonder if she wasn't just a tad butch.

Allie looked out onto the living room full of kids. The light streaming in from the seaside windows turned the scene into a tableau. A twisted moral. Titled *Life After Children,* Allie thought. The twins were in a tussle certain to turn violent. A plump Asian boy (Rip and Grace's kid, Allie guessed) stood in the corner, his hand sunk into a bowl of M&Ms. There was just the one little girl, a long-limbed beauty whose scabbed knees peeked out from under her flowered sundress. Allie knew this was Harper, daughter of Tiffany—a child Susanna loathed almost as much as the girl's mother. Harper had just won a tug-of-war over a jump rope, and the loser, a flaxen-haired boy with an upturned nose, wailed. *Oh yes,* Allie thought, the crier must be Chase. She had heard Susanna speak of Chase's "behavioral issues" in a whisper, as if the boy had an unspeakable disease.

But it was the mommies that frightened Allie the most. *The mommies.* Must she really use that word, she had asked Susanna on the drive. Their sugary smiles, their kisses like pats on each other's cheeks, the exaggerated rolls of their eyes at their children. The daddies seemed harmless enough, shoulder shrugs punctuating most everything they said, as if they were embarrassed at the "crazy" situation they'd gotten themselves into. *Aw, shucks, parenthood.*

And where did Allie fit in?

With the mommies? Oh no, she thought, she was too much of a dyke, too part-time mommy for them.

With the daddies? Nah, a woman could never join those ranks.

She belonged to neither. And that was exactly the way she liked it.

out of sight,
out of mind

Leigh

Leigh closed her eyes and sank into the wicker chair, into the coppery sun that streamed through salt-streaked windows. Four-month-old Charlotte sucked sleepily on her nipple.

It was just as Nicole had promised. A lovely end-of-summer getaway filled with the scent of sunscreen and BBQ.

Maybe the last, Leigh thought with a shiver. Before autumn bore down, before everything withered in anticipation of the imprisonment of winter—every parent's cross to bear.

She wished she could lock herself in this moment forever. She and Charlotte. The warming sun and the shushing sea. A current of seaweed-scented air trickled through the window and the swaddle blanket draped over Charlotte rippled, tickling Leigh's naked breast. She shivered and pulled her cashmere cardigan over her shoulders. The screen door thwacked gently in the breeze, and beyond it, Leigh heard Tiffany's throaty laugh rise from the beach. Leigh had almost forgotten about the others, even about her own son Chase, who, Leigh thought with a guilty wince, was certain to disrupt this peace.

They would return soon.

It had been at least an hour since Tiffany had led the parade of children—like a voluptuous pied piper, Leigh thought—along with Nicole and the other parents down to the beach for what Tiffany had promised was *a seaside dance-a-thon*!

Tiffany's voice, the elongated vowels that sashayed from her ever-pouty lips, had always seemed seductive to Leigh, even when Tiffany was being playful with Chase and the other boys in the Monday afternoon Tiff's Riffs music classes. Especially, Leigh thought, when Tiffany's attention focused on Rip, the playgroup's token dad, whom Leigh found inauthentic and undergroomed.

Once a week, Leigh, with Chase and Charlotte, and the other playgroup parents and children, clapped, danced and even squirmed like caterpillars on the colorful mats at a local yoga studio in Tiffany's Tiff's Riffs classes. They sang songs about mermaids who drove taxicabs under the sea, about children who rode the F train to the moon—songs written by Tiffany herself. Songs that Leigh had, at first, disliked for their fantastical nature. She'd felt compelled to explain to Chase that cars couldn't really drive under the ocean.

As the familiar melodies trickled through the screen, as she stroked baby Charlotte's pale arm, memories of the day before crept in. The Olive Tree Preschool Fundraising Committee meeting. The sour heat of the rec room where the committee had met—just a few doors away from the classroom where Chase spent four mornings a week. The slither of queasy fear that had snaked through Leigh's gut as she, committee treasurer, had presented the group with the latest account balances—numbers she had tweaked again and again in the week leading up to the meeting.

Stop, she told herself, willing herself into the right now, into *mindful presence,* which is what Leigh's nanny, Tenzin, a Tibetan Buddhist, had taught her.

"Too much worrying not good for mommies," Leigh imagined Tenzin saying as she pressed her palms together—pleading or praying, Leigh wasn't sure which. "And worrying not good for mommies' babies either."

Now, now, now, Leigh chanted, in sync with the baby's sucking.

She's a Tibetan peace activist seeking U.S. asylum, Leigh had told the mommies four months ago when she had first hired Tenzin.

Wow, they had said, *how interesting.*

As if it were Leigh who was special.

She was relieved that her husband Brad had gone away that weekend. Giving her the excuse to book Tenzin for the trip to the beach house. Brad had been a pill since the stock market slumped three weeks ago, and Leigh had urged him to get away. Finally, he had arranged a four-day "man-cation" golfing in North Carolina with his three older brothers. Brad had openly disapproved of the weekend at Nicole's. Only because Tiffany was there, Leigh thought. He'd become suspicious—jealous even—of the time Leigh spent texting with Tiffany each night. He claimed to have a *feeling* about Tiffany.

"She's a slut," he'd said after a weekend playgroup brunch at their own brownstone, an event orchestrated to include the playgroup parents' significant others.

Leigh hadn't bothered to defend Tiffany. The woman did have a stripper-esque name, and there was something overtly sensual in the way she swiveled her hips and puffed her lips out cutely. But Leigh was certain Brad was making room for sluts of his own that weekend. A ritual of the Marshall boys' getaways was the mandatory visit to the local titty bar.

Since Tiffany had introduced Leigh to Tenzin over a year ago—Tenzin's effortless smiles and girlish laugh filling Leigh's life, she had needed Brad less and less, a sense of freedom she hadn't felt in years, not since Chase's birth al-most four years ago.

Never had she imagined that she would rely on Brad as she had in the months after Chase's birth. After the emergency C-section that had punctuated the failure of her dream birth plan, she had been grateful to Brad, who had taken a monthlong leave from his position at Manning & Lambert, the invest-ment firm founded by Leigh's father, August Lambert, III. They had strolled around the neighborhood on brisk spring mornings with their blue-eyed blond baby boy. The neighborhood grandmas in their polyester housedresses and slip-pers had climbed down their stoop steps to ooh and ah over cherubic Chase. *God bless him,* they said, and Brad had beamed.

But as soon as Chase's *behavior* (a term his therapists used) revealed itself before his first birthday, as soon as it became impossible to take him out of the house without an *episode* (more therapy-speak), Leigh had watched Brad retreat. Once they'd accepted that Chase was likely to have global delays that would affect the rest of his life (and theirs), Brad had emotionally disowned doe-eyed Chase.

Leigh knew Brad found it difficult to admire their son, even when Chase behaved. The first time Chase had sat at the table for an entire meal, instead of wandering around it (*Helen Keller–style,* Brad often joked aloud), Leigh had praised Chase, promised him they'd tell his therapists what a good boy he'd been, even served him a small scoop of ice cream for dessert—breaking the no-sugar commandment preached by those same therapists. Brad had sat there quietly, forcing a smile, and later suggested to Leigh that she was "handicap-ping" the boy by rewarding him for normal behavior. Brad had used the word most outlawed in the coded therapy-speak of the special-needs world. *Normal,*

Leigh thought now as the sun warmed the crown of her head and she let herself drift into half-sleep.

Charlotte had finally surrendered Leigh's breast, her blond-fuzzed head falling back, her lips parting, her sweet milky breath wafting upward.

And then they returned. A tsunami of whining and whimpering, the half-language/half-grunt speak of children between the ages of three and four.

There were demands of "juice, juice!"

Dimple-cheeked Wyatt and the twins—dark-haired Dash and honey-complexioned Levi—slid to their bellies, grasping for toy cars and trucks.

"Mine, mine!"

Leigh looked for Chase but did not see her son.

She did spot Rip's son Hank standing a few feet from the door, already whining, "*I* want a car too." Hank's eyes were swollen with tears. Angry red splotches rouged his plump cheeks.

Hank was sensitive, which created a unique challenge for Leigh—mother of the rough kid, which was how she imagined the other playgroup parents might describe Chase, especially on one of his off days. Her mission was to keep sensory-seeking Chase, with his hug-tackles and impulsive grabbing, away from the sensory-avoidant Hank.

"Aaaaah," Hank wailed, "I got sand in my eyeball!"

Chase appeared, galloping to where Leigh sat. His freckles seemed to glimmer over his sun-pinked skin.

He exclaimed breathily, "Mommy!" as he jumped in place—his long limbs swinging. Even with his jerky movements, he was stunning. Anyone would think so, Leigh thought. Other mothers, especially her friends on Facebook, where her status updates were all photos of Chase and Charlotte, commented on how Chase should be a model. *Get that kid an agent! He needs to be in a J. Crew catalogue! He would totally win that GAP cutest kid contest!* She smiled and nodded gratefully in person, or responded with *Thanks! We think he's cute too!*;) on Facebook, not bothering to point out that models had to sit still and follow directions. Not pointing out that Chase could follow through on a *task* (therapy-speak) only if it was *self-directed* (more therapy-speak).

"Hi, sweetie," Leigh said. "Did you have a fun time on the beach?"

Chase's cheeks were flecked with grains of sand, and when Leigh's fingers brushed his cheek, he recoiled like a stretched spring.

"Did you have fun at the beach, honey?" Leigh asked again, knowing she wouldn't get a response. Chase was too excited to hear her. "What did you do? Did you go in the water?" She heard the sugarcoated strain in her voice.

He tugged at his wet swimsuit, and drops of cold water stung her naked calves.

"I can't do it. I can't do it," he moaned.

"Oh-kay," Leigh said in a slow voice. Chase's therapists claimed speaking slowly had a calming effect. "Try not to get frustrated."

She sang a song from his favorite television show as she searched the room for Tenzin.

"Keep trying, keep trying," Leigh sang quietly. "Don't give up. Never give up."

"Don't! Sing! That! Song!" Chase lifted to the balls of his feet, the tendons in his neck stretching.

"Peepee-making time!" Tenzin sang as she hurried over. She laid one large hand on his back and escorted him toward the bathroom.

If it wasn't for Tenzin. The thought of life without her nanny blew a bubble of anxiety in Leigh's chest. Her Tibetan Mary Poppins.

"Thank you, Tenzin," Leigh called over her shoulder.

She smiled appreciatively because she was grateful for Tenzin, but also just in case any of the other parents were looking. Although they weren't necessarily people Leigh would call friends, their opinion of her mattered.

The neighborhood mommies' acceptance of Leigh was the currency that determined status in this new life with little children. *Before* she had measured her worth by her salary as an art educator, by the success of the benefits she planned, the annual 5k race she organized in honor of her late cousin, who had died from Lou Gehrig's Disease. And there had been the more superficial successes—her tennis-trimmed body and her rigorous schedule of exfoliation and moisturizing. There was no denying the importance of appearance in the weight of a woman's worth, she thought, you'd be naïve to think anything else.

Now, her identity boiled down to a) good mommy or b) bad mommy. She scanned the room, relieved that Rip was nowhere in sight. Daddy Rip, which was what an often inappropriately flirtatious Tiffany called him, was the most judgmental of all. Leigh knew Rip thought himself a better parent than the mommies, and he spent most of each Friday's playgroup time criticizing the mother who was absent that week. He was probably out on the deck chugging beers. She had felt his alcohol-flushed cheeks earlier as he'd given her that awkward *hello, how are you* kiss when Leigh, Tenzin, a groggy Charlotte, and a carsick Chase had first arrived at the beach house. Leigh disliked the exuberant hellos and good-byes that bookended playdates, but the way of the mommies was to hug all around.

Grace, Rip's wife, was tugging a wet swimsuit off whimpering Hank. She wore pressed capris and a plaid headband that pulled her thick Asian hair into a flawless curtain down her back. Leigh thought she seemed like the last match on earth for Rip, with his baggy shorts and hippie sandals.

"Stop!" a shrill voice piped into the room, and everyone, even the boys sifting through the bins of toys, fell silent and looked to the front door.

The source of the command was Harper, the playgroup's only little girl.

As Harper watched the spastic throng of boys, the sun glinting off her tight red-gold curls, the girl's upper lip lifted. Leigh tried to push aside the dislike she felt for Harper. It made Leigh feel like some kind of monster.

Harper was a pint-sized early-childhood package the elite private schools were sure to drool over. Tiffany was aiming high and had begged Leigh, whose niece Peyton attended the crème de la crème St. Ann's School, to arrange for an interview, and so Leigh had called her sister-in-law Caroline, who was secretary of the school board.

Leigh had texted Tiffany with the news that the interview was on. And Tiffany had responded with thank you!!! fingers crossed!!! trailed by a row of plump, red, heart emoticons.

Leigh had no trouble envisioning Harper at St. Ann's. Not even four years old, Harper had a precocious self-control. Leigh had studied the girl. In music class. At the public library's storytime. While the other children fidgeted, and Chase careened around like an entranced whirling dervish, Harper sat with her little hands folded in her lap. During snacktime, she sipped from an open cup without spilling a drop, even patting her lips with a napkin when she was finished. A perfect performance. One moment, the girl was a miniature version of the debutantes Leigh had come out with so many years ago at the Waldorf Astoria. The next, she was a fearless tomboy leaping off the roof of the playhouse at the park.

Just then, Chase dashed past and gave a shriek of excitement when he spotted the plastic bin of matchbox cars.

"Slow down," Leigh called right before Chase fell to his knees with a thud.

Grace gasped, but Leigh knew Chase didn't feel pain like other children. He had "sensory issues"—the term his therapists used again and again, as if they were casting a spell, and Leigh had been enchanted, because she found herself using the term more with each week as she apologized for her son. At the playground. At playspaces. At the playgroup. *I'm so sorry,* she whispered, like it was a secret. *He has sensory issues.*

The preschool, (which was, Leigh thought, little more than an overpriced day care) had called her twice this month to pick up Chase because he'd bitten someone, and just that week, the director, a sweaty woman who put on grandmotherly airs, had suggested Chase might need a school with a smaller class size, where children had the same "issues." Leigh had parroted the therapy-speak: *Chase has trouble relating his body within the space around him. Chase can't measure his movements, his pace, the volume of his voice.* She felt like a proselytizer trying to convert the preschool director to see (and believe) that Chase's behavior wasn't intentional, just a side effect of his faulty neurology. He was a good boy.

"Are you sure he's okay?" Grace asked. "Hank would be hysterical."

Hank was hysterical about most things, Leigh thought.

"He's fine," Leigh said, remembering to smile.

She knew the weekend would be full of her commands.

Stop running, Chase.

No grabbing, Chase.

Use your inside voice, Chase.

Hands to yourself, Chase.

"The boys are sooo out of control," Harper said, rolling her eyes in a perfect mime of the mommies.

The parents laughed—Michael the hardest.

In the harried pace of life after children, Leigh rarely noticed men. But Michael's long lean torso and his lash-fringed eyes reminded her of a young Sylvester Stallone. He was noticeable.

"I don't know where she gets this stuff from," he said, and Leigh heard the hint of a rural upbringing in his accent.

"Hello?" Nicole said as she hurried past Michael with an armful of damp beach towels. "Have you met the girl's mother? She's a B-A-L-L buster."

"That's our ginger-haired girl," Tiffany said, appearing in the doorway. Her hair was a radiant mess of kinky dark waves. Her cleavage glistened with oil when she leaned over to comb the sand out of Harper's curls with her fingers.

Leigh knew what Tiffany was thinking. *That's our exceptional girl. So advanced. So much better than all these testosterone-laden spastic little boys.* Tiffany talked about Harper's intellect as if it were a burden, but Leigh knew it was false humility.

Tiffany looked up, searching the room, as if she had heard Leigh's thoughts.

"Hey, Leigh," Tiffany asked. "Isn't that your mom's name? Ginger?"

Leigh nodded, smiling. "Ginny," she said.

"You got to love those country-club names," Tiffany said.

Leigh felt a prickle of annoyance. Tiffany was always pointing out Leigh's family, and their money, as if they were something immoral Leigh had done. Despite the many times Leigh had tried to explain to Tiffany that the family firm had taken a huge hit in the crash of 2008. Brad's poor investments had nearly ruined them and Leigh's father had cut her off, as if she should be punished for Brad's mistakes.

Leigh thought of the lockbox in the back of her closet, under the stacked shoeboxes of heels she hadn't worn since Chase's birth, and which she knew she would never wear again. Inside that lockbox sat a pile of financial papers, the last year of bank statements for the Preschool Fundraising Committee, numbers that Leigh had to fix before Monday.

If fixing was at all possible, she thought.

Tiffany rolled on. "Bunny. Muffy. What else?"

"Don't forget Baby in *Dirty Dancing,*" Nicole called from the kitchen.

Susanna sighed as she lowered herself onto the sofa, one arm searching behind her, the other supporting her pregnant belly. "God, I had such a crush on Jennifer Grey. That movie was, like, my coming out."

A tour commenced, Tenzin left in the living room to look over the children. Leigh trailed the playgroup parents, with Charlotte stuffed into the baby carrier—the straps already damp with Leigh's sweat. They started outside, where Nicole pointed out the public beach in the distance, past the wall of boulders. Leigh could make out the colorful dots that were beach umbrellas, and the silhouettes of fishermen waist high in the water. Nicole explained that they were to find her immediately if any stragglers from the public beach made their way past the boulders, especially if they had dogs.

Also, Nicole added gravely, her eyebrows lifting. They were to be on the look-out for any of the children slipping into the woods. She pointed to the dunes that rose between the public beach and the woodland. Beyond the fluttering sea grass that sprouted thickly from the sand, Nicole told them there was a trail that led to hundreds of acres of untouched state-park grounds.

Predictably, Nicole warned them about ticks. Leigh imagined fat, blood-sucking ticks clinging to every leaf, waiting to drop on the children, embed in their soft skin and infect them with Lyme's Disease.

They filed back into the house and up the narrow stairs, stopping in each cramped room of the shabby beach house, which, Nicole informed with an eye roll and a disgusted chuckle, her parents had named Eden. Leigh assumed Ni-cole's parents had believed that by decorating their home with eastern Long Island's famous lighthouses (in the form of wallpaper, soap dispenser, lamps, and even salt and pepper shakers), they'd imbue it with the elegance and status of the Hamptons. She could only hope that Nicole's parents would remain blissfully ignorant of their lack of taste. Although, with a daughter like Nicole, sharp-eyed and sharp-tongued, Leigh was sure their precious lighthouses had been critiqued often. Even then, Nicole served a healthy dose of condemnation.

"And this," Nicole was saying, "is my parents' library. The finest collection of Danielle Steel you'll ever see!"

Leigh knew it must have taken courage for Nicole to invite them here. Nicole, the published novelist. Nicole, with her sophisticated academic friends. Leigh could barely follow some of their pompous Facebook conversations. Nicole, who was elitist about her claim that she was nonelitist. So why had Nicole in-vited them? It was the equivalent of (Leigh thought with a shudder) stripping naked, revealing every varicose vein and pucker of cellulite. For heaven's sake, the bathroom reeked of old people's urine, and the shower curtain was streaked with mold. If this had been *her* childhood home, *her* parents, Leigh would have kept her friends far far away.

taking stock

Nicole

Nicole hovered over her laptop in the dim garage that smelled of fertilizer and gasoline. Sweat dripped from her chin onto the keyboard as she searched for a wireless signal, the splinters on her father's nail-scarred workbench digging into her fleshy forearms. She felt that pulsing restlessness unique to plugged-in life. Those rare occasions you were cut off. Denied access. What if something did happen? Something the TV stations wouldn't pick up until it was too late. Everyone knew Twitter was the most reliable source these days.

Finally, the five bars in the corner of her laptop screen glowed. She went straight to www.urbanmama.com and posted:

Any updates with this end-of-the-world Web bot thing?
posted 3:37pm

Nicole refreshed the site, her index finger tap-tap-tapping, looking up at the house only when she heard a dull thud or the muted squeal of a child.

Finally, a reply:

—what the hell are you talking about? 3:40pm

A moment of relief. It's nothing, Nicole thought and even allowed a slow exhale.

But she refreshed the site. Just to be sure.

If only she had left it alone, closed her laptop, put it out of reach, and gone on with the weekend. Because there were more responses. Some anxious, *Oh god, I can't handle anything else. I was at the towers on 9/11* and *I saw someone in another post say they were leaving the city,* which brought forth multiple posts of *what?!* and *wtf!*

Of course, there were the naysayers, the responders who, in their breezy "whatever" tones, dismissed the slightest hint of hysteria.

Okay, conspiracy mom, relax and *I bet you were stockpiling water and duct tape during Y2K.*

And these rational voices calmed Nicole for a moment, enough that she could post once more. She had to. She *had* stockpiled supplies for Y2K. She still did. And look at what her single post had created. She owed it to these women to follow through.

Is something terrible going to happen tomorrow? Are these "Web bot" rumors true?

posted 3:48pm

(5 replies)

—no. relax. 3:50pm
—OMG. No. You're FINE. 3:51pm
—yes. search Webbot 3:54pm
—can you really be this stupid? 3:56pm
—pay no attention to the fearmongers, sweetie. 3:57pm

Nicole stood in the driveway and searched the windows of the house before popping the trunk of the car.

There they were. The product of months of saving, researching, and purchasing, then organizing and reorganizing, until she was certain she had the best Go Bags in the tristate area, even more thorough than the official OEM (Office of Emergency Management) *Ready New York!* Go Bag.

She began her inventory, checking the items against the NYC.gov Disaster & Preparation Checklist. The iodine tablets, the "Space Emergency Blankets" and first-aid kit, the whistles and toilet paper and plastic plates and utensils, the camping stove and bottles of water and nonperishable food, including twelve cans of gluten-free organic Alphabet O's from Trader Joe's, Wyatt's favorite. She had packed changes of clothes for all three of them and a few toy cars for Wyatt, as well as his lovey, a cuddle-worn blanket named Blue, which he'd given up a few weeks ago after several sleepless nights. There were matches and flashlights and packs of batteries, and an envelope with five hundred dollars cash. A to-go package of tampons. A thick paperback, *The Complete Works of William Shakespeare*. The print was so small, she had added a magnifying glass. Not her ideal reading material, but more bang for the buck space-wise.

Nicole's fingers dragged over each object as if, by touch alone, they imbued her with a kind of protection. A force field, Wyatt might say. Her sweet boy needed to organize the world into two ranks. He was always asking her if so-and-so (the gruff UPS guy, the angry taxi driver) was a good guy or a bad guy.

Entwined with this feeling of safety was self-loathing. How could an intelligent person buy all this crap? Yes, she was neurotic, she thought, as most creatives were, but she was a high-functioning member of society. She paid her bills on time, she made sure her child had all he needed to thrive, she taught at a well-regarded city college where her classes were among the students' favorites. She was a professor, damnit. The trunk of this car belonged to a militia member of a paranoid fringe cult, not a liberal, educated upper-middle-class mother.

The checklist lay on top of the bags. She'd recently had the single page laminated at a drugstore, but she could see the creases where she had folded it time and time again. In the last few months, it had been massacred by check marks and scribbled notes.

She felt love for this list, which had, in many anxiety-flushed moments, comforted her. Now, in her parents' driveway, she pressed it to her face and breathed deeply. The plastic was cool against her sunburned cheeks.

The Go Bags had taken her months to complete. First, she had saved the money, then she had spent it, using a PayPal account she had opened in her mother's name, arranging for the items to be shipped to her parents' house—$50 for an economy bottle of Cipro antibiotic, $250 worth of gas masks (+ extra charge for child-sized), $100 of Mylar blankets, $185 for the walkie-talkies.

She had scoured the Web each night after Josh and Wyatt had fallen asleep. Her insomnia had worsened in the winter, after the ice and salt had deepened the pothole in front of their building. In the early mornings, when Nicole finally made it to bed—the list of still-needed supplies running like ticker tape through her dream state—every garbage truck rumbling down Union Street felt like a test by a cruel god. Each time a truck hit the pothole, the echo of the metallic shudder flung her into consciousness, into a nightmarish light, the bed trembling under her. It took her a few seconds to realize it was the mellow light of dawn, not the blinding white of a nuclear blast.

She gave the same kind of meticulous attention she had once given to writing her graduate dissertation to her Go Bags. To the precious goods she prayed would help them prevail, not perish, when and if *it* happened.

She was about to zip the bags when she heard the grinding brakes of an ancient car. An orange-and-white taxi pulled into the sea-pebbled drive, its bumper as rusted as the hinges on the beach house's shutters.

The taxi door opened, and a red-faced Josh stepped out.

"Honey, you're here," Nicole called. She slammed the trunk closed.

Josh walked toward her in an exhausted half limp, his overfull messenger bag—briefcase of the creative world—bouncing against his thigh.

"I'm sorry. I'm late," he said, breathless. "The train. I had to walk from downtown."

He doubled over with his hands on his knees, and Nicole wondered if it was an exaggeration, an attempt to guilt her.

Josh took a slow breath, blew it out Lamaze-style, and said, "I was scared you'd be mad if I was late."

She tried to squash the reflex but couldn't stop herself. "You know I H-A-T-E it when you say you're scared of me."

She smiled. She knew the air must remain conflict-free if Josh was going to tolerate their weekend guests.

"I've been calling you for hours," Josh said. "What's wrong with the phone?"

"Oh, sorry. One of the kids must have been playing with it."

He looked at the house, startled, as if seeing the line of cars crowding the driveway for the first time.

"Jesus, I forgot. The playgroup."

"You said it was okay," Nicole said, knowing he was just pretending to have forgotten about that weekend. She'd been reminding him for weeks.

"I'm just so exhausted. It would've been nice if it were just us."

There was bloodshot exhaustion in his eyes. He did, she thought, work so hard for them. And she knew he was correct the many times, midargument, he had called her a leech. She also knew that wanting to be selfless, wanting to be a good wife, wasn't the same as actually being one.

"Did the *whole* group come?" He looked up at the house and winced.

She guided him up the driveway, pulling away when her hand touched the sweat-soaked dress shirt clinging to his back. She knew that once they were inside, in front of an audience, his protests would subside.

"You can't invite one and not the others, honey."

"You said," he spoke slowly, like a storm gathering, "we needed more family time."

"It *is* family time," she said, hoping the shrug of her shoulders served as an apology. "It's just that, we're sharing the time with other families." She paused, "With the h1n1 stuff and all, I thought it would be good for us—all of us—to get a break from the city."

This wasn't necessarily a lie, she thought. At the start of the summer, when the flu numbers had spiked, she had begged Josh to commute to work from Long Island each day, where she and Wyatt, alone and essentially quarantined, would be safe from the flu. Like the Tudors, she remembered thinking, who had fled London for their country mansions every summer to avoid the sweating sickness. Now Nicole was embarrassed by the comparison. Josh had refused, claiming he would barely see Wyatt, he wouldn't be able to tuck him in at night, and Nicole knew she'd be crazy and cruel to deny her son the hour of sweet prebedtime book reading and lullaby singing with his father, whom Wyatt called his best buddy.

Josh stared at the back door, beyond which rumbled the screeching, chattering, and banging of the children. His brows lifted in what, for a moment, looked to Nicole like fear, sending an arrow of panic through her chest. Josh was her rock, her given in the formula of her life. He'd been there those last ten years to tell her *no, nothing bad is happening* and *yes, everything is okay.* If he was worried, she was ten times as worried. Before she could ask him if he was okay, if everything was okay, he opened the door.

As they walked inside, the clamor of family time washed over them. The noise had reached predinner-bullhorn pitch.

Josh's face shifted into a smile as Wyatt appeared from within the band of boys and galloped to him, yelling, "Daddy! My daddy is here!" He tackled Josh's knees.

Nicole registered the adoring smiles on the other parents' faces, and she was able to recognize that this was a happy moment, and she wanted to stop herself from yanking Wyatt away from his father. Truly, she did. She even thought about walking out of the room, running upstairs, locking herself in the bathroom, and lighting up.

But she had to protect Wyatt. Think of the masses of people whom Josh had shared, first, the subway with and, second, the commuter train out to Long Island. Surely, she thought, the number of people increased the odds that at least one of them had the h1n1 virus, and before she knew it, she was gripping Wyatt's shoulders and lifting him out of Josh's arms.

"Wyatt, go wash your hands, please," she said. "Right now."

When Wyatt rolled his head in protest, she bent over, and whispered, "You don't want to get sick, do you? You touched Daddy before he changed out of his yucky germy city clothes."

Wyatt looked down at his hands.

"Daddy?" Wyatt looked to Josh. "But"—he paused before gathering his breath to cry—"I don't want to wash my hands!"

Nicole could feel the mommies moving away from the three of them, toward the dining table. All except for Tiffany, who plopped onto the sofa. Nicole knew Tiffany would find her later, to ask if Nicole wanted to talk about *what happened earlier*.

"Relax, Nic," Josh said with a laugh that was clearly for the benefit of their guests.

Nicole pointed to his messenger bag sitting in the middle of her mother's heirloom afghan.

"Was *that* on the floor of the train car?"

The voice she heard belonged to a caricature of herself, like a character in a sitcom with a laugh track. But this was important. To think of the filth! Of man, beast and/or machine; the dog shit, hocked-up spit and garbage juice that thrived in the grooved floor of the subway car.

Josh moved his bag to the floor.

Harper stepped forward, her fists on her hips.

"Take turns, guys," Harper said, and shook a finger at Nicole. "Be nice."

An intervention Nicole was both annoyed by (*that bossy little . . .*) and grateful for, especially when the room broke into laughter, nodding heads, and smiles that said *well how about that*!

"You little peacemaker," Tiffany sang as she ushered the little girl away.

Tenzin intoned from the corner where she was building a castle made of blocks with the twins. "As the great Dalai Lama himself says," she began, and Nicole almost whirled around to tell Tenzin not to hurl another Dalai Lama quote her way, but Leigh saved her by calling, "Tenzin, can you please take Charlotte for a sec?"

The roomful of parents seemed to sigh in unison. Their obvious collective relief made Nicole feel like more of a fool. One who had to be rescued by a three-year-old and an infant.

"Daddy?" Wyatt said, then paused, thinking, his lash-fringed eyes looking upward. "You said, Daddy, we could go to the carousel this weekend."

"I did," Josh said, smoothing Wyatt's hair. "Mommy wanted to come to the beach instead."

The sting of the passive-aggressive dig made Nicole worry—not for the first time—about how Wyatt would soon be old enough to see how his mommy and daddy used him as a weapon in the tiny battles they waged against each other.

She interrupted with a cheery exclamation, "And here you are, Wyatt. With all your best buddies!"

"Daddy's my best buddy," Wyatt said, pouting. "Now is the carousel weekend."

"The carousel will be there when we get back, Wy," Josh said. "It'll be there all fall. And we'll go for the whole day. And ride it twenty times. Okay?"

Nicole imagined the carousel in all its renovated glory, the wooden horses with their flowing manes and muscled bodies, and behind it, lower Manhattan in apocalyptic smolder.

She waited until Josh was busy brushing his cheek against the cheeks of each of the mommies in pretend kisses, then she went into the kitchen, and dug the sliver of Xanax from her pocket. It was only a half of a pill, she told herself. She downed it with a swig of flat root beer, the crumbling pill bitter on her tongue.

She snapped the rubber band on her wrist five times. The quick bite of the rubber catching her arm hairs refocused her.

Then she washed her hands.

Nicole had read and reread the CDC's guidelines on how to wash to avoid disease. Hot water. As hot as she could stand. Wash top and bottom, between fingers, under nails, and up your wrists. *Due to the overuse of sanitizers,* the site had informed, *the Supergerms' favorite hiding place is the wrists.* Finally, you wiped your hands with a towel, and then—this was the tricky part—used the towel to turn off the faucet.

Josh walked into the kitchen and stopped in front of her, his hands on his hips in a stance she had always disliked because it felt effeminate, and she wanted him to be manly. Rocklike. Unbreakable. She also expected him to banish her daily worries with maternal-style tenderness—a hypocrisy he had pointed out in their couples' therapy. Since they'd met at college, so many years ago, Josh had been the first and only person who could put Nicole almost at ease, who made her feel almost safe, and despite his gentle voice that was just a note too high, he'd always had muscular forearms, with thick cords of vein that wriggled under his skin and indicated pumping blood and strength.

"Nic," Josh said, his voice nearly a whisper. His chin was tucked to his chest, and his large brown eyes (Wyatt's eyes, she thought) looked up at her—one part concern, one part inspection.

He stepped closer and took her in his arms and into the warmth of his body. Its solidity was a sudden comfort. His smell, which had always reminded her of cinnamon, made her feel as if she was home, made her realize how exhausted she was and how badly she wanted him to lift her, like a sleeping child, and carry her upstairs to the bedroom, where she would lie next to him, sleep comalike all night and through the next day. Dead to the mommies and daddies waiting below. Dead to the relentless forward momentum of the world. Oh, how she wished she could die and come back to life after the doomsday warning had expired. Because it wasn't the end she feared, so much as the waiting for it not to happen.

Josh massaged her scalp with his fingertips, and said, "You've got to relax. This worrying isn't good for you. Or for Wyatt."

She closed her eyes and let her head rock back and forth with the sliding of his fingers.

"Are you okay?" he asked.

She knew what he really meant was, *do we need to have a talk?* Do I have to call Dr. Greenbaum to schedule an intervention where we can discuss upping your meds? Do I have to hide the dish sponge so you don't scrub your hands raw, Nicole? Do I have to conceal the knife block behind the microwave so you don't perseverate (a verb he'd gleaned from their couples' therapy) about slicing yourself every time you walk into the kitchen?

"Aw, you are so sweet, honey," Nicole said, in a voice she knew sounded both appreciative and condescending. "I'm fine."

The Xanax spread through her like liquid calm, and as she blew on her hands that burned pink, she almost believed herself.

domestic bliss

Rip

It had been over a year since Rip first began calling himself a mommy.

In the beginning, it had been a joke.

Now, *they,* the mommies, were the only ones who understood it was no longer a joke. Nicole, Susanna, and Tiffany.

Even Leigh. Although, Rip thought, the discomfort Leigh felt around him was obvious. Like that afternoon, when she'd turned her head as he kissed her hello.

Rip stood on the deck alone, the cool sea air lapping at the back of his sunburned neck. He looked out at the Long Island Sound, as dark and still as a lake, only the occasional hesitant wave kicked up by one of the motorboats in the distance. It saddened him, this sea without any waves, as if it had been rendered impotent by the land on each side, as if it were cowering between two bullies.

He was buzzed. Or maybe more than that, because he'd lost count of the beers he'd put back since he, Hank, and Grace had driven out that afternoon. Grace had insisted they listen to some peppy kids' album instead of Rip's music, claiming the mix of grunge and rock was far too mature, that it "terrified" Hank, an argument that had led them, somehow, to a revisiting of that past week's most popular debate. To buy or not to buy Hank the princess dress set (gown, tiara, and plastic shoes included) their son had coveted for so long.

"Just like Harper's," Hank had lisped, a dreamy look sedating his features.

As if, Rip thought, Hank was envisioning himself in a faraway land, he and his friend Harper frolicking among singing animals and Technicolor toad-stools, a fairy-tale castle sparkling in the distance.

Rip was pro princess dress. Grace, con. He urged Grace to be open-minded, to let Hank express his unique fantasies. This was 2010, after all, a boy *could* wear a princess dress.

By the time they had crossed the causeway, Rip had opened his window to let in the mix of tangy brine and aging honeysuckle, and to drown out Grace's half of their argument, which had now graduated to what had been their #1 hit on the squabbling chart for the last six months. The debate over whether they should have another kid.

Once again: Rip, pro; Grace, con.

Now, as the sun slipped closer to the sea, Rip dug his elbows into the con-crete seawall and ran his hands over his stubbled face. Yet another perk, he thought with a smile, of the stay-at-home-daddy life. Not having to shave every day.

His fingers still smelled like the coconut-scented sun lotion he had lathered on the kids. At playdates, the undesirable child-care tasks often fell to him, and soon after he and Hank and Grace had arrived at the beach house, he'd been silently elected sunscreen applicator and grappled with one squirming kid after another as he applied, and reapplied, the BabyGanics organic sunscreen.

He had invited Grace along that weekend with hopes that a few days among his mommies would inspire her, would pluck at her biological heartstrings. Maybe the sight of the kids on the beach—their sun-browned skin, their bound-less enthusiasm, their wonder over every shell, crab, and minnow, would change her mind. His plan was already backfiring. Hank had loathed the beach, acting as if each grain of sand was a personal assault. And there was already tension between Grace and Tiffany. He could tell, as soon as he'd introduced them, that there'd be pecking between them before the weekend was over.

But, Rip thought—and there was always a *but* for Rip. He considered him-self a believer. Not in God per se, but in man. In Rip. In self-actualization. When the doctors had told him and Grace that it might be difficult for Rip to have children, he had torn the reins from Fate's gnarled hands and steered that chariot to fatherhood. With a little help from an anonymous sperm donor, of course. Still, the day Hank had been born, wrinkled and swollen, Rip knew the boy was his own. He had wanted to shout down the pale yellow corridors of the maternity ward. *Fuck Fate! I have a son!*

The screen door flew open and out dashed Nicole's son Wyatt, clad in nothing more than *Spider-Man* underoos. Nicole's husband, Josh, followed, his face reddened with what Rip interpreted as embarrassment and fury.

Rip waved hello and received a tight smile in return as Josh jogged after Wyatt, who skipped around the deck, effortlessly dodging his weak-chinned father. Josh wore wrinkled suit pants, and the armpits of his button-down shirt were dark with sweat. Rip looked down at his own ensemble. Frayed camo shorts and a tee shirt, stained, most likely from Hank's greasy fingers. He took a swig of his beer and congratulated himself. The last time he'd worn a suit was just before Hank's birth, when he had become an official stay-at-home parent, and when he had (with relief) quit his temp IT job at Grace's investment firm.

When Nicole's husband had arrived a half hour earlier, fresh from the Manhattan commute, Rip had caught the pale shadow of terror on the man's face as he walked into the early-evening chaos; overtired children, wine-flushed parents, the floor carpeted with toys and cookie crumbs and puddles of spilled juice.

"Wyatt," Josh called through clenched teeth, as Wyatt skipped across the deck, "Mommy says it's time to go potty."

Passive-aggressive parenting, Rip thought. Blame it on the other parent.

"He'll make a decent soccer player," Rip called out with a short laugh.

"Yep," Josh said.

Whatever, Rip thought. Not like *he* was dying to make chitchat with the mommies' SOs, aka Significant Others.

SOBs, Rip often joked toward the end of the playgroup dates, when everyone (except for Leigh, who was too almightier-than-thou to drink before sunset) had imbibed enough liquid courage for a bit of honesty to seep out, and with it, a collective venting about their partners, their kids, the monotony of life as a parent to small children. Rip played his part, griping about his fourteen-hour days alone with Hank, but, in all honesty, it was the best life Rip could imagine. Lately, the reality of that life running out (Hank would be in preschool next year) had Rip up at night, in a panic, strategizing over rum and Diet Coke on how to maintain his stay-at-home-daddy status.

Of course, he knew there wasn't much strategy needed, though his mind still trembled in an endless cycle of *what to do, what to do.* It was simple. He had to convince Grace to have another baby, to accept the role of an anonymous sperm donor back into their lives, along with the hormone shots in the soft brown skin of her ass, the egg extraction, all leading to *in vitro*.

On the first try, it had seemed like science fiction to Rip, like one of the dog-eared paperbacks he'd loved as a kid. *Brave New World.* It had seemed routine by the third try, when the egg had finally stuck. Stuck was what the women on the trying-to-conceive online message boards called it, as in *I hope to God this one sticks.* Rip had spent hours (mostly during Hank's afternoon naps) lurking on the anonymous boards of www.TryingToConceive.com, watching as the women sent each other good wishes (*sprinkles of sticky baby dust!!*) when they signed off. Off to check their basal temperatures, he assumed, or to pee on a plastic ovulation detector stick—all so they could time sex perfectly and catch that window of procreative opportunity.

As the sun slipped closer to the water and the pools of seawater on the sandbar caught its tangerine light, Rip thought of how he envied those women on TryingToConceive.com. Even if they were barren, at least their wombs ensured it was they who held the reins. He admired their bottomless optimism. Like him, they were believers, unwilling to surrender to that stubborn old bitch, Fate.

If only Grace had an ounce of the reproductive fervor those women had, he thought. Then he would have his baby.

Wyatt's flip-flops slapped against the deck as the father-son pursuit wore on.

Josh hunched forward, hands on his knees, gasping for breath. "Wyatt! Come to Daddy already. It's time to get dressed and go potty." He coughed. "You can't walk around half-naked, now can you?"

First mistake, Rip thought, kids don't do reason. Second, do not ask your kid a question. *Uh, yeah, Dad, you can walk around half-naked. I'm doing it right now!*

There were a thousand Joshes in Brooklyn, Rip thought. All with the same sixty-dollar haircut and thick, black, Buddy Holly glasses. They dressed their offspring in tee shirts with ironic sayings, like the kids were their own private billboards. They wrote blogs describing life as a dad with an irreverence Rip was plain sick of. As if there were something uncool about loving your kids.

On weekends, the daddies came crawling out of the brownstones, numerous as cockroaches. Nervous they'd fuck up their kid in the few hours they had watch, they were either too lenient, trying to discuss the crime (*Now, Finn, you know we don't grab*), or overbearing, giving their kid a time-out if they forgot to cough into their elbow. They wore self-doubt like a wet blanket, Rip thought, and left the playground as if they'd surrendered to an enemy.

Even now, Rip could see defeat coming, Wyatt running toward the edge of the seawall as a look of terror contorted Josh's sweaty face.

"Stop," Josh screeched.

Rip scooped up Wyatt just as he started to scale the wall.

"Little man," Rip said. "You have got to chill."

He handed the balled-up boy, still giddy with the chase, to his father.

"Thanks," Josh heaved. "It's Rip, right?"

"Yep."

"Great to meet you," Josh said.

Rip didn't bother telling him they'd met before. Several times, actually.

As Josh walked back to the house, Rip watched the man whisper furiously into Wyatt's ear. The boy sat upright, peeking over his father's shoulder.

Rip gave him a wink, and Wyatt covered his mouth to stop a laugh.

Yep, there was no way in hell he'd be friends with that Josh dude. A dad who couldn't have fun with his own kid.

Grace, and even Tiffany—who, lately, was the closest thing Rip had to a friend—had been urging Rip to make some guy friends. Someone to grab a beer with. A pal for a daddy double playdate to the zoo. They didn't understand he couldn't befriend just any guy. *He* wasn't just any dad. He felt most comfortable with the mommies because, in the last four years, he had become a mommy.

Could they hook him up with a dad who made his own soap, shampoo, and lotion after his son was diagnosed with eczema? Who baked his own gluten-free bread, so not to aggravate Hank's allergies? Who knew the names of all his son's creatures, the stuffed animals (Mortimer, Polly, Pinky, Boy-boy, Nuk-nuk, Greenie) that Rip and Hank had christened together over the last four years. The only BFF daddy for Rip was the guy who, like him, spooned with his child every night while he told stories about the alien boy Zank and his pet robot Zork, and who, like Rip, was psyched to live in a time and place where daddies could be mommies, where they could embrace their domestic gifts, where they could nurture their offspring without being made to feel dickless. Rip baked a mean rhubarb pie and nobody (at least nobody in his mommy circle) would consider him less the man for it.

It didn't hurt that Rip knew he embodied what the women of creative, yuppie, hipster, artisanal-obsessed, whatever they were calling themselves these days Brooklyn wanted in a man—the very opposite of their own fathers, whose duties had been limited to conception, financial support, and the occasional advice from on high. Today, the urban, and even suburban, streets were sprinkled with stay-at-home daddies pushing a toddler in a stroller on their way to a Tiff's Riffs music class, an infant in a Baby Bjorn hanging like some mutant appendage from their chests.

In the last three-plus years, Rip had logged hundreds of hours at playgrounds, playspaces, and playgroups, and every playdate was a lesson in the new boundaryless definition of gender. He'd be lying if he didn't admit to enjoying the more obvious perks for a hetero (very hetero, he liked to think) guy living the stay-at-home-dad life. Mommies smelled nice and served delicious snacks. Never was there a bottle of vino under $13 at the playgroup. Each day held umpteen chances he'd catch a glimpse of cleavage, or the curve of a butt cheek winking at him through those tight jean leggings the mommies loved to wear.

Rip often felt as if he were living a kind of fantasy, the setting for a clichéd porn. Like when Tiffany, the extreme-domestic goddess in the group and (let's face it, Rip thought) the hottest mommy, had invited Rip and Hank over so Rip could help her can the blueberries they'd picked upstate. While Billy Holiday had crooned, and Hank and Harper built snowmen with homemade playdough, Rip held the mason jars as Tiffany poured the jam that slid, almost seductively, into each hot glass container. He had watched Tiffany's braless breasts quiver through the thin cotton tank top, smelled the nectar covering her hands, her slender forearms, staining her puffy lips. He'd felt a compulsion to taste her, and felt certain, in the way she let her tongue slide over her bottom lip, the way she let her long hair tickle his cheek as she bent to screw on the jar tops, that she too wanted him to slip his hand over the breasts he had seen so often.

Breasts, breasts, and more breasts, it had been four years of nipples, all shades of pink and brown, erect and glistening, fresh from a satiated baby's mouth. Only Leigh was so modest as to breast-feed with a swaddle blanket shielding her. He'd known Susanna's breasts (small but perfectly shaped), Nicole's breasts (large with wide, purplish nipples) and Tiffany's, his favorite, full and white, almost translucent, a network of blue-green veins radiating from her petal pink areolae. Tiffany had zero qualms about unleashing her breasts for Harper to nurse anywhere and anytime, and Rip had seen them enough to memorize them, to think of them as old friends. These weren't women to hide themselves. These were the daughters of the daughters of the feminist revolution, after all. They'd taken monthlong prenatal breast-feeding classes, they'd given up trying to hide a wriggling baby under their fifty-dollar hooter-hider nursing covers, and Rip could see in their eyes and in their relaxed smiles, a gratitude toward him, for giving them permission to let their breasts roam free.

The mommies thought of him as Mama Rip. Diaper-changer, boo-boo kisser, nose-wiper, playground pal. A sensitive shoulder to cry on when the monotony of motherhood felt like just too much. How little they knew about how grateful he was for their breasts.

strings attached

Leigh

The room hummed with the business of children. After a glass of white wine, Leigh felt as if the noise in the room had elevated. The revving of toy cars and the clatter of plastic blocks. The jabber of half-formed language and shrieks of fury in the never-ending battle of toy sharing. The giggling chatter of the mommies and the sobbing that followed a boo-boo; all of it plucked at the growing pain behind her eyes. *Mommy! Mama! Mommy! Mama! Mommeee!*

Wine was poured, Brie and crackers nibbled. Leigh smiled and nodded appropriately as the mothers alternated between admiring the children in the moments they behaved (*Look at them. They're so cute!*), and critiquing them when they fussed (*It's a good thing they're cute*).

Hank was crying again, rubbing at his swollen eyes with fleshy fists.

"There's still sand in my eyes."

Grace looked around the room, caught Leigh's eye, and said, "He has a hard time at the beach. Everything's so intense."

Leigh nodded; there was a hint of a question in the woman's stiff voice, a silent plea for commiseration.

"Yes," Leigh said. "It *is* a very sunny day."

Then she caught sight of Chase creeping closer to Hank. Chase's head was tilted, as if mesmerized by Hank's despair. Leigh started to stand, to intervene, but the weight of the baby in her arms pulled her back, and just as she was about to call for Tenzin, Chase backed away.

"Yip, yip, yip!" he sounded off as he galloped around the room.

"Give people their space, Chase. Honey," Leigh said.

Chase continued to race around the room, skirting the other children. It was a game he played, to see how close he could get without bumping someone. He sounded off as he galloped, yips and tongue-clucks and fluttering of his lips.

The soundtrack of Chase, she had once joked with his speech therapist, who assured Leigh her son did not have a tic. Still, Leigh feared a Tourette's diagnosis down the road. She had always been proud of how still she could hold herself, even as a child. In the polished pews of Saint John's Episcopal Church on Sunday mornings. At the *barre* in Miss Posey's ballet studio. In cotillion class, her white-gloved hand sweating in the viselike grasp of a pimply thirteen-year-old boy.

Grace wiped the tears from Hank's reddened cheeks with the corner of a towel, and said, "Chase just wanted to cheer you up, Henry."

Hank summoned the breath for an even louder wail. "My name is Hank!"

"If you don't calm down," Grace said, pausing to search the room, "I'm going to have to get Daddy."

"I want Daddy!"

"Okay, that's it." Grace's lips were a thin white line. "You're getting a time-out."

"Daddy!" Hank screamed, raw and phlegmy. Leigh covered Charlotte's little ears with her fingertips.

"Actually," Tiffany began as she knelt in front of Hank and rubbed his back.

Leigh saw Nicole's eyes flicking to catch Susanna's, a *here she goes* look passing between them. The air in the room fell flat, the same tense silence that always accompanied Tiffany's lectures on child development.

Tiffany continued, sweetly. As if talking to the children during music class, Leigh thought. "Studies show time-outs don't work as effectively as we might think they do."

"Oh. Really?" Grace said. A skeptic's wrinkle creased her forehead, and Leigh could see she was a woman unused to criticism, trigger-quick to bat down any challenge. "Where did you hear that?"

"Well," Tiffany said, "I don't know if you've heard of the Waldorf philosophy? It focuses on imitation. It suggests you guide the child to more appropriate behavior. In a gentle way." Tiffany gestured toward Harper. "Harp goes to a Waldorf school."

As if to say, Leigh thought, *look at this perfect specimen.*

Tiffany took Hank's free hand, and the little boy, his sobs ceasing, looked up at her expectantly. Leigh could see that Grace's lips had parted. In astonishment, or irritation.

"I'll start on the kids' dinner," Nicole called out before vanishing into the kitchen.

"Let me give you a hand," Susanna said, waddling after Nicole.

The fear Tiffany inspired in the playgroup parents baffled Leigh. Tiffany had been nothing but kind toward *her*. Even loving.

"For example," Tiffany continued, "if a child was acting in a disruptive manner, the teacher would redirect. By leading them away with an outstretched hand." Tiffany mimed the gesture. "Suggesting an alternative activity."

Tiffany grabbed a beach towel hanging over the back of a chair. She held it out to Hank and smiled. Her voice was soft. Seductive even, Leigh thought.

"Here, Hank. You may help me fold the towel."

The little boy reached for the towel, but his mother jerked him away and, for a moment, there was an absurd tug-of-war.

"That's so very interesting, Tiffany," Grace said with a beaming smile of her own.

Grace's calculatedly cordial tone made the back of Leigh's neck prickle.

"I'm a child-development specialist." Tiffany shrugged modestly. "With a master's in music therapy."

"And where was that?" Grace asked. "The Columbia School for Teachers?"

"No. City College."

"Oh," Grace said, and smiled. With a barely perceptible nod of pity, Leigh thought. Then Grace ushered the still-whimpering Hank to the screen door and out onto the deck.

Even before the screen door thwacked shut, Tiffany had pulled out her phone and was jabbing at the keypad.

Three seconds later, Leigh's phone vibrated.

The text message read:

ok! she's a fucking cunt!

Leigh's hand jumped to her mouth to smother a laugh. When she looked up, Tiffany winked at her, seemingly unscathed.

Tenzin rushed by, shuffling after Chase, singing, "Potty time! Make a pee-pee on potty time!"

Chase cried, "Can't get me!" and leapt onto the sofa seat next to Leigh, jumping up and down, his hip knocking the arm cradling Charlotte.

"Chase, sweetie, careful," Leigh said. "You'll wake the baby."

"You can't get me, Tenzie," Chase sang with an openmouthed smile.

"No, no, no, Chase, my boy," Tenzin clucked quietly, reaching for him.

With each jab of his elbow, Leigh felt the coil tighten in her chest.

"Stop, Chase. Please!" she heard herself begging. Then she took a slow breath and tried a more rational approach, "You're not doing good listening, Chase."

With each thudding jump, each dip of the cushion seat, Leigh felt a sense of unsteadiness grow, and when he fell against her, his fingers catching in her hair, a white-hot stinging at her temple, she almost laid her palm on his bare chest, imagining his skin still sun-warmed under her fingers, him on the floor, on his back, his elbows skidding across the thin carpet at her feet.

But Tenzin was there to save Chase (and Leigh) again, scooping the boy up under the armpits and swinging him up in the air and away, his giggles trailing behind them.

Leigh relatched the baby's mouth around her nipple, the hot gush of her milk letting down a relief. Only then did she dare to look around the room, bracing herself for the disapproving stares. But no one looked her way. She couldn't tell if their busy chatter was intentional. Maybe they were embarrassed for her. More than once, Nicole, and even Susanna (a mother to twins!) had said things like *I don't know how you do it, Leigh.* As if Chase were a trial she must endure, as if she were a mother to be pitied.

But now she had her Charlotte.

Nicole, Susanna, and Tiffany stood in the kitchen doorway, their shoulders touching in a conspiratorial huddle as they watched Tenzin hop among the boys, plucking brightly colored foam sandals from their sun-browned feet. Leigh sensed a hint of mischief in their amused smiles. Even from Tiffany, who, as Tiffany loved to remind Leigh, had "discovered" Tenzin, and who called Tenzin a goddess to her face.

The Tibetan woman did look a bit comical, Leigh thought, and instantly felt it a betrayal to think this, as if she had joined forces with those judgy mommies against her precious Tenzin. Tenzin didn't own a bathing suit and was wearing one of Leigh's. It was too small in the trunk and left her hip bones exposed. But it was too big in the chest; the empty cups two pockets of air-filled fabric. She wore white men's athletic socks and sweatpants rolled up to her knees. Her SAVE TIBET! baseball cap was perched atop her head. Still, Leigh thought, there was beauty in Tenzin's effortless smile, in the simplicity of her unwrinkled golden skin that left little to distract from those loving black eyes.

When Leigh saw children look at Tenzin with lip-curled disgust, as Harper sometimes did, as the parents in the playgroup did now, Leigh felt a swelling urge to defend her.

"Tenzin going to clean up," Tenzin sang in her usual cheer.

The only way Leigh could make sense of Tenzin's playful energy, and her habit of referring to herself in the third person, was that she'd been a first-grade teacher back in India, where her husband and three children still lived. Leigh preferred to think of Tenzin's clowning as intentional. An act. Tenzin's daily performance was just as seamless as Leigh's own. But lately, as she grew to rely on Tenzin for more than child caregiving, but also for comfort and even for guidance, Leigh sometimes feared that Tenzin was as clueless as she appeared. The nanny might actually believe there was goodness in everyone. After all, Leigh thought, Tenzin's most-used American cliché was *look on the bright side.*

The din had woken the baby, who, unlike big brother Chase, was all smiles after a nap, even one interrupted. Leigh tried to avoid comparing them, but it felt impossible when they were such opposites. When the Leigh who was Chase's mommy was a stranger to the Leigh who was Charlotte's mommy.

Leigh jumped when she felt the hand on her shoulder.

The scent of Tiffany's musky perspiration swarmed her.

"Jumpy, a bit?" Tiffany asked with an amused lift of her eyebrows.

"You scared me, silly."

She gave Tiffany's cool dry fingers a squeeze, counting *one-two-three* before releasing. Recently, Tiffany had pointed out, with a tone of exaggerated hurt, that Leigh didn't hug her back, so Leigh had been making an extra effort.

Tiffany tucked herself between Leigh and the arm of the sofa, curling her naked legs under her. Like a cat looking to be scratched, Leigh thought. Harper ran over and climbed onto Tiffany's lap. The girl's long legs, spotted with yellowing bruises, spilled across Leigh's thighs. The soles of Harper's feet were filthy, and Leigh scooted over to make room.

"Milky-time, Mama," Harper pleaded. She fell back so her head rested in the crook of Tiffany's elbow. A cradle position. The same way Leigh held Charlotte.

But Charlotte was three months old. Harper nearly four *years* old. Again Leigh wondered when Tiffany would put an end to the sullying of this naturally beautiful act that, in Leigh's opinion, Tiffany had made wholly unnatural.

Tiffany lifted a heavy breast over the neckline of her shirt, and Harper cupped it in her hands, closed her eyes and opened wide before pulling the bright pink nipple into her own pink mouth.

"Gentle, Harp," Tiffany said, "I know you love mama's yaybies and all, but ouch."

Leigh smiled, more of a reflex, when Tiffany used her embarrassing alternative for boobies. *Boob has negative connotations*, Tiffany had once explained.

Leigh pressed her fingertips into the hollows above her eyes.

"Do you have any painkiller?" she asked.

"Nope. But," Tiffany's voice fell to a whisper, "Nicole has like a grab bag of pharmaceuticals in the bathroom upstairs."

Leigh was about to stand and head for the stairs when Tiffany clutched her elbow and pulled her back into the sofa.

"Did you get a chance to think about the babysitting schedule?" Tiffany asked. "I really *really* need those hours on Thursdays."

Not this again. How many times did she have to tell Tiffany no, without actually saying no? Tenzin was hers on Thursday—the only weekday Chase's preschool did not have a spot, which meant twelve hours alone with the kids. Twelve hours trying to protect Chase from himself while she nursed the baby through the 5–7 P.M. witching hour. *Don't jump headfirst off the couch, Chase. Don't stick Cheerios up your nose, honey. Don't chew on Mommy's cell phone, please.*

"I'm sorry," Leigh started, but Tiffany interrupted.

"Tenzin says she's cool with it. She really wants the cash."

Leigh felt a blush of humiliation at the thought of Tenzin and Tiffany conspiring behind her back.

"Other side," Harper demanded, and swiveled around in her mother's lap. Wordlessly, Tiffany tucked one breast back into her shirt and extracted the other.

"And Tenzin said she's super happy to do a share," Tiffany said, leaning close until Leigh could see the depression in the woman's nostril where her nose had once been pierced. "Which would be great, Leigh. 'Cause it would save sooo much money."

And, Leigh thought, I'd come home to Chase in hysterics after hours of Harper-abuse. No one riled Chase like Harper, and Tiffany's *laissez-faire* discipline only made matters worse.

The lusty suck of Harper's nursing deepened, and Leigh felt the girl's shining eyes watching her, waiting for a reaction. As if Harper hoped Leigh would defy Tiffany, knowing it would make for entertainment. All the kids were drama junkies, their little noses in the air, sniffing out the slightest hint of blood drawn between the mommies. Especially Harper.

Leigh slid out of Tiffany's grasp and stood. She sniffed at Charlotte and wrinkled her nose. "Oopsy! Got to change this baby girl's diaper."

"Just think about it, okay?" Tiffany tugged on the hem of Leigh's seersucker skirt. "Okay? If I can't promise Shabbat Tots Tuesdays *and* Thursdays they won't give me either."

"Okay," Leigh said, hoping she could smooth this Tenzin business out later because suddenly she was exhausted. Her mouth was so dry that her lips stuck together when she tried to speak, to explain that she needed more time to think about it, but Tiffany interrupted her again.

"Oh my God, I love you!" Tiffany squealed and pounced on her, pulling Leigh into a hug, nearly jostling the baby out of Leigh's arms and sending Harper tumbling to the floor.

Tiffany's hot breath was in her ear. "You really *are* my best mommy friend. I'll make this up to you. I fucking swear it."

Leigh couldn't tell Tiffany right then she'd meant okay, as in *okay, I'll think about it*. Not *okay, you can have the hours*. You can have Tenzin. The throbbing behind her eyes sent a wave of nausea crashing over her, and Leigh thought she'd vomit right there, with the baby in her arms. Tiffany had pulled her knitting project from her tote bag, and her fingers were already dancing at the tips of the bamboo needles, the yarn trailing over Harper's boob-absorbed face.

Leigh retreated to the darkest corner, by the fireplace, trying to avoid the sun that glinted off every surface in the white-walled room.

Nothing is permanent, she told herself, yet another Tenzin mantra. This pain is temporary.

She was no different from the other mommies, she thought. She was scared of Tiffany.

She remembered the night at Jakewalk a few weeks earlier, when Susanna, with Nicole's assistance, had tried to coax Tiffany into leaving the bar with them. Tiffany was practically sitting in that guy's lap, Leigh thought, remembering Tiffany's eyes, which had grown impossibly wide with rage, the look of someone unhinged.

Harper, her cheeks flushed pink, climbed off Tiffany's lap and joined Hank in threading yarn through tiny nature-made holes in the shells they had collected. A task Leigh knew Chase would never sit for.

Chase skipped over and planted a kiss on Harper's cheek.

"That's very sweet, Chase," Leigh said, trying to mask the surprise in her voice.

Her son stepped back and chewed his lower lip in shy satisfaction.

Harper scoured her cheek with the heel of her hand. "Yuck!"

Leigh longed to yank the girl's red-gold hair.

"But. I miss you, Harper," Chase said.

Leigh knew this was his way—his only way—of saying I love you.

He was a good boy. He was. Despite what the city's Early Intervention psychologist had said about Chase's "social-emotional delays" preventing him from forming "purposeful relationships" with the other children, on and on until Leigh's eyes had stung with contained tears.

Her boy loved people. Why couldn't they see that?

bosom buddies

Rip

Rip had just cracked open another beer when the screen door opened again, and Hank appeared, squinting against the fiery orange globe that rested on the horizon. Grace stood behind Hank, her hand nudging him out the door.

"What's up?" Rip asked.

"Go to Daddy," Grace said.

The screen door slapped shut.

"Hey, buddy," Rip said, taking one of Hank's warm hands in his own, pulling him gently away from the door. "Mommy sounds frustrated."

Mommy sounds effing pissed off, Rip thought.

"Are, are there buggies?" Hank asked as his fearful eyes scanned the deck.

"Hey, bud," Rip said. "Come on over here and check out this awesome sunset."

Hank shuffled forward like a timid baby penguin. "No 'squitos?"

"No mosquitoes," Rip repeated, and wondered, for the hundredth time, how Hank was going to survive the big bad world.

"Daddy?"

"What's wrong?" Rip asked when he saw Hank's raised eyebrows and the tremor in his chin.

"I'm sad," Hank said in a breathy whisper.

"Why, sweetheart?" Rip asked as he ruffled the boy's hair, as thick and black as Grace's and, Rip imagined, the generations of Chos before her.

"'Cause Mommy got mad at Mama Tiff."

"Oh, I see," Rip said, making a mental note to tell Grace to cool it. These were his friends, after all. "I'm sure Mommy was just being a silly old thing."

"And 'cause I missed you, Daddy."

Rip felt as if he'd been punched in the gut. He wanted to run into the house and drop to his knees in front of Grace, beg her to give him another baby so that this feeling of being needed could be prolonged, even if just for another few years.

He pulled Hank into his arms and squeezed, breathing in the apple-scented shampoo he (*he!*) had made for his little boy, until Hank squealed, "Ouchy, Daddy!"

He lifted Hank and slung the boy's pudgy legs over the rail. Hank stiffened, scrambling for Rip's neck.

"Don't worry. Daddy's got you." He wrapped an arm around Hank's waist. "See?"

Hank relaxed and looked down at his feet dangling over the massive boulders that formed a double seawall. The occasional wave splashed over the rocks, spritzing foam up onto Hank's naked brown feet.

"Oooooh, Daddy," Hank giggled. "It's freezing."

The pink light of the sunset magnified Hank's delicate beauty. The cherubic face and rose-tinted cheeks. The puckered mouth, lips ever apart, and those thick lashes Rip both loved and despised because they made strangers on the street stop and exclaim, *What a beautiful little girl!* Those weren't Grace's lashes, and they certainly weren't his, and he hated himself, as he always did when he ruined a moment full of love for Hank with that reminder. Hank wasn't his. He was Grace + anonymous sperm donor #1332.

The still surface of the water rippled, and a slice of silver rose against the bruised sky. Rip's breath caught in his throat. Then another flash rose and another, until the air just above the blue plain was slashed with tiny glimmering fish flipping in and out of the water.

"Daddy! Do you see? Do you see?"

"It's a school of magical fish," Rip said, and winked.

"Daddy, look! You missing it," Hank cried, and laid one warm, cookie-scented hand on each of Rip's unshaven cheeks, turning Rip's head to the water.

"Okay, buddy, okay." Rip laughed, certain the fish had been sent, their dance choreographed, just for him and his son.

He heard the screen door squeak open behind them and when he turned he saw Michael, Tiffany's fiancé, step onto the deck. He wore a scuffed black motorcycle jacket, and the sun made the silver studs wink a fiery light. Harper ran out from behind him.

Hank shouted with breathy excitement, "Hah-per! We saw magic silver fish. Jumping and flipping."

Harper was Hank's only real playmate in the group, and Rip knew this friendship was born from necessity. Only Harper had the focus to sit for the passive activities Hank loved, like drawing, painting, or making necklaces from Cheerios and uncooked elbow macaroni. And only Hank would do whatever Harper commanded when the other boys abandoned her for a game of you-can't-catch-me or superheroes.

As if she could read Rip's mind, Harper ordered, "Come on, Hank," and pointed to the corner of the deck where they had secreted their hoard of seashells, pebbles, and a few pieces of blanched driftwood.

"Okay!" Hank said.

Rip lifted Hank off the seawall and then Harper took Hank's hand, tugging him to the corner.

Rip had heard Tiffany brag about her baby's father at many a Friday afternoon playgroup. Michael had knit Harper's stroller blanket, white sheep on a green pasture. *With wool he had spun and dyed himself!* Michael had his yoga certification. Michael had been a potter in an earlier life. *There's nothing sexier than a man who can throw his own vase,* Tiffany had said with a smoky laugh, then her voice had fallen to a conspiratorial hush, forcing Rip and the other mommies to lean even closer. Michael *always* pleased her first in bed, she had whispered before breaking into a deluge of drunken giggling.

Rip had imagined a mild, maybe even effeminate man, but it was true what Nicole had said one Friday, on a day Tiffany and Harper were absent from the playgroup. Michael had looks. Like indie-film-star looks. Even Rip could see that. The punkish tangle of brown-black curls, short in back, long on top. Just enough grease to claim hipsterhood. Thick sideburns that accented his chiseled jawbone. Cool in the most casual way.

Of course, the topic of Michael, especially as Tiffany's wineglass emptied, had also opened the gates to a flood of complaints, all delivered Tiffany-style; big gestures, exaggerated expressions, a choreographed performance. But didn't they all gripe about their significant others on Friday afternoons?

Michael gave Rip a slight nod of recognition and walked toward him with a disinterested saunter. Rip was certain Michael had been *that guy,* the aloof bad boy all the girls had swooned over in high school.

"What's up, man?" Rip said, holding out his hand.

Michael clasped his hand, and Rip caught a whiff of something both sweet and heavy, like pipe tobacco.

"Yeah," Michael said slowly, "sure. I know *you.* You make the balloon animals at the park, right?" Michael continued, "Hank's dad. Sorry, I suck with names."

"Rip," he said, hiding his displeasure. Was he so forgettable?

"Cool. Yeah. Rip. Of course! Tiff's wild about you."

There was something in the way he said that, the escalation of recognition, that made Rip think of Tiffany and Michael in bed, their lithe, naked bodies like two serpents writhing. He shook the scene from his head with a slug from his beer.

Michael bowed his head to light a cigarette that seemed to have magically appeared. He cupped his hand around the flame, but the wind had picked up, and it took the two of them to get it lit, their hands cupped together.

"Hey, man," Michael said, and thumbed over his shoulder at the door. "Shhh." He winked at Rip as he lifted his cigarette.

Rip knew that if he had tried to wink at someone, especially another man, he'd look like a fool.

"Got you, dude," Rip said and plunged his hand into the cooler's icy water, retrieving two Coronas. He handed one to Michael.

"Thanks," Michael said. "I'm down to just a few smokes a day. And treasure every single drag. If you know what I mean."

Michael held the cigarette between his thumb and forefinger. Like the Marlboro Man, Rip thought. The way Michael's eyes squinted with pleasure when he took a drag made Rip hunger for a smoke, but he knew if Grace caught him, it would give her yet another excuse to put off trying to get pregnant the old-fashioned way. *Your body is full of toxins,* she'd say.

"Yeah, I hear you," Rip said. "Grace made me quit when she got pregnant." He found himself wanting to say something clever. "I used to sneak them out on the fire escape. But one night I was drunk and almost fell off."

This wasn't necessarily a lie but also wasn't necessarily the truth, and Rip was surprised by how much he enjoyed Michael's response. A knowing smile. Like they were cut from the same cloth. Or the same piece of badass vintage leather, Rip thought.

Then Rip realized, with a jolt, that his eyes had been off Hank for too long. He imagined Hank's head dashed against the seaweed-strewn rocks, his little boy's body floating facedown. He whirled around and there were the two kids sitting quietly in the corner of the deck, a mound of sand between them. Hank was removing each wave-washed pebble with great precision and dropping it in the bucket. Ping, ping. Delicate and fastidious as always. Like a detective on one of those CSI cop shows, Rip thought. Harper sifted through the sand with her toes, her skirt hitched at her waist, panties bared, shins dotted with bruises.

"Whoa," Rip said, taking a breath and slapping his chest as if he'd choked on something, "Sorry. I just freaked out. I never forget him like that." Just in case Michael might think he was one of *those* dads, the kind that left their kid dangling from the monkey bars while they updated their Facebook status on their iPhone.

"Don't sweat it," Michael said, "I've had plenty of moments like that. Where it's like Harp has vanished from the playground."

Rip felt a decline in their conversation, a momentary pause, like a record skipping, a common side effect in the sleep-deprived and distraction-rich early years of parenthood.

"Look at these guys," Rip said, nodding at Hank and Harper's pebble-sorting project. "Some sand. A few rocks. And they're in heaven."

"They're pretty awesome," Michael said. "They know what's up."

"What do you do for work again?" Rip asked, sheepish as usual. He loathed asking the question since he'd been asked it so often, forced to admit he was doing his job right then and there. His J-O-B was watching his kid.

Michael shook his head. "Meaningless crap. I edit videos for infomercials. Internal films for corporations. Like," Michael altered his voice so he sounded like the Moviefone guy. "There are five points in the star of teamwork!"

Harper and Hank looked up. Harper shouted, "You're silly, Daddy!"

Michael smiled and gave them a comical bow. Still, there was something unintentionally graceful and James Dean-esque about it, Rip thought.

"It's a paycheck," Rip said.

"Yeah," Michael said, a smile lifting his stubbled jaw. "You got it."

He likes me, Rip thought, and felt his cheeks flush. What was he? Some kid in freakin' grade school?

"But like I was saying," Michael said. "Kids have got their S-H-I-T together, if you know what I mean. They got, like, perspective. We don't give them enough credit."

"Totally," Rip said, nodding in agreement, thinking this was exactly what he'd said many times at the playgroup, where it seemed the mommies demanded too much from the kids. The mommies expected the kids to have the self-control of adults. *No one wants to be friends with a nose-picker. Only babies suck their thumbs. Cookies are for good boys only.* Why would you want a child to feel shame when you knew adult life was chock-full of it?

"I like to ask Hank what he thinks about things," Rip said, hoping he didn't sound like a self-important fool, what the mommies called sancti-mommies.

"Exactly," Michael said, and nodded knowingly. As if, Rip thought, it was just the two of them on some mountaintop. Two guys dishing the meaning of life.

"I say the same thing at playgroup," Rip said. "But the moms, you know. They think I'm crazy."

He laughed to hide the truth—their giggles at his earnestness made him burn with humiliation.

"They're just jealous," Michael said, rolling his eyes.

"Yeah," Rip said, nodding, as if it was a revelation. And it was. He felt taller, and there was a sharpening in his vision, like he could see all the way across the Long Island Sound. He was the one who deserved the status (the honor, he corrected) of main caregiver. He was the one running around the playground while a kid clung to his back, he was the one rolling across the blacktop while Wyatt, Dash, and Levi piled on top of him, while the neighborhood mommies (*those jaded bitches*, he thought, surprising himself) sat on a bench, watching their kid show off his or her monkey bar skills—*watch me, Mommy!* But the mommies weren't really watching, Rip thought. Sure, their pretty little heads were turned to watch, and maybe the kids were fooled, but the women continued to yap away—Yadda, yadda, *the cost of living in Brooklyn was outrageous!* Yadda yadda, *another preschool rejection came in the mail!* Yadda, yadda, *did you hear how little Milo bit little Celeste at Toddler Tom-Toms class—better get that kid evaluated!*—remembering to pause once in a while to yell, "Way to go, Wyatt!" or "Super job, Dash!" with half-hearted interest.

He was a professional, full-time, stay-at-home parent. And he was awesome at his job.

He was ready to tell Michael. Normally, he waited a while to dish it all out. Most guys weren't comfortable—TMI and all that—but Michael felt different.

"You wouldn't think it," he whispered to Michael, "but she and I have a lot in common."

He pointed his beer at Allie, Susanna's partner/wife/whatever, who was curled up on a chaise lounge at the far end of the deck, where she'd been hiding out with her iPhone ever since the lesbians, twins in tow, had arrived. With her chin resting on bony knees, her sweatshirt hood slung over her head, and her face barely an inch from the screen of her phone, she looked more like a teenager than a mommy, Rip thought.

"You both like to have sex with women?" Michael said, straight-faced.

"Heh. Well, yeah"—Rip smiled—"there's that."

The men shared a laugh, and Rip took a leap of faith and clinked his bottle against Michael's.

"Me and her," Rip said, looking back to Allie, "we're both nonbio parents."

The difference is, Rip thought, she's about to get her own kid. A surge of resentment wormed through his gut.

Michael gave him "the look." People paused, their mouths fell open, and their gaze moved just a bit off center. It was always the same when he came out to people, when he revealed he wasn't Hank's biological father. Frankly, Rip thought, it was a stupid look, but as soon as they got it, the intelligent light returned to their face, and they practically beamed at their aha moment. Like they were freaking geniuses or something.

"That's right. I'm not Hank's biological father. We used an anonymous donor. Donor #1332." Rip sang the combination of numbers, as he often found himself doing. As if the absurdity of it—the fact Hank's real father was nothing more than a jumble of symbols—called for a song and dance.

"Wow," Michael said.

"Yeah," Rip turned to look over the concrete seawall. The sun loomed large and red, a corona of gold simmering around its rim. "My sperm is kind of slow."

Rip knew, from experience, that guys didn't dig sperm talk and it was better to avoid eye contact. He wasn't out to make anyone uncomfortable, and he sure as hell didn't want pity. He was happy to tell the tale, to perform it even, if it made for a smoother delivery.

"Yep," Rip said. "At first, the doctors thought we'd be able to do it. That the boys would rally."

Michael laughed, and Rip was able to turn around and face him again.

"So we," he looked over at the kids, "you know . . . A lot. Then we did it less. Because, apparently, too *much* depletes the sperm. So then we did it on a schedule. Two years later—after hormone therapy, artificial insemination." He stopped short and lifted his beer. "To turkey basters!"

Michael answered with his own raised bottle and "Here, here."

"We picked a donor. One who had my coloring and height. A good old Ashkenazy Jew-boy. And after the third in vitro try." Rip pointed at Hank, who was huddled in the corner of the deck, his tee shirt pulled over his knees. "Voila! Henry Elijah Cho-Stein."

"Bravo," Michael said, and this time it was he who reached out and clinked Rip's beer with his own. "We're glad you guys made Hank. Harper adores him." Michael paused, then continued in a half whisper. "And it's tough sometimes. For Harp to make friends. She prefers to lead. If you know what I mean."

"Yeah, well, Hank prefers to follow," Rip said, finding it impossible to hide the disappointment in his tone, a tone he'd found himself using lately when talking about Hank. Hank who was so sensitive. Hank who cried over everything. Hank who wanted a princess dress.

"So," Rip continued, "Harper's devoted to her followers. That's a good thing."

"I worry about her," Michael said, looking out into the sea, where a shimmering corridor shot out from the falling sun. "Charles Manson was devoted to his followers, too."

There was a pause, filled by the screech of a gull, then they laughed. The laugh of friends, Rip thought, who make you feel better about how fucking ludicrous life can be, who remind you how, all of a sudden, joy can fill a deflated heart.

He knew he could hang with this guy.

The sun was ready to drop into the sea. There was a sense in the air, Rip thought, like surrender.

A flock of geese flew overhead in perfect V formation, honking as if saluting them.

Rip watched as Michael, as if he had read Rip's mind, saluted up to the sky.

"Hey," Rip said, "Tiff tells me you knit. We should get a beer or something and you can teach me how."

"Man," Michael said with a quick wink, "I can knit the shit out of a baby sweater."

tit for tat

Tiffany

Tiffany was grateful for the break when the children, along with Tenzin and a terrified-looking Josh, marched upstairs for their baths, their squeals dulled by the closed bathroom door.

Of course, Tiffany thought (in defense of her good mommyhood), she wasn't as grateful for the children's absence as some of the mommies. Leigh's face had grown chalk white with exhaustion as the night neared, and Tiffany had noticed an agitated tremor in Nicole's hands all afternoon. Maybe Nicole had run out of her secret pink pills.

Tiffany watched as Grace stood up from the sofa and moved toward the kitchen.

"I guess I'll go ahead and make the kids' bedtime snacks," Grace said.

Clearly a passive-aggressive ploy, Tiffany thought. Grace wanted someone to say, *No! Sit down and relax. We'll take care of it.*

Tiffany jumped up from her seat. "I'll give you a hand."

Grace froze. For a moment, Tiffany wondered if they were going to have it out right then and there. But as quickly as Grace's eyes had dulled with suspicion, she smiled.

"Would you rather do it?" Grace said. "I know I'm just the visitor here."

"Don't be silly!" Tiffany said. For fucksake, she thought.

"I'm sure you don't need me."

Tiffany sighed. "Grace," she said, "let's do this."

As she and Grace moved toward the kitchen, Rip hurried over. Like some kind of servant, Tiffany thought.

"I'll help out," he said, his hand flat against Grace's wide back, as if he were pushing both Grace and himself through the kitchen doors.

"No, no, no," Tiffany said, turning him toward the main room and giving him a shove. "I know you have some important stuff you wanted to discuss with Michael." She looked at Grace and winked. "Guy stuff," she added in a dramatic whisper.

Rip slunk back to his chair, staring back at them and reminding Tiffany of the mangy shepherd-mix mutt they'd had for a while when she was a kid. The same hurt it wore when her shithead stepbrother gave it a kick.

"We'll be fine, sweetie," Tiffany soothed, fluttering her fingers at him. She felt Grace stiffen at her side. *Sweetie.* Tiffany stopped herself from blowing Rip a kiss.

Not only had Grace humiliated Tiffany when she'd been trying to help calm a hysterical Hank. Not only had the woman cut her down in front of the whole playgroup. Tiffany's playgroup. She had then heard Grace ask the room, as if Tiffany and Harper (there was her little girl's feelings to think of) were invisible, "What's the normal age for kids to stop breast-feeding?"

Normal. A declaration of war.

Tiffany had waited for the perfect opportunity to enact revenge.

Which was now.

Of course, Tiffany thought, how could Grace know breast-feeding was a sore topic between Tiffany and Michael? That Michael had made a request (it felt more like a command) just last week that she quit nursing, which had boiled over into a three-day battle? *Please stop,* Michael had pleaded. Even if only (her jaw tightened at the memory) to return her breasts to him. He'd claimed it was having a negative effect on their intimacy. Simplistic psychobabble that sounded nothing like Michael. As if he'd googled "wife won't stop nursing" and copied some pediatrician's misogynistic advice verbatim.

She had admitted to the few times she'd accidentally sprayed him during sex, but that had been when Harper was a baby, Tiffany's breasts engorged, the flow out of her control. And wasn't there, she had pointed out, like a whole online-porn fetish based on lactating women?

Secretly, part of her was grateful to Michael. She knew nursing a preschooler was unnecessary. She wouldn't call it "ridiculous" (Michael's choice), but she'd wanted to wean for a few months—tired of Harper's fingers pulling and tugging, trying to squeeze a few more drops from breasts that held little more than a few ounces each. Tiffany knew that if she'd made the decision herself, she'd have come to regret it, come to label it selfish, an abandonment of her baby, a failure at mothering. She knew she'd think, *you are just like your goddamn mother.* Michael had given her permission by demanding she stop. So she would play out her anger for a few more days—she couldn't let him catch wind of her gratitude—and then she would quit, cold turkey, when they returned to Brooklyn. Or at least she told herself she would.

Now, in the small kitchen of the beach house, Tiffany stood a few feet away from Grace, whose breasts—Tiffany was sure of it—had never been put to their intended use. Rip had told Tiffany that Hank was a formula baby. *Maybe,* Tiffany allowed, Grace had nursed for a few weeks after Hank's birth, until the nipple blisters and engorgement and performance anxiety had grown too challenging, then a plastic nipple replaced flesh, synthetic formula replaced mama-milk.

"How about you do the apples, and I'll do the carrots?" Tiffany suggested, her voice bright and friendly as she unpacked the fruit and veggies that would accompany the small bowls of yogurt for the children's prebedtime snack. As if they were two women in a television commercial advertising organic toddler snacks.

"Sure," Grace said.

"Mmm," Tiffany said with exaggerated pleasure (she still had the TV commercial in mind) as she pressed the bunch of carrots to her nose, her eyes squeezed shut. "Nothing better than fresh CSA veggies!"

"What's CSA?" Grace asked casually as she sawed into an apple, straining to break the skin with the dull knife Tiffany had chosen for her.

"You're kidding, right?" Tiffany stared at Grace with what she hoped would translate as shock.

She held the expression until Grace was forced to look at her and ask, "What?" with a catty little wave of her head.

"I thought you knew Rip was a member. You know? Of the Community Supported Agriculture group? That he, like, picks up a huge crate of ultrafresh locally grown food each week?"

"I do know," Grace said, interrupting her. "I just didn't know what it was called."

"CSA," Tiffany repeated.

"Yeah, CSA."

"I'm sure you know how lucky you are," Tiffany said over the swish of the faucet as she scrubbed the carrots with the EcoClean Bamboo Brush she'd brought from home, whose bristles were guaranteed to absorb 50 percent more of the toxins that lay in wait on the seemingly clean skin of a carrot or an apple. "Rip really, truly cares about what goes into his son's body. Michael would feed Harper Cheetos and Kool-Aid if he had his way!"

"Oh, I sure am lucky all right," Grace mumbled before letting out a long sigh, so full of quivering self-pity that Tiffany almost felt sorry for her.

As Tiffany sliced the carrots into neat two-inch-long sticks, she wondered if Grace's sigh was meant as a surrender of sorts. Maybe Grace wasn't a bitch after all but only wore a bitchy armor, as so many insecure mommies did. Maybe Tiffany had pierced its iron girdle, and they could even grow to be friends, brainstorm over the issue that consumed Rip day in and day out. And, Tiffany thought, surely drove Grace mad. If Michael started nagging Tiffany to have another baby before she was ready . . .

She imagined Rip, back in the living room, talking to Michael, nodding in that overeager way of his, all the while imagining how he'd love to siphon Michael's sperm. The way Tiffany and her friends had stolen gas from their daddies' pickups for the four-wheelers they took off-roading in the woods. She could still remember sucking on the thick plastic tube until golden gas sputtered up, gagging and growing dizzy as she stuffed the tube into the dented plastic milk jug they used as a gas canister.

Tiffany was about to introduce the topic of Rip's bomblike biological tick—maybe she'd even be able to help Grace talk through it—when Grace's voice cracked the silence.

"I've never met anyone named Tiffany before," Grace said, and looked over at her with the most genuine smile the woman had worn all day. "Only read about them in romance novels," she paused. "Or seen them on *The Jerry Springer Show*."

No, Tiffany thought. Grace was a self-righteous bitch after all.

"You know," Tiffany said, pointing at the apple slices on the cutting board with the tip of her knife, close enough so the blade was an inch from Grace's squat fingers, "Hank won't eat that if there's even a speck of peel on it. No way José! Not a speck. But you probably know that already."

"He's picky," Grace said as she lifted a slice of apple and scrutinized it.

"Not just picky," Tiffany said with a snort of a laugh.

"That's what happens when your father insists on coddling you." Grace sighed.

"We always joke—in the playgroup—that Hank's religious about food. But," Tiffany paused, "maybe you don't really see that. What was it Rip told us?" Tiffany screwed up her eyes and mouth (a thinking face), enjoying the certainty that Grace was stewing.

"*What* did Rip say?" Grace asked.

"Oh, that you're with Hank, like, no more than fifteen hours a week. Wow, that's less than a single day! I sure am jealous."

Grace let the knife fall to the cutting board with a *thunk,* turned on her heel, and left the kitchen. The breeze from the swinging doors sent a delicious shiver over Tiffany's bare arms.

She arranged the apple slices on the plate in the shape of a pinwheel. Not a speck of skin. Sure to please even Hank.

Tiffany had just finished scrubbing the cutting board and started on the teetering pile of dirty dishes, when the kitchen door swung open, sending a blast of little children noise into the kitchen.

"Hey, Tiff," Rip said softly. He touched her elbow. As if he were consoling her. "Do I have to apologize for Grace?"

"What do you mean?" Tiffany said, staring down at the pinwheel of apples, making sure there was a quiver of hurt in her voice. Whatever Grace had told him, or whatever Rip had deduced, Tiffany knew that in a conflict, it was always best to act like the wounded party.

"I don't know." He slumped over the counter and dragged his short fingers through his unruly hair.

The sun caught the stubble on his jaw, making him, she thought, momentarily attractive. In a nineties Seattle-grunge kind of way.

"What's up?" Tiffany said. "You can tell me anything. You know that, silly."

"Well"—he paused—"Grace came out of the kitchen. And she was wearing that look. I know that look. I get it when I'm in deep shit with her."

Tiffany laughed. "Oh, sweetie. Everything's fine. My skin isn't as thin as you think it is."

"So she *did* say something!"

Tiffany liked the churning anger in his voice.

It was her turn to sigh, and she did it nice and slowly. The only thing better than playing wounded was playing forgiving and wounded.

She nudged him with her hip, and the hair on his legs tickled her naked calf.

"She must feel like such an outsider with all of us moms. You know?" Tiffany said. "I feel kind of sorry for her. I really do."

Rip lifted his head and looked at her from under arched brows, "You're such a good person, Tiffany. I just don't know"—he stopped and checked the kitchen door—"how much longer I can take this," he whispered. "This life with her."

He let his head fall heavily into his hands.

"It's okay," she said as she rubbed his back. His muscles were small hard hills under the curve of her hand. Had she noticed them before? Or the V that started with his shoulders, tapering to his waist?

"I can't remember the last time she, like, asked me how my day was," he mumbled into his folded arms. "Or when she last touched me without . . ." He stopped.

As her hand moved in circles, heat rising through his shirt, she smelled him. Something both sweet (honey?) and sour (the brine of the sea?).

"You do the best you can," she said. "No one. And I mean, no one, is as good a daddy as you."

"I'm not sure Grace would agree with you," Rip said with a sigh.

She knew what he wanted to hear, what he'd heard from all the moms in the playgroup at one time or another. He had a way of making them want to comfort him. *Poor daddy Rip.*

She whispered, "Hell, you're a much better mommy than most of them out there."

He looked up at her. Their faces were close, close enough that she could see he really was near tears, and to her surprise, instead of repulsing her (she liked her men tough), this pulled her in with a magnetic force, and she felt that urge to jump, the way she had as a girl standing on the balcony of her grandmother's condo in Florida, the delicious longing to give in to the very thing that would destroy you. It would be so easy to lean in. When had she last felt that shiver of recognition, a hum in the air calling her, commanding her to move closer to someone? With Leigh—yes. But with a man? Sure, she and Rip had teased each other before. A playful slap at his chest. Or their bodies pressing together briefly as they squeezed past each other in a hallway jammed with parked strollers. When they tweeted at each other—mostly comically mundane details of their parenting life—they always used the hashtag #favorite.

But this? This was different. She felt hunger.

"I better go back," Rip said, and spun toward the door, but not before she saw him shuffle a bit. Ever-nimble Rip was a bit off-balance, which meant she hadn't been the only one. Even as a girl, she'd known what that shuffle meant. A guy trying to hide his boner.

She moved back to the sink, turned on the hot water, and picked up another cereal bowl. The back of her neck tingled with heat. The running water sounded like the booming rush of a waterfall. He was at the door, one hand raised to give it a push, when she said, "Wait. Oh my God, I'm having that déjà vu thing."

"I love it when that happens," Rip said, smiling in that half-cocked way she'd grown to think of as almost handsome. The smile of a lead actor's sidekick.

"It's crazy. It really feels like this has happened before. Like we've been here. Done this already."

"You getting all new age on me? Going to pull out your crystals and shit?"

"Whatever." She laughed. "You know what I mean."

A wail sliced through the door. It was Chase. Tiffany knew all the children's cries, each with its own specific pitch.

She remembered the pinwheel of apples. The children's snacks. If they weren't fed before they slammed into that wall of hunger, it spelled tantrums, and she would be the one the mommies blamed. Especially grudge-holding Susanna.

"Fuck!" She waved Rip over. "Can you reach me something?" She pointed to the shelves above the kitchen sink. "See those little plates? The plastic ones. You got them?"

As he brought down the plates, his shirt lifted, and there was her favorite part of man—the hollow above hip bone and below ribs, where the pelvis arched like a rainbow down, down, down.

Follow the rainbow.

It was easy. She took a few steps forward so she was in front of him, at the sink, the sponge and a soapy dish in her hands like props, like the wooden kitchen toys the children used. Make-believe time. His breath was hot on the back of her head. He was close, but still not close enough.

"You can just put them over there," she said, pointing at the far corner of the counter with a soapy finger, so he had to move into her—she as stationary as a block of stone. And it was so easy to take a little step back. How wrong could a baby step be, she thought, when nothing was even happening, they weren't *doing* anything, and when his dick pressed against her ass, they both froze, the hot steam from the running water billowing up into her face so her skin felt dewy. As if lost in a cloud.

She picked up another dish, soaped it, and began to rinse it clean—ignoring the water that was so hot it felt like ice sheathing her fingers. She shifted her hips as she wiped the dishes dry—circles with her hands, circles with her hips—and she felt him grow harder.

She reached behind her. She wanted Rip to touch her nipples. She liked Michael to tease them over her shirt, the friction of fabric between his fingers and her nipples just right. Rip flinched when her hand grazed his thigh, and she stepped back to meet him. To return him to her, as if to say, "Come on back, boy."

When his hand cupped her hip bone, they arched forward together, and Rip whispered, "Um," and then she felt the wet warmth in her bikini bottom.

Just like that, he was gone, and there was cold empty space behind her, as though a gust of wind had picked him up and carried him out to sea. She turned in time to see Rip's sandals disappear up the back stairs leading to the second floor.

Tiffany returned to the living room, her thighs tingling, the crotch of her bikini bottom damp. She wondered if she should change, then imagined Rip upstairs. Jerking himself off as he thought of her.

Dusk settled, and the crickets took up song, reminding Tiffany of back home. A hole-in-the-earth town another two-hour drive out east on the North

Fork that stank of rotting clams and the potato chip factory on its shore. A memory she chased away with another swallow of wine before refreshing her drink at the makeshift bar Nicole had set up on a wobbly card table.

Rip returned, passing her on the way to the kitchen without a second look, asking the room, in typical Rip cheer, if anyone wanted another beer. It was easy to pretend things had never happened. She'd been practicing forgetting most of her life. She laughed at the melodrama of the thought—nothing *had* happened.

The children returned from baths just as the white moths began to flutter against the window screens. The boys rushed down the stairs in their tighty whiteys and undershirts—or, as Tiffany's father had called them, wifebeaters. Tenzin had combed their wet hair back, slick and parted, and Tiffany thought they looked like an old photograph from *Life* magazine. A distant boat blew its horn, and the boys rushed to the window, their hands cupped against the glass reflecting black sky and silver sea. Then her Harper was there, leaping off the third step, the wide skirt of her nightgown a ballooning sail. *Mommeee!* Tiffany tried not to think about Rip, or Michael, or Grace, as she held her little girl, buried her face in Harper's saltwater-crisp curls that smelled like sun and baby shampoo, and she remembered she was Mommy now, nothing like the old Tiffany, who put men and sex before everything else because she confused them with love—and, she thought (to be honest), because sex just felt fucking good.

Tiffany had bought Harper's nightgown just for that weekend, knowing how Harper would look, the pure white cotton vibrating against Harper's bronzed skin. The mommies' eyes wide with envy of her girl. She had splurged nearly $200 on the dress of handspun organic cotton, using the MasterCard she kept hidden from Michael, tucked in the dusty breast-pump bag at the top of the closet.

"Aw, sugar," Tiffany said, and dropped to her knees to flatten the wrinkles in the dress with her palm. "You look so pretty!"

Harper pushed her away with a sharp twist of her torso. "Mama, I don't wanna look pretty. I wanna look cool!"

Tiffany released her, and the little girl skipped to join the boys, the hem of her dress fluttering like moth wings. "Let *me* see!"

Tiffany looked around the room, talking to no one and everyone at once,

"My little prima donna." So it was clear to all that she was a patient mother. A good mother.

The baths had soothed the little beasts, and they turned the pages of books lazily as they nibbled carrots and spooned yogurt. The mommies and daddies were loosening, too, Tiffany thought. Thanks to the wine. Even Grace, who acted as if their kitchen duel had never happened.

Michael built a fire, and trills of laughter rang through the cozy living room. Tiffany's wineglass had been filled once, twice, then she lost count. The cool, salt-tinged air filled with bossa nova and she felt a thrill in her chest that meant she was buzzing. She felt as if she could sashay from person to person, light on the balls of her feet, and touch them with her magic, sugar-plum-fairy wand to make them love her.

Michael pulled her into his lap, and she stayed, even though it made her feel small, and these were surely not people who appreciated PDA. Tiffany had learned quickly that the urban sophisticates admired subtlety over all else. Anything loud, lewd, or lascivious should be filtered through irony or irreverence.

Susanna and Nicole were whispering, their foreheads nearly touching. Tiffany wondered if Nicole had really wanted to invite her that weekend. Leigh might have convinced Nicole, Tiffany thought, and reminded herself to be grateful for the bond she'd made with Leigh.

But if Leigh honestly loved her, then why was she so hesitant to loan Tenzin for three freaking hours a week? Maybe, Tiffany thought, she'd be doing Leigh a favor. Extra time with Chase might be what Leigh needed to accept that Chase would always be Chase.

Tiffany had seen many Chases. She thought of all the mothers who brought their "busy" sons to Tiff's Riffs classes, those super sophisticated women with perfect hair, and perfect teeth—women so thin that Tiffany wondered if they ever ate. They were models of refinement. Their sons the very opposite. They had their lines memorized. *He's just so excitable! He's a real boy-boy, never sits still!* Tiffany had seen many boys like that, a year or two away from a diagnosis on the spectrum, from neurodevelopmental-pediatrician visits and tours of private schools specializing in behavioral disorders.

She was blessed with her girl. Her Harper. Her mind sailed into a harbor she seldom visited, where the waves were the same crimson as her wine, as dark as the blood that lines the womb, and she wondered if the babies she'd aborted had been boys. Maybe it had been for the best, she thought as she tipped the velvety wine back, back, back. Maybe Fate had intervened so that the baby she did choose to keep would be a girl.

In the mellowed light of the wine, the conversations dotting the room were each its own little planet, and Tiffany their sun. It was her energy making them spin, she thought, as she danced from one constellation of mommies to the next.

word of mouth

Tenzin

The babies were upstairs asleep.

The mommies and daddies were in the living room, speaking with the excitement of children. Tenzin couldn't capture the meaning of their conversation, only phrases and words.

She had made it a habit to repeat new words in her thoughts, reciting them to herself, to God, and to her children in India. To the memory of a free Tibet, where her great aunts still offered secret prayers to the supreme Buddha. She even practiced with her boy Chase.

Tenzin's memory had improved in the three years and seven months she'd lived in America. She could hold many words in her head, carrying them on the long train ride from Brooklyn back to Queens, back to the apartment she shared with five other Tibetan women, most of them nannies like her. Each night, when she arrived home, she hurried to the envelope-sized electronic dictionary hidden under her pillow and unveiled the meaning of those words she had cupped in her mind all day.

Her favorites were the phrases that sounded like one thing, but meant another. *Over the moon. Promise the moon. Once in a blue moon. Many moons ago.*

Nicole had lined the dining table with the most precious cups Tenzin had ever seen. Thin glass globes that sat in the palm of a hand and long-stemmed ones that made Tenzin think of lilies. It was as if the liquid in each glass, like red and gold shifting seas, absorbed the candlelight of the living room. The mommies held them fearlessly but Tenzin had refused a glass offered by Tiffany.

She was certain she would break so fine a thing. As if God himself had blown it with divine lips.

It had been Tiffany who had scratched at the door of the bedroom Tenzin was sharing with Leigh and the children, insisting Tenzin come down and join everyone else. Tenzin had whispered *no, no, no* as Charlotte and Chase's snores hummed like tiny motors, but Tiffany's desire burned brightest of all the mommies. Tiffany hated to be refused. Tiffany wanted Tenzin to be her *bosom buddy*.

Now, as the candlelight stretched their shadows up the walls, Tenzin watched Tiffany as she sashayed from one group to the next, like a princess in one of the Disney movies, greeting the guests at her great big party. It was as if all the mommies and daddies were dancing in celebration of the children's absence. Tenzin understood the adult mind needed a rest from the busy-ness of children. She had three of her own. And, as the Dalai Lama himself says, *Love is the absence of judgment.*

The mommies' and daddies' voices reminded Tenzin of glass bells, ringing loudest when someone made a joke. Startled, they froze—peering up the stairs. *On pins and needles.* Then, the dance resumed. The rhythm of the mommies' chitchat was the music of Tenzin's American life.

This was the first thing she had learned. The Americans, especially the wealthy, educated ones, it pleased them to talk. About the things they loved and the things they did not love, the people they knew, and the people they dreamed of knowing. They very much liked to talk about what they imagined the people they knew (and even those they did *not* know) were thinking and feeling. As if they could read the mind, as the ancient Tibetan shamans had read dreams to reveal past lives. Tenzin saw how the mommies and daddies delighted in the stories they told, especially the stories about before. *Before Chase, before Hank, before Wyatt, before Levi and Dash and Harper.*

Tenzin circled the room slowly, smiling at each drink-flushed face that looked at her kindly but without invitation. She knew how to appear as if she understood. She lifted her chin and gave a soft nod when a pause cued. She was able to grab a phrase here and there, peeling the shell away until the translation was clear. Like the thin skin that wrapped a piece of tangerine.

"Out of sight, out of mind," a pink-cheeked Susanna said, and the circle of mommies and daddies giggled. As if pleased with their naughtiness, Tenzin thought as she smiled along.

"I know I'm not supposed to say this," Nicole half whispered. "But the foie gras there is to die for." Nicole's eyes lifted to the ceiling. As if in prayer, Tenzin thought.

What could this mean? It sounded essential.

To die for. Tenzin thought of that morning's news—the two monks who had self-immolated in protest at the Chinese embassy in Qinghai Province. She had just finished packing the children's things for the trip to the beach and had asked Leigh if she could check her e-mail on the family's home computer. When the images appeared on the Tibetan news site, the computer monitor even bigger than the TV she shared with her roommates, Tenzin had recoiled. It was as if the flames would leap from the screen and wrap around her. But as she had sat there, fingering her prayer beads, asking for Buddha to bless those brave souls, the longer she stared at the men ablaze, the more they seemed like two wax statues aflame.

Those monks had desired so little. Taken so little. Suddenly, the ringing of the mommies' and daddies' laughter made Tenzin feel tired.

She rubbed the prayer beads she kept tucked in her pocket, passing the wooden balls under sea-softened fingertips until her skin burned. She imagined the Dalai Lama's face, his ever-laughing eyes.

Hatred is like a fisherman's hook. We must not be caught by it.

Leigh appeared from the kitchen, a plate balanced in each hand.

Poor Leigh. Leigh played the part of the sad princess, the one who did not know she was a princess. Not until her glass shoe was returned. Not until the good-looking golden-haired prince unlocked the tower door. Despite the smile on the pale woman's face, Tenzin could see the Cinderella-sadness pooling behind her good employer's damp blue eyes.

"I'm so relieved," Leigh said, handing Tenzin a plate. "There's food for you. I forgot to tell Nicole you were a vegetarian."

"No worries," Tenzin said, and patted Leigh's bony knee.

"I hope this is okay," Leigh said. "I mean, I don't know if it will be enough. You might still be hungry. But tomorrow you can take the car and go to the supermarket." Leigh spoke quickly. Tenzin could see she was nearly out of breath. "Oh, wait. Shoot. I forgot. You can't drive."

"There now," Tenzin said, as if she were hushing a frightened Chase. It was a phrase she'd heard the mommies use to comfort the babies. She put an arm around Leigh's shoulders and felt the woman's slight frame bend under her own thick arm.

Leigh laughed. "Yes, no worries. You like that. It's your favorite thing to say."

There was a slight quiver in Leigh's chin, and Tenzin was certain the mommy felt a near-bursting terror, like a river pushing against a dam.

"No worries," Leigh said. "I'll try."

How different the mommies were from the little children, Tenzin thought. When the children fell, skinning a knee or scraping the meaty part of their palms, they hopped to their feet, eager to rejoin the game.

Tiffany slid into the seat next to Leigh, curling her legs under her. Like a little girl playing shy, Tenzin thought. Tiffany was the mommy the other mommies liked to complain about the most. Tiffany was *too* this, they said, Tiffany was *so* that.

Tiffany leaned over Leigh and linked her long white fingers in Tenzin's. The woman's rings, one on every other finger, were warm against Tenzin's skin. Tiffany gave off heat like an infant.

Tiffany sighed, and said, "I love you, Tenzin. Like, really. We're so lucky to have you. Aren't we, Leigh?"

There was a blurriness in Tiffany's voice that made Tenzin think of one of her old employers, the mother of an excitable two-year-old, who'd had cases of alcohol delivered to the family's town house each month, the glass bottles a brilliant blue.

"Of course we're lucky," Leigh said.

Leigh pointed to the two pools of creamy puree resting next to a piece of triangle-shaped bread. "That's hummus," she said, "I think. And the bread is gluten-free."

Free, Tenzin thought, as in freedom, which was what she had left her family to seek.

"This no meat? You sure?" Tenzin asked.

"Yes," Leigh said. "I promise. Vegetarian."

She was relieved when Leigh understood, as she so often did, without explanation.

She scooped some of the hummus with the bread. The tangy paste stuck to her tongue.

"Mmmm," she said, nodding, not wanting to insult.

Leigh's relieved smile was worth the lie.

Tiffany stroked the long braid hanging down Tenzin's back.

"I think it's so wonderful that you've given up meat. You know, in sacrifice for asylum?" Tiffany said. "But can I just say, personally? I think you've sacrificed enough." Tiffany's voice fell to a whisper, "And if you *do* get asylum at the next hearing, and you *do* end up eating meat again, I wouldn't beat yourself up if I were you. Life's no picnic."

Beat yourself up. No picnic.

Leigh interrupted with a quick bark of laughter. "Well, you're *not* her, Tiffany. And it's probably . . . I mean I'm just guessing"—her eyes searched Tenzin's face—"it's probably impossible for us to imagine what Tenzin feels."

Tenzin interrupted, "No, I am all done with meat. Okeydokey with no meat."

How could you feel anger, she thought, when Tiffany was so much like a child?

"So," Tiffany asked slowly, "no meat? None? Forever and ever after?"

"I think that's what she said, Tiff," Leigh said, eyes lifting up. Making a joke out of it, Tenzin thought.

"Happily ever after," Tenzin said.

"Every. Day," Tiffany said, leaning close, her breath warm and spicy, "I think about what an amazing woman you are, Tenzin. A true earth mother. A pinnacle of revolutionary woman-ness!"

Tiffany continued, "Not like us pathetic American mommies. With our whining. And our bitching and our oh-my-life-is-so-fucking-hard."

Tiffany waved toward the room, and red wine splashed across the coffee table.

"Oh, oh," Tiffany said, and Tenzin had to giggle with her. "Don't tell Mommy Nicole."

Leigh gripped Tiffany's freckled shoulders and turned her toward the kitchen.

"Come on, Tiff," Leigh said, "let's find some paper towels."

Tenzin knew the mommies and daddies thought her simple—her enthusiasm with the children silly. She could tell. But all that mattered was she had done her duty that day. Her best. This karmic certainty was the blanket she wrapped herself in each night, thick and warm, in place of her husband's arms, in place of her children's bodies, in place of her mother's small figure, with whom Tenzin, even as a married woman, had shared a bed most nights of her life. She and her husband Lobsang had their time together each week, but she returned to her mother's bed after, her husband's seed trickling down the inside of her thigh as she curled into her spot on the mattress, still pressed with the shape of her body.

She could barely grasp the memory of wet warmth, the shiver inside her, the taut veins in her Lobsang's arms as he arched above her, but as she watched Tiffany pour another glass of wine, liquid sloshing over the rim, Tenzin's thighs flared with heat.

Tenzin watched as Nicole stepped outside the cluster of mommies, tap-tapping on her phone. The mommies and daddies loved their phones and were made very happy by the things they read on the glowing screens, the pictures they took, the clever things they wrote on the Facebook they mentioned so often.

She would miss her computer these few nights away.

The night before, when Tenzin had Skyped with her family, her husband and sons and daughter coming to life on the monitor, she had felt the swell in her throat and the croaking cry escaped.

Lobsang had surprised her by begging she come home.

"This is too hard," he said. "Four years is too many."

The three round-cheeked children she had left behind had vanished. Her daughter was a woman. Her oldest son's voice would soon change, and what if she couldn't remember what it had once sounded like, as clear and high as a bell? He walked out of the small square screen when she began to cry, and she wanted to pull him back, to feel the new stubble on his cheeks, to lock him in a room with her until it was her time to die.

"No," she said to Lobsang as she wiped her face dry with the heel of her hand, "we are too close. No pain, no gain."

Her second asylum hearing was in two months, three weeks, and four days, and if she did her duty, if she did her best, as the Americans were fond of saying, soon they would be together. Leigh and Tiffany, and even Daddy Rip, they were always saying, *You are the best, Tenzin! What would we do without you?* Surely that would be enough to make the officials at her next hearing grant her asylum.

As she watched the mommies and daddies enjoy themselves, their backs arching in laughter, their arms waving as they impersonated other mommies and daddies and told silly stories, she thought of the children asleep upstairs, holding the dolls and stuffed animals the mommies called loveys. The mommies had made it clear to Tenzin that the loveys should never be lost. But how was Tenzin to protect the loveys when the children begged to keep them close? The cuddle-worn plush puppies, limbless dolls, and ragged blankets accompanied them to playdates, to story time at the library, even to the playground. The loss of the loveys was a terror looming over Tenzin every minute of every working day. There was always a part of her watching, for Mr. Nuk-nuk, Kitty-face, and Blue, keeping an eye on these soft pastel objects, just as she did on their miniature owners.

She thought of climbing into bed with Chase, but knew she wouldn't tonight. Not with Leigh sleeping in the same room.

She had never slept alone, and on the nights her employers stayed out late, Tenzin spending the night in the big drafty brownstone, the warmth of Chase's body replaced the memory of her mother's heat.

Of all the American children she had cared for, she knew her Chase had the best heart. It was her duty to guide him through the betrayal of his body that told him to grab, hit, bite, that robbed him of his peace. And that of his mother. Tenzin knew he was a child of God. Full of light. He greeted her each afternoon with *I missed you, Tenzin,* and when she left at night, her legs throbbing from housework and piggyback rides, Chase stood at the tall parlor window, watching her standing on the street, so they could mime great big hugs. Chase was her *silver lining.*

"I can't believe she'd stab you in the back like that." Tiffany's voice rose like a siren.

"That's why they call them golden handcuffs, dude," Rip boomed.

"Their oldest son just got the diagnosis," Grace whispered. "He's on the spectrum."

"Well," Nicole said, "the warning signs can differ from kid to kid. But they usually start with a sore throat."

"And I was like, *no way!*" Tiffany's face was shiny with sweat.

"There's always strings attached, man," Michael said.

"I'd give an arm and a leg for a country house," Susanna sighed as her swollen fingers drew circles around her belly. "Someday."

The mommies lived in the future, Tenzin thought. *Ever after.* Where they imagined they would have all they wanted. How could they when they wanted more and more? Their list of wants was a teetering, tottering tower, just one want away from crashing upon their pretty heads, the hair they had painted at the beauty shops with so many colors like the palette of the sun.

It was not for her to judge them, she reminded herself. She, like all men, was just one observer. It was not her place to tell them, as the benevolent Dalai Lama says, *Happiness is not something ready-made. It comes from your own actions.*

She walked up the stairs into the cool, still silence of children dreaming. *Strings attached. No picnic. An arm and a leg. To die for . . . to die for . . .*

silver lining

Rip

A more-than-buzzed Rip tiptoed into the dark guest bedroom, the light from the hallway spilling onto the bed where Hank and Grace lay, Grace's lustrous black hair fanned over Hank's rising and falling chest. Rip closed the door slowly until he heard the click of the lock echo in the hallway, cursing under his breath when Hank moaned in his sleep. The only light in the room was the white pillow under his little family's heads, glowing blue in the moonlight filtering through the thin shades. Rip peeled off his clothes, trying not to stumble despite the darkness and the spinning of his head. Why had he stayed behind with Michael after the rest had gone to bed? Why had he downed those shots—one after another, he and Michael toasting irreverently to: *health insurance! twenty-four-hour sushi delivery! the good old days!*

Down to his boxers, Rip climbed into the cot next to the bed. The coils screeched under him, and he froze. The alcohol churned in his stomach, and he clutched a pillow against his gut. Their family doctor had diagnosed his nightly discomfort as irritable bowel syndrome. Grace's mother had diagnosed it as—translated from Korean by Grace—*nervous American stomach*. His stomach felt extra nervous tonight as memories of that afternoon in the kitchen returned. The beads of sweat on the back of Tiffany's neck as the steam had billowed up from the sink. He had wanted to taste them. The wet pop of her lips parting as she gasped. Had she gasped, he wondered, trying to remember, trying to hold on to consciousness, and as he crept into that netherworld of half sleep, half memory, he grew hard and hoped he would cross into a dream-world where all that had not happened in the kitchen that afternoon could and would.

The dewy Tiffany-scented scene cracked with a high-pitched little-boy voice. Rip opened his eyes to the cool, still darkness, and Hank's moon-shaped face looked down at him.

"Sleep with me, Daddy," Hank demanded.

"This is a teeny tiny bed, buddy," Rip protested, even as he was pulling back the thin blanket, making room for Hank.

Hank climbed in, and Rip was comforted by the familiar scent of jelly sandwiches and fruity shampoo.

"Pacis," Hank demanded.

"Come on, now," Rip whispered into the boy's neck. "We talked about this. Pacis are for babies. Are you a baby?"

Rip knew Hank was thinking. The boy was silent, his breathing slowed.

"No. I a big boy."

"And who uses pacis?" Rip asked again, adding gruffness to his voice.

"Babies," Hank said before he hiccuped.

Rip knew a wail was imminent.

"Okay." Rip sighed. And then added, his lips tickled by the soft fuzz of Hank's earlobe, "Don't tell Mommy."

"'Kay, Daddy. Cross your heart," Hank said. Rip heard the pacifier-anticipating glee in his boy's voice. He knew Hank was smiling.

Rip rolled off the bed, crawling around the dresser until he found the diaper bag, and, at the bottom, the plastic baggie he'd hidden with the three pacifiers he'd sterilized before they left home. One for Hank's mouth, one extra (just in case) and one for Hank's nose. Hank liked to pop one in his mouth and half suction/half balance another on the bridge of his nose, switching the two until he fell asleep—a ritual Rip found both odd and ingenious.

He tucked the two pacifiers in Hank's sticky palm.

The pacifiers were Rip's golden ticket. Insurance. The one sure way to soothe Hank during a meltdown, and Rip knew *he* was the one who wasn't ready to retire them.

"Arm around, Daddy. Arm around."

The pacifier garbled his words, but Rip knew what Hank was saying. It was the same every night, and Rip knew he wouldn't want it any other way. Rip curled his body around Hank until there wasn't an inch between them. Like one teaspoon inside a tablespoon, he thought. Until his ass hung off the narrow cot, and there was room only for his breathing and Hank's breathing. No room for thoughts of Tiffany.

"Okay, buddy," Rip said, "Quiet down now. Sleep time."

That was how Grace found them each night when she returned home from work, her suit wrinkled from the subway ride. She stood in the doorway, blew a kiss to Hank if he was awake, gave Rip a weak wave if Hank was asleep, then retreated to the living room, where Rip had placed a plate of food for her on the coffee table. Rip didn't mind doing it all, or doing it alone. He relished the effect the nighttime rituals had on Hank, the predictability that made Hank's limbs loosen and his eyes shine with security. Every parenting book Rip had read preached the importance of consistency, especially at bedtime. Rip fed, bathed, and dressed Hank for bed (always in that order), read him three books, and then they brushed their teeth together.

"Make sure you do your fives," Rip said every night, which meant brushing for five seconds front, back and on each side.

Of course, Rip wasn't beyond reminding Grace what a trial it was to be the sole caretaker day in and day out, but he did miss her. He missed the way she'd let him rest his head in the curve of her thigh while they watched movies. The thrill of spontaneous sex on a Saturday morning, followed by sleeping in past noon. But what else was there to miss? Certainly not the crap job at Goldman Sachs, a temp IT gig Grace had found him, with just enough responsibility that he'd been able to memorize his audition lines when his boss wasn't hovering, but which had earned just enough to pay a quarter of their rent and tuition for his improv class at the Upright Citizens Brigade.

Now, as he breathed in the sugary scent of Hank, he knew there was little in life before Hank to be missed. Still, now that he was technically unemployed, Grace had begun to treat him like some loafer crashing on her couch, instead of the university-trained thespian she had met (and even admired, he'd once believed) in college. In conversation with other couples, and at painfully dull dinners with her colleagues, Grace explained that Rip was a "stay-at-home dad," her manicured fingertips curling to indicate quotes. Her laugh was a quiet hiss that both included him and alienated him although he always laughed along, assuming this was the kind of teasing grown-up couples did.

At the small, New England, liberal arts college he and Grace had attended, Rip had felt as if he belonged. There, in a class of less than a hundred, he'd

been the lead in every theater production—Seymour in *Little Shop of Horrors*,
Pippin in *Pippin*, Tevye in *Fiddler on the Roof.* He'd been named *Most Musical*
and *Most Likely to Be on TV.* Ever since, he'd been adrift in a world of cliques
whose language he didn't speak. Social life in college had been simpler—he
had hung with a crowd and met Grace, a business major with an appreciation
for the arts, who had made him believe his performance in *Jesus Christ Super-
star* was something after all, that he might have a chance of making it in the
city with its off-off Broadway theaters. After graduation, he'd shuffled from audition to audition, and in the post-9/11-economy slump, the only work he could
find were temp gigs at Grace's firm.

Then they couldn't get pregnant. It wasn't that Rip was sterile, the doctor
explained, his sperm had *mobility issues.* Another man's swimmers were
pumped into his wife's body. Some random dude's discharge. Something Rip
normally wiped away with paper towel, or washed off in the shower. Rip knew
he should think of it as sacred stuff, the seed that sprouted life, but it felt dirty
each time Grace was inseminated, and words like *cum* and *jism* filled his head.
He secretly preferred the later in vitro procedures, though he knew it was more
painful for Grace and a helluva lot more pricey, but at least some anonymous
guy's ejaculate wasn't filling his wife's holy harbor.

He'd begun to wonder if he'd ever feel necessary again.

Then Hank was born, and with the mewling brown-skinned boy came a new
life for Rip. Once Rip's role officially cemented to stay-at-home dad (finally, he'd
joked, he had a title!), he was needed day and night. Life-or-death needed. If not
for Rip, baby Hank might have rolled over on his stomach and suffocated, suc-
cumbed to the mysterious SIDS the pediatricians spoke of in hushed tones.

Babies are the most helpless creatures in the world, Rip had read in the go-to
baby book, a loan from a fellow "primary caretaker" at his mommy and me
yoga class. The author was a California pediatrician, who, in his author photo,
held a serene infant swaddled like an Eskimo baby. The gist was that babies
were born three months too early. They could barely handle learning to breathe,
eat, and shit at the same time, so why would parents expect them to know how
to fall asleep on their own, or soothe themselves? *Holy crap*, Rip had thought in
genuine epiphany, and from that moment on, he had looked upon Hank with
sympathy and was a true convert to the "attachment parenting" method. His
sole mission was to soothe baby Hank. Hey, Rip remembered thinking, he
needed a six-pack some days to soothe himself.

Rip wore the Baby Bjorn baby carrier most of each day, and after months of living life with Hank dangling from his chest, Rip wondered (not in front of Grace, of course) if he knew a little bit about what it might feel like to be pregnant.

He wore Hank on walks, on the subway, when he cooked, when he vacuumed, and even, on occasion, when he took a shit. Baby Hank was a whole lot happier. Rip had worn Hank every night from five to eight, what the veteran mommies at the playground called the witching hour, when, according to old-world maternal superstition, babies' crankiness peaked. Rip and Hank bobbed to his old alt-rock mixed tapes as Hank fussed, farted, and face-mashed until he finally surrendered to sleep.

When he joined the playgroup after Hank's six-month birthday, invited by Susanna, whom he'd met at the shrimp-level newborn swim classes at the Y, Rip was the sole stay-at-home-daddy, or SAHD. He'd quickly learned the lingo of the newest generation of connected mommies. For the first time in years, he knew what it was to belong, and he was still grateful to the mommies. Especially to Tiffany, who never failed to ask Rip how *he* was. Tiffany, with her oil-scented embraces and the reliability of her texts that made his phone dance all day, reminding him—even on lonely winter days, he and Hank stuck inside—he wasn't alone. Tiffany's smile. Her lips. Her tongue darting out to catch the cherry-flavored ice dripping off Harper's Popsicle. Her hand reaching for him, pressing him into her. What if all those layers of clothes had disintegrated? His dick would have slid up and down, up and down, snug between her ass cheeks. Tiffany. Tiffany. Tiffany.

"Daddy," Hank moaned.

Rip jolted, almost rolling off the cot.

"What? What is it?"

"My tummy feels sick."

Rip sighed and rearranged himself, tugging at the elastic of his boxer briefs.

"Did you make a poo-poo today?"

"Um"—Hank hesitated—"no?"

"Okay, potty time," Rip said, groaning as he slid off the cot and lifted the boy in his arms. His back was aching from the dozen piggyback rides he'd given that day, and from racing across the uneven sand as unofficial lifeguard. A night on an ancient metal cot certainly wouldn't help.

"Okeydoke," Rip said, trying to sound cheerful once he and Hank were in the small, pink-tiled bathroom whose fixtures were relics from the sixties. "Take off your 'jamas."

"You help me," Hank whined.

"Come on now, big boy."

"But, I can't." Hank's arms hung slack, zombielike.

Both he and Hank knew that if Grace were present, he wouldn't give in, Rip thought, he would make Hank undress himself.

But she wasn't there. She hardly ever was.

Rip tugged Hank's *Toy Story 3* pajama pants down, and then his *Toy Story 2* underoos, careful not to slide the elastic over Hank's penis. Rip had insisted on circumcision. He was a Jew (albeit a lackluster one), and he wanted his son's junk to match his own. He'd stood strong against Grace's insistence the circumcision was "mutilating" their child's genitals, and every time he bathed Hank, helped him onto the toilet, or watched him run nude through the sprinklers in the backyard, he thought of how Grace had made him fight. And how he had won.

He helped Hank position himself on the toilet seat and watched as the boy's eyes neared the epiphany-like glaze that accompanied each bowel movement. Like pooping was a spiritual experience. Like the kid might start talking in tongues. Rip chuckled, congratulating himself on his ability to find humor in the mundane.

"Don't. Laugh. At. Me," Hank said as he strained. "Privacy. I need privacy!" he yelled.

Rip hurried out of the bathroom, shutting the door behind him, almost colliding with Grace in the hallway.

"What are you doing?" she whispered. Asking him—as usual, he thought—the obvious. "He'll wake the other kids."

Her hair was mussed. Her eyes puffy in the bright hall light.

"I hate it when you sneak up on me like that," Rip said. "It's creepy." He smiled to show he was joking, but she glared at him.

The memory of Tiffany gripped him. Her back arching in pleasure. The ends of her dark curls tickling his mouth.

"Are you hearing me?" Grace said, returning him to the stuffy hallway. Like one of his wet dreams, Grace appearing just in time to spoil his climax.

"What's wrong?" he asked.

Grace's nostrils flared as she took a breath, preparing to speak, and Rip was certain she knew. Her eyes weren't just swollen. They were ringed red. Had she been crying?

"Why don't you ask your BFF mommy friend?" Grace said. "She seems to know sooo much about you. And me." She took a shaky breath. "And our very private personal family life."

His mouth opened, but he couldn't speak. He heard himself say, "Wha? Wha?" Stuttering.

"Wait," he got out. "What are you talking about? I have no idea."

Grace interrupted him, her words launched by a breathy humph that made him feel as if he'd been blasted by hot wind.

"She just made me feel"—Grace paused—"like a really shitty mom."

He heard the girl-like hurt in her voice and knew, with a cooling cascade of relief, Grace knew nothing of what had happened at the kitchen sink that afternoon. If she did, there'd be no room for sadness. Only anger.

"Grace, sweetie," he said.

He cupped her elbows in his hands and drew her close, so her forehead rested on his chest. Groggy and loose-limbed, she let him. She shuddered—with a sob or a sigh, he wasn't sure.

Hank yelled from the bathroom. "Come here. Daddy. I want you. Dah-day!"

"Forget it. She's just an immature B-I-T-C-H," Grace said as she lifted her head and pushed him toward the bathroom. "Hurry. Before our kid wakes the whole house and everyone *really* has a reason to hate me."

"Why are you yelling, Henry?" Rip snapped, as the bathroom door shut behind him, but then he saw that Hank was leaning over, his chin almost touching his thick knees. His face twisted in pain.

Rip knelt, peering up through the boy's glossy bangs.

"You having a tough time going, buddy?"

Hank let out a groan, and the vein in the center of his forehead wriggled.

"Oh, poor guy," Rip soothed as he rubbed the back of Hank's cold, sweaty neck.

After consoling Hank, and promising a good poop would make him feel better, Rip convinced him to lie back on the pilled bathroom rug. He helped Hank pull his knees to his chest, a bowel-loosening trick via their pediatrician.

They were in the bathroom for another half hour—the air sour with Hank's intermittent farts. Rip scanned his memory to think of any slip of his (or Tiffany's) that might have given their brief—whatever that was—away. Tiffany would never throw him under the bus, especially when nothing had happened. He thought of the playgroup mommies—Nicole, Susanna, Leigh. Oh God, he thought. Leigh. She'd have him ousted from the playgroup, never cc'ed on a group e-mail again, if she knew he'd even looked down Tiffany's shirt—which, he had, of course, frequently. Hank would be devastated. And the new baby. Think of the loss he or she would suffer? What would Rip do without the play-group? Who would he be? One of those aimless stay-at-home dads, the ones without a clique. He thought of them as floaters, hovering around the margins of the playground, like ships without a port to anchor in.

"*What* is going on in there?" Grace whispered through the door. Rip could hear the irritation tweaking her voice. Not *Is everything okay?* Or something comforting, like *You'll feel better, Hank, honey.*

Rip was the one trapped in the bathroom. He was the one who made Hank's lunch every day, making certain there wasn't the tiniest hint of crust on his cheese sandwich, not a speck of skin on his sliced apples. He was the one who bought Hank new socks and underwear, who kept track of the sales on kids' clothes at the Gap and Old Navy. It was Rip who had bought a lead test to check the water in their apartment, and even the water fountain at the playground—though he'd never admit that to Grace, certain she'd call him a worrywart. Rip remembered to cut Hank's toenails. If it had been up to Grace, Rip thought, as Hank's face turned purple from straining, the boy's toenails would grow until they curled over his toes. Like some freak in the old *Guinness' Book of World Records* Rip had loved as a kid.

Rip did it all alone. He needed the playgroup. They were his port and his anchor.

"Answer me, Richard," Grace sang from the other side of the door. "Please."

"Almost done," Rip sang back, his jaw clenched. "Right, Hankster?"

"Don't let him push too hard," Grace said.

Always the manager, Rip thought.

"He'll get another hemorrhoid," Grace whispered as if it were a four-letter word.

He leaned his chin on Hank's knees. Hank placed his warm hands on Rip's cheeks.

"Daddy?"

"Yeah, my special guy?"

"It hurts."

Rip winced. Still, he savored the yearning in Hank's voice. His son wanted him. No. He needed him.

"I'm here for you, buddy," Rip said. "Promise."

"Forever and ever and the end of time?" Hank asked, his voice squeaking as he strained.

"You betcha."

Finally, a small ball of tarlike foul-smelling poop plopped into the toilet.

"Daddy?"

"Yeah, bud?"

"Constipated poops smell worser than regular poops."

"You got that right, stinker."

on pins and needles

Nicole

The living room emptied, the wine-drowsy moms and dads climbing the stairs in socked feet. As if, Nicole thought, they were teenagers sneaking in after curfew.

She checked the front windows of the house for movement before opening the trunk of her car and reaching over the duffel bags for the lever that released the lid over the spare tire. With a satisfying pop, the lid opened, leaving her just enough room to reach in and feel for the tampon box she had tucked into the center of the tire. She withdrew the three joints she'd rolled the night before while Josh and Wyatt had slept.

Her technique was improving. After several failed attempts, she'd found a site online with instructions on how to roll a traditional joint, including a few specialty rolls; the Saturday Night Special, the Magic Carpet, and what the site claimed was a favorite in the hash bars of Amsterdam, the Tulip. She had decided to stick with the classic basic, the Knee Trembler. At least until she could roll a joint that burned smooth.

The first hit was strong. When the smoke filled her lungs, she doubled over, coughing. *Fuck, fuck,* she whispered, checking the house through watering eyes.

She'd already thought of what to do if she got caught. Put on a sheepish smile and say she'd snuck a cigarette. To most of the moms (except Tiffany), a cigarette was an adventure. The mommies accepted the need for a bottle of wine here, half a Xanax there, to get through tough times, like when your child was going through a tantrum phase, a hitting phase, a waking-at-four-in-the-morning phase.

Nicole tucked the tampon box into one of the Go Bags and slowly shut the trunk.

She walked around the side of the house, past the piles of sand, shells, and seaweed that had washed through the seawall's drainage holes in the last high tide, past the toolshed her father had decorated with the buoys and fishing net that washed ashore. A skeletal fence of silvery driftwood gleamed, anchored with thick, rusted nails (a childproofing hazard if she ever saw one), squaring off her father's garden—a tangled mess of squash plants, bean vines, and black-eyed Susans.

It seemed to Nicole, that since her last visit six months ago, the house had aged twenty years. The white aluminum siding was rust-streaked, as if the salt water, in the last nor'easter, had given the house a manic embrace, digging its barnacled claws in as the tide pulled the storm back to sea. Her father's purple petunias, potted in rusted, stewed-tomato cans, had shriveled. She thought about watering. But what did a few flowers matter when the rest was such a mess? The grass, bare in spots, was littered with sunbaked figs slashed in half by eager raccoon claws. Even in the night's darkness, Nicole could make out the cloud of no-see-ums swarming the sweet, rotting mess.

She knew she should be grateful for her parents' home. *How many city boys have a private beach on the weekends?* her mother shot back when Nicole complained about the toilets that backed up, the dust and grime and cobwebs and clutter. This, she thought, as she stepped over a twisted hunk of driftwood, was all the inheritance she'd get, and once the economic crisis had squatted on her parents' doorstep, they'd had to sign off on a reverse mortgage. She'd have to repay the government. She'd have to buy this piece of junk.

She knew she sounded like a spoiled brat. But, she thought, isn't that just what she was?

Her parents had moved to this affluent suburb so she'd come of age amid the privileged, so she'd adopt their manners, absorb their way of seeing the world, and she'd been damn good at it: pruning, reshaping herself, sprouting expectations and entitlement like new leafy branches.

Was it any surprise she felt disappointed in her parents, who couldn't splurge for family vacations—the whole clan flying to Turks and Caicos—or pay for preschool, or karate classes, or thirty-guest birthday parties for Wyatt? Who couldn't "gift" them money for a down payment like so many of her friends' parents had, because wasn't that the only way one could afford a home these days, even on a decent salary like Josh earned?

She plucked a plump purple-black fig from the tree and tore it open with her nails. She ate the sweet meat, made sweeter after she pulled on the joint and her mouth filled with smoke. The tiny seeds cracked between her teeth. Her father had eaten figs as a boy in southern Italy during the war—handfuls of them until he shit his pants, he'd told her. It was the only food left. And here she was, she thought, whining about family vacations.

Times were *relatively* tough for everyone. She had seen the guilt flickering across even her wealthiest friends' faces when the check came at the end of a pricey dinner out. But, still, they ate out, they vacationed at Club Med, they drove BMWs, Audis, and luxury SUVs, they hired women to clean their less-than-1,000-square-foot apartments. They bought handbags that cost double her parents' weekly grocery bill. She knew she was just like them, living way beyond her means. Saving zilch. Acting as if the future would never arrive, with its overdue notice.

She cringed when she thought of what the moms in the playgroup might have expected of her parents' home, and the disappointment they had surely felt when they pulled up to the house. Nicole's own apartment was tastefully deco-rated with midcentury pieces, including a pristine Danish teak dining table and two leather armchairs, perfectly worn. The look was minimalist, the very opposite of her parents' home, with its mismatched furniture, the synthetic drapes her mother insisted on despite the way they blocked the view of the water. *Too much light aggravates my uveitis,* her mother complained. Nicole's home smelled of sixty-five-dollar organic candles with scents like Moroccan mint tea and woodland violets, while her parents' home, despite Nicole's at-tempt to air it out, smelled of mildew and the sulfa pills her diabetic mother took for her urinary tract infections.

Nicole was sure the mommies—especially Leigh, who had grown up sum-mering out East at the Lambert clan's country home—had imagined a scene out of *Sex and the City*. A turquoise pool vanishing into the horizon. There was a leaking kiddie pool. The mojitos Nicole had promised were poured from a scratched Tupperware pitcher, and her childhood Pac-Man and Smurfs sheets covered the guest beds instead of fresh white linens. Thank God she had found, and then hid, her mother's feminine deodorant spray—*guaranteed to alleviate vaginal odor!*

Yet, in the silvery night air, wrapped in the perfume of the fading honeysuckle, as Nicole looked up at the windows, warm portraits of light, and thought of the women and men who filled the house, she felt a glowing approval that made her blush. They liked her enough to travel all the way out to the Island, she thought, before quickly reprimanding herself for acting so junior-high.

She spotted a light in the kitchen. Someone was awake, and they were downstairs. Only twenty yards from where she stood.

She ducked behind the car, then slunk past the shed. She ran, hunched over, in and out of the shadows to the side of the house. She crouched under the deck stairs, the crushed shells cutting into her bare feet.

As the sea air rippled through her thin shirt, Nicole relit and sucked greedily on the joint.

no picnic

Susanna

Susanna had waited, curled up on the sofa, pretending to sleep, fearing Rip and Michael might never leave their shared bottle of booze. When they finally staggered upstairs, she had gone to the dark kitchen.

Now sauerkraut dribbled down Susanna's chin. She took a bite of a hot dog and dunked an onion ring in ketchup. Already, she could feel the acid mingling with the grease, all of it a roiling mess in the small pouch of a stomach perched atop her ballooning uterus. At thirty-five weeks, it seemed as if just two or three bites of food filled her. One too many detonated the heartburn. Sometimes, and especially after she binged, she stood over the toilet and stuck two fingers down her throat, hoping a good puke would extinguish the reflux.

In the last eight months, Susanna's world had been a rainbow of puke. Bright pink after she ate a pint of cherry-flavored ice cream. Speckled green after the spanakopita from the Mediterranean Kitchen down the block. And once, after the boys' third birthday party, a rainbow of pastels from their Thomas the Train birthday cake.

So, she had reasoned a few weeks ago, why not eat what she craved if puking was inevitable? As she stood in front of the open refrigerator in the beach house kitchen, the cold air spilling over her sweating body, she bit into a fat pickle, knowing it wouldn't be long before it rose.

She had vomited at least once a day for nine months. She no longer feared the heaving return. It had become part of the routine of everyday life. She woke. She ate breakfast. She puked. She brushed her teeth. She got the boys ready for preschool. Hadn't she puked practically everywhere by now? Outside the F train Carroll Street stop, into the gutter in front of their building, in the bathroom at the hair salon. In practically every restroom of what *used* to be her favorite restaurants. She had puked in the ladies' room at a Broadway show. At the spa midmassage. In a marble-floored bathroom stall the day before at the courthouse where they'd gotten married. She had even puked on Levi one night, as he lay sleeping in her arms. Once a week, he reminded her, "Mama? 'Member when you throw up on me?"

Dr. Patka, their diminutive obstetrician, insisted the vomiting was fine. It even had a long Latin name. *Hyperemesis Gravidarum.* Which, to Susanna, sounded anything but fine.

Don't worry, Dr. Patka soothed in her singsong, North Indian accent. The baby was gaining weight, the heartbeat perfect. As if throwing up every day for nine months was no big deal. Susanna fought the urge to defend herself. She wasn't some wimpy prima donna. She'd been captain of the MacArthur High School field hockey team. She'd pierced her own belly button in college. She had tolerance. For pain. For Allie's bullshit. For her parents' disgust that she was gay. *A pretty girl like you,* her father had said, shaking his head, when she'd come out to them after college.

But this was 247 days of retching until her throat was sore, heaving until she felt like she'd been kicked in the ribs. She had calculated it one night, as she sat in piss-soaked maternity sweatpants, her cheek resting on the puke-mottled lid of the toilet. And she still had a month to go.

She had tried everything. The cotton seasickness wristbands whose pressure points were supposed to alleviate nausea. She had taken extra vitamin B-12, usually vomiting the pill along with milk she'd chased it with. And there were those darn Preggie Pops lollipops ($4.99 a box). Oh the promises those lollipops had made with that smiling pregnant woman on each wrapper. *A natural way to ease nausea! Great for labor! Alleviates dry mouth! Quick energy boost!* She had ordered a box from drugstore.com, tried one, and thrown the rest away.

The OB nurse had given her a handout with yet another photo of a happy pregnant woman, her smile so placid that Susanna wanted to tear the paper into pieces, throw it in the toilet, and puke on it.

SUGGESTED SNACKS FOR MORNING SICKNESS:
Lemons (eat them, suck on them, sniff them)
Ginger (ginger soda, ginger tea, ginger jam on toast, ginger snaps)
Peppermint tea
Crackers
Jell-O
Flavored Popsicles
Pretzels

It wasn't morning sickness, Susanna thought. It was all-goddamn-day sickness. And peppermint tea was not a snack.

There were more DON'Ts in this pregnancy than DOs.

Don't eat spicy. Don't eat greasy. Don't eat foods with a strong odor. Don't drink with your meals. Don't overeat. Don't nap after you eat.

At first, she had followed these suggestions. She was a do-gooder after all, she thought as she squirted a zigzag of ketchup on the half-eaten hot dog. After the birth of the twins, Allie had started calling her Miss Goody Two-shoes, especially when Susanna insisted they stop swearing in front of the boys, they eat strictly organic, they try to be more positive, less cynical, have more fun. They were mommies now, after all.

Susanna reached into the refrigerator (*aha, Brie! Screw your no-soft-cheese rule, Dr. Patka*), and the baby kicked hard, a low jab that made her lean on the cold freezer door for balance. She gave her belly a few firm pats, and shushed, "I know, sweetie, that lemonade's got you all excited now." The baby responded with a roll and Susanna's thin tee shirt rippled.

She remembered her first pregnancy with the twins with a nostalgic yearning. Despite the scheduled C-section (they were six pounds each) and double the hormones, the pregnancy had seemed effortless. Susanna had felt that proverbial glow, as if the life coiled within had painted every part of her, inside and out, with a magical luminescence.

Friends said they'd never seen her so lovely and asked if they could paint her and photograph her. She had modeled nude for their friend Brett, a bisexual sculptor with a graying ponytail, and as the spotlight warmed her naked shoulders and the cool air hardened her nipples, Susanna had been certain she had never been so beautiful, because this beauty was necessary. Allie, and all of Susanna's art school professors, had preached passion, guts, ferocity. Nothing as mundane as necessity. But every one of Susanna's paintings paled next to the work of art she had become, and after the twins were born, the unthinkable happened—the photographs Allie had shot, some of which lined the walls of the country's finest museums (and the walls of their lives), photographs that had once seemed like tiny miracles to Susanna, withered in the resplendent light of the double miracle of Levi and Dash.

Now, in this pregnancy, Susanna felt shriveled. *Un*miraculous. The tedium of slogging through each vomit-scented day, the hours of napping, the afternoons lying prone on the couch while the boys played Chuggington Traintastic Adventures on their iPads. Her once Pilates-toned muscles had slackened. Her skin was so dry, it itched, despite the cups of water she drank and the shea butter she lathered on before bed. What a waste of time, she thought, and quickly reminded herself it would be worth it in the end. Wouldn't it? Wasn't creating life enough?

Allie remained radiant. Although she was seven years older and did practically nothing to take care of herself. No exercise. No makeup. She hardly moisturized! Susanna imagined what everyone saw, especially Allie's adoring Parsons students, who were perky-breasted and newly out, ready to spring into Susanna's place as younger lover.

Allie was still beautiful. Unbroken.

It seemed as if even the twins' eyes were all for Allie. Susanna had watched Dash lean into Allie, like a cat rubbing up against a visitor, asking to be stroked. Casanova, they called him because he sought female attention.

"Mommy," Dash had said after Allie let him climb into her lap, "you're a pretty girl. Like a princess."

Susanna had to stop from laughing. He was certainly the first male to call Allie a princess. Allie, who was butch in appearance, in swagger, with her bow-legged gait, like that of a soccer player, and whose idea of "dressing up" was a plain silk tank with frayed skinny jeans and a dab of lipstick. But she knew what Dash had meant. Allie sparkled. Especially next to Susanna—Mama—in her baggy maternity dresses that could not hide the newly bulging saddlebags that made her feel squat. Ordinary. Like one of her middle-aged middle-American aunts.

This baby had also destroyed her love affair with New York City. The smells! Brooklyn would empty, she thought, as she dunked a cold french fry in mayo, there'd be a mass exodus to the suburbs if everyone had the superhuman smelling ability of a pregnant woman. If they could smell the filth that lay, like a sleeping demon, under their renovated brownstones and organically designed gardens.

There were whole blocks she had to avoid because of the stench that wafted up from the drains. She confined herself to the apartment on Tuesday and Friday nights, when the sidewalks were crowded with black garbage bags pulsing with odor. Safe in her scent-controlled apartment, Susanna fantasized about her someday home. Far enough outside the city for peace and quiet but also cushioned in one of the small liberal enclaves populated by those fleeing the city for a better life. They'd have a chicken coop (fresh eggs for breakfast), a kitchen garden, and honeybees. A wood-burning pizza oven on the redwood deck. Right next to the hot tub. But she had so much money to save, and she had to convince Allie to leave the city, all of which took energy she didn't have, not when she was so sick, so weak, so scatterbrained.

Every Friday, $500 was deposited from her Babes-on-the-Go! business bank account into a savings account she had opened online. Allie didn't need to know, Susanna told herself; Allie had a different definition of investment, which included a trip around the world with stops in Paris, Egypt, and Morocco to experience the art they had talked of so often before the boys were born and, Susanna thought with a twinge of guilt, they had spoken of less often after.

Susanna would certainly not let Allie spend the Babes-on-the-Go! earnings on frivolous things, not after she had toiled over those filthy strollers, pulling hair out of wheel spokes with a pair of tweezers, scrubbing car-seat cushions that smelled like spit-up. Susanna remembered that afternoon in the car—to think Allie actually thought she wanted to clean strollers, as if it were a hobby Allie was giving Susanna permission to dabble in!

It was Allie who kept them trapped in the city. City of Shriveled Produce. City of Foul Air. City of Obstacles, where a simple food shop became a test of endurance, navigating narrow supermarket aisles with the ever-jostling twins, and now her enormous belly. Screeching at the twins as she waddled to the park, their scooters zipping half a block ahead. *Stop! Freeze! You stop or I'll give you the biggest time-out ever!* She longed to live somewhere where her neighbors weren't a few feet away, witness to her shitty parenting.

Susanna knew she only had herself to blame. She had convinced Allie to have another baby. She hadn't thought of her motivation at the time, but she'd had a lot of time to think in the last eight months, alone in the bathroom, her head hanging over the toilet, the overhead fan a meditative drone. She had nagged Allie. *Think of the meaning it will add to your art.* When Susanna had only wanted to keep her job. As mother. As main caregiver. What else could she do except mother and create mediocre art? She'd gone straight from high school to art school to Allie.

You don't have to work, you can focus on your art, Allie had said when they'd first moved in together. Someone wanted to take care of her, Susanna remembered thinking—and they had lain in bed all day, the sun passing over the twisted white sheets and their naked, sweat-slick bodies as they planned their future. The art they would travel to experience, the art they would make together. Even then, Susanna hadn't felt the passion for art that Allie did, but she knew Allie needed to see her as an artist. She wondered now if Allie loved Susie the painter more than Susanna the mother.

She had meant it that afternoon in the car. There wasn't room for two artists in this family, not when one had photographs hanging in the Met, and had designed award-winning covers for *Time* and *Newsweek,* and it was this that had driven Susanna, over a year ago, to beg Allie to carry their next child. To take her turn. To make another baby for Susanna to mother.

The twins' birth hadn't transformed Allie into a mommy. Maybe, Susanna had hoped, carrying a baby would. Allie had agreed, though her resignation was clear, and she'd lasted for only two months of inseminations, which involved Eric jerking off into a sterile cup in one room of their apartment and Susanna transporting the cup to the bedroom, where among scented candles and *Les Nubians* on the iPod, Allie lay, waiting for Susanna to inject Eric's sperm at the moment of climax.

After the second failed attempt, Susanna had done some googling and informed Allie that oral sex was off the plate for the next try. Apparently, she'd explained matter-of-factly, saliva could kill sperm. Who knew? And that had been that. A few hours later, Allie, her speech blurred by alcohol, had woken Susanna, and said, "There will be no more turkey basters in my vagina."

Without pause, Susanna had said, "I'll carry the baby. Your baby."

At first, it had felt as if they were pioneering activists. There was nothing they couldn't do! Allie had seemed excited, too, promising she would work her ass off to make the extra money they'd need for the egg extraction, the in vitro, the adoption fees, the works.

As Susanna rewrapped the food, replacing tops of containers and returning them to the overstuffed refrigerator, she caught a whiff of food gone bad and gagged. She froze, breathing rapid little yoga breaths through her nose. A bubble rose from her belly and escaped as a rumbling belch. The pressure was relieved. She turned to make her way up the stairs and caught sight of a figure, startling so she almost lost her footing.

An older woman with a tired slouch.

It was her reflection in the grease-stained mirror.

the chicken before the egg

Rip

Hank was snoring softly; Nuk-nuk the bunny crushed by one plump arm.

Rip rolled out of the cot and tiptoed past the bed, where Grace lay still and unmoving. He slipped Grace's laptop from her bag and set it on the dresser. So sleek, so untouched by grubby little hands. His own laptop, which Hank used to watch children's shows on Netflix, was always sticky, the white handrest stained, the keyboard missing the letter H, which Hank had peeled away.

The cool blue light of the screen made Rip's fingers on the keyboard glow alien-like. He logged onto TryingToConceive.com under the username Hanks-daddy76. He had visited the site daily the past few months, ever since Grace had given him a *we'll have to think about it* shrug when he brought up having another baby.

He had been surfing the net, googling "wife does not want another child" when he'd found TryingToConceive.com.

A sense of belonging had blanketed him. His situation fit several of the forum categories. *Trying to Conceive in Your 30's* or *Trying to Conceive Baby #2* or *Trying to Conceive with In Vitro*. But the forum he longed to join, the one that reached out to him, whispering, *we will understand*, was:

I'm Ready . . . He's Not! (Do you want to TTC but don't have the support of your partner?)

Yes! He had wanted to post a confession full of exclamation points and capital letters, releasing the flood of resentment and shame he often hid from his friends, some of whom were still bachelors, and from his family, who seemed embarrassed by his infertility. He wanted to confess that if he were the woman (not that there was an unmanly bone in his body, he'd joke, wink wink), and if his husband didn't want a baby, he would sabotage the birth control, poke holes in the condom with a pin.

He had been wary about joining. Worried the women desperate to become mommies-to-be would resent his intrusion. The womb was the ticket, after all. In the end, it was the memory of the warm welcome the playgroup mommies had given him that bolstered his confidence, and he decided (at the risk of rejection) to remain honest, picking the über-revealing username Hanksdaddy76. He introduced himself in a post in the *Newbies* forum; he was a father who wanted to conceive, or at least have the right to try; there was nothing he wanted more than another child, and his wife was not on board.

His first posting received over 2,000 views and 252 responses. Most were supportive and welcomed him, praising him for his dedication as a father. A few were cruel, calling him an imposter (even a misogynist!) and claiming he'd never understand what it meant to have a barren womb.

Weeks went by, and he posted daily. He made friends, officially called girlfriends on the site. He and three other members even formed a group. They called themselves *3 women and a daddy*.

Rip learned everything about his new friends' trials to conceive, much revealed by the icons (or blinkies) following each member's signatures. The *Addicted to the Stick* blinkie was a pregnancy test icon that flashed from a − sign to a + sign. The *Fertility Issues* blinkie sported a bottle of pills and a hypodermic needle. There was an infinite variety of blinkies, including a dancing smiley face that did a robotic jig, and most women reserved this for when they finally got their positive pregnancy test.

One of the women in his group—Mama2Angels—had miscarried three times. Mama2Angels' username was followed by a stack of winged smiley faces, one for each of the babies she'd lost. In her most despairing posts, she referred to the column of angels as *my poor lost babies,* which overwhelmed Rip with self-loathing (how could he take Hank for granted?) and pity for poor Mama2Angels.

Though Rip hated to admit it, as he signed in that night at the beach house, he hoped Mama2Angels wasn't on. He knew her presence would dampen his already hopeless mood. Her baby angels with their flapping computerized wings, her long list of miscarriages and failed IVFs; it was like watching a base-ball player with horrific stats take his place at bat.

As soon as he logged on, he saw Mama2Angels was lurking, having posted in the *Please Pray* forum ten minutes earlier. *Please Pray* was where women re-quested prayers to be said in their name, for a conception, or for their new pregnancies to "stick"—a phrase that riddled the posts on the board, where Rip guessed most of the women had miscarried, many more than once.

Rip saw that the other two women in their clique were also online. Hope-ful80 popped up first. She'd been hanging out in the *Two-Week Wait* forum, where women in the two-week purgatory between ovulation and menstruation gathered, hoping their period (*the witch* was the members' preferred pseud-onym) didn't show up.

HOPEFUL80   OMG!! This two-week wait is taking forever!!! Only symptoms are a pinching feeling on my right side and bloating. I really hope this is my month. Do you ladies (sorry, HANKSDADDY76! hee hee) think this sounds promising? 💜 💜

Me: 28 (Polycystic Ovary Syndrome)
Dear Hubby: 30 (Normal Swimmers)
Married: August 2007
2 Fur Babies (Brandy & Bailey)
TTC #1 since Nov. 2008
Miscarriage 8/13/10 6w1d (ectopic) Looking more and more like IVF in 2012 . . .

MAMA2ANGELS   I'll pray for you, HOPEFUL80! Put your trust in the hands of God! 🙏

Me: 39
Husband: 42
👼 June 2005—mc @ 6 weeks
👼 July 2007—mc @ 8 weeks
👼 March 2010—mc @ 9.5 weeks
On the TTC journey as of January 2005

XCITED_2BA_MOMMY   Hi ladies and gentleman!

Re: HOPEFUL80—Your symptoms seem promising!! Fingers crossed that the WITCH 🐛 doesn't arrive for you. She sure is one tricky lady! I had a chemical preg last month and it was so hard when the witch showed up two days later!!!

Hoping for sticky beans this month! 😀

Me: 32
Fiance: 38
Daughter: Mackenzie DOB 5/22/07
TTC #2 since December 2009
Diagnosis: Unexplained infertility
Member of "Clomid Chicks"

HANKSDADDY76   ahem, ahem. hello, ladies! Poor Hank is all stopped up. Anybody know of a good natural remedy that can loosen my boy up? 😀

Me: 36
My Wife: 35
Son: Henry (aka Hank the Tank) DOB 8/3/2006 (IVF #3)
TTC #2 since December 2009
Diagnosis: Sperm mobility

The responses came rapid-fire, and Rip tapped the REFRESH button again and again (loud enough to make Grace stir on the bed) as post after post of suggestions appeared.

A tablespoon of syrup, suggested Hopeful80.

One teaspoon of ground flaxseeds sprinkled over his morning cereal, offered Xcited_2BA_Mommy.

Fluids, fluids, fluids, Mama2Angels chanted.

HANKSDADDY76   Thanks, future mommies! I knew you'd have great advice. OF COURSE, the wife was NOWHERE to be found when our poor son was in pain.

MAMA2ANGELS   Your son is blessed to have such a good-hearted daddy, HANKSDADDY76!!!

XCITED_2BA_MOMMY   Woot! Woot! You're an honorary mommy.

HOPEFUL80   HANKSDADDY76, I'm sorry to hear that. We can't all be BORN TO PARENT. ♥

HANKSDADDY76   Thanks. Your comments mean so much. ♥ Just a few minutes with you ladies might be enough for your great mommy vibes to rub off on her.

XCITED_2BA_MOMMY   Send her to us HANKSDADDY76! We'll whip her into shape LOL ☺

HANKSDADDY76   In OTHER news, I made a daddy friend today.

HOPEFUL80   Swoon!!! Maybe . . . you can *borrow* some of his swimmers, HANKSDADDY76?

HANKSDADDY76   Hahaha we'll see. I just met the guy. Let me ask him on a date first! ☺ Thank you, ladies! Truckloads of BABYDUST your way!!!

Rip signed off and erased the online history.

He stood over Hank, whose soft whistling snores were so sweet, Rip knelt and kissed the boy's cool forehead. He longed to wake his son and tell him what a great big brother he'd be. Hank was patient to a fault, and Rip imagined the two boys (in his fantasies, the second baby was a boy) wrestling in their apartment. Hank was all happy squeals as the slobbering toddling baby boy nibbled on Hank's chin. The baby would be gushed over at playgroup, and now that Hank was off to full-time preschool next year, Rip and the new baby would settle into the routine Rip had treasured when Hank was an infant. Naps every three hours (a chance for Rip to take a little snooze and bake a loaf of gluten-free bread). Ready-made formula bottles (no messy finger foods until four months). Strolls in the park, where young women in their mid-to-late twenties, their biological clocks recently wound, would stop to admire his baby, to place their hand gently on Rip's arm, and coo, "oh, he's sooooo cute," as they buzzed with procreative hunger.

Almost, Rip thought, as if it were the baby's daddy they wanted.

He thought about leaving Hank on the cot, squeezing in next to Grace on the bed. It was a full-size (their bed at home was a king) and he knew their bodies would press together, and maybe, just maybe. Then he heard the sound coming from next door.

Moaning. Each long moan punctuated with a grunt.

"What the fuck?" Grace muttered.

He froze, standing over his wife, listening to Tiffany. And getting harder and harder.

make-believe

Leigh

Leigh sat in the rocking chair in the corner of the guest bedroom and held a sleeping Chase in her lap.

He had fallen asleep with his cheek pressed against her milk-heavy breasts. She was scared to move, in case she woke him and lost him to his bed, or Tenzin's arms, which he often preferred. She felt like a teenage girl in bed with a slumbering boy for the first time—possessive, proud, and fearful. She rocked him and cuddled him the way she couldn't—the way he wouldn't let her—when he was awake.

A sleeping Chase was easiest to love.

The baby was asleep in the ancient crib in the corner. Tenzin was asleep on the air mattress under the window.

Then Leigh heard it. A lowing. A moaning.

Tiffany and Michael.

Leave it to Tiffany to bring a little X-rated action into a family weekend. Leigh laughed, and her hand flew to cover her mouth. Just as quickly, she removed it. Tiffany had told her she had a *radiant* smile and shouldn't hide it, the very opposite of what Leigh's mother had told her—that her teeth were too large and she should do her best to smile close-mouthed in photos.

She dared to lean over and brushed her lips across Chase's, tasting strawberry-flavored toothpaste.

Leigh had known Chase was different right away. She had been told by her birthing class instructor, and the how-to-parent books she'd read, that the first

weeks of a baby's life should be filled with quiet nursing, mother and baby doz-
ing in bed, warm naked skin on warm naked skin, the sugary scent of breast
milk on the baby's breath. Baby's eyes locked on Mama's in an unconditional
love–saturated gaze.

Instead, they'd been filled with Chase's cries. His mouth popping off her
nipple again and again. His eyes hadn't met hers. She had tried to stick with
nursing. She had hired a lactation consultant. She wouldn't be one of those
women who abandoned breast-feeding after a few nipple sores, she told herself.
She set her alarm every two hours and felt a nervous sweat spring out right
before the alarm sounded, calling her to what felt like a doomed match.

Leigh had tried to relax. She had even meditated, after the appointment
with that French pediatrician with the shock of greasy hair, the one hipster
parents raved about for his *laissez-faire* approach to children's health. He had
asked Leigh if, *perhaps,* her anxiety was the problem. She had believed him.
She had blamed herself. And her breasts.

She had heard about those "twice-exceptional" kids—who had delays and
gifts. They might not be able to get along with classmates but they learned how
to read at age two, and picked up Japanese by watching YouTube videos. Not
Chase.

Thank God he wasn't autistic, she told herself on Chase's "off" days—
although there were times she wished he'd been diagnosed with something so
they'd have a way to help him. To explain him. As her own mother had said
once, in a casually observant tone Leigh would never forget, there was *something just not right* about Chase. And although Leigh knew Chase loved her,
she still wished for his eyes to meet hers in that look the parenting books had
promised, as if it would act as a marker, proof she'd fulfilled her maternal duties. She was lucky, she thought, if she could hold Chase's attention for more
than ten seconds these days.

Stop, Leigh told herself, and laid her hand on Chase's chest. It rose and fell
in time with his breath and, it seemed, in time with the sigh of the waves below.

Do-over.

"Time for a do-over," Tenzin often sang when Chase's mood turned explosive, and he screeched and gnawed on his forearm with frustrated rage. *Do-over,
do-over,* Tenzin sang until Leigh felt as if their four-story brownstone, the
down payment had been a gift from her father on her wedding day, had been
put under a spell. A happy enchantment.

"Do-over," she whispered in Chase's ear now, picking away the strands of hair plastered to his sweaty cheek.

What was it Tenzin had said a few weeks ago? When she walked in on Leigh in the master bathroom—the cuts Leigh had just made on her own upper thigh a pattern of bright red crisscrosses, the razor still in her hand?

Leigh had watched Tenzin's reflection quadruple in the wall-to-wall mirrors. Tenzin had spoken calmly, as if she hadn't seen the blood rising, filling the paper-thin slashes until a drop rolled toward Leigh's knee.

"Your bad mood only serves your enemy."

Then Tenzin left. The click of the lock catching had seemed to multiply as it bounced off the hand-painted Italian tile, and Leigh had thought, absurdly, *There she goes, quoting the Dalai Lama again.*

Leigh hadn't understood at the time. Enemy? She knew who Chase's enemy was, and when she thought of *neurology,* she imagined a posse of outlaws—black-toothed, greasy-haired, village-pillaging bad guys, running amok inside Chase's brain.

But this was serenity. Her still and silent boy. She examined every freckle on his long, tanned arms. She studied the purple veins branching across his eyelids. It was a chance for Leigh to be still, too. There was no one to impress. No one to apologize to. Just her and her sleeping beauty. A perfect Chase and a perfect Leigh.

At least he had beauty, she thought. It just might be what saved him someday.

She lifted his limp arm and let his palm fall flat on her cheek, sliding his hand up and down.

"Mmm, gentle touch," she whispered.

As Chase accelerated toward boyhood, she feared his physical contact, rough and unpredictable. She tried not to flinch. Or pull away. Like that afternoon, when he'd jumped joyfully on the sofa downstairs, or on the beach afterward, when he had hugged her and squeezed until she had to peel him off her throbbing throat. All of this witnessed by the other mommies, so she had to hide her reaction, reminding Chase calmly, "Gentle touch." She had seen Brad lose his temper and shout, "Jesus, Chase!" when during one of their "wrestling matches"—an assignment from Chase's occupational therapist—Chase's long limbs whacked Brad in the throat, or worse, in the groin.

Chase's therapists—the well-meaning young (and mostly childless) women who came into their home eight times a week and who insisted on calling Leigh and Brad "Mom" and "Dad"—told them Chase needed more "sensory feedback." Deep bear hugs and pillow sandwiches and wrestling matches with Dad. They made it sound as if he needed a padded room.

Give him what he needs, they said, as if offering a cure. Couldn't they see she had needs too? Leigh needed to be able to hug her son when he was awake. But the only touch Chase accepted was the tight pressure of his weighted therapy vest and the rough-and-tumble wrestling.

When her phone vibrated on the nightstand next to the rocking chair, Chase twitched and let out a whimper before his head fell back, openmouthed.

It was a text from Tiffany. She texted Leigh this time every night, after Harper went down, after the bottle of Malbec had been drained, after she'd snuck a cigarette on her balcony (only six blocks from Leigh's brownstone) overlooking the oil-coated Gowanus Canal. They'd text back and forth for hours sometimes, until Leigh's fingers ached from typing on her keypad.

Tiffany:

get down here and save me you biotch. nicole's whining again. but she's got good weed!

Leigh texted back, hoping Tiffany couldn't tell she was lying, hoping the cringe she felt when Tiffany talked about sex and drugs hadn't infected her tone.

ha! you are crazy. baby on my boob. rain check? xo

Tiffany:

um, ok. I guess. (; I need to talk to you 1st thing tom am about what time Tenzin can be w me on thursdays. k?

Leigh didn't respond, hoping that if she avoided the topic long enough, Tiffany would give up. Tiffany had backed her into a corner, and as hard as Leigh tried, she could not ignore the tremor of anger she felt. She tried to chalk it up to Tiff's being tipsy, or her native tactlessness. After all, the woman had grown up practically feral somewhere in the farm country of Long Island. Terrible, awful things had happened to her. Tiffany had revealed snippets of her dark backstory in their late-night texts. Her abandonment by her mother at the fragile age of nine, her father's alcoholism, the rape at a party after she moved to NYC, the drugs, the sex, the abortions.

At first, Leigh had felt smothered under the weight of all that badness, but Tiff's honesty about how utterly soiled and broken she was made Leigh feel safe. After Leigh had taken (at the time, she had thought of it as borrowing) the money from the fundraising-committee account, she began answering Tiffany's texts more often. Leigh's own crime paled a shade or two in the glaring light of poor messy foot-in-her-mouth Tiffany's decades of error.

Every time Tiffany teased Leigh about her family's wealth—all those country-club and debutante jokes, and quips about sorority girls wearing pearls with their letter sweatshirts—Leigh wanted to tell Tiffany the truth. Her family had been rich decades ago, but now they were rich in name only. The family firm had nosedived in the crash of 2008, after Leigh's father had invested big in subprime mortgages. Leigh lost the three-thousand-dollar monthly allowance her father had been depositing in an account under Leigh's name since she went off to college. Brad had to scramble for extra work, consulting jobs he hated, and his resentment of Leigh, of her family, had built a wall between them. The slightest mention of having another baby, the costs of the IVF, set Brad into a rage, ranting about their maxed-out credit cards and mortgage payments, insisting they get back on their feet before spending more money on "getting" (he always used this verb, as if they were purchasing a child, Leigh thought) a baby, usually ending with the front door slamming, Leigh alone with Chase for hours.

She had drained the remainder of her allowance account for the first visits to the fertility doctor, and then the Clomid treatments, and the artificial insemination attempts with Brad's sperm. When Chase turned two and a half, they'd been trying for a second baby for twenty months. Her fortieth birthday loomed. She knew other women would have been patient, kept trying until they conceived naturally. Forty wasn't that old, especially in Brooklyn. Twenty months wasn't that long. But Leigh had never wanted anything so badly. Enough to steal. When Charlotte was finally conceived, Leigh felt certain that the risk she'd taken—the first of her life—had been worth it. She had sworn to herself that, when her new baby was born, she wouldn't love Chase any less.

Now, rocking slowly in the chair, staring at the blue light of her phone screen, an anxious sweat coated Leigh's upper lip as she remembered Tiffany's grip on her arm that afternoon when Leigh had tried to walk away, tried to avoid surrendering Tenzin.

She had almost fallen asleep in the rocking chair, her chest sticky with Chase's sweat, when her phone vibrated. Another text from Tiffany.

look out your window at exactly 12:35 don't forget!!

When her phone read 12:32, Leigh rose from the rocking chair, Chase dead-weight in her arms. Her back throbbed, but still she went to the window, Tiffany's command like the call of a mythological siren luring her forward.

blast from the past

Allie

Allie set matching sippy cups of water at the foot of the air mattress where both boys slept in that tangle of arms and legs that still amazed her. Levi's sunburned cheek rested on Dash's shoulder. Dash's right arm was flung across Levi's chest.

Susanna waddled into the room, looking depleted, her perfumed wrist tucked under her nose.

"You okay there?" Allie asked.

Susanna let out a gassy burp, and Allie laughed. It was so un-Susanna. Allie guessed Susanna had been on one of her secret fridge raids.

"It's not funny," Susanna said. "I just puked my brains out."

"Well," Allie said, "it's a good thing I'm the smart one in the family."

Allie was relieved—comedy was her personal ice-breaker—when Susanna smiled.

"I hope they're best friends forever," Allie said, nodding at the sleeping boys and thinking of her own brother, a banker (a Catholic, for fucksake) and how he and she couldn't have been more different. "You know, so they can look out for each other. Levi might need Dash to take care of him."

"Come on, Allie," Susanna said, "we have to create positive expectations, so the boys can strive to meet them."

When had Susanna turned into a walking, talking inspirational poster? Allie wondered.

Susanna struggled to reach her bra clasp, the globe of her belly swerving from side to side.

"This effing bra's killing me. Can you help me get it off, please?"

"Not until you say the F-word properly," Allie said.

"Fine. Fuck." Susanna stamped her foot. "Fuck. Fuck. Fuck."

The tops of Susanna's heavy breasts jiggled, and Allie imagined kissing the milk white skin, using her tongue to trace the green veins that glowed so vividly in pregnancy, leading, like a map, to Susanna's dark nipples.

"Good girl," Allie said.

She slipped her hands inside Susanna's maternity shirt, something shapeless and pastel from Old Navy or one of those stores that should be making uniforms instead of clothing.

Allie tried to remember Susanna's flirtatious confidence, the self-righteous tilt of her head that had gripped Allie's attention in the studio class she'd taught at Parsons years ago. Susanna the girl. Her dark hair in a ponytail that swung when she nodded during Allie's lectures. Allie had gone home after each class with thoughts of that ponytail. Of winding it around her fist and pulling it so Susanna's torso (unmarred by pregnancy) arched like a bow, Allie's hand sliding into Susanna's panties from behind. A living sculpture of taut curves.

She unhooked the three clasps of Susanna's maternity bra. Her double-D body armor, they joked. Susanna's breasts had been sore, filled with fibrous cysts, and Allie hadn't held their weight in months.

"I miss your ponytail," Allie whispered as she combed Susanna's neat pixie cut with her fingers. "Remember? That first night?"

Allie dropped to one knee, and then on both, lifted Susanna's shirt.

Susanna swatted her away and looked to the boys, her eyes wide in warning. She tried to step back, but Allie pulled the end of her long tee. Susanna stumbled forward.

"So?" Allie asked, ignoring the pain of her knees against the hardwood floor.

"The first night," Susanna said, her voice deeper. Relenting, Allie thought.

She kissed Susanna's navel. It had popped a week ago and was visible under her thin summer clothes. Allie had caught people looking at it when they walked down the street at home.

"Oh, yeah. The concert," Susanna whispered. "You were such a god to me then."

"And I'm not now?" Allie asked.

She ran the tip of her tongue around Susanna's belly button; she could see the silvery pink scar where Susanna had pierced herself in college. Allie hummed quietly to imply pleasure and to hide the fact that she found the protrusion grotesque. Tumorlike. *Remember,* she told herself, this is where the umbilical cord begins, the life-sustaining nourishment. A fucking miracle.

Allie had been teaching at the Parsons School for Design less than a year when Susanna had registered for one, then two, and finally three of Allie's four classes. Their relationship remained innocent although the tension of attraction was so strong that later Susanna would admit to dizzying panic attacks during student/teacher conferences in Allie's small office overlooking Union Square. Mid–second semester, Allie got the call from her agent. It was the ten-minute class break, in which her classroom emptied, the students rushing outside to suck down a cigarette and refill their styrofoam coffee cups at the convenience store across the street. Her hand shook as she wrote down the details—the time of the Amtrak train, the hotel in Philly, and the name of the band's manager, who would meet her in the hotel lobby in eight hours.

"Oh my God," she said as she looked out into the classroom.

Susanna was sitting at a front-row desk, chatting with a friend of hers, a mousy and opinionated girl who annoyed Allie.

"What?" Susanna asked, and the breathy excitement in her voice startled Allie, made her want to share the thrill. So she told them. She was going to Philly to shoot Aerosmith in concert. For motherfucking *Rolling Stone.* The booked photographer was ill or something, and it was her gig now. After much oohing, aahing, and holyshitting, Allie had asked the girls if they wanted to come along, they could split the hotel room, and she'd score them some tickets. *Hell yeah,* the girls said, and Allie cut class short. They hopped in a cab, stopping only at Allie's studio in Alphabet City to pick up her equipment, where Allie had liked the way Susanna studied every photo, book, tchotchke. Allie bought the train tickets, then food in the dining car, and they talked about art. Well, Allie talked mostly, and the girls listened with eager eyes and parted lips. Like delicate glass pitchers waiting to be filled, Allie remembered thinking.

It would become one of the most important nights of her life, the story that she'd tell for years after; at conferences, in classes she taught, to new acquaintances she hoped to impress, one of the few stories she would use to define who she is, was, and who she had always wanted to be.

She had taken her position onstage in darkness. The dim lights in the massive amphitheater seemed a primordial glow, the shuffling and whispering and intermittent shouts of the crowd like a dam ready to spill. She could just make out the silhouette of the band. The chords rang out, and the crowd detonated.

"More lights," she called into the wings, and then louder, louder, shouting. It was too dark. The shots would be weak. She moved out onto the stage, standing where she knew the lighting dude could see her. She lifted her arms from her waist to above her head, again and again, like some crazy fucking referee in a football game, and there was an explosion of light, and a maelstrom of noise from the crowd, and it would always seem to her that the band let loose at exactly that moment. Allie would always feel as if she, like a conductor, had brought it all to life.

Allie tugged at the thick waistband of Susanna's maternity pants until they lay in a pile at Susanna's feet.

"We fucked our brains out that night," Allie said, as she slid Susanna's peach-colored panties down her legs, the fraying elastic stretching under her fingertips.

"That's a romantic way of putting it." Susanna laughed breathily.

Allie slid her palms up Susanna's thighs.

"Oh, now, come on," she said as she led Susanna, one hand in hers, to the bed. "You used to like talking dirty. What was that fantasy you had? The one in the stable? With the saddle?"

"The boys will hear," Susanna whispered.

"They're wiped out, babe," Allie said.

She gripped Susanna's elbow with one hand, Susanna's hand with the other, and slowly guided her down onto the bed. Allie's arms shook under the strain. Susanna had always been bigger—in height, in personality. In the impromptu photos they had taken over the years, their faces side by side, crowding the frame, even the features of Susanna's face seemed more three-dimensional next to Allie's own child-sized mouth and close-set eyes.

"Scoot back," Allie commanded as she crawled onto the bed, using her toes to kick off her black motorcycle boots.

She felt sexy. Like a jaguar stalking prey, its haunches rising and falling. But the sight of Susanna trying to pull her body back on the bed snagged the moment. It was an awkward scuttle that made Allie think of the crabs the children had squealed over on the beach that afternoon.

Finally, Susanna fell onto her back with a groan, her knees falling apart in a position that felt too gynecological, like yet another appointment at the fertility doctor, where the waiting room was filled with sad women, their eyebrows lifted in a pathos that revolted Allie, as if they could see nothing more of themselves than an empty shell waiting to be filled. Once upon a time, she had been attracted to the kind of girl who wore that look, the ones that needed a teacher, not at all as innocent as they thought themselves to be.

Susanna had been different. Sure, she had been impressionable, eager to see meaning in every tag of graffiti on a concrete wall, every dead pigeon at the park, every Manhattan sunset burning with radiant colors only smog can birth. But it was Susanna who had been Allie's teacher, who had transformed Allie from a photographer who shot celebrities and supermodels with unblemished bodies and symmetrical features, to an artist who photographed the wrinkled hands of an Iranian peasant. The scabbed limbs of a Sudanese refugee. The ravaged body of a Bronx AIDS baby.

The tip of Allie's tongue circled Susanna's clit until Allie heard her sigh from beyond the massive globe of flesh that stood like a wall between them.

"Oh," Susanna whispered. "Yes."

But Allie wanted to focus on what *she* was feeling, the zing in her throat the memory of the concert had awakened, that made her want to touch herself and think of other women, the young and lean and horny girls of her past—including herself—who lived on in her fantasies.

She rose to her knees and pulled her tee over her head. She'd never needed a bra, and the male glances at the dots of her nipples poking through her thin tee shirts satisfied her in an almost-intellectual way. A little curious. A little vengeful.

The cool breeze sifting through the window screen made her skin ripple with a chill, and she leaned over Susanna's belly (*Tell me if I hurt you,* she said) and rubbed her hardened nipples against Susanna's chest. But the way Susanna's breasts fell to each side, the flat field of skin between a sickly white in the moonlight, made Allie close her eyes. As they slid together, Allie's prickled skin warmed and she conjured another Susanna—a ponytailed Susanna, her breasts high and firm, a V of young cleavage resting between them as she sat atop another Allie in a hotel room in Philly, their pelvic bones grinding, their tongues twining, the bedsheet wet.

They tried, but Susanna's belly was like an unscalable mountain, and Susanna let out a giggle (*Sorry, the baby kicked*), and Allie was certain Susanna's moans were too even to be authentic. Finally, Susanna tapped, then slapped Allie on the shoulder, whispering, "Stop, stop. Help me up!"

Allie lifted her face from between Susanna's legs, wiped her mouth with the back of her hand, and gripped Susanna's forearm. Susanna slid off the bed and onto her knees, a blur of loose white flesh. She wrapped a towel around herself, a butt cheek exposed, and hurried into the hall.

A few minutes later, Allie heard retching in the bathroom next door. Then the sound of water running through pipes. Then more retching.

Should she go in there? What could she do, really? Susanna had thrown up so many times with this baby. *My baby,* Allie thought, and then, *our baby.* It was part of the day's routine, Susanna running to the bathroom to puke.

Allie lay on the bed and listened for more of the moans she'd heard earlier from down the hall, hoping (she surprised herself) that Tiffany and her man had gone for another round. But there was only Susanna's heaving, Levi's snoring, and Dash's even breathing. The sounds of family.

She rolled onto her stomach, slipped her hand under her hips, and touched herself, rubbing in circles, the way she had always liked it, her face pressed into a pillow. She imagined Tiffany, one breast loosed from a diaphanous gown, her stare coy but inviting. Like Drost's *Bathsheba,* whose eyes, Allie had thought on her first trip to the Louvre, shone with desire. She held her breath when she came. Levi mumbled. Dash's hand crawled around his head until he found his pacifier.

She cleaned her fingers with a diaper wipe and pulled on a tank top. As she rummaged in her duffel for a pair of leggings, she heard feminine laughter outside, drifting up from the deck below. Then a voice: "Don't! The rocks. You'll kill yourself."

Allie moved to the window and parted the thin synthetic curtains.

On top of the seawall, illuminated by a bright moon, stood Tiffany. She was naked, her hair loose around her, black against the blue-white of her back. She gazed straight ahead, as if in a trance.

She's going to jump, Allie thought with a wave of panic as Tiffany rose to her toes—the shift of muscle under skin catching the moonlight—and dove off the wall.

There was a soft splash, then the black water rippled.

the coast is clear

Nicole

Nicole huddled on a lounge chair on the deck, her sweater pulled over her knees.

She sucked hard to keep the joint lit against the whip of the wind. Each gust pulled a trail of sparks over the seawall.

The weed had done little to numb her dread. Under the vast starry dome, the unknowable dwarfed her, and she felt more mortal than ever. Insignificant. Impermanent.

"God, you are such a narcissistic self-pitying freak," she whispered aloud to crack the chain of worrying.

She thought of her mother, who was always calling Nicole to tell her that she was praying for her and for Wyatt, and *even* for Josh (aka the Jew Nicole had married). When something good happened, like when her first book sold, or when Josh was promoted, her mother's response was, "My prayers have been answered!" As if, Nicole thought, her mother was trying to take credit for Nicole's life, for the never-ending pile of decisions she struggled to make.

She picked a piece of rolling paper from her lip and watched the yellow-tinged wisps of cloud hurry across black sky. She tried to imagine God, the white-bearded Father in flowing robes she had known as a child, who, she had imagined, hovered somewhere up there, his muscled arm reaching down toward his children on earth.

"Thunder's just the angels bowling," her mother had told a young Nicole when she'd been frightened during summer storms. What a comfort that had been. When Nicole had learned, in seventh grade Earth Science, the real cause, the clash of cold and hot air, she'd been ashamed, wondering how could she have been so stupid.

What she'd give to be a girl again, believing in prayers, sleeping under the simpatico eyes of a Jesus who hung above her bed in a gold plastic frame. Before her mother left for Florida that July, they'd had the same futile God conversation.

"I can't make myself believe, Mom."

"Well," her mother had said, "you certainly could try a bit harder."

Nicole flinched as a fantasy shot through her mind like a film. Couldn't *it* happen any minute now? Like in the movies? A flash of light that fills every inch of the sky with the purest white, then a vacuum suck and a huge expelling, a wind trampling the earth with the force of a billion rabid horses with plutonium hooves.

She heard movement behind her and spun around with a frightened sound, more animal than human.

A tittering Tiffany appeared in baggy sweatpants and Michael's black motorcycle jacket.

"Shit," Nicole whispered, rolling her eyes. "You scared me."

"Don't drop the joint, whatever you do," Tiffany said with a smile.

Nicole laughed and raised the joint along with her eyebrows. An offering. A howl of wind carried off orange sparks.

Tiffany huddled next to her, each on one of two chaise lounges pulled side by side. They wrapped beach towels around their shoulders and tucked them over their legs. The thick black leather of Michael's jacket creaked as Tiffany lifted the joint to her mouth. Nicole cupped her hands around the glowing ember and saw the smudged mascara ringing Tiffany's eyes.

"Fuck," Tiffany said into her thick, smoky exhale. "It's freezing. This is totally messing up my postorgasm high." She laughed before a gale picked up her giggles and flung them into the sea.

"I thought there was something different about you," Nicole said, not mentioning it was the musky scent of skin and come and sweat that now seemed so foreign to her own life. "You're glowing."

"Isn't that what they tell pregnant women?"

Nicole tucked her head between her knees, her legs shielding the roach, and took a drag.

"Things must be great between you two," Nicole said, trying to remember the last time she and Josh had sex somewhere other than their bedroom.

"Well," Tiffany started, and Nicole could hear the calculating note in her voice, "I asked Michael which of the lesbian mommies he'd like to fuck. *That* set him off."

"Jesus, Tiff." Nicole laughed, although she had often admired and envied Tiffany's damn-the-world attitude.

With a whine of impatience, Tiffany said, "Listen! So that led to which one I'd fuck." She paused to take a hit off the joint. "In front of him, of course."

"And?" Nicole asked.

"Who do you think?" she asked. "Allie, of course."

"And Michael?"

"Susanna," Tiffany said, with a tut-tutting headshake that made Nicole suspect Tiffany was hiding something. A bit of jealousy? Sometimes, Tiffany couldn't stomach her own little mind games when it was her turn to be the underdog.

"I hope I wasn't too loud," Tiffany said, a new energy lifting her voice. "It's a good thing Harper was pooped. Out like a light."

Tiffany gripped Nicole's arm. Her eyes widened.

"Do you think anyone heard?" she asked.

Nicole knew Tiffany by now, and she knew Tiffany hoped the whole house had heard.

"It wasn't actual *sex*," Tiffany said, "Just oral. But it's really doing it for me lately. You know?"

Tiffany's matter-of-fact tone threw Nicole off-balance. What could she say? Yes, she wished Josh were doing anything for her lately. Yes, she wished her libido hadn't been flattened by antidepressants for the past three years.

"Ugh," she groaned. "It's been ages for me."

Another reason not go back on her meds, she thought. As a girl, she'd masturbated daily, sometimes multiple times a day, and when she and Josh were first together, she'd been filled with a churning desire, which had only just now, almost three months meds-free, begun its shy return.

A clang of metal rang out from the side of the deck, and Nicole jumped.

"You'd think I'd be a bit more chill," she said. "Under the stoned circumstances."

Tiffany took a hit, and, holding her breath, squeaked, "Who, you?"

"Who me?" Nicole sang in tune to the "Cookie Jar" song Tiffany had performed in many a Tiff's Riffs class.

"Yes you!"

Nicole finished, "Couldn't be!"

Smoke trickled out with Tiffany's laughter.

"I hate that song," Tiffany said as she poked at the spit-flattened base of the joint with a nail polished green. "It's all about guilt and shame." She took another hit. "It's enough to give some poor kid an eating disorder. I mean, who cares who took the cookie from the cookie jar?"

"You crack me up," Nicole said. "Have you ever thought about writing? Or blogging? I bet you'd be great at it."

"Maybe," Tiffany said. She pulled the sweatshirt over her knees until only her toes, also painted in green polish, peeked out. Her silver toenail winked as she wiggled her toes. She wore a dreamy look, Nicole thought as she followed Tiffany's stare across the Sound to the blur of industrial Connecticut that had always reminded Nicole of the lights of a distant carnival. But then she caught a befuddled look masking Tiffany's face. It was the look Tiffany wore when the playgroup parents talked about books or films or politics, topics Tiffany dismissed with a wave of her hand, and, "You guys are too smart for me!"

Nicole thought it strange the way Tiffany played the ditz card when it suited her. When everyone knew Tiffany was smart in the ways that mattered most. Nicole remembered the ugly scene a few weeks back at the Jakewalk bar, on the group's Girls' Night Out. It was the kind of intelligence that snuck up on you when you least expected it.

They passed the joint back and forth until it was a brown-stained nub of wet paper. Nicole let it slip through her fingers into the black night.

"Lookie what I have," Tiffany sang, and pulled a cigarette from behind her ear. "And I've got more." She tapped the pocket of Michael's jacket.

"Nice," Nicole said.

"So," Tiffany said, hugging herself, the lit cigarette dangling from her lips. "Why don't you tell me what's really going on, Nic?"

The emphasis on *really*, the questioning trill, made Nicole flinch, and she wondered if she'd heard Tiffany right, if the wind hadn't mutated her words.

"What do you mean?" she said, when what she meant was, *how on earth could you know?* She had been so careful on urbanmama.com, not to use any details that would give her identity away, a choice that had made her think, *Well, how crazy can I be, if I'm covering my tracks so well?*

"Sweetie," Tiffany said, "it's obvious."

"What?" Nicole laughed, hoping she sounded genuinely clueless.

"You were so doom-and-gloom all afternoon," Tiffany said, "I mean, that whole thing with Josh and his bag on the sofa?"

Tiffany lifted her eyebrows, an expression that reminded Nicole of her own mother; disapproving.

"Maybe," Tiffany continued, passing the cigarette to Nicole, "if you share, you'll feel better. So, what's up?"

"I don't know," Nicole said.

"You *do* know."

"It's embarrassing."

"Worse than your thing about swine flu? Worse than when you thought the city was being attacked by terrorists and texted Josh, like, twenty times?"

"Fuck," Nicole said. "I'm a freak." She squeezed out a small laugh.

"Just tell me, dammit. I'm not going anywhere until you do." Tiffany pulled the lit cigarette from Nicole's hand. "No judging, promise." She took a drag, squinting against the smoke as the tip blazed red.

"I'm happy," Nicole started. "I mean, I know." She nodded somberly. "I seem miserable. Josh reminds me that every day. But I swear. In many ways, this is the happiest I've ever felt."

"But are they the ways that matter?" Tiffany asked as she reached over and patted Nicole's wind-chilled hand. "Look, Nic, if there's anyone out here that understands, it's me? I'm broken, too. Remember? I should be on a ton of drugs!"

How did Tiffany know she had stopped taking her meds, Nicole thought. What if Tiffany outed her to Josh, motivated by what Tiffany would call *friendly concern*? Nicole imagined Tiffany's slinking next to him, hooking her arm in his, whispering, *You know, Josh,* her hot breath in his ear, *I'm worried about Nic.*

Tiffany, Nicole thought, was not the frenemy any mom in her right mind would take on.

"I'm sorry," Nicole blurted.

"What's there to be sorry about?"

Tiffany pulled the crushed pack of American Spirits from the jacket pocket.

She tapped two cigarettes out, tucked one between her puffy lips, gave the other to Nicole, and tossed the empty pack over the seawall.

Nicole stopped herself from mentioning pollution.

"I've been meaning to text you about last week," Nicole said. "You know." She paused. "The thing at the bar. With Susanna."

"Pregnant women," Tiffany said with a huff. "They're certifiable."

"Susanna was just"—Nicole paused—"so upset. You know how she is. Always mommying everyone."

Tiffany mumbled something Nicole couldn't hear.

Nicole continued, "She thought that—maybe—you were drunk. Vulnerable. That the guy was going to take advantage of you. And I got caught in the middle."

What Nicole didn't say was that they'd all been on Susanna's side. Susanna had been the only one brave enough to tell Tiffany she'd had too many Cosmos, she was being loud, she was embarrassing them on this one night they'd all managed to get sitters or secure husbands to watch the kids, after they had squeezed into their *before children* clothes and straightened their hair and tweezed their eyebrows and shaved their legs in anticipation of Girls' Night Out.

Nicole was anxious to change the subject now that she'd performed her apology, and she felt that shivering sense that time was both slowing down and speeding up, a precursor to her panic attacks.

"You know," she said, "when I was a kid, I didn't really appreciate this place." She nodded to the thick woods at the end of the beach that led to acres of tangled and marshy nature preserve. "The woods—especially at night—creeped me out. I had two cats go in there and never come back. Oliver and Casper."

"Probably coons," Tiffany said.

"The ocean scared me, too," Nicole said. "It's not like in a pool. You can't see what's under you."

"I don't know. I was a big-time skinny-dipper growing up out east," Tiffany said, as she arched her back in a stretch. The black leather creaked. "So, I guess you weren't?"

"Nope." Nicole felt her urge to confess rising. Instead of washing her hands two dozen times a day, or obsessively organizing—habits she'd learned to kick—sometimes, reciting her fears momentarily freed her from them. "It started, maybe around when I was nine. On summer nights when the tide was highest, I'd come out here after my parents were asleep. And I'd dare myself to jump off the wall into the water."

"You?" Tiffany said. "I'm impressed."

The *you* stung Nicole, though she knew it shouldn't be a surprise. She was scared of everything. Just as Josh had said in countless arguments. *Your life is one giant fucking phobia.*

As if she needed to be reminded.

"Yep," she lied. "I jumped in. And I made myself stay out there 'til I counted to a hundred. I treaded water with my heart pounding so fast I thought I'd drown."

Details came to her, the way they once had when she was writing fiction.

"And there was this green stuff. Phosphorescence, I think it's called. This green, glowy stuff that kind of, like, sparkles in the water at night. When you wave your arms around."

Tiffany stood. She peeled off Michael's jacket and let it fall to the deck with a leathery thud. "That's all just lovely, Nic," she said. "But if you're going to keep avoiding my question, I think I'll go for a swim."

"What?"

Tiffany wriggled out of her sweatpants. Then she pulled off her shirt and stepped out of her underwear. "Obviously, you're not going to tell me why you've been acting like such a freak all weekend. So I'm going to let you keep fretting, and I'll keep enjoying myself."

"Tiffany, seriously, what are you doing?"

Tiffany stepped toward the seawall. She was all pale curves except where her pubic hair formed a shadowy triangle. Tiffany was the only mom in the playgroup who'd had a vaginal birth. No pouch of hardened flab hanging like a shallow shelf over her vagina like the rest of them had, a vestige of their C-sections that no amount of exercise would banish.

"What are you doing? It's freezing out here." Nicole realized she was whispering, as if they were teenagers trespassing, pool hopping in a neighbor's backyard.

"Your challenge," Tiffany explained. "I'm supposed to count to a hundred, right?"

Nicole nodded, unable to speak.

The rocks.

"Don't!" Nicole yelled as Tiffany climbed onto the seawall, her breasts swinging with the effort. "The rocks. You'll kill yourself."

Tiffany looked down at her. The wind whipped her dark hair.

She rose to her toes, her body a luminescent column, and dove into the black water.

Nicole ran to the seawall.

Tiffany's face was a white oval bobbing in the black water.

Nicole flooded with relief.

"You're the crazy one!" she yelled.

This time, when Nicole laughed, she meant it.

She tried to hold on to what was she was feeling. To make it last. The openness in her chest, like a door unlocked. The lift at her heels, as if she were standing taller, as if she, too, could climb onto the wall, strip away her layers, leap out over the water, and never land.

Fly to the moon.

Part 2

Saturday

URBANMAMA.COM A Community and Forum for Parents

Welcome to UrbanMama, an anonymous forum where you can interact in sincere and open-minded conversation with other parents.

Speak your mind and share your thoughts about parenting, family life, marriage, relationships, and everything that makes you an urbanmama!

Sign up now!   Already a member, log in!

Ok that's it. I'm keeping my kids home today. No park, no playground.

Posted 9/4/2010   8:38am

(*14 replies*)

—where do you live? i feel like I should pack up the car and leave town 8:38am

    —huh???? what are you talking about? 8:39am

—Anything new happen? 8:40am

    —all this discussion is making me nervous. WHAT is going on? 8:41am

—because of the Webbot prediction? 8:41am

    —yes 8:41am

—The market fell below 10000 two weeks ago. *IT* ALREADY HAPPENED. 8:42am

    —but today will be horrible. 8:42am

        —why? 8:43am

            —cause that's when it's supposed to happen. 8:43am

—what's supposed to happen?
8:44am

—THE END. 8:46am

—^^^just kidding
8:47am

—Oh. My. GOD!! 8:48am

golden handcuffs

Leigh

Leigh had always been a good liar. Most of the lies leapt from her lips without thought or planning. Uninvited and, sometimes, unwanted, but she had always escaped detection. Who would suspect such a pleasant person—ever-smiling, neatly dressed, polite, and agreeable? She wasn't one of those contrarian women, like Nicole or Susanna, who felt it their duty to have the last word, particularly if a man was involved. She had even changed her name to Marshall to appease Brad, a choice she knew the other mommies disapproved of.

Since Chase's birth nearly four years ago, Leigh had felt as if the lies she had accumulated, stacked into a tower of infinite height, were teetering over her, and she had begun to fear she'd trip and fall, the lies smothering her.

Lately, she doubted every choice she made. There wasn't enough time in the busy-ness of motherhood to weigh every consequence, and she felt herself spilling like a leaky milk carton—a spurt here, a drip there.

Two days earlier, Leigh, treasurer of the Fundraising Committee at Chase's preschool, the Olive Tree Academy, had attended the first committee meeting of the year. Even before she'd conceived Chase, she had added their name to the waiting list for the co-operative school renowned for its donation drives and silent auctions that brought in close to a hundred thousand dollars a year.

The chairwoman of the Fundraising Committee, Kat Richards, had approached Leigh before the meeting, while the members sipped herbal tea and nibbled homemade orange-scented scones in the recreation room of the preschool. Kat, a pleasant woman, whom Leigh had found a touch too flaky to vote for, had asked if she and Leigh could set up a meeting to go over the latest financials.

"I keep making errors," Kat said, "I just can't get those numbers to fit."

The woman twittered on as that hateful blush crawled up Leigh's neck. She was certain her ears glowed pink. Like an alarm sounding.

"Of course, Kat," she said. "How's Monday work for you?"

The rec room had once been a benign place, even cheerful, where Leigh had volunteered to run a monthly bake sale and assisted in setting up the Fall Festival. But that night at the meeting, in the fluorescent light, the air damp with late summer heat, sweat pooling between her milk-heavy breasts, the room was vibrating danger. She had gripped the arms of her assigned chair. The fund-raising treasurer sat to the left of the chairwoman.

When it was Leigh's turn to speak, she found her voice, and to her relief, was able to train her eyes on the number-filled sheet in her hands and share the latest fundraising-account financials. Her voice quivered, and she stopped to wipe sweat from her upper lip, joking that the postpartum hormones were still kicking her butt, which received nods of empathy from the other mothers, many of whom knew how long she had tried for a second child. They had comforted her when she'd miscarried, and had congratulated her when her Charlie girl, just a twelve-week-old fetus, stuck.

Leigh made it through the remainder of the meeting—Luisa Kaufman (mom to Leo and Lux) reminding the committee (again) of the harmful GMOs in their children's food, quoting studies on the side effects of hormone-injected meat, such as boys growing breasts; Maggie Yun (mom to Izzie, Gus, and Anya) pleading for $5,000 to renovate the playground; Simon Clifton (dad to Posey), a stay-at-home dad active in the protests against idling ice-cream trucks at Carroll Park, suggesting a compost bin behind the school, to show the kids "green in action." Leigh imagined rats the size of cats but applauded with the other parents.

By the end of the meeting, her fingers were itching to pluck her eyebrows. The ritual had brought comfort to her as a girl. Pluck. Pluck. The sting of each root dislodging from her scalp was a blessed distraction. Each as innocuous as a white lie. Her mother had driven all the way to the Evenhill Academy for Girls in New Hampshire to usher Leigh to dermatologists, neurologists, and finally to a psychologist on the Upper West Side.

At the end of the meeting, the committee secretary, Marian Ravensberg, read the minutes back slowly, until Leigh feared she would stand on her chair and scream something outrageous like, you fucking fools! There's no money for your stupid compost bin! Or she might run up to the loft and jump from the window looking out onto the rec room so she was a splatter of blood and crooked limbs on the waxed blond wood.

They were released. A quick wave good-bye and Leigh was out into the blue night, her engorged breasts aching as she ran home. She took the stoop steps two at a time until Tenzin stood before her, baby Charlotte in her arms.

All was well. All was as it should be. Mother and child. Small lips nuzzling at Leigh's breast until the baby's mouth caught her nipple and there was the pull of her suck and, finally, the release of milk, the letdown like a gentle current coursing through the blue veins branching across her breast. Leigh was reminded of the need this child (*child of my heart*) had for her, and only her. This was her redemption.

She sat in a deck chair, her feet on the seawall, the concrete biting into the back of her ankles. Still the same smooth muscles and delicate ankles that had made her proud to wear tennis whites to the Locust Valley Country Club as a girl. She rearranged the swaddle blanket over Charlotte, asleep except for the occasional suckle at Leigh's nipple.

Leigh chewed her nails, her mother's voice in her head.

Leigh, dear, no boy will want to hold your hand with those ragged fingernails.

She watched Tiffany run across the sand with the children down on the beach. Though it was only a little after nine and the morning sun weak, Tiffany wore a red-and-white, polka-dotted bikini. With her yoga-toned curves and her hair pulled into a ponytail, she reminded Leigh of one of those long-dead Vargas girls.

"Somebody decided to turn up the sun today, monkeys!" Tiffany's voice rang with cheerleader-quality glee.

It was an energetic frolicking that had been foreign to Leigh for longer than she could remember. Surely, she must have moved like that before Chase had been born. Some of the other mommies had aged in life after children, even in their affluent neighborhood, with its countless yoga studios and salons and spas. With money came babysitters, and time away for the gym and private training sessions and hours sweating off pounds in the sweltering heat of a Bikram studio.

Tiffany was still beautiful, yes, but it wouldn't last much longer, Leigh thought. Not if she kept filling her plate, as she had at breakfast that morning. Two thick pads of butter on her toast. Half & Half in her coffee. At that rate, Leigh thought, Tiffany would be just like the rest of them in five years.

The children scurried away from the seaweed-speckled foam of the waves, back onto the sand dotted with red, white, and blue inflatable beach balls, which they kicked, threw, covered with sand, and the most daring (Harper, of course), set afloat in the cold, dark water. Chase sat on his ball, rocking gently.

How foolish she'd been to think coming out to the beach house might make him happy. Chase couldn't be content, or comfortable, anywhere, it seemed. Or was it her? Was her own unhappiness infecting him? When all she had ever wished for him was less suffering? If only everything would be okay. If only Monday's meeting with the fund-raising-committee chairwoman went smoothly, she would be happy, she promised. She would make Chase happy.

But Leigh knew that wasn't true. She knew they would take her to jail. A series of concerns popped into her head, all of which seemed trivial. But what was more important than preserving the children's day-to-day life? How would breast-milk-exclusive Charlotte thrive? Who would remove all the tags in Chase's clothing so not one stray thread rubbed against his skin? Who would remind him to howl like a baby wolf in the bathtub, chin lifted to the moon, so soap didn't run into his eyes? And brush him with the soft-bristled surgical brush his occupational therapist had given Leigh? Up his back, over his shoulders, and down each arm, just the way he liked it, soothing him before bed.

That morning at breakfast, recharged after a good night's sleep, as she had spooned scrambled eggs into Chase's mouth and dabbed his smile with a napkin, the sea outside the window stretching endlessly under the bluest sky, she had felt hope.

Sure there had been the usual grumbling from Chase about not wanting to eat, his fidgeting, spilling a whole cup of juice across the table (Leigh had apologized to the room—*we're working on our fine motor skills*), but once they walked out into the blazing sun, Chase had fallen apart. The sand was too sticky, the wind too cold, the sun too hot. The seagulls hurt his ears. The sea snails, which the other children squealed at gleefully, were scary. The greenhead horseflies were biting him.

"They're going to get me!" he had screeched.

No, Chase.

Gentle, Chase.

Share, Chase.

Use your words, Chase.

Careful, Chase.

Calm down, Chase.

No throwing sand, Chase.

By nine, Leigh's patience had been obliterated.

Then a bikini-clad Tiffany had appeared, skipping down the sun-blanched wooden stairs that led from the deck to the beach, the tops of her tanned breasts jiggling. Chase had left Leigh, running to clasp Tiffany's hand, looking up at her in a shy but also, Leigh had noted, flirtatious way. His mouth twisted as he tried to hide a smile.

"Go ahead, Leigh. Take a break," Tiffany had said with a wink, nodding up to the deck. "Get some sun. We got it covered. Don't we, Chase, my dear?"

And so Leigh had retreated.

Now, over the flapping of the deck umbrellas, she heard Tiffany on the beach.

"Say cheese! Say cheese!" Tiffany sang.

Tiffany loved to be photographed, and it made Leigh feel embarrassed for her. Couldn't Tiffany see how vain she seemed? Not long after the barrage of *cheese*, Leigh heard Tiffany's demands. Now to Michael, she imagined.

"Let me see," Tiffany commanded. "Are there any good ones?"

Leigh knew Tiffany would post the photos immediately to her Facebook page, especially the ones showing off her bronzed cleavage. With cheery status updates like: *A day at the beach with the Tiff's Riffs kids!*

Leigh sat up when she heard Chase's cries, carried up to the deck on a gust of wind.

"Everything okay down there?" she called out.

She spotted Tiffany with two children, one at either side. Harper and Chase.

Leigh shielded her eyes and waved. "Hey! Should I come down?"

Tiffany shook her head and waved Leigh back, as in *we don't need you.* But Chase was hopping from foot to foot like a furious little elf. She followed his pointing finger to the blue-and-white ball floating out to sea, tossed by the waves. Chase pointed to Harper, and Leigh could see that the little girl's hands were balled on her hips. Leigh read the distress in Chase's widened eyes, his stretched mouth.

"Harper," Leigh whispered. "That little . . ."

She readied herself to go down, tucking the edges of the blanket around Charlotte so it wouldn't fly away, but then Chase was in the air, laughing, landing on Tiffany's shoulders. Leigh felt relief spread through her limbs, like a drug taking effect, warm and fluid.

Could Tiffany really be so bad? No one made Chase smile that broadly. Definitely not Leigh herself though she tried, she was sure of it.

Tiffany was devoted to her, wasn't she? Not a day went by without a text from Tiffany. An expression of adoration. *miss you buddy!* or *luv ya lots!!*

Leigh had woken that morning to her phone vibrating on the dresser. Texts from Tiffany.

The first had read:

Cool if I book Tenzie for Thurs afternoons? Can you let her go at noon, so she's w me at 12:15? Thx again! U r the bestest!!

Another text had arrived only ten minutes later:

Did u get my text? Let me know! Thx xoxo

Followed by:

Everything ok? Need to confirm thursdays asap

Leigh had been changing Charlotte and trying to coax Chase out of bed where he lay puffy-faced and snoring. Then she had dashed into the bathroom after Rip had finished (the air freshener barely disguising the smell of his bowel movement) to shave her bikini line.

She had decided to ignore the texts, hoping Tiffany got the hint. Thursday afternoon Leigh was free. Free to sit on the Brooklyn Heights Promenade while Charlotte took her nap. Free to browse for curtain fabric on Etsy, to share photos of the kids on Facebook, and to strategize on how to get out of this goddamn fundraising-committee mess. She was Chase-free. Didn't she deserve one afternoon of *me time*? Wasn't Tiffany always urging Leigh to do something nice for herself? And there was no one else to ask for help. The weekend sitter, a college student studying education, had admitted to feeling overwhelmed by watching both Chase and Charlotte, or at least when Chase was awake. The few times Nicole had asked her mother to come into the city to sit, her mother had left harried, her meticulously quaffed perm misshapen.

There was only Tenzin.

Tiffany's final text that morning read:

Ok! Confirmed with Shabbat Tots so it's all set. Thx a million my mommy bff (;

Leigh felt she'd been slapped across the face. Tiffany taking Tenzin from her, as casually as one child might pluck a toy train from the hand of another. Leigh's single peaceful afternoon, undone by her so-called friend.

A huge loss, Leigh thought, when you had so little time left to lose.

Monday was coming. Her meeting with Kat Richards scheduled for eleven o'clock.

no worries

Rip

Rip watched as Michael chased Harper around the sandbar, a dollop of sunscreen on his outstretched hand. The little girl flitted around like one of the dragonflies skimming the dried seaweed on the beach. She shrieked when her father neared her and giggled as she took off again. Finally, Michael caught her and dabbed gobs of white goo across her forehead and cheeks.

"Stop! It!" Harper screamed.

Hank clamped a hand over each of his ears, looked at Rip, and moaned, "Too loud, Hah-per. Make her quiet, Daddy."

Hank had been sitting alone on the sand, hiding from the sun under the floral umbrella whose fringe was dotted with dead ladybugs. Hank had folded what Rip guessed was at least twenty origami bunnies. Hank had learned origami at *Green Hill*, an elite gifted and talented program Grace had bent over backward to secure. Hank's origami skills were a source of pride for Rip (clearly, the boy was *beyond* G&T), but who wanted twenty paper bunnies?

"Get! Off! Me!" Harper screeched, as Michael struggled to complete the sunscreen-application challenge. She flung her head from side to side, and Rip wondered if brain damage was in order.

Tiffany stood ten feet away, facing the water, silent, unmoving, not even glancing over her shoulder. Tiffany's blind approach to parenting riled the other mommies to no end, but Rip believed in having a personal philosophy. And what were they going to do about it anyway? Tell Tiffany to give Harper a time-out? As if.

"Harper, please," Michael begged.

Rip jogged over.

"Hiya, sweetie," he said to Harper, crouching next to the little girl. Her wiry muscles tensed in defiance.

She stopped writhing for a moment, just long enough for him to scoop a glob of lotion from her cheek.

"What's this?" Rip asked. "Mmm. Vanilla frosting."

He pretended to eat it with one hand while the other rubbed in the lotion streaked across her cheeks.

"Noooo, Daddy Rip." Harper giggled. "Ew. Don't eat it!"

"Yum-yum."

He continued his charade as he rubbed the lotion along her hairline and down her nose.

Harper's face turned serious. "Your tummy will get sick. And then you'll have to go to the doctor. And get one hundred shots. And maybe even"—her catlike eyes squinted—"get dead."

Rip stood and pulled the bottle of organic sunscreen spray from his back pocket.

"Thought you might need this," Rip said, and tossed the bottle to Michael. "Single best invention ever. A gift from the parenting gods."

Michael sat back on the sand and leaned his forearms on his knees.

"You sure you don't need it?"

Michael looked up at Rip, one eye squinting Marlboro-Man style.

"Dude," Rip said shrugging. "Take it."

"Thanks, man," Michael said. "Wow, I was without a paddle there."

Rip grabbed two beers from the cooler, opened one with his car key, and handed it to Michael. With a quick wink. Their fingers touched as the icy beer passed, and Rip almost flinched, remembering, with a sharpness that felt like a hallucination, the citrusy tang of Tiffany's sweat the day before in the kitchen. Suddenly, he was there again, but this time grinding into her, lifting her skirt up, and—he stopped there, the wild cry of the kids chasing seagulls like an alarm sounding.

Rip slapped Michael on the back, in the way only dudes do, when he spotted Harper peeling off from the group and skipping toward the end of the sandbar, where the waves resumed.

"She's on the run," Rip said, and pointed toward the little girl—a speck of pale skin topped with flame red, like a birthday candle.

Michael stood and ran toward the sea. "Catch you later."

The next chance he got, Rip decided, he'd invite Michael for a kayak trip out to the marsh. A man-to-man excursion. Maybe he'd even ask Michael for his opinion on Grace and the whole convincing-her-to-have-another-kid dilemma.

Rip glanced over at Josh, whose face was reddening as Wyatt and Dash tackled him, tugging on his arms, his legs, his swimsuit, trying to pull him into the water.

"Okay, guys." Josh laughed. "Let's take it easy now."

Even Tiffany was more of a man than Josh, Rip thought. He had seen her wrench the cap off a beer with her back teeth.

Fuck it, he thought.

"Hey, man," he called to Michael, who was lifting Harper onto a large, barnacle-coated rock.

Michael gave an up-nod, as in *yeah*?

"Want to take the kayak out later? We can head over to the marsh. Nicole says it's awesome back there."

"Hell yeah," said Michael with a pleased look. One of those *uh-huh* looks Rip had seen pass between jamming musicians locked in on a groove.

"Cool," Rip said, as nonchalant as possible because inside he was a-titter with a thrill he hadn't felt in years, like the rush after a shot of whiskey, like before he stepped onstage for an improv show. And he wasn't going to ruin it by asking Michael if he'd ever kayaked before, or by admitting this would be his own first kayaking trip. They were two grown men. They'd figure it out.

He tilted his head back and let the beer course down his throat.

all's fair in love and war

Allie

In life before the twins, Allie had described parenthood, to the amused tittering of her unburdened artist friends, as having houseguests who'd overstayed their welcome.

As she stood at the edge of the water, rolling the soaked cuffs of her black jeans, cold sand oozing between her toes, she felt like that clueless guest right now and wished she could hop in the car and flee to Brooklyn.

It wasn't that she didn't *like* children. She appreciated the purity of their enthusiasm, their unfiltered view of the world. But her jaw ached from smiling. The mommies smiled so damn much. They smiled when the children fell and when the children cried. They smiled at each other, they smiled as they looked out over the water, where, as far as Allie could see, there was nothing to smile about. They smiled even when the children were bad. When the minibarbarians deserved the very opposite of a smile.

Like right then, as Harper, clad in just the bottom half of a pink bikini, her tiny nipples as nut brown as the rest of her torso, flung sand at Hank.

Despite Hank's cries of "Hah-per, Hah-per, stop!"

Tiffany just smiled and stood with her hands on her hips—which were gorgeous, Allie couldn't help but notice. The woman was Marilyn-esque.

"Harp, sweetie," Tiffany said, "are you doing good listening? 'Cause it sounds like Hank wants you to stop. What do you say, baby?"

Allie's own mother would have yelled, through cigarette smoke, *I'm watching you, Allison!* And her father? Forget about it. He would have been in front of Harper in two strides and walloped her on the butt, right there in front of everyone.

These people were definitely not raised by the kind of people who had raised Allie. Her people had worked with their hands and disciplined with their hands and let it be known when they were pissed off so there was a sharp rise to each conflict, an explosion, maybe a bit of violence, then the matter was quickly forgotten. Life went on. Pass the peas.

The playgroup parents, especially Tiffany—despite the working-class roots under her perfect highlights—disciplined through talk.

"Talk, talk, and more talk," Allie had complained to pale-faced Susanna before breakfast. "Do they ever say no?"

"Would you rather they hit them with their belts?" Susanna had snapped, which was unfair, Allie thought now, as the waves rippled over her toes, because Susanna knew Allie's father had used his belt on Allie and her brother.

If she could just get a break, catch her breath for an hour, away from the talking, the two streams—the children's chatter and the mommies' chatter crossing right in front of her, catching her in its crosshairs.

She couldn't leave Susanna, who sat with her legs outstretched, the small waves breaking against her enormous belly. Allie tried to imagine the baby in the echo chamber of Susanna's womb, listening to the waves.

Poor Susanna.

How many times had Allie heard people whisper this and shake their head? Allie found herself wanting to say, as if in her own defense, *It was Susie's choice.*

Allie had participated as much as she could. First, there were the months of crack-of-dawn fertility appointments in a pastel-walled office all the way on the Upper East Side, with its waiting room full of desperate women and hangdog husbands. Next, the hormone shots she and Susanna injected into each other's butt cheeks in the weeks leading up to *her* egg extraction (and it had hurt). Finally, the wait-and-see anxiety of the in vitro procedure—Susanna lying immobile for days while Allie threatened the boys to *leave Mama alone!* Not to mention the costs. Allie's work had paid for their baby. Two in vitro trials equaled a trip around the world, where, Allie imagined, they might have visited the art they'd worshipped in the years before the boys were born.

"Allie!" Susanna shouted. "You watching the boys? I can't see them."

Allie's view swung away, and for a second, she panicked, the movement of the waves beyond the sandbar making her dizzy.

The boys were standing at the foot of a massive black boulder that had appeared gradually in the last few hours as the tide went out, and the ripple-streaked sandbar revealed itself, creating a perfect playspace. Atop the rock was the long-limbed Harper, her wind-teased hair a red-gold crown glinting in the sun.

"Boys!" Allie yelled through cupped hands. "Stay close."

Harper shouted, "Come here! I said . . . Come! Here!"

Allie shielded her eyes. All the boys stood in front of the rock, peering up at Harper worshipfully. Allie wanted to make a joke about a sea witch and her minions, but Michael was just a few feet away. For once, she thought proudly, she would hold her tongue.

Susanna waved Allie over to help her up. Allie had to lift Susanna from behind and, finally, after a grunt or two, Susanna climbed to her feet. The pebbles had pocked the backs of Susanna's fleshy thighs. Cellulite gone viral, Allie thought, embarrassed for Susanna, and for herself.

A few minutes later, they, along with Tiffany, Michael, Rip, and Josh, had joined the boys at the rock.

It was clear to Allie that Harper was calling the shots.

"You!" Harper commanded haughtily, pointing a finger at the boys. "You are my subjects. And I am Queen Priscilla, ruler of all the seas in the universe."

"You go, girl!" Tiffany whooped, and the adults laughed, flinging words like *precocious* and *advanced* into the sea breeze.

Harper shot them a glare. "Don't laugh at me!"

Allie was relieved when Michael chimed in, "Now, Harper, that's no way to talk," but she heard hesitation in his voice.

They were afraid of the little girl. Just like the mommies were afraid of Tiffany.

Queen of the Universe, my ass, Allie thought. More like a budding sociopath. She wished she and Susanna were standing closer, so she could whisper in Susanna's ear. They would laugh together the way they once had. When it had been Allie and Susanna vs. the rest of the world.

Harper clapped her hands. Like a coach gathering the team for a pep talk. All that was missing, Allie thought, was the whistle.

"Listen up, everybody!" Harper shouted.

The crowd fell silent. There was only the lapping of the waves and the complaints of seagulls.

"You got your buckets?" Harper asked the boys, who stared up at her mutely.

"Answer me," Harper ordered. In a remarkably authentic fed-up-mommy tone, Allie thought. "You got to answer me by saying, Your Royal Highness!"

The boys parroted *Your Royal Highness!* before scattering across the sandbar in search of containers. Wyatt, Levi, Dash, and Chase returned with plastic buckets in hand. Hank with an empty plastic water bottle.

"Make me a royal feast," Harper commanded. "Go for" (Allie assumed she meant *forth*) "and collect crabs and snails for my delish lunch!"

Harper opened her arms wide and tipped her head skyward. For a moment, Allie saw an exquisite photo. Scarlet hair and knobby knees, long limbs dotted with bruises, ribs pressing through browned skin. A warrior child staring up at the heavens as if testing God himself. Damn, that girl was fierce.

The children scattered, away from their queen and toward the Sound, and when they reached the water, their shoulders hunched and their heads bowed as they studied the sand that lay under a few inches of clear, sun-dappled sea. Their focus reminded Allie of search parties on crime shows. Even Levi, usually distracted, walked slowly—heel-toe, heel-toe—looking for a bit of sea life to serve up to his queen. A squeal of delight erupted here and there with each find, as the boys plucked tiny brown or black barnacle-speckled shells from the sand, the miniature claws and antennae creeping out, flailing before the crab went *plunk!* into the bucket with its kin.

Allie dipped her hand into the cool water and scooped up a shell, resting it in the center of her palm. She waited, breath held, and miniscule claws appeared, then two glistening eyes.

For the first time in a long time, she remembered how nature trumped art and how easy it was to forget this in the city, where all beauty seemed man-made. She thought of her baby and looked to Susanna, who stood with her round face turned to the sun, her eyes closed.

I should be more grateful for her, Allie thought.

There was a tickle on Allie's palm as the shell scuttled across her hand. She shrieked and dropped the crab.

Then there was a hand on her shoulder. It was Tiffany, an arm outstretched, the brown dot of a shell crawling up her arm.

"Don't be scared, silly," Tiffany said with the hint of an intentional lisp, as though the tip of her tongue were caught between her teeth.

Tiffany moved her arm to accommodate the crab's path, an undulating dance that reminded Allie of the curvaceous Odissi dancers she and Susanna had seen perform in India on one of their preparenthood trips. Although it was a religious dance, Allie had felt there was something delightfully impure about their wide, painted eyes and come-hither looks, their bare midriffs and gyrating hips, the way they cocked their heads left and right, beckoning, *come closer.* And wasn't that what Tiffany was saying now as she let the crab crawl across the sand-dusted hills of her breasts? As she giggled like a schoolgirl?

The children returned to the rock Harper had claimed as her throne and emptied their buckets onto the smooth shelf at the base of the boulder. Josh pointed out hermit crabs, humped sand crabs, sea snails, and even an orange-speckled Lady Crab. It was a pile of flailing legs, searching antennae, and twitching, googly eyes. Allie pitied the slow-moving sea snails, their slimy tongues stretching out into the sunlight to see what the fuck was going on.

The children whooped and jumped and did a little dance around the rock, kicking mud-dark sand in the air. Harper watched with a satisfied smile stretched across sun-rouged cheeks.

"Now what?" Allie asked, looking to Josh and Rip, who stood in a daze, eyes trained on the wiggling mass.

Josh shrugged. Rip took a swig of beer.

"Okay," Susanna sang. "Time to put the creatures back in the sea."

"No way!" Harper shouted. "Now we make soup for our big feast."

Tiffany laughed. "Harper loves playing pretend. Should we have a picnic? That's one of our favorite play activities at home. Right, hon?"

"Soup!" The boys shouted, in a perfect unison that creeped Allie out.

"Rocks! We need rocks for our stew!" Harper commanded, and the boys scattered again, each returning with an armful of stones. Poor Hank's short arms shook under the weight of the rock he chose, one almost as big as his head.

"Not *that* big, Hank," Harper said. "You'll get a boo-boo. And we don't like to hear you cry." She rolled her eyes. In perfect mommy replication, Allie thought.

"Now," Harper instructed calmly, "when I count to three, use the rock to mash my food."

"Harper," Susanna warned, tottering forward to the base of the rock, an arm stretched up toward the little girl. For a moment, Allie thought Susanna might pull the girl-queen off her throne.

Harper counted slowly, "One . . ."

"Harper, sweetie," Tiffany said. As if, Allie thought, she were calling the girl to the dinner table. "We don't hurt animals, now, do we?"

The dads, Allie noticed—even Michael—had stepped back, as if they feared the residual spray of mashed sea life.

Harper continued, a smile skipping across her lips, "Two . . ."

"Tiffany!" Susanna screamed, a strangled plea that made the hair on Allie's arms tingle. "Do something!"

The little girl looked the happiest Allie had seen her that weekend. Like she'd eaten something mouthwatering. Like she'd won the biggest prize at the fair.

Harper chirped, almost cutely, "Three!"

The massacre commenced. The children fell upon the sea animals with raised rocks, and there was crunching and cracking and the echo of rock hitting rock and Susanna was screaming—*Stop! No!*—pulling one and then another boy away, tearing scum-covered rocks from their hands and flinging them to the sand, and Allie heard herself say something dumb, like "Okay, I guess they've gone a little *Lord of the Flies* on us," but no one was laughing.

It was as if they'd landed on some foreign planet and were surrounded by a clan of small, bloodthirsty aliens.

She hurried to Susanna, who stared at her hands flecked with brown-and-black goo. Susanna gagged, her chin jutting forward in the prevomit, chicken-like movement Allie knew so well.

"Come on, baby," Allie soothed, nudging Susanna toward the open sea, a hand on Susanna's lower back.

"The smell," Susanna croaked between heaves.

"Let's wash off in the water," Allie said.

Puke was coming. Better to get Susanna as far from the others as possible.

"Mama?" Levi whimpered behind them. "Mommy?"

Allie looked over her shoulder. Levi's nostrils flared. Dash's hands were balled at his side. What was he so angry about?

"Don't worry, guys," Susanna said, her voice wavering. "Mama's okay." She turned to Allie, "Tell them."

"Tell them *what?*"

"Tell them I'm okay!" Susanna commanded. "Comfort them, dammit. Comfort them!"

"Everything's fine, boys," Allie said. "Mommy and Mama are cool."

They didn't make it to the water. Ten feet from the rock, Susanna leaned over and puked into the sea snail–dotted sand. A foul fountain of half-digested eggs. Allie stroked Susanna's shuddering back as the mother of her children heaved again and again.

knife in the back

Leigh

Leigh woke in the deck chair, her mouth dry and face sweaty from the blazing sun overhead. She had indulged in a rare Charlotte-free nap, since Tenzin had offered to put the baby down for a nap in the house.

Tiffany stood at the foot of Leigh's chaise, toweling her trim legs. Her tan breasts were dusted with flecks of sand, and seawater dripped from the curled ends of her hair.

"Why, hello there, Sleeping Beauty," Tiffany said. "Oopsy, did I get you wet?"

Leigh looked up, shielding her eyes, but all she could see were the curves of Tiffany's silhouette, black against the dazzling blue sky.

"Don't you wear sunblock?" Tiffany asked. "You'll be one of those wrinkly old ladies playing bridge at the country club."

"Very funny," Leigh said.

"Oh my God, Susanna just puked her guts out on the beach."

"Oh no," Leigh said. "Is she okay?"

"Yeah. She just got worked up over the kids. You know how she is," Tiffany said, one eyebrow raised.

Tiffany plucked a beer from the cooler by the seawall. She wrenched the cap off with her back teeth, her purplish lips spread wide, big square teeth bared.

"Jeez!" Leigh said, forcing a laugh. "You're going to break a tooth."

"That's what they teach you at community college," Tiffany said. "Here, live a little."

She pushed the beer toward Leigh in a gesture that implied a command, and although Leigh didn't want it, she took it, figuring she could dump it out later.

She leaned forward and playfully slapped Tiffany's leg.

"Michael's such a cutie! That's awesome that he came out this weekend. I think Nicole's got a crush," Leigh said, and lifted her beer in a toast, knowing Tiffany would like the idea of someone's desiring her man.

Tiffany's cocktail glass clinked against Leigh's bottle, and beer splashed onto Leigh's white shorts.

"Sorry about that, babe," Tiffany said, easing down on the end of Leigh's lounge chair, and leaning in toward her. "You didn't hear us last night, did you?"

"Hear what?"

"Liar!" Tiffany's eyes danced as she tried to suppress her grin. "Shit. I knew it. The whole house must've heard." She bounced on the chair and its rusted springs groaned.

"Careful," Leigh said. "This patio furniture might be older than Nicole's parents."

"Well, honestly, I don't care if Michael and I pissed everyone off. It was totally worth it."

"Good," Leigh said, as matter-of-factly as she could.

Tiffany lowered her voice. "It was hot, Leigh-Leigh," she said. "I mean, it's always hotter in someone else's bed, right? But that mattress Nic put us on is about a thousand years old and disgusting. I was thinking I'd never sleep on the thing, let alone fuck around on it, but Michael wanted a BJ the second we turned off the light. We didn't have sex-sex. Just oral. But he wouldn't quit! It was like he was on E or something. I think spending all day with mommies in bathing suits worked him up. He hardly ever goes down on me like that, but—"

"You can't get me!" Tenzin's melodic voice rang out from the beach below. "I'm too fast!"

Tiffany paused, and Leigh took the opportunity to escape from Tiffany's porny story, hopping up from the chaise and striding over to the seawall.

"Hey, Tenzin!" Leigh called out, marveling at her nanny's typical perfect timing. Just when she'd been prickling with discomfort from Tiffany's oversharing.

"Hel-LO, Leigh!" Tenzin sang back.

Leigh turned back to Tiffany, who had stretched out completely in the chaise, like a sleek jungle cat basking in the sun.

"God, I love Tenzin," Leigh said, impulsively.

"I love her, too," Tiffany said, her eyes half-closed. "Though I wish she'd come down a dollar an hour. I keep asking, but she's not budging."

"Really? I'd pay her twenty dollars an hour if I had to."

"Well," Tiffany said, "you have money." She paused to detangle her hair from the sunglasses atop her head, then lowered them over her eyes. She smiled up at the sky dreamily. "Hell, *I'll* watch Chasey for twenty bucks an hour. I love that kid."

"You do?" Leigh said.

"Of course I do," Tiffany said, as if Leigh had asked an obvious question.

Leigh felt teary with gratitude. Tiffany had never expressed affection for Chase so plainly. No one had. She took another small sip of the beer Tiffany had forced on her. Less than a third of the bottle was gone, but under the hot sun, it had gone straight to her head.

Squeals from the children collided with screeches from the gulls.

"Let's get 'em!" a boy yelled.

"Um, while we're on the topic." Leigh began, her pulse quickening, the way it did when she knew she was about to confess something to Tiffany. Usually, these confessions were via text. In person, she was blushing. "I wanted to ask you something about Chase. And school for next year."

"Shoot," said Tiffany, crooking her elbow over her forehead. "Damn, it's hot. I need another drink and half a cigarette."

"Well," Leigh said, "you know I respect Chase's therapists. They've changed our lives immeasurably. But"—she paused—"they're saying he needs a closed classroom next year. One of the small ones for special-needs kids."

Tiffany nodded solemnly, "Okay. Well, there were twenty-nine in the gen-ed pre-K classes last year."

"Jesus," Leigh whispered.

"I know. It's fucking tragic."

"I mean, I just thought he was doing so much better," Leigh said. "There's been more listening. Less hitting. He's even telling stories. Like little fantasies he has in his head. It's so sweet. And age-appropriate! It just seems"—she paused—"I mean, have you seen those kids? The kids in the closed classrooms? They're just so delayed. I mean . . . there are kids with Down's."

"You don't have to whisper the word." Tiffany laughed. "It's not like they have cancer."

Before Leigh could defend herself, explain that she certainly did *not* mean *that*, Tiffany spoke again. "Chase has been regressing in music class." She squinted, as if it hurt to be the bearer of bad news. "And he did bite Harper last week."

Leigh felt as if time had slowed. A shift occurred. Hadn't Tiffany just said she adored Chase?

"I guess," Leigh said slowly. "But they were both bugging each other. You know how they are? Harper kind of nags at him."

She wanted to say, *Harper incessantly criticizes him, picks at him. Tells him he's too loud, too messy, too this, and too that.*

"She *is* going through a bit of a bossy phase," Tiffany whispered, as if Harper were nearby.

You mean an oppositional defiant phase, Leigh thought, plucking a term from Tiffany's own early child development–speak.

"It's hard for Chase." Leigh knew she was defending him. Worse, she was defending herself. "Harper is so"—she searched for a safe word—"*attached* to her toys."

Your little girl was breaking the cardinal rule of playgroups, Leigh thought. Harper wasn't sharing. She was torturing Chase, taking away toy after toy, every single pony (and there were a dozen at least) and hiding them in her bedroom. Tiffany, as usual, had done nothing, ignoring Harper's cruel game until Leigh had worried she couldn't trust her own interpretation, that maybe she was just falling prey to her dislike of the little girl.

"Like you say in music class," Leigh forced herself to say, "sharing is caring."

Tiffany picked at the peeling green polish on her toenails.

"I don't know, Leigh. A contained class might be the best fit for Chase."

How could she say that? That Chase would be better off with the kids who had behavior issues so severe they were destined never to be mainstreamed? Her Chase didn't even have a diagnosis. He was just a little slow at developing. Wasn't it Tiffany herself who had reassured Leigh that most boys like Chase caught up by age four?

"There's a difference," Leigh said, "between biting and being stuffed in a class with retarded children."

As the R-word—absolutely forbidden from the lexicon of a sancti-mommy like Tiffany—flew from Leigh's mouth, she knew there was no turning back. She had crossed the line.

Tiffany pushed herself off the chaise lounge with a dancer's grace, keeping her back to Leigh.

"I'm going to pretend you didn't say that," Tiffany said, pressing both hands onto the seawall and lifting up onto her toes to stretch. "I mean, come on, Leigh. What century are you living in?"

"Sorry," Leigh said, reclaiming her spot on the chaise lounge, emboldened and fearful at the same time. "I'm just so stressed out about this. On top of potentially losing Tenzin on Thursdays . . ." She trailed off intentionally.

Tiffany whirled around, hair flaring. "Not *potentially*, Leigh. It's a done deal. Tenzin is with Harp on Thursdays. Period."

"You misunderstood me. I didn't say yes. I still need to talk to Brad about it. I need a few more days. I'm sure Shabbat Tots will understand. Or maybe you can teach another afternoon? Or bring Harper with you. You can just . . ."

Tiffany interrupted her. "No, I already accepted the job."

Leigh was at a loss. "Oh-kay," she said with a huff of a laugh. "We'll talk about it later."

"Please don't be mad, Leigh-Leigh." Tiffany sashayed back to the chaise and ruffled Leigh's hair. "I'm sorry."

Don't touch me, Leigh wanted to say. Tiffany's apology was as fake as her engagement ring, which she claimed was IF grade and two carats, supposedly inherited from Michael's grandmother. Leigh had been embarrassed for Tiffany when she told Leigh this; the ring was obviously flawed and no more than a carat and a half. But she'd said nothing. She'd been kind. Now, she wanted to fling the lie back in Tiffany's face. Remind her that she, Leigh, was a Locust Valley Lambert who could spot a good diamond from ten feet away.

"I'm going to find a cigarette," Tiffany said. "Allie looks like a smoker, doesn't she? Be right back."

Before Leigh could answer, Tiffany shimmied off the deck and into the house.

Leigh stared at the clots of thick cloud that seemed to float atop the water and thought of her family's country house in Sag Harbor—the lawn that rolled into the sea and the swarms of fireflies that lit upon it in the blue dusk. She wondered if she would see it again.

Tiffany had been the only one she'd trusted. The only mommy to whom she'd bared her soul. The only one who praised her parenting, who soothed her guilt.

Don't be so hard on yourself. You're doing your best.

And there had been the months of late-night texts, the two women tapping out secrets and confessions to each other for hours. All the affection that poured from Tiffany, the empathy via cartoony emoticons. Little red hearts. Smiling suns. Smiley faces with their mouths pursed as if blowing a kiss. I Love U and U r the best and BFFs 4evah. Tongue-in-cheek, of course, Leigh knew, but Tiffany had chosen her from all the other mommies. The more confident, educated, hipper, and wittier masses of mommies who filled their neighborhood playgrounds and playspaces.

Tiffany was her only friend.

waste not, want not

Tenzin

Tenzin examined the half-eaten banana sitting on top of the trash, still wrapped in its skin and nestled in a pile of used coffee grounds and globs of yogurt. She glanced out the kitchen window and counted, *one, two, three mommies. One, two, three daddies.* She wasn't sure if Allie was to be called a mommy or a daddy.

The coast is clear, she thought, a phrase she had heard on an American television show.

She stepped closer to the trash can.

After breakfast, during cleanup time, Tenzin had watched Susanna hold the half-eaten fruit by her thumb and finger—the same way the mommies held the poopie and peepee diapers of the children (*peeyou!*). Susanna had complained about the smell, gagging as she exiled the perfectly good banana to the trash.

They were a mystery, these lesbians and their life. The night before, Tenzin had asked Leigh if it was okay to give Susanna and Allie congratulations on their wedding. Leigh had laughed, "It's not a secret, Tenzin. Of course you can!"

Tenzin had tried to explain they didn't have lesbians in Tibet, but Leigh had looked at her in the same way you look at a silly child.

Poor Mommy Susanna, Tenzin thought as she stared at the banana. So much throwing up of food. That morning, Tenzin had walked on the beach with Susanna, while Chase and the twins played pirates with sticks of driftwood. Susanna had invited Tenzin to visit the twins' home in Brooklyn, to see if she was a *good match.* Tenzin had added this to her vocabulary list to look up later, but Nicole had told her that the twins' mommies needed someone to watch the new baby, and so Tenzin had guessed the walk was a kind of interview. She knew she had passed Susanna's test because the woman had hugged her afterward, her swollen belly pressing into Tenzin's own belly, soft and slack from three pregnancies. It had sparked a brief, but bright, yearning in Tenzin for a baby. A child who would never know a day apart from its mother.

Now, staring at the banana, Tenzin felt her mood sink. She and Leigh, and maybe the other mommies, too, were due for their flow. Women everywhere, in Tibet, in India, in America, when the routine of women's lives matched, so did their cycle. She wanted to blame her tears during her last Skype with her family on this.

In one swift movement, Tenzin plucked the banana from the garbage, peeled back the mottled brown skin and ate the remaining fruit in two big bites.

"Tenzin?"

She turned to face Leigh, who stood with her mouth open, an alert and sweaty Charlotte in her arms. Leigh's face was red with what Tenzin guessed was too much sun, but as her good employer walked closer, Tenzin saw it was the flush of emotion that pinked Leigh's cheeks.

Tenzin smiled with her eyes and nodded, pointing to her banana-stuffed mouth.

"The baby's up," Leigh said.

The concern on Leigh's face made Tenzin wish she could give her good employer a great big squeezie-hug, just like the kind Chase's therapist had taught her to give Chase when he was so excited that his hands shook, and he clucked like a little chicken.

"You didn't have to eat that, Tenzin."

"Yes, I do. No biggie."

She thought of the two-day-old rice she once ate from out of Leigh's garbage. There was nothing wrong with the rice, and Tenzin had wondered if the newspaper laid over the mound of rice had been too neatly placed, as if Leigh had been trying to hide her wastefulness. The Dalai Lama says not to waste life, then why not avoid wasting anything at all?

Leigh had passed on many things to Tenzin. A set of pots and pans the color of poppies, flawless but for a few scratches. A plastic pitcher for cold tea

Leigh no longer used. A pretty diaper-wipe holder with a Velcro flap that Tenzin used as a purse. Tiffany had given her dresses that wrapped around your body and tied at the hip, and red clogs so shiny Tenzin only wore them to temple on Wednesdays and Saturdays.

God had been so good to her. Why should she choke on perfectly yummy two-day-old rice and stale cereal and cans of cold beans past the expiration date? This is what she ate for lunch at Leigh's house, choosing an item she predicted might be thrown away because it had sat in the cupboard too long, or because Leigh had found a brand she liked better.

"Okay," Leigh said. "That was terrible to throw away food like that." She paused, closing her eyes. "I'm sorry, Tenzin."

Leigh was still wearing the same shocked look, and Tenzin knew it had nothing to do with her eating the rescued banana. There was something wrong.

"Tenzin," Leigh said. She stopped and wiped at her face with baby Charlie's swaddle cloth. "I'm so happy you are here with us."

Her good employer was near tears.

Tenzin had seen this expression on the faces of protesters in India outside the Chinese embassy, as gangs of officers approached, destined to leave many broken and bloodied in their wake.

Terror.

The protesters had not run, even as the officers' approaching boots made the ground tremble. They sang of the sun, moon, and stars, songs that would have had put Tenzin and her husband Lobsang on trial in China, maybe cost them their lives. Tenzin had sung the forbidden name of her God-King, the Dalai Lama. It had been her last protest before leaving India for America, and she had sung until her throat ached and sweat and tears darkened the front of her silk chuba. She'd felt fierce and satisfied—praising him, the great Sun—but she had also felt broken, for she and all the Tibetans were homeless.

The mommies, even sweet Leigh, did not understand. *Tenzin,* they laughed politely, *but you're not homeless!* How could she explain, or make them understand, that it was only in exile in India, far from the Chinese government, that she would dare sing of how *the sun, moon, and stars are no longer in Tibetan lands. The lands are dark, and we are very sad that we can't see them.*

Her daughter Samten had wept, her chin wrinkling, her nose running, as the police dragged Tenzin and her husband away. Tenzin had smiled at her, shouting again and again, one of the few sayings Samten had taught her, in anticipation of Tenzin's trip to the U.S., *Do not worry, do not worry, do not worry!*

She said the same now, to Leigh in the beach-house kitchen, wrapping her arm around the woman's narrow birdlike shoulders.

"No worries, my good employer. No worries."

try your luck

Rip

Rip woke to Grace's tossing a piece of paper on his chest.

"What's this?" he said, as his eyes came into focus in the sun-filled room.

He felt the empty space next to him and sat up so quickly his head spun. "Where's Hank?"

"Oh," Grace said, feigning surprise. "You're up. He's with Harper. Michael's watching them. He's definitely Tiffany's better half."

She was refolding the clothes he had already folded and stacked on the bed-side table.

"Well," he said, "it's kind of hard not to wake up. When someone opens every shade in the room."

No apology from Grace. Which meant, he knew, that she was still pissed, and she was about to introduce a *discussion*.

"Is this a love note?" he asked, smoothing the paper she'd tossed at him.

There were numbers written in Grace's precise handwriting, an equation of sorts. How did she get those zeros so perfectly round?

41 hours had been circled twice.

"It's the number of hours I spend with Hank each week," she answered casually, turning away to look at herself in the mirror, to adjust her headband and smooth her glossy hair.

"Oh-kay," he said slowly.

Definitely trouble, he thought.

"Tiffany told me you told the whole playgroup . . ." Grace said, still looking in the mirror, where he knew she could see him sitting disheveled and puffy-eyed on the bed behind her. "She smells like body odor, you know?"

"*What* did I tell her?"

And what else could Tiffany have told Grace? He knew Tiffany was a little wacky, but not crazy. Not mad enough to tell Grace about the kitchen the day before. Or was she? She'd be risking everything. Their children. Their marriages. Their lifestyles, because when it came down to it—and it hurt him to admit this—he was in the same boat as Tiffany and the mommies. They were all dependent on their partners, their breadwinners. Without Grace, he was nothing. He had nothing. Not even a savings account in his name.

"You told all of them," Grace said, her voice creaking with restrained emotion. "Tiffany, and your *mommies,* you told them I'm never around. That I'm at work all the time. That I'm not there for Hank."

"I never said you weren't there for Hank."

"Then what *did* you say, Richard?"

What could he say? She really was gone all day every weekday, and on the weekends she had routine errands. Gym at 9 A.M. on Saturday and Sunday. Lunch with her sister every Saturday at 1 P.M. "Alone time" in her room where she read a book or crocheted little squares she then stitched into blankets for her friends who were expecting babies. And he understood her need for "me time." Her job was demanding, the stress of managing so many people who were juggling so many millions of dollars had to be exhausting. Frankly, although he would have had his chest hair waxed before admitting this to Grace, or anyone at the playgroup (even Tiffany), it was easier when Grace wasn't around. When she *was* home, she was like a shiny object distracting them from their routine, making Hank restless for her attention. Hank didn't understand why mommy needed her alone time. If Rip didn't take him to the park (and in winter this was a chore), the boy stood at the closed bedroom door and cried until Grace came out, annoyed with Rip and frustrated with Hank.

"I may have said you worked long hours. Or that there were some days you didn't see Hank," he said. "Isn't it the truth?"

She turned to him, and he saw she was close to tears. The woman his sister had once called The Ice Queen began to sob. A tickling thrill shot from his stomach to his throat. This vulnerability was new, and anything new was better than how things had been—he and Grace arguing in the same dizzying circles until the air in their apartment felt stale and claustrophobic.

"How could you betray me like that? In front of all of . . ." She paused. "The mommies!"

Then she was kneeling by the side of the bed, her lineless face cracked in tears, her back shuddering with sobs. He hadn't seen her like this since—he searched his memory—not since she'd given birth to Hank and been struck with what their OB had called the baby blues.

He stroked her hair and tipped her chin so their faces were a few inches apart. She was a teary, snotty mess. But beautiful. Vulnerable, for once.

"I'm sorry, baby," he said.

"I really try," she said, then a hiccuping sob escaped. "I try to do my best. Maybe I'm just not meant to be a mother."

"That's ridiculous," Rip said. "Hank adores you."

She looked up at him, her eyes squinting in suspicion. "Don't give me that shit. You don't really think that. I know it. You have to have it this way. It's like a sickness. Your martyr complex. You're like some passive-aggressive house-wife!"

"Sure," Rip said, with a bitter laugh. "That's right. I *like* your never being home. I *like* having no help. I can't take a shit by myself, without you or Hank . . . You're both demanding in the same way, you know? Always taking. Sucking the life out of me."

Grace pitched face-first into the mattress. "I know!" she cried into the com-forter. "You're right. Why is everything I do so un-mommylike?"

He'd won, and it made him feel awful. He lowered himself onto the bed beside her and stroked her back.

"That's not true, sweetie," he murmured into her ear. "You make every-thing possible for our family. Hank and I are so lucky to have you."

As he stroked her back, he felt her soften beneath him. Respond to his touch. He kissed her neck first, cautiously, and when she didn't brush him away, he made his way to her mouth. He undressed her, he licked her, he tweaked her nipples while he made her come with his tongue. He pulled down his boxers and spread her legs—his penis is his hand. But then she was on her knees, tak-ing him into her mouth.

He hadn't brought the condoms she always made him wear. Just in case one of his swimmers picked up speed.

"I want to be inside you," he moaned.

She ignored him.

When she stopped midsuck to adjust her hair, he could tell she was getting tired. She was growing impatient. Her head bobbed up and down. Too fast. She'll run out of steam, he thought, she's got to pace herself, or this would end up like most of the blowjobs she'd given him in the years since Hank was born. Half a blowjob.

"Honey"—he held her head in his hands, stopping her, as painful as it was—"that's enough."

She looked up at him, spit glistening on her lips.

"I want to come inside you," he said.

"No," she said. A single, flat denial.

Instantly, the mood flattened, too. She put in another five minutes of decent work, tiring out toward the end (*sorry, my neck is sore*), practically handing his penis back to him, then crawling up to nibble on his earlobe while he jerked himself off. As he came closer to climaxing, he thought about the text Tiffany, definitely drunk, had sent him the night before. The text had been a tease because he knew that she knew the answer, especially after she'd felt his hard-on in the kitchen.

who would u rather fuck? allie or susanna? ;)

You. The answer he never sent.

Now, as Grace lay limp next to him, performing the bare necessities—her cheek pressed to his chest, her hand between his thighs cupping his testicles, he conjured a vision of all three of them—Allie, Susanna, and Tiffany—naked and writhing on the beach. When he finally came, Grace was still lying dutifully beside him, but he'd flown far away from her. He was no longer in the dusty bedroom but beside the sea, entwined with Tiffany, inside her.

Twenty minutes later, Rip was on the deck with the rest of the mommies and daddies. The children had a surprise, Tenzin had told them with her usual hand-clapping vigor, and she and the kids had been out of sight since.

Rip and Michael were wrestling. They had both wrestled high-school varsity, it turned out, and were now grappling in the middle of the deck while Grace, Susanna, Tiffany, Nicole, and Allie sat side by side in deck chairs, their oversized sunglasses turned toward the afternoon sun.

"Get a room already," Tiffany said.

"Gross," Grace said, "You're practically dripping sweat into each other's mouths."

"Oh, God," Susanna groaned. "Don't make me puke. Again."

"Ha-ha," Rip said between grunts, as the mommies tittered, but the truth was, he was winded. Michael was going practically no-holds-barred. Rip had Michael in a headlock, but he could feel his grip loosening as they grew sweatier. Although the thought embarrassed Rip, he wondered if Michael could smell the sex on him, and he found himself hoping Michael could feel the muscles Rip had once sported. When they'd first moved to the city, right after college, Rip had been struck by the fear he felt; the panic when, during a block party, some Italian-American teens from the neighborhood had picked a fight with kids from the projects. Bottles had been smashed, a folding table collapsed, and a girl was thrown to the asphalt. Rip had jumped up from his seat on their stoop and pulled Grace into the dark hallway of their apartment building, daring only to peek through the small window in the door. In short, he'd been a fucking pussy, he'd thought afterward, recalling the icy fear that shot through his body and the roadrunner rate of his heart.

He had begun lifting weights at the City Gym nearby—nicknamed Shitty Gym because it stank of body odor. After a few months of daily weight sessions, one of the serious gym dudes, the beasts who wore weight-lifting belts on their walk *to* the gym, asked Rip to spot him while he benched what appeared to be at least three hundred pounds. Only then did Rip know he'd put on enough muscle to maybe hold his own in an actual brawl, or just make him less approachable if some bad guy (as Hank would call him) picked on him and Grace.

"You never have to worry, sweetie," he had said one night at dinner as he took a slug from his protein shake. "I'm pretty sure I could kill someone with my bare hands now if I had to."

"Um. Okay," she had said, and smiled. He'd been grateful to her for putting up with him. She was the daughter of immigrants who'd seen war and political persecution, whose father used a rusted machete to kill the rats he caught in the basement of their convenience store, and she had pretended to understand why Rip, a sensitive Jewish kid from the 'burbs, had to convince himself he was capable of defending her.

After Hank was born, the visits to the gym waned, and then stopped. Rip gained weight, and his muscles shrank. His only exercise was pacing around the apartment shushing the crying baby. When Grace returned to work, Rip was lucky if he could squeeze in a shower and a quick bite to eat while Hank took one of his twenty-minute naps, never mind a run across the Brooklyn Bridge or a session at the gym.

Now, as he pressed against the resistance Michael created by arching his back and tightened his hold on Michael's neck, like a vise, squeezing, he wondered if he could cut off Michael's air, if he could make the guy black out. He'd seen it done at an impromptu jiujitsu match between two trainers at the gym. All you had to do was increase the pressure until your opponent went limp and slipped to the ground, waking a moment later with no memory of passing out.

Michael submitted with a firm tap on Rip's arm, and Rip released him with a triumphant roar that startled Nicole, so she gasped, choking on her drink.

"Shit," Tiffany said. "You'll give Nicole a heart attack and make Susanna go into early fucking labor!" She laughed, and the tops of her breasts jiggled.

"Damn, man," Michael said, massaging his throat. "You're not kidding."

Rip saw a new respect in Michael's nod, an appreciating squint in the man's eyes.

"For crying out loud," Susanna said. "The daddies are going *Spartacus* on us."

The women tittered, and Rip gave a prissy little curtsy before he picked up his beer and downed it in three big gulps.

"Boys will be boys," Tiffany said, a lazy slur in her voice. Her eyes were hidden behind mirrored sunglasses, and Rip let his eyes travel from her baby-oiled legs up to the pool of sweat resting in the clutch of her cleavage. Their eyes met. Or at least he thought they did, but then Michael was slapping him on the back. "What do you say we take that kayak trip?" he said.

"Awesome, man. Can't think of a better way to cool off."

Grace's voice broke through. "Don't forget life preservers."

Rip stopped himself from saying something like, *We don't need those.* And he was relieved when Michael didn't reject the idea.

Nicole let her sunglasses slip down her nose, and said, "Susanna and Allie are making a quick trip to Stop and Shop. Anyone need anything?"

"You think they've got organic out here in the 'burbs?" Tiffany asked as she drained her wineglass.

Rip watched Michael lean over the back of Tiffany's chair and finger the wisps of hair at the nape of her long neck. The neck Rip had thought about so many times those last few years because of the breasts it led to.

"We haven't traveled back in time to the Dark Ages, babe," Michael said.

"Oh, is it one of those amazing twenty-four-hour supermarkets?" Tiffany asked. "With the fluorescent lighting and the Muzak? And the indifferent checkout girl doing her nails?"

She held her phone up to Michael. "Look at this sweet pic of Harp. I mean, the expression on her face!"

"You've posted too many online this weekend already. Enough," Michael said.

Rip felt the subtle click of the other mommies' heads swiveling to look at Tiffany.

Michael dropped his voice and whispered into Tiffany's hair. Her hand shot up and swatted him away. It looked like an accident, the way her green-painted fingernails snagged Michael's bristly upper lip, but Rip could see she'd meant to do it.

"Everyone knows you're a fantastic mama, Tiff," Michael said as he shuffled over to the cooler and lifted a dripping beer. "You don't have to go posting a billion photos of our little girl out there for every weirdo to see. I'm just being a daddy. Right, ladies?" Michael looked to Rip. "And gentleman?"

"You're just being controlling," Tiffany said as she tapped away on her phone. "Everyone knows there's no such thing as privacy anymore."

There came a shattering sound from the side of the house. Nicole gasped again, and Rip saw her hand shoot up to her chest, the tendons in her neck tightening. Take it easy, he thought.

Wyatt, Levi, and Dash appeared, walking slowly to the deck, heads bowed with guilt. Wyatt held the remains of a potted plant. A shard of terra-cotta, a clump of black soil, and a few heat-withered petunias. Dash looked the most ashamed, his grubby fingers gripping the metal car and launcher that must have caused the accident.

"Oopsy-daisy," Dash said.

"Dash oopsied!" said Levi, and all three boys laughed.

Susanna groaned and patted her belly, "Please let this one be a girl."

Like she had anything to complain about, thought Rip. She was a goddamn baby-making machine.

"Oh, the testosterone," Tiffany warbled dramatically, and threw her hand up to her forehead.

"Seriously," Nicole said as she reappeared with a broom. Rip saw she had recovered. No doubt, Rip thought, with the aid of some pill. "Testosterone has *got* to be responsible for at least half the evils in the world."

The women laughed.

"What?" Nicole said. "I'm serious."

"You are?" Allie said.

"Ignore her," Tiffany said before Nicole could answer. She reached over and linked her arm through Allie's.

Next to stick-thin Allie, Tiffany's curves were even sexier, Rip noticed.

"Yep, don't pay attention to Nicole, Allie," Rip said, smiling. "She hates men." He winked at Nicole, so she could see he was joking, or at least half joking because she *had* spent many a playgroup lamenting the inferiority of men. *They're just not emotionally stimulating,* she'd say, with Rip sitting just a few feet away.

"I do not hate men!" Nicole said.

"Well, I do. Hear, hear!" Allie said with perfect timing, lifting her cup. "To women!" she trumpeted.

"To women," Rip and the other parents echoed, their cups lifted.

"And thanks to those rare men whose testosterone flows in moderation," Allie said, clapping Rip on the shoulder.

She had meant it innocently, Rip knew, a friendly poke, but later, it made his cheeks burn with humiliation.

Harper appeared, wearing a mass-manufactured princess dress, all shimmery polyester and synthetic satin—clunky plastic iridescent gems glued so you could see where the adhesive had dried. She walked up the stairs that led to the deck and stopped to curtsy in front of the mommies and daddies.

"Good evening, You Highnesses," she chirped.

"Welcome to our palace," Rip said before making a musical-theater-quality bow. "M'lady."

The little girl's eyes sparkled, and later, Rip would realize it wasn't with pleasure but with anticipation.

Harper turned back to the steps and announced with a flourish, "Princess Harriet!"

Hank appeared at the top of the steps, wearing a pink princess dress. His face was garishly painted with haphazard makeup.

Tenzin stood behind Hank, her hands clasped in front, her face somber.

No, Rip thought, she couldn't have had anything to do with this. She looked mortified. This had to be all Hank and Harper's doing.

Harper asked, "Doesn't Harriet look beayouuuutiful?"

"He sure does, sweetie," said Tiffany.

Rip tried not to react, he really tried, but his head was swirling, and Hank was so pink, so glittery, and the silvery thread trimming the skirt and the sequins dotting the bodice caught the sun until Rip felt blinded. Everyone was looking at him—Grace's eyes saying, *You were the one who was all pro princess dress. You are the one responsible for our son in a dress.* He knew he should say something, anything, but the lump in his throat made it hard to speak, and he felt Michael's sweating presence so close, and so he said, in the voice of a different man, a different father, "Henry Cho-Stein, go wash your face!"

He heard Grace's voice behind him but didn't dare look.

"Rip?"

Although they stood on the open deck in the cool, late-summer breeze, the air around Rip felt unnaturally still and impossibly silent, so when Hank asked, "When can I get my own princess dress?" it felt to Rip as if the whole world were listening.

It wasn't the dress that pulled Rip forward like a giant pulsating magnet, until the uneven deck floor was cutting into his bare knees and he was using his own shirt and spit to rub at Hank's face. It was the makeup.

Someone, clearly a child, had painted Hank's face. Surely, Rip thought, they had meant to mock his little boy. For a moment, he forgot they were small children, barely preschoolers. It looked like a cruel practical joke a gang of boys in high school (bullies!) would play on the effeminate boy. Hank looked like a victim from one of those goddamn after-school specials Rip had watched as a kid.

Hank's cheeks were heavily rouged, and glittery blue shadow arched clownishly over each eye. But it was his mouth that made Rip scour his son's lips with the heel of his hand. The thick lipstick circling Hank's mouth had dried in the creases between his plump lips.

Later, Rip would wonder if it was Hank's smile he had tried to erase.

"Daddy," Hank cried, swatting at Rip's hand, "Stop. You're messing it!"

But Rip rubbed until Hank's skin was hot and flushed under his fingers. Why was he doing this? he asked himself. All those arguments he'd had with Grace, urging her to be open-minded about the princess dress, pleading with her to respect their son's unconventional desires. Yet now, as he looked at his son's smudged and tear-streaked face, cracked in sobs, he knew he didn't want his son to be a *sissy, pussy, homo, theater fag,* all those names the jocks at his high school had hurled at Rip years ago, so much that he'd avoided walking past the senior commons area each morning, slipping in the back doors by the gymnasium.

The children were ushered inside. Snacktime, someone mumbled, and there was the sound of chairs scraping against the deck floor.

Then Grace was there, her warm hand on Rip's arm as she gently pulled him away from Hank.

"Don't worry," she said. "I'll take care of this."

Hank said, "I just wanted to look pretty. Like Hah-per."

Rip heard Grace take sniffling Hank inside.

He sat on the deck and stared at the plastic tiara in his hands. The silver heart read Princess in curly script. Rip wanted to fix it, to tell Hank he looked awesome, but he couldn't. He couldn't see his son dressed like that. Not today at least—maybe another day.

He twirled the tiara around his finger. He was grateful he'd been born into this new wave of daddy domesticity. This was the age of men who were emotionally intelligent, who said they were sorry, who asked for the box of tissues in therapy, who planned their kid's birthday party.

But a princess dress? Wasn't that asking too much?

URBANMAMA.COM A Community and Forum for Parents

Welcome to UrbanMama, an anonymous forum where you can interact in sincere and open-minded conversation with other parents.

Speak your mind and share your thoughts about parenting, family life, marriage, relationships, and everything that makes you an urbanmama!

Sign up now!   Already a member, log in!

This webbot shit is freaking the fuck out of me.

Posted 9/4/2010   2:08pm

(7 replies)

—then quit reading it. 2:09pm
—get over it. there are tons of websites predicting all kinds of disasters. 2:10pm
—has it been picked up by mainstream news at all? 2:10pm
    —not at all. 2:11pm
—people predicted back in January the banks would fall. I thought then: these people ARE NUTS. And NOW look at us. 2:13pm
—what is a Webbot? 2:24pm
—does the guy on the corner with the sandwich board scare you too? 2:26pm

worrywart

Nicole

"No climbing on the rocks!" Nicole shouted at Wyatt and Dash.

They ignored her, scrambling on all fours up the steep gray boulders that formed a barrier in front of the seawall. She leaned over to catch her breath. Her thigh muscles thrummed from the sprint across the uneven sand. She had chased the boys down the beach, yelling at them to stop, her anger growing with every second she could feel her ass jiggling.

Wyatt's head had been turned to look at her as he ran, leaping over clumps of seaweed, as effortless as a gazelle, a smile dimpling his cheeks. Pure glee in the chase.

They had reached the boulders before her and, like two lithe lizards, scurried to the top with little effort. The boys stood tall, their hands shielding their eyes as they looked to the horizon. Two arrogant explorers, Nicole thought, as her need to get them off the jagged rocks grew more desperate.

They raised their arms high in triumph, and Wyatt laughed, and said, "Look, Mommy, we didn't fall. Toldya!"

"You might. And if you do, you'll hit your head. Hard!"

"I see a seal. A whale!" Dash said.

"Me too!" said Wyatt.

"If you two fall." She paused. "There'll be blood. A big big boo-boo!"

Then, calming herself, she looked over her shoulder at the staring faces of the other parents down the beach. She begged, "Please, sweetie. Please. Do you want there to be no more Wyatt? No more Mommy?"

Wyatt looked down at her and studied her face.

"If I fall and get a boo-boo, I have to go to the doctor and get a shot?"

Without thinking, she answered, "No, the doctor won't be able to fix you."

His face clouded with confusion. "Like Humpty Dumpty?"

"Yes," Nicole said. "Just like Humpty Dumpty."

Don't go in the water alone. You could drown.

Don't put so many grapes in your mouth at once. You'll choke.

Don't touch that knife. You'll cut your finger off!

The day had been filled with warnings, Nicole thought, and it was only midafternoon. A chorus of *don't!* and *watch-out!* As the mommies' and daddies' exhaustion had surged, the routine parental reprimands had morphed into ominous threats and prophecies.

Nicole had always feared the unexpected. Disliked surprises. Even the roller-rink birthday party her mother had sprung on her when she was nine, and the surprise tea-party baby shower her sister-in-law had thrown her. It was embarrassing to be caught unaware. To be fooled.

It was that feeling of not knowing what would happen that made her, now, in the kitchen, amidst fruit-bar wrappers and crumpled Dixie cups dripping apple juice, reach for the knife some careless parent had left on the cutting board. *In reach of a child!* She washed it, dried it, and returned it to the wooden knife block. She knocked on the block five times, her lucky number, chanting quietly—*knock on wood knock on wood knock on wood knock on wood knock on wood.*

The children cheered from the living room. It was afternoon snacktime. What joy they could feel at the drop of a pin. The pop of a straw into a juice box. The crackle of a package of bunny-shaped pretzels.

She was about to join them when she caught the glimmer of metal by the sink. The parer. She pushed it against the wall. Definitely far enough, she thought, and was about to walk into the living room, when she realized one of the taller kids—Wyatt, Chase—might reach the parer with a stool. So she gathered the parer, as well as the meat and fish knives that gleamed menacingly on the magnetic strip over the stove. The thwack each knife made as she pulled it from the strip made her feel nauseous. She could, she thought, slice through her skin with one quick flick of her hand. Plunge the sharpest knife—the one her father used to flay fish—into her soft belly. She didn't want to, but the fantasy of the event flashed through her mind so vividly that she could almost smell the metallic scent of blood. See the red-black pools of her own insides spreading out across the kitchen floor.

She gathered the knives—a dozen or so—into a pile on the kitchen counter. Each with its unique purpose—filleting, carving, bread slicing, butchering—verbs that induced fantasies of her own skin being flayed in thick pale sheets. She added the parer, the apple corer, and a bottle opener whose hook, she thought, was definitely sharp enough to gouge out an eye. She had to stop and knock five times on each wooden knife handle, whispering *knock on wood knock on wood knock on wood knock on wood knock on wood* as fast as she could until the words melted into each other, and there was only the soft clicking of her tongue against the roof of her mouth. She was running out of time. Someone could walk into the kitchen at any moment. Maybe even Josh, she thought as she searched for a hiding place, turning in a slow circle until she found the cabinets above the stove. Empty.

She heard Rip call to the children in the living room with his signature *gather together, gang!*

He began the round of that dreadful song, "Who Stole the Cookie from the Cookie Jar?" in a hushed stage whisper, and the children joined him, taking turns reciting the chorus, their voices amplifying, and by the time they reached the last child (*Harper took the cookie from the cookie jar!*), Nicole had found the stepstool.

*Who me? **Yes you!** Couldn't be? **Then who?***

She was clutching several of the knives in her hands and preparing to step onto the stool when the parents applauded. The boning knife slipped and stuck her finger.

"Fuck." She pinched her finger, and a small dome of blood rose. She sucked on it, her mouth filling with that hot, tinny taste that was like nothing else, when she felt the kitchen door swing closed.

"You said a bad word."

Harper. The little girl's hands were on her hips. One knobby Band-Aided knee jutting forward. Nicole followed Harper's sharp blue eyes to the pile of knives on the counter. Nicole stepped forward, dropping to a crouch at Harper's feet. Smiling.

"Harper, sweetie . . ."

The girl was gone. The breeze from the swinging doors rolled over Nicole, and she thought she might fall to her knees on the cold linoleum. Instead, she stood, climbed onto the step stool and slid each knife, as well as the parer, the apple cutter, even the blades from the Cuisinart, and finally the knife block (*knockonwood knockonwood* . . .) into the cupboard above the oven.

She knew Josh would notice. He knew the signs that she was approaching an episode. He would find her and ask if she was doing *it* again. Was she having bad thoughts? Shortly after Wyatt was born—fucking baby blues, Nicole thought—Josh had to hide the knife block because every time she walked in the kitchen, the thought of slashing herself had popped into her mind, like an unwelcome squatter.

Josh still brought up the knives in their couples' therapy. As if he were outing her insanity to their therapist, Nicole thought. He knew it was the humiliation she wanted most to forget. Who, in their right mind, obsessed over household objects? The washing machine she feared would overflow, checking five times each cycle. Or faucets in the bathrooms, which she tightened and retightened before bed, in case one dripped, drop after drop accumulating until water cascaded through the ceiling of the room below.

Are you having your *thoughts*? Josh would ask, as if their code could protect Wyatt from the obvious.

Nicole stood by the kitchen door and listened.

The children were silent. They must be eating. The only quiet moments she'd had in the last three and a half years were when Wyatt was eating or sleeping.

She thought of the cache of Go Bags in the trunk of the car and wondered if she should visit. A dose of security. A little something to get her through the night. Instead, she poured herself some Prosecco and swallowed a whole Xanax.

She returned to the living room, where Tenzin was leading the children in a merry game of Ring Around the Rosie. Nicole sat in her favorite chair, a high-backed midcentury piece of red-and-gold brocade that had belonged to Grandma Lois. The single soul in generations who'd possessed an inkling of taste, Nicole thought. She had loved that chair as a girl, crowning it the princess chair, and spent hours there, scribbling in her notebooks as stories un-spooled—of unicorns, goblins, and fair-haired maidens stalked by hook-nosed witches. Stories of lost children in dark forests.

Tenzin led the children in a wide circle around the living room. Nicole was walled in by their laughter. She remembered a lecture by one of her grad-school literature professors—a spinster with a romantic pouf of hair, who had reminded Nicole of the heroines in the turn-of-the-century novels that were the profes-sor's expertise. She had reveled in the gothic, and also in revealing how it threaded through today's pop culture.

Nicole itched to stand, to halt the children's carefree song. Don't you know, she wanted to tell Tenzin, that the ring—a red ring, a rosy ring—is the first sign of the plague? That pockets full of posies aren't pretty flowers to wear in your hair, but sachets of herbs, to ward off infection? As for ashes, doesn't it make you think of the burning of diseased corpses?

She imagined herself saying, We *will* all fall down, clasping Tenzin's arm, calling to the other mommies chitchatting on the deck about who knows what insignificant gripes. Death won't be as fickle as us, Nicole would shout, with our never-ending wants and needs! Death loves all its victims. Rich and poor. Young and old.

Instead, she sipped her Prosecco. She chided herself, calling herself names. Insane, melodramatic, and the worst; the word Josh hurtled at her in argu-ments. Sick. She snapped the rubber band around her wrist until she wore a red ring of inflamed skin like a bracelet.

Ashes-ashes-we-all-fall-down!

Please, Nicole. Web bots? You don't even believe in God, how can you believe in prophetic computers?

The children were still on the ground, giggling, Tenzin crouched in the middle of their circle, when Tiffany walked into the living room, an apple in one hand and a butter knife in the other.

"What in the H-E-L-L happened to all the knives?" she asked.

Nicole felt Josh's eyes fall on her.

"Anyone?" Tiffany said.

Nicole chanted silently. *Knock on wood, knock on wood, knock on wood . . .*

"Mama Nicole did it," Harper said.

The little girl was standing, pointing at Nicole.

Mercifully, this was the moment the Xanax kicked in. Liquid calm.

Leigh Marshall
347-555-2027
September 4, 2010 3:10 PM

what up chicca?

paging debutante Leigh
Lambert Marshall . . .

September 4, 2010 3:23 PM

Haha very funny, Tiff.

whats up? where have you
been? you missed CRAY-ZY
scene on the deck. Hank in
princess dress. Rip almost died.

Poor Rip. Miss Charlie fighting her
2nd nap. Chase snoring away.

September 4, 2010 3:29 PM

r u mad at me?

September 4, 2010 3:40 PM

leigh??

That WAS kind of weird. You know, what happened between us. On the deck?

September 4, 2010 3:42 PM

u forgive me? i just hate myself when I do dumb things that hurt the ones i ♥

I hate it when I get so crazy & insecure.

It's okay. we ALL make mistakes. Thank you for the apology.

September 4, 2010 3:48 PM

so . . . did u talk to Brad bout me having Tenzie on thurs? I gotta know. like NOW.

IDK, Tiffany, I'm a bit stressed about the whole Tenzin sched thing. Bummed if I have to give up Thurs afternoons. You know?

It's cute how you ALWAYS use my name in our texts when you get nervous.

September 4, 2010 3:50 PM

how about a share? we can do it at my place if u r worried about yours getting dirty. i know how you are about your fancy schmancy things. ;-)

You KNOW it's not dirt I'm worried about. The thing about the share is that Chase is SO overtired when he gets home from school & you know how intense he & Harper are together & I worry he'll be a pill & he's been going to bed at 6pm on school nights. He's THAT tired! Poor little guy!

September 4, 2010 3:53 PM

hmmm. Tenzie says Chase stays up til 9pm sometimes ???

I'm not going to call Tenzin a liar (she is a VERY good friend) and I don't know why you guys are talking about my kids' bedtimes . . .

LOL. look, leigh. i NEED thurs afternoon. the deal was to share Tenzin. she was MY friend first. i could've kept her all to myself. but i didn't. so you need to be flexible.

I didn't realize there was any "deal"???

i seriously didn't think it was gonna cost our friendship or anything or I would've NEVER introduced you to Tenzie.

Slow down! Are you saying we have to stop being friends over this? I'm sorry but I already arranged (MONTHS ago) to have Tenzin on Thursdays. AND you didn't introduce us, you just gave me her phone #

we r not breaking up. i don't totally trust u right now (sorry, reflex) but we will b even better friends if we can work this out.

IF??

i'm upset. it feels like u don't care about me or love me enough to see that i would REALLY suffer w/o the help i desperately need to run tiff's riffs. And the tiff's riffs kids would suffer too. there's kids who look forward to that 1 music class all week, u know? i'm not trying to cause drama I'm just saying it isn't the issue of Tenzie or no Tenzie, but more the fact that u DON'T care about me after all!

September 4, 2010 4:10 PM

I guess I felt the same way. Like you didn't think I was worthy of the extra help. I DO care about you. More than most people. You know how I am. ;-) And you KNOW I am a huge Tiff's Riffs fan!

September 4, 2010 4:14 PM

Tiff? You there?

September 4, 2010 4:38 PM

Tiff. . . . answer me. Please.

September 4, 2010 5:04 PM

Can we talk about this face 2 face? The kids are up from naps. I can leave them with Tenzin and meet you somewhere private? Please?

September 4, 2010 5:30 PM

Okay then. I guess you're really mad. And that our friendship is over??

September 4, 2010 5:33 PM

I can't imagine that you still love me as much after all this. But I'm sure we can work this out, Tiff.

September 4, 2010 5:35 PM

of course i ♥ you. u r the bestmommyfriend i've always wished for. sorry i missed yr texts. Miss Harper needed her mommy-milk.

ditto ♥ ♥ ♥

so i can have tenzie on Thurs then?

Um, no?! I'm sorry but I really need her that day and she and I arranged it months ago.

September 4, 2010 5:39 PM

What's with the "we'll work it out" BS, Leigh?!

ugh!! how can you hand me all that BS about your gratitude "thank u 4 adding Tenzin to our lives" BS & "thank u for loving Chase unconditionally" BS & then be so greedy?!!!

Can we talk about this later? In person? Please?

September 4, 2010 5:45 PM

Tiffany? You there?

BFFs forever

Leigh

Tiffany had terrified Leigh at first. She was crass. She was a sloppy drunk, and burped and farted, and giggled *excuse me* in a sweet, childish voice that hinted at sex. Tiffany talked about sex often, which served as a reminder to Leigh that she herself was, as Brad had told her, so "fucking uptight." Leigh had even considered dropping out of playgroup, making an excuse, like she'd registered for a Tumbling Tots class on Friday afternoons. She hadn't felt a bond with any of the parents, though she liked Susanna, who was pretty and sweet, especially for a lesbian. Leigh had thought about inviting Susanna to lunch, but she worried she couldn't relate to someone whose perspective just had to be so different from her own. Susanna was elegant. She looked like Natalie Wood. With an extra twenty pounds on her frame.

Leigh knew Tiffany had grown up white trash. A phrase Leigh had heard Tiffany use to describe herself with obvious pride. She had boasted about her inspired decision to meld her and Michael's last names (Zelinski and Romano) into a hybrid surname for Harper—Zelano—and if there was stronger proof that Harper's mommy and daddy came from little, so little that they wouldn't continue their ancestors' names, Leigh couldn't imagine what that might be.

But Tiffany knew how to shop. Her clothes were boutique-quality. At least she was trying, Leigh thought, and began to feel sorry for Tiffany, who painted a childhood of neglect for the rapt parents at playgroup (all the product of privilege), a gritty tale of rural, working-class upbringing. Tiffany's father was a mechanic, who ran a garage out of their front yard. Her stepbrother had kept a pet raccoon. Her sister was a methamphetamine addict, and Leigh had stopped herself from asking Tiffany if her sister's teeth were all rotted out.

There was also the near-miraculous way Tiffany engaged Chase. When she crouched at Chase's eye level and looked straight into his eyes, Chase actually looked back, a marvel that nearly took Leigh's breath away. So Leigh had not only stayed in the playgroup, she had signed up for one, then two Tiff's Riffs music classes. Tiffany seemed unbothered by Chase's behavior during class. The way he whirled his body around with little awareness there were other little bodies nearby. Tiffany gently redirected him when he mouthed the egg shakers and ran around the room in jagged circles instead of sitting and "participating." Leigh was grateful Tiffany never snapped at Chase in frustration as former babysitters and therapists had. As Leigh herself did.

Almost a year ago, Leigh's phone began buzzing nightly with Tiffany's texts. At first they were short and playful, Tiffany's syntax unmistakably alcohol-mussed. A joke about something stupid Rip had said at playgroup. Or Tiffany might send Leigh a message through Facebook, asking for her opinion on a hand-sewn quilt Tiffany had found on Etsy that she just had to have. Did Leigh like the cobalt or the tangerine color best?

Soon, Leigh, newly pregnant with Charlotte, was sitting at the kitchen table, after Chase had gone to bed, staring across the river at the buildings of lower Manhattan silhouetted against a dusty rose sky. Waiting for Tiffany to text her with intimate complaints about Michael, how he smothered her, how he rejected her *true self.* Leigh had responded, revealing how Brad constantly criticized her for being impatient with Chase.

He makes me feel like I'm a terrible mother. Though he doesn't have a drop of patience himself!

Tiffany responded:

U r a great mom! And . . . my fave new mommy friend ♥

What could Leigh do but text back:

ditto ♥

She had erased her text history, even rebooted her phone, to ensure that Brad never read her silly declaration of love.

Two text-filled weeks later, Tiffany probed Leigh on topics as deep and dark as *what's your greatest fear?*

Tiffany shared first:

that I'll die alone & everyone will forget me

Leigh knew she couldn't share her greatest fear—that the truth about the money she'd stolen would be revealed—so she texted:

me too :-(

Tiffany's question the next night was:

have u ever thought about spending ur life w/someone else?

Leigh curled up on the taupe leather chaise in her sitting room, fingers poised over her phone.

Yes I'd leave him. If I had $

With her confession, a blush spread like wildfire up her neck.

Thought you were loaded??!

It's complicated.

She wanted to tell Tiffany the truth. Her family had been rich decades ago, but now they were rich in name only.

The two women texted through the cold winter nights and into spring. Some nights, Leigh's hands grew slick with sweat on the overheated keys of her phone. As her naked newborn suckled at her breast, it seemed as if the world were asleep, except for Leigh and Tiffany, and Leigh's little miracle, Charlotte.

On those text-filled nights that smelled of lilacs and linden blossoms, when time slowed and the spring air pressed in, warm and vibrating like a bear hug,

Leigh wished she could tell Tiffany about her crime. Maybe, by proving its necessity to Tiffany, she could prove to herself it had been the only choice. Thieving from preschoolers *was* worth one perfect Charlotte Lambert Marshall. A second chance for Leigh to prove she wasn't a rotten mommy after all.

Some nights, it was just one or two lines of text that lifted her, that felt like her salvation, a treat to carry her through the next day, until she was back in her leather chaise and texting with Tiffany, the branches outside her window black against the midnight sky.

Leigh: I'm such a bad mom

Tiffany: Me too :(

Leigh revealed secrets she hadn't told Brad:

my father made me call him daddy. ugh. once he took me to a restaurant and i wore my white patent leather heels. i was so proud. But his secretary was there! he kissed her on the lips. the lips!! in front of me!!

Tiffany:

i'm so sorry. he's a bastard. u r a better person than him.

And since the rhythm of their texting was tit for tat, it was Tiffany's turn to share.

my stepbro & his creepy friends made me give them BJs in the woods behind the school when i was in 6th grade. so yeah, guess you could say i'm broken. ;(

It was that winking sad face at the end of Tiffany's confession that made Leigh type:

I wish I could kill them all for you.

That night, when Tiffany signed off, she wrote:

u r the best mommyfriend. i love u. ♥ ♥ ♥

i love you, Leigh had typed. She added a xxxooo before she tapped SEND.

In the morning, after these late-night texting sessions, as Leigh stirred one-half teaspoon of Splenda into her coffee, her sight blurred by fatigue, Brad joked about her *girlfriend* and their *text affair*. Although Leigh laughed and swatted him away, she knew it was a kind of love. A first love. Tiffany was the first, much more so than Brad, with whom she dared to share the ugliness of pretty and pleasant Leigh Penelope Lambert Marshall, of the Lamberts of Locust Valley, Long Island.

x marks the spot

Allie

Allie was watching the boys on the deck while Susanna took a shower.

Dash and Levi ran their Hot Wheels across the top of the seawall, from one end of the deck to the other. This they repeated, along with the requisite *vroom vroom* sounds, while behind them, puddles of seawater on the beach glowed gold with the late-afternoon sun.

It seemed to Allie that every little boy came with a penis and the uncanny ability to mimic car engines and machine guns.

"Mommy?" Levi asked. "We go play in the woods?"

"Aargh!" growled Dash as he squinted one eye and poked Levi with a driftwood stick. "We be pirates searching for buried treasure."

"Yeah!" Levi cheered. "Pirates! Treasure!"

Allie looked to the thick, shadowy woods beyond the dunes, leading into hundreds of acres of protected state-park land.

She was only *in charge* until Susanna finished showering. Surely, she thought, she could manage not to fuck up in the next twenty minutes. Susanna's water would break if she knew the boys had gone into tick-infested wilderness.

"No," she said, as sweetly as she could. "We'll go to the big park tomorrow when we get home. Okay?"

"They don't got trees at that park," Dash protested.

"Sorry, buddy," Allie said. "We'll get ice cream, too."

"Chocolate?" Levi said.

"We can get ice cream anywhere," Dash grumbled.

Allie looked at the fierce half. Her tough guy. The low orange sun simmered behind Dash, and the tips of his ears glowed pink. She wondered when his complaints had become so rational, so grown-up, and she wondered how long it would be until he was arguing with his mothers and winning.

"Well," she said, "that's technically true. But we'll get chocolate-chocolate-chip."

She pulled the hood of her sweatshirt over her head to blot the sun.

"Now Mommy needs to rest. Just for a few minutes. 'Kay?"

Allie eased down into the deck chair and stretched her legs. The rusty springs, missing their cushion, pinched through the pair of Susanna's pants she'd been forced to wear after her jeans had been sprayed by Susanna's puke on the beach. White. Of all colors. She hadn't worn white since her First Communion. Allie figured it was the first time her hairy shins had seen sun in a decade, but there was no grown-up present to appreciate the joke.

After Susanna's shower, the two of them were to drive to the store and shop for the "feast" everyone had been mentioning again and again until, Allie thought, they sounded like a bunch of geriatrics psyched for the early-bird special. The feast was the last major event Allie would have to endure before she could excuse herself for the night and retreat upstairs. She planned to pack their bags so they could leave early the next morning.

The weekend had been exactly the kind of experience Allie had tried to avoid the past four years of part-time motherhood. When the *Times* profiled Allie two months after the boys were born, she had watched as Susanna read. The Arts section had quivered between Susanna's naked fingers—still so swollen from the pregnancy she couldn't wear the commitment ring Allie had given her, fashioned from Allie's grandmother's diamond earrings. Susanna had been there from the start; the rented cameras, the shabby studio on the Lower East Side, back when cabbies refused to take you into Alphabet City. She wasn't the first student Allie had slept with, but surely the first whose opinion of Allie's work, and of Allie, mattered.

So when Susanna's face crumpled as she read, a smear of disgust contorting Susanna's mouth (a paintable mouth, Allie had flattered when wooing Susanna years before), a part of Allie ached.

When the critic had asked Allie about the new effect motherhood had on her work, she had replied, "I'm a part-time mommy but a full-time artist."

The critic—an influential female photographer—had praised Allie's honesty as an act of feminism.

"But isn't it the truth?" Allie asked a sobbing Susanna, who hurried from the room, her puffy hands shielding her face.

The newspaper fell to the floor, and though Allie knew she should go to her wife, the mother of their children, instead she knelt and picked up the pages, gingerly. They were supposed to save them after all, frame them and hang them above the other interviews and reviews of Allie's work they had collected, starting a decade before the twins were born, before the boys were even a thought in their minds. Or, at least, not a thought in Allie's mind.

Though this part-time mommyness had been a blight the day the *Times* had finally, after so many years of dreaming, given her the Sunday Arts feature, it was exactly this that saved Allie, that allowed her to focus on her work and, although she would never admit it to Susanna, allowed her to forget the boys for hours at a time. It was the excuse she had when things with the boys went wrong on her watch, when one of her mistakes—too much ice cream at the park, a missed nap, or her temper lost—caused a minor disaster, usually Levi limp with wailing, Dash brooding and defiant.

Allie could tell herself, "It's okay. You're just a part-time mom."

The *vroom vroom* sounds resumed, and Allie closed her eyes against the glare of the low sun.

Just for a moment, she thought.

When she woke, with a jerk that made the springs in the chair screech, Rip was squinting down at her.

"You okay?" he asked.

The boys. She gripped the ties of Rip's life jacket to pull herself up out of the chair. It took a moment for her eyes to adjust, for the purplish black sunspots to fade.

There they were, still making their slow, methodical rounds, eyes trained on the tiny wheels of their toy cars.

"Oh my God. I fell asleep. Susanna asked me to watch them for ten fucking minutes, and I fell asleep."

"Well, NBs like us can't really be trusted, can we?" He winked at her.

"NB?"

"Nonbiological parents," Rip explained. "Sometimes we don't get full credit, you know?"

"Even you?" Allie said. "I would think Grace would constantly sing your praises. You're such a great dad."

"You think so?" Rip asked, his voice hopeful.

"Hell yeah," she said, feeling the urge to amp it up. This guy needed a boost. She leaned toward him, close enough that she could see the silvery shadow of his stubble. "A lot of these mommies," she whispered, glancing back at the house, "they're just going through the motions. But you . . ." She paused. "You really mean it. You love the kids. You love the *process*."

Rip gathered Allie into a hug, nearly lifting her off her chair. His life jacket pressed up under her chin, and she smelled seaweed and mildew.

"Okay." She laughed, patting his back. "You're suffocating me."

He released her and backed away. "Sorry. That was just a really nice thing to hear."

Michael walked onto the deck, in a pair of shorts and a sweatshirt, stripped of his usual hipster look.

"Alrighty then," Michael said. There was mischief in his smile. "If you two are done making out, Rip, we can go for that paddle now."

Rip chased after Michael, who had started the climb down the ten feet of rocks leading to the beach. Rip slung his legs over the seawall, then turned to Allie.

"Hey," he called. "Thanks."

He made a loud *mwah* sound and blew her a kiss.

Allie pretended to catch it and winked.

"No prob, my nonbio brother."

Rip disappeared behind the wall, then Levi's singular high-pitched wail sliced through the air. The boys were a pile of flailing arms and legs rolling across the weathered floor of the deck.

"Cut it out!" Allie ran over and peeled them apart, hoping it wasn't too late. That Susanna hadn't heard.

Levi gripped a handful of Dash's hair in one white-knuckled fist. Dash pounded on Levi's back with the heel of his hand. Dash's nostrils pulsated and then Levi's head was thrown back, mouth open to the pink-tinged sky in a silent scream.

She had to stop the scream, had to stuff it back into the boy.

"Shhh," she said, "Don't cry. It's okay." Allie was almost whispering, and it reminded her of the fights she'd had with her younger brother as a kid. Her pleas to pacify him—*I'm sorry. I didn't mean it. You can hit me back!*—after she'd walloped him, knowing that if he screamed, her father would come running with an open hand.

"Dash said he was going to throw my car"—Levi paused, mustering steam before howling—"in the ocean!"

The seagulls scattered to the far end of the beach, and Allie wished she had wings of her own.

The boys sat a few feet apart, each singing his own pathetic song, the *it was him, not me—he hit me, no I didn't* routine. Their cheeks were flecked with sand and snot and tears.

When Susanna called, "Hey!" from the window upstairs, the boys fell silent.

"Everything okay, babe?" Susanna asked. "Do you need me to come down there?"

The boys stared at their matching orange water shoes. Why couldn't Allie produce that kind of order in them? What was it about sweet-voiced, ready-to-burst, waddling Susanna that terrified them into gulping down tears?

Allie waved to Susanna.

"We're fine," Allie shouted. "Everything's fine."

She crouched in front of the boys.

"Come. Here," she said, curling her index finger.

The boys crawled forward on hands and knees.

"Stop fighting right now," Allie whispered fiercely. "Or else Mama is going to get really mad at Mommy. Is that what you want?"

Levi shook his head no. Dash rubbed the top of his toy car.

"Listen to me," she said, shaking Dash's scabbed knee. "If you don't cut it out . . ." She felt her lips tighten. "You're gonna be in big trouble."

"No, Mommy," Levi whimpered, his lower lip trembling. "Don't say that!"

"No crying," Allie snapped. She hated when her attempt at discipline backfired—Levi crying harder, Dash grudgingly silent.

Levi clamped a hand over his mouth, but sobs slipped through his tan fingers.

"If you don't start being good," Allie said, "there'll be serious consequences."

"What is *consequences*?" Dash asked hesitantly, garbling the word, so it sounded more like *con-sickness*. Allie saw the promise of defiance in the lift of his chin.

She stopped to think. Her answers to Dash's questions never came out right.

"It's like when you do something bad, and so something bad happens to you in return."

"Something bad is going to happen to me?" Levi wailed, and stood, shouting toward the upstairs windows, "Mama! Mama!"

Allie pulled Levi into her arms, shushing him, but his cries rose like a siren. Her hand flew to his grotesquely stretched mouth. He mustn't disturb Susanna, she thought, as his wet lips blubbered under her fingers.

"Nothing bad is going to happen," she said.

She pressed her lips to his cold, damp forehead and shushed him until he was quiet, his big eyes looking up at her, waiting.

"Mommy," Dash said, a sharp reprimand. He had his hands on his hips, his chin tucked to his chest. "You're making my brother cry. You're doing a bad thing."

She let her hand slip from Levi's mouth. "Levi wasn't listening. I asked him nicely to stop crying." Her eyes scanned the back of the house, searching the windows for the disapproving faces of the mommies.

Calm down, she told herself.

"Boys," she said, as placidly as she could, "nothing bad is going to happen. But you *will* have a time-out if you don't start doing good listening. A big one. No Thomas trains."

Levi gasped.

"No," Dash whispered.

For a moment, she admired the smug look on his face. It took balls to call her bluff.

"Fine then. No iPad for a whole week."

A flicker of rage narrowed Dash's eyes.

"Okay, Mommy. Okay!" Levi cried. "We be good. We do good listening!"

"Dash?" she asked.

Behind them the waves whispered as they ran over the pebbles on the beach.

Dash stared at his knees. He nodded, and mumbled, "Okay."

The screen door opened, and as soon as shuffling Susanna appeared, Levi flung himself into her arms, his head knocking into her belly. Her hair was wet, sleek, and dark, and she smelled like old-fashioned soap—something cheap, like Ivory—but in the moment it felt perfect and almost exotic, and Allie wished again that she and Susanna were alone. In bed. Their damp bodies tangling on crisp white linens. Curtains billowing into their Cape Cod ocean-view hotel room.

"Be gentle with Mama," Allie said. She tried to ignore Susanna's questioning look: *I leave you alone with them for ten minutes, and . . .* Allie wanted to defend herself, to explain that it was the boys who were making her look bad.

"Come on, Levi," Susanna said, taking the sniffling boy by the hand. "Let's get you cleaned up. You can go potty before Mommy and Mama leave."

"Oh," Levi hiccuped. "'Kay."

The screen door thwacked shut, and Allie swiveled to face Dash. He had a metal car in each hand and stood with his legs apart, knees bent. As if ready to run.

"Give me the cars."

He backed away until he was flat against the seawall.

"Okay. Then give me Levi's car."

She motioned toward his right hand, which held the car Levi had named Hawk because a purple Mohawk-like fan rose from its hood all the way to its tail.

"Now, Dash."

Hawk was gone. It happened so quickly she wasn't certain it had happened at all, until she saw Dash's empty hand. He ran from her and she caught him, peeling back his sweaty fingers. Nothing. She leaned over the wall. The tide was coming in, stray waves bumping into the boulders at the base of the wall, exploding into foamy spray.

"Did you throw Levi's car in *there*?"

Dash looked at her blankly. That same fixed stare of rebellion. When had this happened? It was like looking at someone else's child.

"You did it now," Allie mumbled as she swung one leg, then the other over the wall, possessed with the goal of retrieving Levi's car. If not, there would be official proof that she couldn't even handle part-time motherhood. Her back pocket snagged on the concrete and she felt it tear as she scrambled down the rocks. A wave slapped against a boulder, drenching her. Her eyes stung with saltwater.

She called up to Dash, "Stay there! Don't move!"

The drumming of the waves, and the smack of the water into the wall, drowned out any response he might have made. The rocks were slick, and she gripped with her toes so not to slip. As the water tumbled back out to sea, she spotted something shining in the rolling pebbles a few feet out. She jumped onto the beach, underestimating the drop, and landed on a turned ankle.

"Fuck, fuck," she yelled as she hobbled forward. The water grew darker, colder, and deeper with each step. Something slick wriggled over the toes of her left foot. She held her breath, tears rising.

No fucking way was she going to blubber. She could feel *them* behind her, the others; the mommies and daddies, and she wondered if this was some orchestrated practical joke. A *let's laugh at the geeky hipster* moment. She knew they resented her for not carrying the baby herself. She could feel it when they stared at her when they thought she couldn't tell, and in the way they spoke to Susanna. As if she was the playgroup charity case. *Poor Susanna*—married to such a selfish woman. Surely, they would jump at the chance to humiliate Allie. And would it really be surprising if Susanna was in on the joke?

She slipped on what felt like a seaweed-covered rock, and her sole stung with what she knew was a gash, but she didn't dare stop or look back. *Motherfucker, motherfucker.* When the next wave came, she waited until the water rolled back out, and reached down and grabbed the gold car before it was sucked out to sea.

By the time Allie had climbed back up the rocks and practically thrown her body over the seawall, the water had risen to at least three feet, the waves slamming into the rocks, the spray jumping the seawall and splattering the paint-stripped picnic bench.

The surge of relief, of triumph even, washed over Allie's goose-pimpled skin despite her soaked clothes and the chill that arrived with the first hint of pink sky. She lifted her foot, and sure enough, there was an angry red cut in the white meat of her sole, watered-down blood seeping out.

Dash was gone.

She hobbled to the back door.

"Hey," she called through the screen, "is Dash in there?"

Grace, Leigh, and Nicole sipped wine. The kids huddled around an iPad, watching an episode of *Yo Gabba Gabba*.

"No," Nicole said. "He hasn't come this way."

Even through the screen, Allie could see Nicole's eyebrows peaking with worry.

Allie ran to the seawall and scanned the rocks below. Wet, black, and half-submerged, they looked ominous. Would she be able to see Dash if he was down there? If he was stuck in a crevice between two rocks? If he had fallen headfirst, his head was underwater, and . . . She couldn't finish the thought. Should she call to the others for help? What if Susanna heard and came outside and freaked out and went into early fucking labor way out here in the middle of nowhere?

She ran to the end of the deck that looked out on the length of beach, dotted by the occasional beach house, each with its own seawall-and-boulder barricade. No boy-sized figure running across the sand. She ran to the other end of the deck and saw movement by the wooded state-park entrance.

That little shit. She ran along the side of the house to the front yard, jumping through the sun-ravaged cypress trees that stood guard along the path to the beach.

"Dash," she yelled, as branches scratched her arms and face.

She slid down the dunes. Sand stuck to her wet clothes, slipping into the waist of her pants, into her underwear. She ran down the beach, shells jabbing her bare feet.

Dash was sitting on a rock at the park entrance. Like one of Waterhouse's painted sea nymphs. That same satisfied smile skipping across his lips. The woods behind him were shadowy and nightlike. Fairy-tale woods, she thought, as the green flares of fireflies flashed. Red Riding Hood woods. She thought of the mommies with their jewelry and highlights, their platform sandals and push-up bras. Yes, even she—butch Allie—was once a little girl who knew the names of the little girls who'd been lost in the woods.

"You," Allie said, leaning over, her hands on her knees, as she tried to catch her breath. "Look, kid. I'm only trying to keep you safe when I tell you not to do things. It's not like I have a freaking agenda or something. I don't even want to be here!" Her voice echoed against the trees that loomed tall and black behind Dash.

Before she could say *let's go back,* before she could reach for him, take his hand and lead him back to the house, he was off. Into the narrow path someone, long ago, had hacked into the woods.

"Dash! You stop this right now!"

She ran faster than she knew she could, into the claustrophobic confusion of so many branches overhead and on all sides.

She was on him, grabbing him, whirling him around so he faced her.

"You are being so bad, Dash!"

"*You're* bad," he shouted, his voice small and weak after her roar. "Harper said so."

Her vision shuddered as the ethereal light of dusk settled.

"What are you talking about?"

"You're not our real mommy. Mama is."

He bowed his head and drove his upper teeth into the top of her hand. She howled and pulled away, trying to shake him off, but he wouldn't let go. His teeth drove in harder, and she swung back and slapped him across one cheek. Hard enough to turn his head so he was looking at the ground. She saw the spot at the nape of his neck where hair never grew. His beauty mark, Susanna called it. She felt the wetness of his saliva on her palm as she drew her hand back, cradling it against her chest.

There was only the sound of nature, and the silence—after so much noise all day—was a relief. The snapping of branches. The distant waves like a sleeping child's heavy breathing. Dash looked up at her, his head shaking as if he were cold. His tiny nostrils were pulsating, in-out, in-out. No one had ever looked at her with such ferocity. Like he could devour her whole.

"I just wanted to play a game," he said, and his voice broke, the little boy returning. "Pirate treasure."

She waited for him to cry. She knew she had slapped him hard, as hard as she had once slapped her own brother when they were kids because their father only hit Allie when he lost his temper, when he drank, when he was worried about money, and she had wanted someone else to know how it felt.

Allie helped Susanna into the car, the long grocery list fluttering in Susanna's hand.

"We'll be right back!" Allie said, and waved to the twins, who stood at the steps of the front door. Levi whimpered from the gentle prison of Nicole's arms. Dash kicked at a rust-streaked sign staked into the earth by the withered azalea bushes. Refusing to even look in Allie's direction since she'd slapped him.

WELCOME TO EDEN the sign read in hand-painted letters.

After she'd hit him, Dash hadn't cried a tear. Only gone quiet, like a wounded lover, and walked stoically back to the house, where he resumed playing with his toy car on the deck.

As if it hadn't happened.

She would have a talk with him, Allie promised herself, the minute she and Susanna returned from shopping. She'd figure out just what to say.

"Don't worry about the boys," Susanna said brightly once Allie was in the car. "They always cry for the first few minutes when I leave them. They'll be happy again soon."

Allie thought of how some people who met them for the first time—at the park, at a family wedding—asked who the twins' real mother was. Susanna reacted defensively, *we both are.* But Allie was speechless in those moments, desperate to avoid the attention. And her doubt.

Dash was right, she thought as she pulled out of the sea-pebbled driveway and onto the sand-dusted road. That little conniver Harper was right. Allie was not a real mother. Not like Susanna.

She decided the next time someone—a mom in music class, the reception-ist at the pediatrician's office, some kid's grandma at the playground—asked them who the real mother was, she'd tell them to fuck off.

don't rock the boat

Rip

Rip sat in the kayak with the paddle resting on his knees and Michael's broad muscled back facing him. They had lugged the two-seated kayak from the cobweb-filled shack at the side of the house, then searched for the paddles in the piles of Nicole's father's crap, everything from badminton racquets to moldy deck cushions.

Now, finally, the beach house at their backs and the open sea stretching limitless in front of them, they waited to start their journey. As the cool breeze ruffled his hair, Rip felt almost at ease. If only the kayak didn't feel as if it were sinking, then maybe he'd feel even better. He hadn't realized the boat operated half-submerged. Water was already spilling into his seat and he was about to ask Michael if this was normal. Then he heard his name being called from the deck behind them, a punch of urgency in Grace's voice.

She was standing behind the seawall, Hank's head peeping over the concrete. Rip saw, despite the distance, the red in Hank's face, and knew his son was crying.

"Fuck," he groaned.

"Daddy," Hank wailed. "I waaant you!"

Michael turned to face Rip. "Could you just tell him no?"

Behind Michael's casual grin, Rip sensed that Michael was annoyed.

Rip knew Grace wouldn't relent, and even if he argued with her, right there, in front of everyone, Hank would cry until Rip took him along. And he had traumatized the boy earlier with his insane reaction to the princess dress, hadn't he? He owed it to Hank. He tried to find satisfaction in the fact that Hank felt safest when he was with him, his dad, but right now, it felt like a burden.

"No, wait. We *can* go. We can take the canoe instead of the kayak!" Rip said, cringing at the desperate ring in his voice.

"With Hank?" Michael said. His upper lip twitched enough that Rip could see the disgust. "Won't he just cry?"

A small flame of anger flared in Rip's chest.

Sensing his screwup, Michael added, "Cool. Let's bring Harper, too."

After another twenty minutes of complications; searching for the kids' life jackets, pulling the canoe out from under the deck, last-minute potty trips, and last-minute commands from the mommies—mostly Grace, who Rip could see was terrified with the idea of the kids going along—Harper and Hank took their seats, and Michael shoved the canoe into the water, the base grinding against the pebbles.

Rip had wanted to be the one who shoved out, the one who the mommies would watch from the seawall, their delicate, manicured hands shielding their eyes, checking out his tanned leg muscles as they flexed with the effort. Instead, he walked behind Michael. They climbed in the boat once the water was chest high, and amidst Harper and Hank's squeals, they set off.

"And we are on our way!" Michael sang out.

Harper whooped from the head of the boat.

It wasn't fair she got to sit in the very front, Rip thought as he rubbed Hank's goose-pimpled arm. He wanted Hank to prove to Michael he could do more than just whine and cry. For Rip's sake and for Hank's own. *Please, for the love of God, Hank, stay calm,* Rip thought.

The last time Rip had been in a canoe was at sleepaway camp as a kid, one of those Jewish camps where all the kids wept at the end of the session during the good-bye ceremony. Not Rip. He'd wanted to get back to his air-conditioned house, his Game Boy, and the privacy of his room, where he could masturbate when inspired.

Paddling was not how Rip had remembered it. This was hard work, and the current made it feel as if they were pushing their way through pudding. He had imagined that he and Michael would have time to chat, to get to know each other a bit more, and he was hoping he'd get a chance to ask Michael for advice. Maybe another male perspective would help Rip find *the* way that would convince Grace to have another baby. Like a magic spell to transform her into a procreative believer.

Rip's palms stung by the time they'd made it out to the buoys where the Island residents docked their boats. The white cottages, squeezed side by side, stared at them from the shore with their sea-weathered faces. He spotted people lounging on the decks under striped umbrellas and wished he were there instead of here. Then he focused on the twitching muscles in Michael's arms, and it gave him the strength, the competitive boost, to paddle faster.

"Slow your roll back there, man," Michael said without looking back. "Or you'll be pooped before we make it around the bend."

Harper giggled. "Daddy said pooped!"

"Poop. Poop," Hank echoed, looking up at Rip with a grin.

Rip smiled back although he felt a rising dread this trip had been a mistake.

"Sure, boss," Rip said with just enough attitude (he hoped) to send Michael a message.

Nicole had suggested they paddle to the estuary. Rip was vaguely familiar with the term but had no idea what an estuary actually was. All they had to do, Nicole had explained, was paddle around the tip of the island. There, she had promised, they'd spot the families of swans that had made the secluded cove their home for generations.

Michael led, directing Rip in a way that reminded him of Grace, and he wondered if the world wasn't chock-full of micromanagers.

"Don't lean so hard to the left, partner," Michael said. "Let's try to paddle in sync," and finally, what Rip felt was totally unacceptable, especially in front of the kids, "Can you pick up the pace a little? You're paddling like a girl."

Michael followed the dig with a bark of a laugh before adding, "Just kidding, man."

Rip concentrated on the tip of the paddle polished white with wear, commanding himself to play it cool, brush it off; this was just how guys bonded. Through humiliation.

"A girl?" Hank sang, smiling and shaking his head as if he was in on the joke. "Dad's not a girl."

"Michael's just being silly," Rip said, when what he wanted to say was *Michael's just being an asshole.*

"Girls are cool," Harper said.

"They sure are, sweetie," Michael said. "And boys and girls can be friends."

"You are my friend, Hah-per," Hank said quietly.

"And Mommy Tiffany and Daddy Rip are friends," Michael said. "Isn't that right, Daddy Rip?"

"Sure we are," Rip said, unnerved. "Our whole playgroup is pretty tight."

Michael didn't answer. Rip listened to the sound of the paddles cutting through the water and worried: what was Michael implying? Could Tiffany have told him something, about what happened in the kitchen yesterday? Rip's interaction with her had been limited all day, but it seemed normal enough. As if they'd simply go on with the monotony of little kid life—naps and snacks and trips to the potty—as if nothing had happened. Sure, Tiffany was wild and loved to see how far she could push boundaries, but would she really tell her fiancé about what had happened in the kitchen? Or what had *almost* happened, Rip corrected, because nothing had happened, had it? Okay, something *had* happened, he thought. A line had been crossed. Their bodies had reached for each other, and he knew she'd been as wet as he'd been hard, and he was growing hard in the canoe now just thinking about how nothing had happened, goddamnit. Especially, he told himself (convinced himself, by squeezing his thighs together and pushing his weight into the paddling), when you thought about what *could* have happened.

In the twenty minutes it took to round the tip of the island, while Rip tried not to think about Tiffany and her breasts and the slight looseness in her bikini bottom where he had, earlier that day, on the deck while she lay on the lounger, glimpsed something inside, the children talked nonstop. They pointed out a school of silvery fish leaping into the air as the canoe glided past. They spotted an orange-and-black butterfly flitting over the dark blue water.

"Wow, a monarch!" Hank whispered with awe. "What if he falls in, Daddy?"

"He'll be okay," Rip said with a grunt. It was hard to talk and paddle at the same time without losing his breath. The wind had picked up, just enough to ruffle Hank's hair a bit, but it felt as if they were pushing against a wall of water. Were they paddling against the current or what? Not like he would ask Michael and risk looking like a wuss.

"Man, that kid's smart," Michael said. "He'll be like a science teacher. Or some kind of tech geek who invents something and makes a billion."

Rip couldn't help but feel it was a backhanded compliment. He knew all the hipsters were using the term *geek* like it was cool, but hadn't those same hipsters just been geeks themselves back in the day, bullied and persecuted? Plus, it was killing him, the way Michael spoke, almost breezily, as if paddling were a piece of cake. Rip knew what the guys in their weight-lifting belts at Shitty Gym would think of him now, winded by a damn paddle.

The trip was anything but peaceful, despite the gorgeous orange orb of the sun sinking into the horizon, and the clouds that hung low and pink, as if dazed by the sun's beauteous exit. But the children talked incessantly. *A bird! Look, a doggie on the beach! Are we almost there? When will we be there? Another bird! That's onetwothreefourfive birds.*

"Hank. Harper," Rip said finally. "Let's have a little quiet time, okay?"

"They're just being kids," Michael said with a shrug.

"Sorry," Rip said, embarrassed he'd let himself come close to losing it, a term he'd used himself to criticize so many parents on the playgrounds of Brooklyn, mocking them for succumbing to the strain of wrangling a child under five. What was wrong with him?

By the time they made it to the marshy estuary—really just a pond with a narrow link to the Sound—the sun had lost its fire. Under the canopy of the weeping willows that draped the pond's shore, it felt as if night was much closer than he'd thought. What a relief it was to drop the paddle and massage his throbbing arms. The boat turned in a circle. So slowly, he didn't realize the rotation until they were facing a different part of the woods ringing the pond. The air smelled damp and mossy, like the inside of a mushroom. Every minute or so, he had to swipe at a mosquito, bat it away from Hank, whose plump brown skin was a delicacy for the bloodsuckers.

Instead of satisfying the children, the end of the journey sparked a new host of questions. *Why are we stopping? What is this place? Where are the swans? You said there'd be swans. Where are the swan babies? Are there going to be swans, Daddy? Are we going back soon?*

Rip and Michael shushed them gently, reassured them again and again. They lied the harmless white lies of parenthood, like *the swans are napping* and *maybe the swans are still on their summer vacations,* which birthed even more questions like, *Why do swans have to take naps? Where do swans go on vacation?*

Rip came up with a game. Count the trees. Count the different sounds of the birds. And when that was finished, count slowly all the way up to a hundred!

"Anything can be a game," he said, and winked at Michael, feeling like a parenting expert, "if you make it sound exciting."

This gave the two men a window of conversation. Michael turned to face him. The breeze had picked up, and the canoe was turning faster, and it felt disorienting as Rip thought, frantically, about what they should talk about. Time was ticking away. Soon the children would be bothering them again, destroying any chance there was to have a coherent—and just maybe— meaningful conversation. So he brought up an earlier topic, the one on which he and Michael had bonded the day before in their initial (and successful, he thought) tête-à-tête; what they hated about the playgrounds of brownstone Brooklyn.

"So," Rip said, cringing at how much he sounded like a gossip-hungry mommy, "what's the worst parenting you've seen at the playground in our 'hood?"

Michael guffawed, and it sent a cluster of birds shooting through the branches into the small patch of open sky above their heads.

Harper and Hank paused their counting and looked up, their lips parted in surprise.

"I saw some mom at Cobble Hill Park the other day," Michael started.

"Oh yeah," Rip interrupted. "I know where this is going. That's the swanky part of the neighborhood over there."

As if, Rip thought, Grace didn't make close to three hundred thou a year. As if they didn't own a three-bedroom apartment, renovated to boot.

Harper renewed her counting, "Thirteen, fourteen."

Hank joined in and the children chanted in unison, "fifteen, sixteen, seventeen . . ."

Michael continued, "This mom, at the park, she gave her daughter—a quiet little thing—a time-out for walking up the slide!" He huffed in disbelief.

Together, the two dads shook their heads.

"No way," Rip said.

"I mean, look," Michael leaned over Harper so his face was just a few inches from Rip's. His skin was a blueish gray in the fading light. Like he was telling a ghost story, Rip thought, and he felt the sudden chill on his bare arms. "I don't let Harper climb up the slide if there's a kid waiting to come down. But there was nobody up there. It was just plain gross."

Rip wished the way he talked was more like Michael's; thoughtful, unhurried, like he had all the time in the world. Rip had always disliked his quirk of spewing forth anxiously. His jokes falling flat, so that sarcasm was taken seriously, missteps that pushed people away. All because he couldn't just slow the fuck down and because, he thought now, he was worried no one would listen for very long. It had been an issue in his college acting classes, his habit of delivering his lines too fast.

"Here's my philosophy," Rip said, his voice hushed, as if it was a secret. "It's simple. Kids are kids. They don't know what the hell they're doing, and it's our job to teach them. So they can go out into the real world someday and be functioning members of society. This"—he lifted his fingers in quotes—"*we-got-to-share-everything* rule is BS. Who shares everything in real life? The very opposite is the way life rolls!"

Michael nodded. "Totally. You're preaching to the choir, man."

"So why do we expect our kids to act more grown-up than grown-ups? Why do we get P-I-S-S-E-D when they freak out?"

Rip was excited now, as if something truly wise was flowing from him. He straightened his back, and the canoe rocked gently from side to side. "What kind of unpredictable world is that for a kid? It's psychologically traumatic, if you ask me. Like, Oh, hey, Tommy, I know that's your most favorite car *ever,* but this kid here, who we don't even know, is bawling his eyes out, and so you got to hand it over. Give it up. For the good of spoiled children everywhere. That's just crazy."

Michael leaned over and squeezed Rip's shoulder. So hard it felt good.

"You got a good daddy here," Michael said, looking down at Hank. "You're a lucky boy."

"Yep," Hank said.

This was it, Rip thought. There couldn't be any window opened wider.

"Thanks, man," Rip said. "You saying that means a lot to me. 'Cause I think you're an awesome dad, too."

Hank's small, whining voice interrupted him, "Daddy? Daddy. I have to make a peepee." Hank clutched at the crotch of his swimsuit.

"Hold on, buddy," Rip said, patting Hank on the shoulder. "We're heading home real soon." And then to Michael, "It means a lot, 'cause I'm in this total dilemma with Grace. Maybe you could help me out?"

"Sure. Anything I can do," Michael said as he turned to face front, gripping the paddle and lowering it into the still, blue water.

Rip sighed. "I appreciate that. 'Cause here's the situation. There's nothing I want more in the world than . . ."

Michael interrupted him, "Why don't you get that paddle in the water, okay? We'll talk on the way home. It's getting dark."

"And dark-time," Harper said, peeking around her father, her little fingers doing a creepy-crawly movement in front of her face toward a wide-eyed Hank, "Dark is when witches and monsters come."

"Daddy?" Hank mumbled, pressing into Rip's stomach as he backed away from Harper.

"Harper, sweetie, please don't scare Hank," Rip said. "So, like I told you, Michael. There's nothing I . . . And we. Grace, too," he lied. "There's nothing we want more than a brother or sister for Hank. Like I said yesterday, on the deck"—he laughed nervously—"we have to use a D-O-N-O-R to get this show on the road. And, ugh, she *hated* going through the whole process at the clinic."

Michael grunted. "Man, the current is fierce back here. I can't get the boat to move an inch."

Rip continued, "I'm cool with it, but it creeps Grace out, you know."

"Are you paddling?"

Michael's back arched, and Rip could see the effort he was using. The taut lines of his upper arm muscles gleamed in the alien blue light.

Rip started to paddle, and the resistance almost yanked it from his hands.

"It's like we're stuck," Rip said. "Oh yeah, so"—he paused, trying to find the best way to explain what was a stomach-roiling humiliation, that his wife wasn't just antibaby, but that he was starting to suspect she was antihim—"you think you could help me out? With Grace? 'Cause I'm at a loss, man."

Michael lifted the paddle and held it aloft, water dripping from it, cold and black. Michael sat unmoving, his head bent forward, until Hank turned to look up at Rip. The soft down on his son's cheek glowed.

"What's wrong, Daddy?" Hank asked, and Rip could hear the terror in his boy's voice, which sent a shiver of unease through Rip's gut.

"Michael?" Rip said. "What's up?"

"Are you asking me," Michael said, so quietly Rip had to lean forward to hear, "what I *think* you are? You. Me. Grace"—his voice dropped to a whisper—"and a turkey baster?" Michael laughed, but there was an ugly kink in it. "Maybe a few scented candles and Sade on the iPod?"

It took a moment for Rip to understand. Did Michael think he'd been suggesting a threesome? To squeeze some sperm out of Michael like he was a reproductive vending machine?

Anxiety thrummed in Rip's chest as he looked around them; at the still water and the blackening branches above and under and everywhere, like an enchanted forest had closed in around them, and the canoe felt too small and he thought they might be trapped there forever, spinning in lazy circles.

"Let's get out of here," Michael said, and spat into the water.

"Ew, Daddy!" Harper said.

"Whoa," Rip could barely speak. His mouth had gone dry. "Wait. I did *not* mean that, dude. You're not hearing me right. Or I wasn't making myself clear, I mean."

"I heard you fine," Michael said. Rip could see the sweat blooming darkly under the back of Michael's shirt. "You need a"—Michael paused, then finished the sentence as if he had a mouthful of bad food—"D-O-N-O-R."

"In a clinical setting!" Rip said. "A freaking doctor's office. Not a bedroom!"

"Do not"—Michael paused—"use language like that around my baby."

"I didn't even mean *you,*" Rip said. "This is some crazy misunderstanding."

"We're done talking about this. Done. Get your"—he looked over his shoulder, and Rip saw the rage in his clenched jaw, but then Michael paused, his eyes moving to Hank in Rip's lap, and he spelled the next word—"F-U-C-K-I-N-G paddle in the water."

Rip was too mortified to speak. He was stuck in a boat in the middle of nowhere with a pissed-off dad, possibly drunk and practically a stranger. And Rip's child, his precious only child, was with him.

"Michael," Rip said, but Michael ignored him, dipping his paddle into the water, stroking with a groan that escalated until Michael released with a grunt.

Hank gripped Rip's forearm, and Rip could feel the boy's sweat-slick palm.

"Daddy?" Hank said, and there was no need to say more. Rip knew what his son was feeling.

"Can I have a turn paddling?" Harper asked.

"Michael," Rip said. He reached over Hank's head to tap Michael's sweat-soaked back.

"Don't touch me," Michael said quietly. Rip sat back, shifting Hank so his son was as close as possible.

They dug their paddles into the water until it felt to Rip like they were gouging at frozen earth. The back of Michael's neck turned purple and Rip imagined the capillaries bursting under his own skin. The veins at his temples throbbed. But the canoe moved only what seemed like an inch every try.

They did not speak. The birds called to each other—a sad and lonely plea that mimicked Hank's whimpering. The drooping willow branches swayed in the breeze. The frogs croaked. More mechanically, Rip thought, than the way he'd imagined the frogs in the books he had read to Hank or in the cartoons the boy had watched. There was nothing natural about the sound. It reminded Rip of the buzz of a city-apartment doorbell, and he wished he and Hank were at home, and the apartment door was buzzing. *Chinese food!* Hank would shout joyfully, and they'd settle down to watch *Toy Story 3* for the fortieth time, and Rip would cover Hank's eyes with his own hands during the scary parts.

Rip almost had to stop himself from laughing as they clawed and clawed at the water with the canoe barely moving. *This is crazy. Just a silly misunderstanding. A temporary hell,* he thought, *like childbirth. All would be good in the end, once they got back and ate some food, had a few beers.* He'd make Michael understand.

He could smell the sour scent of his nervous sweat.

The frogs and the cicadas grew louder. A relentless, grinding, buzzing chorus.

Then he felt it. A hot trickle on his feet.

Hank sighed. Rip caught the rising scent of his son's urine.

"It's okay, my special guy," he said. "Daddy's here. He's got you."

the grass is always greener

Susanna

The car ride to the supermarket had been puke-free. *So far,* Susanna thought.

As Allie drove, Susanna listened to her talk a mile a minute about how intense the mommies were and *what the hell were GMOs?* And *why was Tiffany so against GMOs?* And *what was up with Rip, could he be gay?*

Susanna nodded and answered in short responses. GMOS were Genetically Modified foods. Tiffany was an extreme domestic sancti-mommy. No, Rip was not gay. Just strange.

She used the opportunity to check her savings account on her phone.

The balance was $4,250. It wasn't much, she thought, but her business was just getting off the ground. She'd scored her first big rental, a Swiss family with three kids under five, who would visit their Brooklyn cousins that fall and had booked a double stroller, three car seats, and two portable cribs. For a whole month! Things were sure to pick up in the spring, when the weather warmed.

Then she remembered. There would be the baby to take care of, which would create at least a six-month distraction from building the business. She could hire a part-time babysitter. Tenzin was lovely—but that would spend money meant for their future home. If only Allie were more interested in pitching in with the child care. If only Allie were more interested in general. Honestly, Susanna thought, even the most disinterested daddies, like Nicole's husband Josh, were more invested then Allie.

The car hit a bump, and Susannah's belly slapped against her thighs. *Fuck!*

She rubbed her bump, an apology to the baby for the shock, and for swearing. Even if it was only in her head. She'd read many an article on pregnancy that warned stress and general negativity had a harmful effect on a life *in utero*. And although Susanna took little Tiffany said seriously, there was that study Tiffany had mentioned not long ago, linking stress to an elevated level of testosterone in a pregnant woman's blood, which just might be responsible for the dramatic increase in Autism and ADHD. As Tiffany had lectured the rapt parents, Susanna had felt her heart beat faster, as if her body temperature were rising right then, as if she could feel her stress level rocketing. She had imagined the endorphins pinballing the testosterone, setting off a toxic rainstorm in her uterus.

So she'd taken to apologizing to the baby each time she cursed. A miniantidote, she hoped. Just like the swear jar her Midwestern mother had kept on the corner of the kitchen counter. A nickel had clinked into the jar for every cussword.

The automatic doors of the Shop & Stop whirred open, and Susanna was reminded of the magical efficiency of suburbia. Ice-cold central air. Starbucks drive-thrus.

Allie veered left toward the dairy aisle and picked up her pace, waving her grocery list, "I'll knock this out fast, babe. You just chill, and I'll meet you at the checkout in a few, okay?"

"Okay," Susanna said as she eyed the few shoppers; an older woman in a housecoat and a few kids trailing their mother, their faces pressed to handheld video games. Had they heard Allie call her babe? Had they reacted? This wasn't the city, after all, as Allie was always reminding her, using it as the principal reason they could not never ever move out of city; there wasn't much love of gays in the 'burbs.

No, Susanna decided. No reaction from the other shoppers. Just a slow, shuffled browsing in time to the mellow Muzak piped from some unknown place above. What song was it? She knew she had heard it before.

She entered an aisle. The order and predictability of the grid was a comfort, the very opposite of the fear she'd had as a little girl of losing her mother in what had felt like a never-ending maze of sky-high walls.

The brightly colored packages popped in Technicolor under the fluorescent lights. The endless assortment (who knew there were enough kinds of crackers to take up an entire aisle?) and the rainbow of little flags dotting the aisle with cheery optimism (SALE! BUY ONE, GET TWO!) emboldened Susanna, and she found a corner by the cereal boxes where her phone had three bars of access. She opened Citibank's mobile app and made a transfer from their shared checking to her secret savings account.

$1,000. Click. Done.

The balance was now $5,250. Much better, Susanna thought.

She knew Allie would never know. Allie was too "artistic" to be bothered with the tedium of bill paying. Allie, who had her head up her ass these days, or to be more accurate, her phone in her face. E-mailing clients and instant messaging her agent. Texting her irresponsible, childless friends. Which Allie had the nerve to call networking! Maybe even, Susanna dared to think it, texting a lover? A student from one of her Parsons classes. Hadn't Susanna been Allie's student once?

No, Susanna thought, she would stay positive. Just as Tenzin had suggested that morning as they walked on the beach, a prebreakfast romp, the boys running ahead, sticks of driftwood raised above their sandy heads. The kind of nature-filled childhood they deserved.

"It is good for the baby," Tenzin had said. "To stay calm. As the great Dalai Lama says, *Choose to be optimistic, it feels better.*"

This had filled Susanna with an instant panic. She had been so stressed, so worried, so angry all the time. What if it *had* hurt the baby?

"You will be okay," Tenzin had said, as if she could read Susanna's thoughts, rubbing Susanna's newly rounded shoulders with her man-sized hand. "You are a good person. I can tell."

Yes, Susanna thought now as she maneuvered her belly through the aisles, *I am a good person.* Then she found her destination.

The produce glowed under the lights. The vegetables and fruit in the over-priced organic market in Brooklyn seem dull and shriveled in comparison. And the smells! Tomatoes that smelled of basil. Cantaloupes that smelled like honey. Peaches that actually smelled like peaches. The perfume felt like a hug from a great old friend. She hadn't been able to walk past the grimy Met Food near their apartment in months. The stench of rotting food had made her gag. But this, this was heavenly, and it was as if the baby could smell it, too, because he/she jerked, and the skin of Susanna's belly rippled with delight.

This was what she needed, what the boys needed, what their new baby needed, and even if Allie couldn't see it, this was what Allie needed.

Fall was just around the corner, Susanna thought as she caressed the fuzzed skin of an apricot. The scent of wet leaves in the woods on a rainy day. The patter of drops on the roof, so present when there were no other sounds to drown it out—no sirens, no cab horns, no shouting on the street. The scent of fire smoke rising off crackling hearths and bonfires on the beach and fire pits in the backyard that had always reminded her of homecoming, of powder-puff football. She had been a runner-up for Homecoming Court queen her senior year, which had been one of the few backstory details she had kept from Allie, until Susanna's mother had mentioned it at the first family dinner Allie had attended. As in, Susanna had translated to Allie later, *how could her precious baby girl Susie be a dyke, when she'd almost been the homecoming queen?*

She lifted a coconut and inhaled deeply. The coarse brown hairs tickled her nostrils. Sure, at home there were a few trees in the grassless yard two stories below them (not that they had access to it) and one cherry blossom in front, which, for a few glorious weeks in April, turned their parlor windows pink. How grateful she was to that little tree. That poor little tree scarred by bike chains and poisoned by dog piss, and whose thin branches were strangled by plastic shopping bags.

She shouldn't have to feel that way about one little tree. It wasn't natural, she thought as she grabbed an empty cart and began filling it with cartons of strawberries and blackberries, a cluster of perfectly ripe (not too ripe) bananas. Then mangoes and kiwis and even a passionfruit.

A pregnant woman, a woman brimming with the power of life, should grow her baby where the air at least *smelled* clean, where the sounds of nature weren't overpowered by the sounds of man. In the city, she and the boys were locked in a cage; their apartment was less than a thousand square feet, after all. They were freed only by the occasional escape to the Hamptons, to the sprawling beach house that belonged to Mitzi, Allie's publicist, where a congregation of childless artists oohed and aahed over the boys, ignoring Susanna, treating her like nothing more than a vessel. A chipped vase carrying the most exquisite flower.

"Babe?"

Allie's gravelly voice returned Susanna to the Muzak, to the fluorescent lights, to the gleaming waxed floors, to the overhead mist drifting down toward the leafy greens. Her hands were filled with soft fragrant peaches, and she was crying.

"I know it," she said to Allie.

"You know *what*?" Allie asked, taking a step toward her. "Are you okay?"

"The music playing right now," Susanna said, through her tears. "It's 'Thank You.' By Led Zeppelin. They played it at my senior prom."

white lies

Leigh

Leigh sat on the lumpy sofa in the main room and nursed a drowsy Charlotte. It was after the children's dinnertime, and the room was filled with oversunned overtired children, and half-drunk mommies anxious to get food on the table before hunger spiked tantrums.

Leigh had to remind herself not to pick at her eyebrows. She had already worried a naked patch over her left eye that afternoon during the children's naps, while her phone had buzzed again and again, skittering across the bedside table with Tiffany's texts.

Tiffany knew, Leigh thought now as the children's whines rose slowly, like the distant rumbling of a storm approaching. There was an underlying hiss of threat in the last few texts, as if Tiffany was hinting at consequences much larger than a lost mommy friendship.

Before she could stop herself, Leigh's hand was in her hair, one finger curling around a single strand at her temple and yanking.

The relief was immediate. A cooling pulse starting at the crown of her head at the root and flowing down through her arms. She turned to the windows— pinkish orange with the setting sun.

"Look, Charlie girl," Leigh whispered to the baby, who was half-asleep, her suck waning. "I think it's an egret. Or maybe a heron?"

The clouds reminded Leigh of day-old bruises, but she waved the image away. Tenzin would call those ugly thoughts and had told Leigh that she was a beautiful person who should have beautiful thoughts. Leigh wanted to believe her.

So she tried. She imagined one last trip with the children to the Lambert Sag Harbor country home, where she had spent her own childhood summers.

"Oh, yes," she whispered to Charlotte, who startled, her hands lifting in the air in sleepy self-protection.

They would eat lettuce and radishes fresh from the kitchen garden and play in the sandbox Hugo, her father's "man" and the caretaker of the country house, had built for Leigh and her sisters decades ago. Chase would learn to love the beach, and the salty sea air would calm his tics. All the hyperactivity in the world, Leigh thought, couldn't make the sand any less soft, the sky any less big.

The children's whining tore her from her fantasy. It was as if they could tell there were fewer parents to reprimand them. The dads were on their canoe trip. Like some male coming-of-age classic, Leigh thought. Susanna and Allie were food shopping for what everyone kept calling tonight's feast and which Leigh was dreading. Just the idea of sharing physical space with Tiffany for one more night made Leigh's eyebrows itch, as if they were asking her hands to crawl up and pluck each hair, one by one.

Grace entered the room, balancing a platter of white paper plates on her forearm. Each plate was topped with triangles of grilled cheese and a small mound of cut and steamed veggies. The children sat quietly, their heads peeking over the tabletop, as a plate was placed in front of each child.

Chase wrinkled his nose. "No sam-wiches," he said, and looked up at Grace, offering her his plate.

Leigh saw the crease of annoyance around Grace's mouth.

Chase's eyes wandered the room until he found her. "It's too hot, Mama."

"Blow on it 'til it cools down. Count to twenty," she said sweetly, hoping he wouldn't ask her to leave the sofa. Her safe place, since the dining table was that much closer to the kitchen, where she could hear Tiffany's voice, the way it swelled in conversation and fell quiet, and then swelled again to make a point. Enough to make a person feel seasick.

"They really are so cute sometimes," Grace said.

"Who?" Leigh asked.

Grace laughed. "The kids, of course."

"Yeah," Nicole said as she hurried out of the kitchen to drop a pile of paper napkins in the center of the table, "*Sometimes* being the key word. But," she paused, "I'm glad I made one."

As Nicole and Grace laughed, Leigh noticed the glassiness of Nicole's eyes.

As if she were already drunk. Or on those pills that Tiffany was always gossiping about. *Nicole's magic pink pills.*

Grace, her hands on her hips, said, "They're cutest when they're unconscious," bringing forth more laughter, even from Tiffany, who had slid into the room. Her sudden presence made Leigh sit a bit taller and tug the edges of her hooter-hider nursing cover more snugly over Charlotte's head.

Some children are cuter than others, Leigh thought, and then wished she hadn't. She was imagining what the other mommies were thinking about Chase. That although he was beautiful (it was undeniable—his long limbs, the gold flecks in his hair) he was not cute.

Leigh sunk into the sofa and closed her eyes. Images of a happy Chase danced across the screen of her mind, across the lawn of the Sag Harbor house. Chase, sun-kissed and salt-tousled, running barefoot over the flawless emerald carpet, and there was Tenzin, smiling as she ran behind him. Dear Tenzin was watching over Leigh's children when Leigh could not, for she knew that in her fantasy she was in jail, somewhere far, far away, somewhere empty of green, of sea breezes, of children's laughter.

The sound of Chase's churning frustration returned her.

"I. Not. Hungry." His voice drowned out Tenzin's patient prodding.

At home, Leigh used television to coax him to eat, a technique a therapist had taught her. She paused the TV and refused to press PLAY until Chase took a bite, despite his little fists drumming the table. After he took a bite, the television show resumed, and this process was repeated until it felt like each meal was a marathon. Leigh would never have let the other mommies know she bribed Chase with TV in order to stuff a piece of (God forbid!) McDonald's chicken nugget in his mouth, one of few foods in his rotation. Especially not Tiffany, who was maniacally pro-organic and anti-TV, often reminding the group that television-watching caused brain damage in children under five.

Chase leaned forward to sniff at the grilled cheese. Before she could stop herself, she was raising her voice, "Chase. Do *not* put your nose in the food."

"I not hungry."

"You have to eat. Or your tummy will hurt. Dash and Levi are eating. Don't you want to be big like them? Are you a baby, or a big boy?"

"A big boy?" Chase said.

Levi laughed. "You a baby!"

Leigh saw it coming, a literal darkening of Chase's face, as if blood had gathered under his forehead and cheeks. She stood, a pinch of pain where Charlotte's mouth was still attached to her breast, and caught Chase's arm before it landed on Levi's head.

"Oh-kay! My big boy," Tenzin said, and, as if reading Leigh's mind, scooped Chase from his seat and carried him away.

Leigh sighed. "Thank you *so* much, Tenzin," she said.

She could feel Tiffany watching her, so she kept her eyes on Charlotte, tucking her nipple back in the baby's mouth, rocking back and forth as she perched on the edge of the sofa seat.

When Tiffany spoke, Leigh thought she might have flinched.

"Once again," Tiffany announced. "Your Tibetan Mary Poppins saves the day."

Leigh could feel the blush coming, the heat starting between her breasts and clawing up her neck.

She had shared that once, in a late-night text to Tiffany, confessing that she thought of Tenzin as her Tibetan Mary Poppins.

Charlotte let out a sudden, piercing cry.

"She must be getting a tooth," Leigh said.

"Well," Grace said as she dabbed at a spot on Hank's cheek, "at least *these* guys are done with teething."

"Actually," said Tiffany, "that's not true. I read a fascinating article in *Holistic Health* about how kids keep cutting teeth until they're teenagers." She drew the next word out syllable by syllable. "Nev-er-end-ing."

Grace peered out the windows looking onto the deck. "Where could they be? Rip said they'd canoe for an hour, max. It's been way longer."

"Oh, come on, Grace," Tiffany said. "He deserves a break now and then, doesn't he?" She took a sip of her gin and tonic and lifted it toward Grace. "Cheers."

Leigh scanned the room. Where was Chase? She spotted him by the door to the kitchen. *Doing his own thing*—Brad's code for Chase dazing out. Chase lay flat on his stomach, pulling a shoelace he had removed from who-knows-whose shoes and hooked around the wheel of one of his cars, inching it forward at a snail's pace, watching the wheels turn as if some mystery were about to reveal itself. It was one of few activities that slowed him down, and his concentration was sharp. She could make out the drool glistening on his lip.

"How you doing, Chase, honey?"

She hadn't expected an answer. She knew that in a room full of noise, the rapid-fire chitchat of adults and cries of children, her voice was one sound melting into an ocean of sound.

This was the child who shrieked when the apartment door buzzed. Who froze when the street sweeper churned down the street, and for whom the grinding frequency of a vacuum cleaner, a blender or a lawn mower was a torment. Once, in the Bloomingdales' powder room, Leigh had used the automatic hand dryer. Poor Chase, almost four years old and recently potty-trained, had peed his pants.

Good boy, she thought now, you do what you need to do to block it out.

"Mommy's going to get you some food, okay?"

"Popcorn," he demanded.

"We'll see what Mama Nicole has. Just watch out for mommies going in and out of the kitchen, okay?"

His eyes were fixed on the slow-turning tires of his car.

"Chase? Chase. Answer me, please."

He was far away.

She was about to turn to the pantry when she saw Susanna waddling in through the front door.

"We're back," Susanna sang, and the twins' heads perked as though they were two pups.

Susanna's arms were hung with bags of groceries, and Leigh saw that the bags blocked the pregnant woman's already limited view.

Chase was stretched out right in front of Susanna's path. Sure to make her trip and fall.

"Chase!" Leigh yelled. "Watch out!"

She rushed over and nudged him with her foot. Although it may have been closer to a kick, she realized just seconds later when Chase began to wail.

"Mommy! Mommy! Mommy!"

The children froze, staring at her.

"Did Mama Leigh kick Chase?" Dash asked, fear in his voice.

"No!" Leigh said. "I just moved him out of the way with my foot."

"MOM-MEEEEEEE!" Chase writhed on the floor. Leigh couldn't move, feeling every eye in the room locked on her.

"I'm sorry, baby." She squatted, but Tenzin was already there, folding Chase into her long brown arms.

"I'm sorry," Leigh said again, this time to Tenzin. The last four years had felt like a never-ending string of apologies to, and for, Chase.

"Don't worry," Tenzin said, reaching up to pat Leigh's arm as Tenzin rocked Chase on the floor. "Incidents happen." Leigh guessed that the woman meant *accidents* but she would never correct her.

Charlotte began to cry, and Leigh was grateful; this was a distress she knew how to remedy. She left Tenzin and Chase on the floor and settled on the sofa to nurse. The thrum of the milk's letdown brought relief. *At least I can do this.*

The children were shooed outside after bathroom visits for a little playtime on the deck before bathtime. Tenzin took Charlotte.

Leigh and Chase were left behind.

"Sit here, honey. Please," Leigh said to a puffy-eyed Chase, and patted the couch. He sat in a tense ball—his arms wrapped around his knees.

She had read an article recently—maybe in *Vogue*—about facial symmetry playing a key role in attraction. It had animated a series of hopeful fantasies that shot through her thoughts, like one of the flipbooks Chase loved to thumb through at the bookstore.

Chase in black tie. His prom date in chiffon.

Chase tossing his mortarboard into the air at graduation.

Chase kissing his bride at the altar in St. John's Episcopal Church, where Brad had once kissed her.

Someone will care for him, she had thought, wouldn't they?

They were alone, but instead of feeling the familiar unease, as if Chase's restlessness were contagious, Leigh felt a sudden vibrating love. He *was* beautiful. His mournful eyes. His heart-shaped mouth. His face, even puffy with tears, was pure symmetry.

"Chase, sweetie? Look at Mommy."

He ignored her, and she pulled him into her arms, his cheek hot against her chest. She held him there for as long as he would take it, until he cried *let go*, and the vein in his forehead bulged, as she whispered *iloveyouiloveyouiloveyou* into his pink ear, and *I'm sorry, Mommy's sorry, you know that, right?*

He wriggled free and ran to the screen door.

"Chase," she called. "Wait."

"What?" he said, impatient.

"Mommy messed up." Her voice almost cracked. "When I put my foot out. Do-over, please?"

Even if he had wanted to comfort her, she knew he wouldn't have known how. She had been elated the week before when he said *helicopter* for the first time.

"You kick me, Mommy," he said flatly, giving her the full eye contact he so often withheld.

"It was an accident." She stood and took a step toward him. Slowly. She knew from experience that if she moved too fast, he'd flee. "I was scared that you'd hurt Susanna."

He thought for a moment, studying his scuffed sandals.

"I like Mama Susanna."

"Of course you do," she said as she knelt, cupping his sharp little elbows in her hands.

She wiped the tears from his sunburned cheeks, then his arms shot out, stick-thin but full of reflexive strength, and she fell back, her elbows scraping against the wood floor. A sob rose from her stomach.

Then Tiffany's voice was behind her. The cutesy tone Leigh had heard her use in music class a hundred times.

"Good job using your words, Chase," Tiffany said. "Right, Mommy?"

Leigh swallowed her anger. "Yes. Good job, Chase." She got to her feet, smoothing her pants, and then her hair.

Chase looked from one woman to the other, and Leigh wondered if he was more aware than they appreciated. Maybe he was laughing at them and their silly games, and their failure to accept that children are not like the projects from life before. Leigh thought of her art history dissertation that had won high honors, her 4.2 GPA, the fifteen pounds she had dropped before her wedding, the perfect dinner parties she had hosted. Life before could be perfect, or at least seem so, if you worked hard enough or if you had enough money to hire someone else to do the work for you. She had had both. But no amount of work or money could fix the broken neurology in her son's head.

"Why don't you go play with our friends outside, Chase?" Tiffany said. "They're having lots of fun."

"Oh-kay," huffed Chase as he shuffled through the screen door.

Leigh peeked out the window and watched him join the other children, who were attempting to play catch with a giant beach ball, coached by Nicole.

"Poor Chasey," Tiffany said.

"I pushed him with my foot. I shouldn't have. He was actually being so good. But can you imagine? If Susanna had fallen?"

"But she didn't. Like our sweet Tenzie would say, all is good."

Coming from Tiffany, Tenzin's optimism sounded like mockery.

"She's fucking amazing," Tiffany said, "Isn't she? Tenzin, I mean."

"Yes," Leigh said, lifting her chin so that she looked over Tiffany rather than at her, "she is."

"Fabulous," Tiffany said with her half-shy girlish smile. "Then she was worth it."

Before Leigh could ask what she meant, Tiffany spoke again.

"I talked to Michael," she said as she swiveled from side to side in one of the little half pirouettes that had always, even in the bloom of their friendship, irritated Leigh.

"And," Leigh probed, "what did *he* say?"

"We both agreed," Tiffany said, "that the share isn't the best idea anyway. 'Cause. Well, I don't know how to say it exactly."

The hemming and hawing was unbearable.

"Tiffany. What is it?"

"Michael just doesn't feel comfortable with Chase's influence."

"What do you mean?"

"Well"—Tiffany sighed deeply, hushing her voice, forcing Leigh to lean in—"he worries Chase is a bad influence on Harper. You know?"

No, no, no, Leigh thought.

"Chase is not the problem," Leigh said. She was surprised to hear how even her voice sounded, especially when it felt as if so much blood was pooling in her head. Hot lakes of blood.

"Oh, Leigh," Tiffany said, "I know you *think* that."

Leigh knew she could do something terrible to this woman. She could slap her. She could pull her hair. She could drag her nails down her face and erase its cocksure sunniness. The certainty of what she was capable of was a shock, and for a second it was as if time slowed, the way it had when she'd crashed her dad's car the night of Halloween her junior year, time slowing as the car spun out of control, movement sloshing as if she were underwater, followed by the electrifying zoom as time caught up to itself, launching her back into the moment.

Before she could speak, the children's voices rose.

"I do, I do!"

Leigh looked out the window and spotted Nicole standing in front of the seawall, waving two fistfuls of squeezable applesauce pouches.

"Who wants dessert?" Nicole yelled cheerfully.

The children were shrieking. *Me! Me! Me!*

Like people stranded on a desert island, Leigh thought.

"I need app-sauce!" Chase hollered.

Leigh called through the window screen. "Tenzin, none for Chase, please." Any sort of sugar before bedtime kept him up an extra hour.

"Come on," Tiffany mumbled. "Let him enjoy himself. Before it's too late."

Leigh felt something soften inside her. Like the slippery queasiness she'd felt with Chase at the start of labor pains.

What had Tiffany meant by *before it's too late*?

"App-sauce! App-sauce!" Chase cried.

The children echoed him. *Me too! Me too!*

The mothers answered in near-perfect unity,

"How do you ask?"

"Ask nicely, please?"

"What's the magic word?"

Then the children in chorus: *Please! Please! Please!*

When she looked up again, she saw Chase was already sucking on the small pouch of fruit puree. She imagined the fifteen grams of sugar coursing through him, heading for a massive orgy in his brain.

stick-in-the-mud

Rip

They paddled and paddled, and still, the shoreline was not appearing. Probably going on an hour, Rip thought, his arms aching with every stroke. The current in the estuary was brutal. Harper and Hank wouldn't stop whining. Michael's grumbling swelled.

"Sit down," Rip commanded Hank each time the boy stood and did the saddest little terrified dance, his chubby legs pumping, his balled fists punching at the air.

"I want to go home," Hank cried. "Ho-o-o-me!"

The lower half of the boy's face was coated with tears and snot, and Rip had given up trying to wipe it away with his shirt. There were spots of blood dotting Hank's own shirt where Rip had killed mosquitoes midsuck.

For the first half hour, Harper had remained as nonchalant as usual, sitting so her head leaned against one side of the canoe and her feet on the other. Like they were on some peaceful fishing trip. But as soon as Michael starting swearing, his voice echoing against the wall of trees, birds scattering into the darkening sky, she had started to whimper, to call *Mama, Mama* in such a sweet and vulnerable voice, like the mew of a kitten, that Rip had wanted to cradle her in his arms.

Not Michael, who seemed oblivious as he dug into the water with his paddle, trying to push off the bottom of whatever lay under the murky black water. Rip imagined that the veins in Michael's forearms might pop through his skin.

Michael hadn't spoken to Rip for a good twenty minutes and was silent except for occasional explosive grunts and *motherfuckers* and *Jesus fucking Christs*. Rip had never heard anyone curse in front of little kids like that. Then Michael turned to look at Rip so suddenly that the canoe swayed, and the children yelped, clinging to the sides, their mouths stretched into gaping holes.

"Michael," Rip said as calmly as he could, because he was frightened, too. "Please, be careful."

"We're not moving," Michael mumbled as if lost in thought, still standing. "Maybe I should swim to the shore over there. Get help." He pointed to the thick trees and lost his balance, the canoe rocking.

"Daddy, don't leave me!" Harper cried.

Michael's wide, unseeing eyes reminded Rip of the wacked-out junkies he'd seen on the F train.

"Look at your daughter, Michael," Rip soothed, despite his pulse making his ears throb. "Look at Harper. She's scared."

Michael sat down, and the fruitless paddling resumed.

Hank buried his face against Rip's chest. Rip could tell that Hank was exhausted and close to falling asleep. He felt the boy's warm breath, a near match to the sluggish pace of their paddling.

With every excruciating minute, Rip's anger at Michael escalated. Was now approaching fury. The panicked pace of his thoughts in time with the cicadas' throbbing techno song. He hadn't done anything to Michael. He'd simply let his guard down and asked him a sensitive question. Big fucking deal. Clearly, he'd misjudged Michael. Thought they were some sort of kindred spirits. Now, Rip sorely regretted opening his mouth. He issued a telepathic apology to Grace for disclosing so personal an issue to this asshole. He hoped to God, Michael, who now seemed shockingly unstable, didn't say anything to Grace.

When Hank woke, they had traveled only half the distance to the mouth of the estuary. Hank peered through eyes swollen with tears, saw the night sky, and let his head drop back. His wails echoed against the trees.

"Stop crying, Hank!" Harper yelled although Rip could see that she, too, was on the verge of weeping.

"Harper," Rip said. "Leave Hank alone. Can't you see he's sad?"

"Hank's *always* sad," she said.

"That is not a nice thing to say," Rip said.

"Don't talk to her like that," Michael said without turning.

"Look," Rip started, daring to stick up for himself. If not for himself, then for his son. "I'm just reinforcing the rules that all the other mommies . . ."

"Listen to yourself, man," Michael said, turning to look at him over a sweat-soaked sleeve. "Calling yourself a mommy."

"I'm more of an M-O-M-M-Y," Rip said as he stood, "than you'll ever be a D-A-D-D-Y."

"I thought he wasn't even Y-O-U-R-S," Michael said coolly as he unfolded himself to stand.

I thought Tiffany was your fiancée, Rip wanted to say. *But then, she really wants to fuck me, so maybe you guys aren't so exclusive?*

But he said nothing. The canoe shimmied hard to one side beneath him, and he put his arms out to balance.

A few minutes later, something changed. Maybe the current switched, or the wind changed direction. Rip tried to think back to science classes he'd taken long ago. One minute, they were pushing against a wall, and the next, their paddles cut cleanly through the water and stroked effortlessly, pushing the boat forward in one smooth movement.

In less than fifteen minutes, Nicole's family beach house appeared on the shoreline, and Rip could have wept with gratitude. As he lifted a half-asleep, mosquito-bite-covered Hank from the boat, he noticed fireflies poking bright holes in the dark woods along the shore.

"Look, buddy," he said to Hank, pointing to the trees. "Over there. Fireflies."

"Cool!" Hank said, suddenly wide-awake. "You know, they were here even before dinosaurs."

"That's right, my little man."

"It's like they're teeny tiny magic fairies," Hank singsonged in that once-upon-a-time tone Rip knew the boy loved.

Rip took his son's hand and guided him up the path toward the deck. Michael and Harper followed a few paces behind.

Hank turned to Harper. "Hah-per. I'll be the sleeping princess. And you be the prince. Okay?"

"No, *I'm* the princess," Harper said.

Michael cleared his throat, and Rip knew instantly that the man's *ahem* was mocking Rip, was mocking his son.

"No, me," Hank said. "I'm the princess."

Rip heard the tremor of tears under his son's proclamation.

Harper began, "Boys can't be . . ."

Rip interrupted her. "Harper," he warned with a new severity in his tone.

No more Mama Rip, diaper-changer, boo-boo-kisser, nose-wiper, playground pal. And, he thought, pushover.

"You can't be the princess every time," Rip said. "You have to take turns."

eat your heart out

Tiffany

Tiffany had loved her mother's white leather dress.

"Zip me, baby," her mother had said as she had tugged the dress on over her black push-up bra, and Tiffany, just eight years old, had stood on tiptoes to make the zipper glide right to the top.

"I could pass for your sister in this." Her mother turned her padded shoulders and smoothed the leather that clung to her hips as she examined herself in the mirror. "Don't you think, Tiff?"

"Totally," Tiffany said because she knew that was what her mother wanted to hear.

"It's going to be a good night," her mother said with a deep and hopeful exhale.

Tiffany's mother always left the house looking perfect on a first date. Not a crease in her dress. Not a scuff on her matching white pumps. Not a crimp in her blown-out and hairspray-stiffened hair. She smelled of Jean Naté body wash and Chloé perfume. Tiffany could still taste the mint on her mother's lips as she kissed her good night, before her mother climbed into whatever pickup truck, Bronco, or Trans Am her date was driving.

When Tiffany's father came home after two years in the service and set up a mechanic's garage in the front yard of their small house in their small town on the North Fork of Long Island, he'd gotten himself a new girlfriend, a waitress from the BBQ place on Main Street who lined her lips with brown pencil and who he took out around town.

"So that every goddamn pair of eyes on the North Fork sees them," Tiffany's mother complained.

One Friday afternoon, when Tiffany, a fourth grader, had come home from school, her mother was gone. Her father's explanation was "she run out on us," and Tiffany had no choice but to believe him and guess that her mother had taken the white leather dress with her. Tiffany only saw her a few times a year after that—on holidays, on her birthday. She never saw the white leather dress again.

Now, as Tiffany looked into the dusty mirror of Nicole's parents' guest bedroom and tweezed a rogue hair from her eyebrow, she could still smell that leather. How silly she'd been, she thought, believing that damn dress the be-all and end-all, when it was the tackiest thing on earth.

She thought of Rip, whom she'd been trying not to think of, still not sure what he made (or she made, for that matter) of the scene in the kitchen the day before. She couldn't tell if he'd been avoiding her all day, or if it was just the routine chaos of the kids, and so many people, then Susanna—Tiffany had to stop from laughing—puking on the beach, plus Nicole's fretting and Michael's drinking too much.

Rip wouldn't mind seeing her in that white leather dress. That she knew.

She froze, listening, the tweezers poised in midair. She had thought she heard Harper's giggle out on the beach. Like chimes in the breeze. They sure had been gone long enough, she thought with a tingle of worry. She knocked back the rest of the wine, and it slid warm and spicy down her throat.

She dabbed golden droplets of Rodin face oil on her chin, her cheeks, and her forehead with a tiny glass wand. It cost $150 an ounce, which she had charged to her secret MasterCard. Worth every penny.

After applying primer, foundation, powder, blush, and eye makeup—the steps necessary in creating a dewy, natural-looking complexion—she painted her lips with Tom Ford's Cherry Lush, $45 a tube, a birthday gift from old Suzie Harcourt, Tiffany's own former good employer. Years ago, when Tiffany had stepped off the Greyhound bus for the second time—her first stab at NYC life having been a failure—and into the grime-coated Port Authority, a twenty-two-year-old worth less than $200, she'd been struck lucky, hired by society semidiva Suzie Harcourt, nee Vanderly, whose twins Tiffany would nanny on the Upper East Side until Harper was born. Suzie taught Tiffany all she'd need to know to blend in with women *several* tax brackets above the couples who filled the beach house that weekend. Suzie had taught her to be a class chameleon, and Tiffany had learned that florals and plaids could go together if you had enough blue blood flowing through your veins, that straight hair vs. curly spoke of refinement, and that anything frosted, bleached, or acid-washed was out of the question, a blinking red sign you were trash.

Suzie had taught Tiffany about quality—of bedsheets, of furniture, of wine and cheese. Of clothes. Tiffany had put money aside each paycheck until she had enough to buy a Miu Miu dress at a chic, secondhand boutique, instead of spending it at Strawberry's. *Quality over quantity.* Suzie's voice still looped through Tiffany's head. Suzie's constant elocution corrections—Tiffany was a live-in, so they were together daily—had eradicated Tiffany's nasal-heavy Long Island accent, and the woman's stylist had colored Tiffany's hair a blond that Suzie had praised as *deliciously natural.*

Suzie had revealed to Tiffany the secret code; which colors to wear (black was always safe), books to read, movies to watch, magazines to peruse (Suzie's word choice) at the salon. Tiffany had thrived, so much so that one night, four years ago, at a theater event (a British immersion play in which the audience had to wear white masks), Tiffany had made Michael fall in love with her. Michael, who had a degree from Syracuse, who ate sushi, who used words like *woodsy, floral,* and *earthy* when drinking wine, who dated women with trust funds, and who was pulling in close to a hundred thousand dollars a year. Michael, now her fiancé. Partner, she corrected herself. She had learned it was better to imply they were indifferent to marriage, on principle. Not that they'd dated for six months, then one morning the pink smiley face on the pregnancy test was staring up at her, expectantly.

First, there'd been Suzie. Now there was Leigh, and Tiffany had moved up. Landing just a few floors shy of the penthouse, she thought as she slipped a loose emerald silk chiffon Isabel Marant dress over her head. The brilliant green made the summer highlights in her hair pop. The silver thread that wove through the toile pattern glittered as she rocked her hips from side to side. No one would guess that the dress was a hand-me-down from Leigh.

Look at me now, Mama, Tiffany thought, as she often did, especially since she'd befriended Leigh. Leigh who gave her designer hand-me-downs—Rachel Comey pink marbled boots with stacked heels, a Marc Jacobs hobo bag made of buttery Italian leather. And there were the almost-full bottles of lotion from Molton Brown, and the bars of Red Flower soap, still in their exquisite boxes, so lovely Tiffany couldn't bear to open them. She had chosen Leigh over all the mommy friends and acquaintances who had coveted Tenzin, who had asked, e-mailed, and texted Tiffany, their smiley-faced emoticons practically begging, to see if Tenzin had any hours available. Choosing Leigh to share Tenzin with had made Tiffany and Leigh equals, Tiffany thought.

The soft silk shifted over her sunburned shoulders as she slipped her strappy heels on. After a few wobbly steps, she kicked them off. She was a little tipsy. She would go barefoot. Like a sprite in *A Midsummer Night's Dream*. Even if it was the end of summer, and even if no one, especially not that snobby bitch Susanna, would believe that Tiffany had ever read a Shakespeare play.

She had nipped the "Susanna conflict" in the bud, Tiffany thought, congratulating herself. Susanna had seemed perfectly fine sitting next to her that afternoon on the deck. Friends turned into enemies and back to friends again. That ugly scene at the Jakewalk Bar forgotten. Fine, Tiffany thought, she *had* been flirting that night at the bar, but it was harmless. No one was going to die from a little whispering, a little touching, a little brush of her knee against the inside of a guy's leg.

She twirled from side to side in front of the dusty mirror so her skirt rippled up in the air. *Look at me now, Mama.* Buying lavender-infused truffles at the Chocolate Bar, and the same luxury scented candles that burned in the bathrooms of NYC's elite. She used cloth napkins, employed a house-cleaner, and paid to have her eyebrows waxed. Move over Gatsby. She was practically a super-yuppie.

If Suzie and her Tory-Burch-sporting friends had known about Tiffany's mother and her morals and her white leather dress, they'd never have let her walk through the doorman-guarded lobbies of their luxury buildings. How their wrinkle-free foreheads would have cracked with concern if they'd known about her mother's slutting around, not to mention her sister LeeAnn the meth-head, and Tiffany's abortions. Tiffany knew rich women had abortions, but *they* didn't have to drive to a clinic in the middle of a small town. They were chauffeured to dim and quiet parking garages in midtown and took an elevator to an office where they were the one and only guest. Their uterus was scooped clean as classical music played over an intercom, and they left *almost* as they came, sight unseen, not a peep to anyone. Money not only equaled time, Tiffany had learned, money meant privacy. Protection. And by the time Tiffany had met Suzie, she'd been screwing up for long enough and she was ready for a little protection, and a lot of change. She was ready to be born again. Into the light of DVF and Alexander Wang and Aqua di Parma. Amen.

Tiffany was seventeen when she'd made it out of her middle-of-fucking-nowhere hick town for the first ill-fated attempt at living the NYC dream. She'd been sick of her father taking half her waitressing paycheck for rent, sick of her friends crying about their loser boyfriends, sick of her stepbrother asking her to suck him off. For four years, she'd scraped by in the greatest city in the world. Bartending, dog walking, working in a souvenir shop in Times Square that sold the Statue of Liberty in a thousand different forms—soap holders, back scratchers, thermometers. Then one night, after a party in a factory loft in Williamsburg, where everyone was rolling on E and laying tabs of acid in the shape of blazing suns on their tongues, she had awoken in a dark room, on a stripped mattress that smelled like puke, unable to speak or move as some guy pounded his cock into her. She'd spent the rest of that night willing her body to move, begging her body to roll off the bed, sit up, (*move, goddamnit!*) and finally crawled to the door, only to realize she couldn't turn the knob.

Her body betrayed her.

They came back. Maybe three, maybe four times that night. She'd never know how many times, how many guys, who. She'd never know if they had drugged her—she had taken the E and the acid herself. She went to parties in the months that followed and found herself staring at her feet, terrified to look up. What if they were sitting next to her, laughing at her in their heads, thinking of the way her tits had flapped around as they slammed into her? At the last party she went to, she had stumbled out and onto the dead street of a neighborhood she didn't recognize. When she finally hailed a cab and made it back to her apartment, the sky a battered violet with the coming dawn, she stayed in her room, leaving only to go to the bathroom and to open the door for the delivery guy from the convenience store downstairs.

Days passed.

Her twenty-first birthday came and went.

Then it was a week. Two.

Her roommates in that mouse-infested loft in Williamsburg, all sweet suburban-bred girls whose parents, in Tiffany's humble opinion, had loved them *too* much, had taken care of her. They fed her microwaved ramen from styrofoam bowls. They washed her clothes. They guided her to the already running shower and massaged shampoo into her hair. They stubbed out her

Parliaments after she'd fallen asleep. But when the first of the month came, and then the seventh, and the fourteenth, and Tiffany still hadn't slipped her portion of the rent into the envelope taped to the fridge, they asked her to leave.

She knew she could have told them she had been raped. But because this wasn't the first time she'd come to half-naked in a stranger's bed, because it wasn't the first time some guy had been inside her while she lay like a corpse, she didn't.

She ate her last bowl of ramen and swallowed her last Klonopin, a gift from her most recent ex, the prescription-drug dealer/Ivy League grad.

Michael was three light-years away, Harper Rose, five. And there'd been nowhere else to go.

So Tiffany had gone back to her middle-of-fucking-nowhere hometown, out on the end of Long Island. She crashed at an ex-boyfriend's place. He was squatting in an unfinished house: pink insulation bulged through the beams in the ceiling. Her possessions had fit into two duffel bags and one cardboard box. They were her clothes, her grandmother's faded quilt, a box of thick biographies she had loved as a girl (Marlon Brando, Anais Nin, Georgia O'Keefe) and the little pewter angel with stained-glass wings her mother had given her at her First Communion. There was a wordless fuck with the ex every night on the sunken couch (the price of rent), but she threw back two of his Xanax twenty minutes before and was half-asleep when he came inside her.

She visited her father and stepmother Shelley over casserole dinners at their ramshackle house, a trailer with ill-proportioned adjoining rooms her father had built himself. The cracks in the wood were filled with tar, but the wind wrenched its way in.

For three brisk autumn nights, she'd sat with her father and Shelley under the oak trees, the night smelling of low tide and fire smoke as they roasted chestnuts over the pit and talked of people in the town. Shelley filled her in on who had had married whom, who had whose baby, who had collected enough DUIs to send them to jail, who had finished at the community college and who had left for the city only to return less than a year later. As she listened to the lilting waltz of Shelley's voice, Tiffany tried to remember how to talk in that way—maybe, she thought, it would help her tell them what had happened, why she'd had to surrender, come home—the slow-paced chitchat that mimicked the swaying branches above. She'd been practicing the speedy scrutinizing discourse of the young metropolitans for years, the quicksilver tongue that jumped from earnest to irreverent in a flash.

As her father recounted the latest nor'easter and the damage done to the town bowling alley in the floods, Tiffany watched the gray-speckled gypsy moths flutter close to the flames, catching fire and diving, wings smoking, into the embers. She told her father that something bad had happened to her, had been done *to* her. She wanted her father to ask *what*? And wanted him to say, *It's okay, baby doll. You can tell your daddy.* And then she'd tell him, and he'd hold her and stroke her hair, then promise he'd find those motherfuckers and tie them to a tree in the woods and cut off their dicks and feed them to the muskrats in the marsh.

But her father didn't ask. He made a sound—a *hmmph*—and after a few moments of nothing but twigs crackling and chestnut shells popping, he said, "Best to just move on. I told you to be careful," he said. "That you'd never survive that rotten city."

"Maybe it's me that's rotten, Daddy," she said, and looked at him, waiting.

She felt a lift in her chest, like she was close to understanding something big, and she knew that even after all she'd ruined, the parts of her she'd let get dirty, she still wanted to live. If she could keep that feeling, she thought, she just might make it.

"Thinking, thinking. Talking, talking," her father said, as the flames sent shadows dancing across his fat cheeks. "Do you got to share every thought that passes between your ears?"

Then she remembered the times her father had said to others—right in front of her, like she was invisible—"Tiff's always thinking on things too much," with an eye roll, his twang garbling the words, but not enough that Tiffany couldn't hear the disgust beneath.

Like he was apologizing for her.

And Tiffany knew. She had to go back.

Later that night, she walked the cracked road that led to town. Walked the three miles, the cold salt-filled wind of the nearby shore stinging her cheeks. She prayed to God as she walked, as her sweat-damp hair froze into solid strips. She slept on the chilled aluminum bench at the Greyhound stop, and when the bus pulled up, she left everything behind her, even her books, even her mother's pewter angel. She'd had a little less than $200 in her pocket, enough for a ticket, a stale bagel sandwich, and three nights at a Times Square hostel.

She wasn't like the other mommies, she thought now as she stared at her image—that of a strong and beautiful woman in her prime. They could feel safe in a godless world, so much so that they'd brag about it, as she had heard them do many times. *It's not like I believe in God or anything. Well, you know, I don't believe in God, only in free will.* Not believing in a higher power was a privilege, Tiffany knew. A woman had to have a shitload of self-esteem to walk around thinking she was the most important part of the world, that she called the shots, that she held the reins of her own fate.

Tiffany opened her silk jewelry purse and found the two pink pills she had snuck from Nicole's room that afternoon. Knowing Nicole, who'd been throwing these babies back every few hours since they'd arrived, she wouldn't notice there were a couple missing. Knowing Nicole, Tiffany thought, it was a Xanax. And if not? *C'est la vie.* She threw one, then the other, into the back of her throat and swallowed it dry. The bitterness spiked her tongue just as her phone buzzed with a text.

Another text from Leigh:

Tiffany, answer me!!!

Three exclamation points, Tiffany thought with approval, and when she looked in the mirror, she smiled, checking her teeth for lipstick.

Her phone vibrated again.

Please, Tiff. We've GOT to talk about this! In person. Like adults.

It was only a matter of time—maybe even minutes—before Leigh gave in, before her resolve cracked, before she agreed to handing over Tenzin on Thursday afternoons.

Tiffany knew how little it would take to ease Leigh's stress. A single text, like:
I'm sorry! I love you too, bff
But she didn't write it.

It wasn't the babysitting hours that held her back, or the fact that her music-class gig at Shabbat Tots was at stake—although the extra money would be nice. It was the principle. There was self-righteousness in Leigh's refusal to share Tenzin, as if Leigh thought she was more deserving than Tiffany. Better.

Other mommies—strangers Tiffany didn't even know—made her feel like this every day. On the playground, at the playgroup, even in her own music class, the scrutiny of women who looked her up and down, trying to figure out exactly what it was that made Tiffany just a bit *off*. She'd become accustomed to it.

But not from Leigh.

She would have to compose herself, Tiffany thought. There was too much at stake with Leigh to lose her. Leigh was crucial to Harper's acceptance at St. Ann's School, which was an absolute necessity. Everyone knew an elite private school was the golden ticket, the first and most important step.

Tiffany knew she'd been too messy this whole beach weekend. With Rip in the kitchen. The things she'd let herself say to Leigh. She'd have to decompress next week, reboot: a massage, an aromatherapy session, maybe she'd see her therapist twice. Just until they got through the stress of the upcoming interview at St. Ann's. She couldn't afford to fuck up now.

URBANMAMA.COM A Community and Forum for Parents

Welcome to UrbanMama, an anonymous forum where you can interact in sincere and open-minded conversation with other parents.

Speak your mind and share your thoughts about parenting, family life, marriage, relationships, and everything that makes you an urbanmama!

Sign up now!   Already a member, log in!

Is anyone else freaking out over this Webbot thing? What are you doing to prepare?

Posted 9/4/2010   7:36pm

(7 replies)

—Hi Webbot mommy! Tomorrow night, when all is calm, come on here & say 'sorry.' Ok? 7:38pm

　　　—There will be no Internet tomorrow 7:41pm

　　　　　—LOL 7:43pm

　　　　　—The Internet will be wiped out??? 7:44pm

　　　　　　　—the EARTH will be wiped out 7:45pm

　　　—can't wait until she's proven wrong 7:51pm

　　　—Our collective anxiety is overwhelming me 7:53pm

fear the worst

Nicole

Wyatt was jumping on Nicole's parents' king-size bed. Each time he jumped *(look at me, Mommy!)*, her mother's army of dust-covered Madame Alexander dolls quivered on the dresser. Nicole felt the dolls' fixed eyes watching her. *Be careful,* they said, *Josh knows.*

She was waiting for Josh to finish in the bathroom. He had called her upstairs, and she knew what was coming. The knives. He knew. Part of her was relieved, almost looking forward to the release her confession would bring. That she *was* having an episode. That she had hid the knives and hoarded Go Bag supplies and obsessed over paranoid online rumors of the Apocalypse. That she was fucking up.

She rapped on the bathroom door. *Knock wood.*

"Josh? You said you wanted me?"

"Yeah, hold on. Five more minutes."

"All right," she said. "Everyone's downstairs. We don't want to be rude."

No response from Josh though she was certain she heard the soft click of his fingers against the screen of his phone. She knew he played the Texas Hold 'Em app all that time he spent sitting on the toilet, his pants around his ankles. Hiding.

When he finally left the bathroom, a cloud of baby-powder-scented air freshener trailed him.

He was dressed in shorts and a tee shirt.

"Is *that* what you're wearing?" she asked.

"Yeah," Josh answered. "It's not black tie, is it?"

She was wearing Spanx.

She stood behind him as he scanned himself from head to toe with an appraising look. He could still look in the mirror without looking away, she thought. Without wondering, as she did, where the person she'd once been had run off to. The light-footed, slim-waisted beauty.

"I put the knives back," he said, without looking at her.

"Okay. Thanks. Sorry. I won't touch them again."

He smoothed his hair, tousling it with his fingers.

She had always disliked his neatness. Even in baggy shorts and two-day stubble, he looked prearranged. He'd been able to mask it in college, in the haze of marijuana and the din of jam bands. It wasn't until years after they were married that she realized it wasn't just a surface polish but a rigidity fused to his core. Lately, his outward perfection, which led her mommy friends to ooh and aah about Nicole's incredible luck in finding such a catch, was a reminder that she was the flawed one. Inside and out.

"Josh?" she asked.

She knew he wouldn't be any help when he answered her with a long sigh and, "What is it now, Nic?"

In a voice she felt certain was calm, she asked, "Did you get a chance to read any of those links I sent you yesterday? You know, about the Web bot thing?"

"Work was busy."

"Could you just google it? It would only take a second to look at that one site," she said. "The one that explains everything."

He turned to look at her. His eyebrows lifted in pity.

"Do we have to call Dr. Greenbaum, Nicole?"

Wyatt held up her iPhone, the little muscles in his forearms twitching as the birds flew across the screen.

"Look, Daddy. I made it to the next level!"

"Wyatt," Nicole snapped, "that's enough Angry Birds. Give Mommy back her phone."

Wyatt handed her phone over with a slow roll of his eyes. When did he learn to do that? she thought.

A sizzling sound came from the beach, then a pop and a boom, and Nicole jumped back, bumping the dresser. Marie Antoinette landed on the carpet upside down, her ruffled bloomers exposed.

"They're just fireworks, Mommy," Wyatt said. "Don't be scared."

The look on his face made her want to nail the windows shut, to weep, but instead she said, "Aw, you're so good at taking care of your mommy."

Josh said, "You're not watching any more of that doom-and-gloom stuff on Netflix, are you? I thought we talked about that."

"No, no. I'm not, I swear. I know it sounds crazy." She gripped Josh's arm to show him she was serious. "But these are intelligent women posting these warnings. The demographic that visits this site is supersmart. And they're really concerned."

"That mommy site?" Josh said. "Nic. Please. You've got to get a grip."

He gave her an apologetic smile. Or maybe it was pity again. She had little faith in her ability to read him.

"I don't know," she said.

He surprised her by pulling her into his lap. She laughed and jerked a bit. The bedsprings creaked.

Wyatt covered his smile with a cupped hand, and said, "Dah-ad."

Josh hugged her to his chest, his breath warm on her neck.

"Have you talked to Dr. Greenbaum about raising your meds?"

Now she felt like a child, her feet dangling just above the floor, her skirt hitched too high, her fleshy white thighs flattened against his legs.

"You're right," she said. "I'm sorry. I don't know what's wrong with me." She wriggled out of his arms and stood.

"Mom, can I play your phone?" Wyatt begged. He stretched to reach her phone on the dresser.

"You've had your half hour of Angry Birds time," she said.

"Bu-hut," Wyatt whined. He turned to Josh, "Dad, what's your favorite angry bird? Mine are the yellow ones. Wait, no, the white ones. You know, that drop the egg bombs. Those are really very really cool."

"He needs more attention," Josh said. He was holding her earphones, she had left them on the dresser, and he was winding the cord into a perfect spool with furious care.

"I give him plenty of attention."

She yanked the headphones from Josh's hands. His mouth parted in hurt.

"I like my headphones this way," she said.

"In knots?" Josh asked.

"Wyatt," she said, "while Daddy finishes dressing, why don't you go downstairs and tell everyone dinner will be ready soon."

Wyatt chanted, "Angry Birds! Angry Birds!" He marched in a circle around her. "Play Mommy's phone!"

"Okay," she said, "no sticker on your good-listening chart today. And that means you're one sticker further from getting your Buzz Lightyear costume for Halloween."

"I don't think threats are the way to go, Nic. They just don't work," Josh said.

"They're not threats. They're rewards. Tiffany says they work best with defiant kids like Wyatt."

"He's a perfectly normal little boy. But, of course," Josh said, his voice warbling with sarcasm, "Tiffany's the expert. And what does Tiffany say about these Web bots?"

Josh smiled. Not unkindly, she thought. She pulsed with the urge to ask him again if he thought they would be okay, if terrorists wouldn't detonate a bomb with enough force to wipe out the Eastern Seaboard, if a reactor at the Indian Point power plant wouldn't melt down, if the entire planet wouldn't crumble with a shattering blast from one of those electromagnetic pulses.

"I'm sorry," she said.

Josh sighed and rubbed her back in warm circles. "It's okay."

"But do you think you could just take a peek at the link I sent you?" She pinched her thumb and forefinger together—a sign of the smallness of the request. "I just need you to do a little search for this Web bots thing and then you can tell me there's nothing to worry about."

"You need a lot," he mumbled. "I don't have time to check the dozens of links and articles you send me about bird flu. Swine flu. West Nile virus. The rising fucking mercury levels!"

He paused, staring at the carpet. "Are you getting your period?"

She wanted to hurt him. To tell him that the garishly patterned socks he'd starting wearing to work weren't hip, just desperate. That she knew he jerked off in the shower every morning; his bloodshot eyes the proof. She wanted to carefully choose the ripest, most potent insult and fling it in his face.

He spoke in a quiet command, "Take a Xanax. Call your mother and cry to *her*. Get a grip. You don't want make a fool of yourself in front of your friends."

As he walked toward her, she readied herself for his embrace, but he was no more than a breeze of aftershave, that citrusy musk he'd worn for years because, once, she'd told him it made her wet for him. They had practically bathed in it back then—when they pleased each other, when they had the time and energy and desire. When the bathroom cabinet held massage oils and flavored honey dust that he brushed across her nipples with a miniature feather duster; a silly Valentine's party grab-bag gift they had surprised themselves by enjoying. Now the cabinet shelves were crowded with cartoon Band-Aids and hemorrhoid pads. And his aftershave smelled artificial, as if it—like them—was trying too hard.

"Look," she said quietly, nodding, "I'm trying. Really." She laughed. "I have some issues, I know."

Josh turned to look at her. He pushed his glasses up his nose and blinked. "Your whole life is an issue."

The door slammed. She knew the echo reproduced, traveled through the house, found the mommies, who paused their chitchat, their cocktail-shiny eyes meeting as they exchanged a silent message. About Nicole.

"Fuck," she whispered.

He was right.

when pigs fly

Tenzin

The children were, as the mommies liked to say, snug as bugs in their beds when Tiffany came to invite Tenzin downstairs.

Tenzin thought Tiffany looked like a real princess that night. In a green silk dress that trailed behind her bare feet. Tiffany had insisted Tenzin join them for the feast, and Tenzin had tried politely to decline, but Tiffany had drunk many cups of wine and would not stop saying, *Please eat with us. Please.* And so Tenzin had changed out of her nightclothes, a matching pink set that Leigh had passed on to her, and back into her day clothes.

Tiffany clutched Tenzin's hand as they walked downstairs for dinner. Twice, Tiffany almost tripped on her dress, so Tenzin picked up the hem and walked behind her.

"Like a bride!" Tenzin said.

"It might be the only chance I get, Tenzie," Tiffany said.

All the mommies and daddies were downstairs in the main room, all except for Hank's mommy Grace, who had gone to bed early. Tenzin saw right away that the kitchen table had been made longer, draped in a white tablecloth and decorated with candles.

So much food! A bowl of pasta salad as big as the wheel of a bicycle. Sticks of corn glistening with melted butter. Tenzin tried not to look at the plate piled with grilled meat. She had made her no-meat sacrifice to God after all, in the hope he would grant her asylum at her next immigration trial—the first step to bringing her family to America. Still, she suspected she was allowed to enjoy the smell of fat crackling with heat.

The chairs around the table sat empty, and so Tenzin waited, telling her stomach she was sorry, but that polite is more important than hungry. She could see, from one quick sweep of the mommies' and daddies' faces, that they were sad. They looked as cranky as the children did when they took a too-long nap, waking with their mouths glued in a pout. Even Daddy Rip looked sad. He sat on the edge of the sofa, looking into his cup as if searching for his fortune.

The Sun God, the Dalai Lama's words were with her then.

Your bad mood serves your enemy.

And who, Tenzin wondered, were the mommies' and daddies' enemies to-night?

"Tenzie's here!" Tiffany said. With a *Ta Da!* in her voice, like when Chase pretended to be a magician and wore the black cape and tall hat from his costume box.

"Hello, everybody. Good evening," Tenzin said brightly, hoping the cheer would give them what Leigh called a boost of their spirits. And that then they could sit down and eat all that delicious food.

"I think," Tiffany said, too loudly for a house full of sleeping children. Tenzin could hear the drink in her voice.

"Shhhh," said Nicole.

"Sor-RY," said Tiffany, "So as I was saying . . . what *was* I saying?"

"Something about Tenzin," Allie said, and Tenzin could see Allie was trying to hold back her laugh.

"Yes!" Tiffany said, poking her empty glass in the air. "That's it. I was saying, I think Tenzin should be our guest of honor tonight."

"Hear, hear," Rip said, standing and lifting his own glass.

Every beautiful mommy and daddy was smiling at her with raised glasses. They all looked happy again. For the moment, Tenzin felt like they belonged to her. She thought of the things they did for her, and a lump rose in her throat. So much, to make her life good. Income, bonuses, gifts (whether brand-new or hand-me-down). Extra money for doing silly little things, like the time Michael had paid her, without Tiffany's knowing, to do his laundry at the laundromat down the block.

And there was even more to be given. There was friendship, Tenzin thought, as she stood there, surrounded by grateful, shining faces. Her friends. Yes, she could call them that. Friends are people who need each other. Surely, the mommies and daddies needed her just as she needed them.

Some, like Rip and Leigh, had performed Tenzin big favors, like calling immigration services and acting as her translator when her alien status had been delayed. Leigh had sent presents to Tenzin's children in India at Christmas, and even a silk scarf (in the colors of an American autumn) for Tenzin's mother. Of course, there were times when they made mistakes, like when Tiffany forgot to pay for Tenzin's weekly Metrocard fee, and when Leigh had wished her a Happy Chinese New Year, and there were many times when the mommies and daddies acted more like spoiled children than like all-knowing gods, but Tenzin loved them still.

Their cups lowered and as quickly as their faces had brightened, they fell dark again.

"Let's eat," Susanna said, pushing herself up from the sofa with a groan.

"Mustn't keep the pregnant lady hungry!" said Tiffany. Tenzin could hear she was poking fun at poor Susanna.

Susanna's mouth fell open, while Allie covered her mouth once again to hide a smile.

"I'm just kidding, sweetie," Tiffany said, laughing.

Tenzin laughed, too. It was better this way. Better not to take the silly things Tiffany said too seriously. She felt sorry for Tiffany although she knew, from the expressions on the other mommies' faces, especially Susanna, who Tenzin feared might cry, that Tiffany was being a bad girl.

Michael took a seat at the table, and Tenzin wondered if she should also. There was a big platter of grilled vegetables drizzled with oil. She thought of how she would take two pieces of bread and make a sandwich with veggies stacked in the middle. Delicious. Or as her Chase said, *delish*.

But the mommies did not move toward the table. They stood, waiting.

Waiting for what?

Nicole fiddled with the rubber band on her wrist, snapping it. Nicole did some funny things. Tenzin had seen her throw salt over her shoulder, knock on her head when she talked about something that pleased her, and, that afternoon, she had seen Nicole flipping the light switches up and down, as if it were a private game only Nicole knew how to play. Tenzin knew there were many different ways to pray, and she had seen from the very start of the weekend that Nicole was in a pain worthy of prayer. Now she watched as Nicole hurried over to Josh and whispered in his ear. She was asking for something very important. Tenzin could tell from the mommy's arched eyebrows. He shook his head without looking at his wife, and Nicole clung to his arm, her lips at his ear, moving fast.

Tiffany had been watching, too, because she sashayed over to Nicole, the toes of her naked feet pointed.

"You love to read, right, Nicole?" Tiffany asked.

A silly question, Tenzin thought. Everyone knew Nicole loved her books very much, so much that she organized them according to subject, instead of by color like some of the other mommies, whose bookcases were rainbows.

Nicole nodded at Tiffany. Her fingers snapped the rubber band faster now.

"What's that book you just read, babe?" Tiffany asked in the direction of the table, where Michael's head was bowed over his plate. "You know. The one about the end of the world? They made a movie out of it."

"*The Road*," Michael said with a mouthful of food.

"That's the one!" Tiffany cheered, and she even did a little hop in place. Like one of the dance steps Tenzin had learned in Tiff's Riffs class. "Come on, that must be like your favorite book, Nic. The end of the world and all that stuff?"

Nicole drew in her breath sharply, as if something hurt. Then she made a choking sound. But she didn't have any food in her mouth.

The mommies had told Tenzin that she must always be on the lookout for the children's choking, and Leigh had paid for Tenzin to take a CPR class, where she had pushed with all her weight on the chest of a small child made of plastic.

"Nicole," Tenzin said as she hurried over, "are you okay?"

She took Nicole's hands into her own, which, despite the sweat that rolled down the woman's cheeks, were chilled. She pulled Nicole to the sofa and helped her sit down. She fanned Nicole's pale face with a magazine from the coffee table.

"Are you sick?" Tenzin asked.

Nicole looked as if she was about to throw up. Like the time Tenzin had spun Chase too fast on his therapy swing, and he had vomited all over the playroom carpet.

Josh appeared beside Nicole.

"Nic," he said, and Tenzin heard a new sternness in his voice. As if he were talking to an overtired little girl.

Nicole's hands were clenched together in a tight ball.

"Did you take something?" Josh asked her, loud enough for the others to hear.

Tenzin thought of the many white-capped bottles in Nicole's bathroom cabinet, bottles of medication with X and Z in their names. She didn't know many words in English that had an X or a Z and so she had memorized the words that had been typed across the bottle labels. *Xanax. Zoloft. Diazepam. Clonazepam.*

Nicole did not answer.

Michael cleared his throat from where he sat at the kitchen table. "That book, *The Road*, was pretty awesome," he said. "What a rush."

"A rush?" Leigh said, and Tenzin watched as her good employer straightened her back. Like a shy child working hard to assert herself.

Leigh continued, staring toward Michael, "It's about the end of humanity," she said. "There are cannibals in it"—she paused, her voice falling to a whisper as her eyes hurried toward the stairs—"eating little children."

Michael laughed, and Tenzin watched a piece of food fly from his mouth and land on the pure white tablecloth.

"So," Michael said, scanning the room, "who here would do away with their own kid, in a doomed world full of cannibals?"

"Well," Leigh said, "I wouldn't have let them suffer. Or die some horrible death. Yes," Leigh said, and Tenzin could see that the woman was holding her chin higher. "I would have put them out of their misery."

"Not me," said Susanna. "I'd probably die trying to protect them."

Allie coughed very quietly, but Tenzin heard. Like Allie was trying to keep something inside.

Nicole made a mewling noise from her seat on the sofa. The way one of the children sounded during a movie's scary part—like when Ursula, the sea witch in *The Little Mermaid*, stretched her octopus-legs across the iPad screen.

Josh squatted in front of his wife. "What is it, Nic?"

The room was silent, but Tenzin could hear the whisper of Tiffany's bare feet slipping over the wood floor as she swayed from side to side.

Nicole spoke. "It's almost time."

Tenzin saw Allie creep behind Susanna and start up the stairs.

"Uh-oh," Tiffany called loudly, so that everyone's eyes followed hers. "Alert! Someone's trying to escape. Alert!"

"Al? Where are you going?" Susanna asked, and Tenzin heard fear in the pregnant woman's voice.

"I'm just going to check on the boys," Allie called over her shoulder as she took the stairs two steps at a time.

"Wait!" Susanna said. "Let me come with you." She tried to heave up from her chair, and Tenzin saw her big belly shudder.

"Here, let me help," said Tiffany, moving over to Susanna and gripping her arm. "You shouldn't walk up the stairs by yourself in your *condition*." She said it sweetly, but Tenzin knew she was being bad again.

Susanna shook off Tiffany's hand. "I'm fine."

"Oh, but you're not fine, honey," said Tiffany, her voice sweet as sugar. "Having to live in the dirty nasty city and all. I can see how hard it is on you."

Tiffany's lips were puffed out—like in the pretend-sad faces the children wore when they wanted Tenzin or their mommies to pay attention to them. But instead of comforting Tiffany with a gentle pat or hug, Susanna's round face bloomed red, and with great effort, she pushed herself up out of the chair and toddled toward Tiffany so quickly that Tiffany had to step back.

"You," Susanna said. "We should never have let you into our playgroup." She whirled around, her arms out at her sides, and Tenzin stepped forward, fearing the heavily pregnant woman would fall, but Susanna regained her balance and pointed at Rip. Susanna seemed to be possessed. By something bigger than herself, like a sort of god, Tenzin thought. She had never seen this mommy angry before.

"But you, Rip!" Susanna cried. "Mr. Mom. You were the one that made us take her. I *told* you."

The baby. Tenzin imagined the anger, flame-hot, inside Susanna's body. It will hurt the baby, she thought, then saw that Michael had left the table and was now towering over Susanna.

"Don't talk to my fiancée like that."

Susanna looked up at him, her hands on her hips, her belly pushed forward so far that Tenzin thought the baby might bump Michael.

"Your fiancée?" Susanna asked, with a fancy accent and Tenzin saw the animal fierceness in the pregnant woman's eyes. Like a mother protecting her young. "Ha! You should've seen your so-called fiancée at the bar a few weeks ago. If it hadn't been for me . . ."

Then Leigh was between Susanna and Michael, her arms outstretched, interrupting Susanna with, "Okay now. Maybe it's time for everyone to eat."

But Tiffany was pointing at Leigh, her voice rising like a siren above their heads.

"I don't need you, Miss Debutante." Tiffany spoke strangely, like when Chase had a lollipop in his mouth and his words had to climb around the candy to get out. "I don't need you to defend me."

Leigh turned to Tiffany, and Tenzin saw that her good employer Leigh's face was as still and pale as Tiffany's was stirred and feverish.

"My dress looks nice on you, Tiff," Leigh said, and then to Susanna—but still loud enough that they all heard, Tenzin noticed. "I got it at a sample sale. Paid nothing for it. But the fabric felt so cheap. I never wore it out. Just around the house."

Tiffany sighed long—ending in a phlegmy laugh that made Tenzin wonder if Tiffany wasn't getting a cold. Or maybe it was those stinky cigarettes she smoked.

"We need to go to the car," Nicole said, staring blankly at Josh. "The bags. They're in the trunk."

Finally, Tenzin thought with great relief. Something she could do, a task she could complete to help these troubled mommies and daddies.

"I go get the bags!" she announced.

As Tenzin passed Nicole on the couch, Nicole reached out and grabbed her arm.

"Please," Nicole said. "Stay with me, Tenzin." She looked up at Josh. "You go, honey. Please."

Josh's voice was shaking. "Where are your pills, Nicole? You tell me. Right now."

"It's hopeless," Nicole said meekly. "They're not working. They're not enough."

"Oh, those little peach-colored pills?" Tiffany said. "Yummy yummy Xanax. It's really the best. Don't you think, Nic? 'Cause it's like you feel totally calm. But you don't feel like you're drugged. Man, they really hit it out of the ballpark with that one, those pharmaceutical geniuses." She giggled and sat down on the arm of the couch beside Nicole.

"Hey, Nic. I've been meaning to ask you," Tiffany said, then she leaned close and whispered to Nicole so Tenzin could barely hear, "You never did jump off that seawall, did you?"

Leigh walked to the sofa and laid a cool hand on Tenzin's wrist. "It's okay, Tenzin," she whispered. "You can go back upstairs."

Tenzin nodded, relieved. Her place was with the children. With the innocent. Praise peace.

She patted Nicole's hands and rose from the sofa.

"I think Tenzin should stay," Tiffany said. "She *is* our guest of honor, after all. And she's a grown woman. She doesn't need to be told what to do. Right, Tenzie?"

"Then treat her with honor," Leigh said. "You can start by calling her the name her mother gave her. Her name is Tenzin."

The way Leigh said her name made Tenzin blush. Yes, it was terrible that the two women were working so hard to hurt each other, their words like sword blades. But it was she they were fighting over with an emotion that bordered on love, and this made her not exactly happy, but not unhappy either. She would be lying if she did not admit to a bit of pleasure.

"I treat her with honor," Tiffany said, and Tenzin saw that, for the first time that night, Tiffany was not smiling.

"You don't own her," Leigh said.

Tiffany laughed. "Sorry that your kid is challenging, Miss Leigh Lambert Marshall the third. But there are other people in the world besides you."

"Stop it, Tiffany," Leigh ordered. "Stop this right now. Before it's too late."

Tenzin wished she could stand between them, like she had stood between the children so many times, her arms spread, a wall between two stormy children. She could share with them the wise words of the Dalai Lama:

Every being, even those who are hostile to us, has the same right as we do to be happy and not to suffer. So let's take care of others wholeheartedly, of both our friends and our enemies.

Leigh turned to walk away. And that was when Tiffany gripped Leigh's thin arm, and Tenzin almost cried out, begging Tiffany not to hurt her beloved Leigh. Tiffany twisted Leigh around. Leigh's hair was a gold fan in the candlelight.

The women's faces were inches apart.

"If it wasn't for me," Tiffany said, pointing a finger in Leigh's face, "you'd have no friends. I welcomed you into the group."

Leigh looked around the room—for help, or maybe consent, Tenzin thought—then took a deep breath, and was about to speak, to say what Tenzin knew was something terrible, and Tenzin wanted to run to Leigh and demand that she stop, that she take a breath, that she *smell the flowers, blow out the candles,* just as they urged Chase to do when he was inconsolable.

But Tenzin knew that Leigh had to make Leigh's choices.

"If it wasn't for me," Leigh said, her voice bolder and brighter than Tenzin had ever heard it, "you would've gotten kicked out of the group ages ago."

"Me? Me?" Tiffany laughed, her head thrown back, mouth open. As if she were waiting for raindrops to fall from the ceiling.

Tenzin could see Tiffany struggling to contain herself. She wasn't a bad person, Tenzin wanted to explain to the roomful of hurt mommies and daddies. Just a broken one. She knew Tiffany wanted to stop herself from saying and doing ugly things.

"Your kid is the problem," Tiffany said. "There is something seriously wrong with him. Everyone knows that, and it's time you accepted it."

The room drew in a sharp collective breath.

Tenzin knew there was one rule at playgroup that could never be broken—the mommies and daddies *never ever* said ugly things about the children.

The room was so quiet that Tenzin could hear the hum of her own heart. Her hand crawled into her pocket to rub her wooden prayer beads.

Silence is sometimes the best answer, the great wise Dalai Lama once said.

Tiffany wagged a finger at Leigh's nose.

"I know the truth," Tiffany sang. "I know your big bad secret. Why didn't you just ask Daddy for the money? I mean, is there anything you've ever wanted that you didn't get, Leigh?"

Tenzin knew what Tiffany was speaking of. She had known for months about the money Leigh had taken. Ever since she had accompanied Leigh to a school meeting—so Leigh could show Charlotte to the other mommies there. Tenzin had seen the sweat beading on Leigh's forehead, had watched her pull one and then another hair from her head when she thought no one was looking.

Now Tenzin knew that Tiffany was stripping Leigh naked in front of all the mommies and daddies, then lashing her with a whip, and for a moment, maybe for the first time, Tenzin did judge. She judged Tiffany as bad.

Leigh leaned closer to Tiffany, then closer still, until it seemed that Leigh's chin was resting on Tiffany's shoulder, and Leigh's lips were moving, and Tenzin saw the change come to Tiffany's face. As if Leigh had whispered a magic spell and entranced Tiffany, just like in the children's *once upon a time* stories. Leigh had told Tiffany a scary story.

Then Leigh was in Tenzin's arms, pushing her face into Tenzin's chest.

Leigh's sobs vibrated through her as Tenzin smoothed big circles into her mommy's back. She closed her eyes and pretended it was her daughter. Samten. She kissed Samten's soft hair. She spoke in Tibetan, telling her that all would be okay, that the storm had almost passed.

Tiffany stepped up onto the couch. Gripped the back of it for a minute, to steady herself, then straightened up, so that she stood high above everyone in the room, the skirt of her green dress fluttering.

"What a fun feast this has been!" she called out. She shook her long curls and wiggled her hips, as if dancing to imaginary music.

Tenzin cupped a hand over Leigh's ear. The woman's shudders quieted.

Meanwhile, Nicole had begun to pace around the room, mumbling, "We should wake the children now and get them ready."

Josh trailed her. He reminded Tenzin of a child lost in the supermarket, not sure who to ask for help.

Daddy Rip walked to the sofa and offered Tiffany his hand.

"Come on, Tiff," he said with his gentle smile that Tenzin loved as much as the children did. "Come on down. Before you get a boo-boo."

Tenzin saw him give Tiffany a quick wink.

"Oh, you," Tiffany said, her hands on her hips.

Then, as if they were in music class, Tiffany sang, "Michael told me about you-ooo. About what you asked him in the canoe-ooo. You naughty little boy, Rippy-poo."

Rip closed his eyes, and Tenzin thought he might put his face in his hands and weep.

With his eyes still closed, he said, "It was a gross misunderstanding."

"It sure was gross, all right!" Tiffany laughed. "Does Grace know? No? I didn't think so. She's never around, is she? Let's get her down here."

Tiffany cupped her ring-covered fingers around her mouth and yelled toward the stairs, "Oh, Grace!"

Rip reached up and seized Tiffany's bare arm, pulling her off the sofa. She landed like a cat on its paws.

Michael's voice rolled across the room like thunder. "Hey!"

Leigh was still slumped in Tenzin's arms, quietly weeping.

Nicole said, "Josh, I need you to go to the car and get the bags *now*."

Rip released Tiffany's arm and stormed across the room to the front door, throwing it open so that the screech of the cicadas filled the room.

Then he was gone.

For a beat, the room was silent. Tenzin rubbed Leigh's back. The mommy finally wasn't shaking so much.

Then Allie bounded down the stairs.

"Dash!" she yelled, piercing the lull, "Dash isn't there! He's not in the bed!"

Susanna appeared behind Allie, plodding down each step with effort, clutching her belly. Her face, Tenzin saw, was bloodless.

Tenzin heard the patter of footsteps, and a thin voice call from above. "Mama? What's happening?"

Levi. Standing in his PJs at the top of the stairs. With Wyatt and Harper.

Tenzin gently detached herself from Leigh. Now she could really help.

"Hello, sleepy babies!" she called, hurrying up the stairs.

the world turned upside down

Allie

Allie yelled, spewing disorganized orders, "Check the deck! The rocks! Check the basement!" Was there a basement?

Why were they still standing there in the living room, staring at her? Why weren't they moving? They had to find Dash before he fell into the rocks, under the rocks, before the sea took him, and he floated away. Alone. They'd already put him through swimming lessons, hadn't they? She couldn't remember. She almost turned to Susanna to ask.

They were staring at her. Josh, his hands resting protectively on Nicole's shoulders. Leigh, red-eyed on the couch. Michael, his hand latched to his beer bottle.

No one moved.

"Go!" Allie said, "Go find Dash. Please!"

And like a hammer hitting glass, they splintered, Nicole running toward the kitchen, calling out, "I'll see if he's in the basement." Michael, his voice thunderous, "I got the deck and the rocks." Josh, taking the stairs in long strides, "I'll check upstairs."

Susanna had dropped into a chair and was crying, a sound that made Allie think of an animal. A keening.

Tenzin helped the children downstairs, and they crowded around Susanna, their arms goose-bumped, their eyes unblinking.

"Mommy," Levi said to Allie, on the edge of tears, "where's Dash?"

"Do *you* know where he is, sweetie?" Allie knelt in front of him and cupped his cold elbows in her palms. "If you do, tell us right away. So we can get him and bring him here where's he's safe."

Levi began to cry.

"Levi! Listen to me!"

Then she looked at Susanna, whose eyes were open but unseeing and remembered that afternoon on the beach right before Susanna threw up, Susanna demanding Allie comfort the boys.

"Everything will be okay," Allie said, wiping at Levi's cheeks with her thumbs. "Stay here with Mama. I'll go get Dash."

She remembered the windows upstairs. Did they have screens? Definitely not bars. Oh fuck, what if she left the windows open?

As she took the stairs two at a time, she heard Tenzin say, "Come, Levi, put your hand on Mama's belly. Feel your new baby kick."

Allie tripped and righted herself at the top of the stairs, remembering that friend of Susanna's whose three-year-old had fallen through a window screen to his death and how Susanna had cried in the bathtub for hours after she'd heard the news. His head on rocks. A splash of blood. Still alive when they made it to the hospital. But not for long. They had planted trees in the park in his memory. Fucking trees for a beautiful boy.

She saw that the bedroom windows were open just a few inches, and yelled up at the top floor. "Josh? Anything?"

"Nothing," he called back.

No Dash on the deck.

No Dash in the basement.

No Dash in the bedroom closets and the bathrooms.

No Dash anywhere, Allie thought, and the lines of one of the boys' favorite bedtime books hopped through her mind, like an absurd tic:

Goodnight stars

Goodnight air

Goodnight noises everywhere

"Do you want me to call the police?" Josh asked.

"Yes!" Susanna cried, and then Levi was wailing again, "Mama! Mommy! I want my brother now!"

"Motherfucking shit," Allie whispered, running her hands through her hair, tugging at the roots. *Think,* she told herself, trying to focus through the two glasses of wine she had drunk. Was this happening? The cops?

"Sure. Call the cops. Do it now." She barreled down the stairs and leapt out the front door. As gravel spit out behind her, she heard Susanna's bellow, "You find my baby!"

The moon was high and full, an immaculate white, animating every shrub, every stone with shadow. A world of secret hiding places. Her boy could be anywhere. She spun in a slow circle, searching for movement, for the sound of pebbles under little bare feet. A giggle. Anything. Something. Please, Dash.

She sprinted to the weathered shack on the side of the house and threw the door open, so that the hook fell with a ping on the gravel behind her. She yanked on the string overhead. It tore off in her fingers, and the explosion of light revealed clear plastic bags filled with old teddy bears and stuffed animals. Like some demented carnival, and it made her think of the state park and the town beach, both just a short walk from the path she had chased Dash down that day, and what if some fucking pervert had seen them. He could have seen them, she thought, trying to measure the distance in her mind, couldn't he? And then lay in wait like some predator, maybe even lured Dash out that night, maybe he had her boy somewhere right now, somewhere dark and distant and cold and fucking terrifying. Right now.

She yelled toward the front door, "Call the cops!"

Allie ran to the cars that lined the driveway. She opened the doors on the two closest to the house, not bothering to close them, and as she fell to her stomach to check under each car, the pebbles pressing through the thin cotton of her shirt, the ding-ding-ding sounded. She climbed to her feet and paused to look up at the house, the bottom windows glowing gold under a moon-tinted cloud-streaked sky.

There was one more car to check, a dark SUV. She jiggled the handle and the alarm went off, a blaring siren punctuated by a honk. No Dash in there, at least not as much as she could see in the flashing taillights.

"Dash!" she screamed over the alarm. "Dash! Where are you? Come here now!"

"Hey! It's all clear up front!" Michael shouted from the deck. "I'm going down on the beach to check the boats."

"Did you check the rocks?" Allie called back. "Check the rocks!"

The rocks. *Oh fuckfuckfuck,* she chanted, and a sob lifted from her belly and stuck in her throat and she thought she might choke if she didn't let it loose and she screamed, *dashdashdashdash.* Until her throat felt raw.

Then, suddenly, she knew where he was. The woods. That afternoon.

"I need flashlights!" Allie yelled at the house, then whirled to face the tree-and-bramble-lined path that led to the dunes, and beyond them the woods. The car alarm stopped. She stood for a moment, listening as her ears rang. Maybe she could hear her boy, the shush of his pajamas rubbing together, his sniffles, the little clucking noise he made when he laughed, his cry for help, but there was only her pulse screaming in her ears—*move, fucking move, you moron.*

She was sliding down the dunes—the sand once again filling her pants, slipping into the back of her underwear, stinging her eyes—when she saw the cop car pull onto the beach by the park entrance. The hum of a motorboat engine made her look to the sea. *Oh God no!* she cried aloud when she saw the blue searchlights of the police boats sweeping the water.

what dreams are made of

Rip

Rip ran down the aisles of Target, the soles of his sneakers squeaking across the gleaming floor. He stopped in front of each aisle, read the sign, and took off running again. Like the sprints he'd done as a kid on the junior varsity basketball team. There were shiny toys in primary colors for infants. A whole aisle of toy cars. Cars that talked, cars that blew bubbles, cars that shot up a track of intersecting circles and into the mouth of a giant, roaring dinosaur.

He almost ran right into a mom in a windbreaker and sweatpants.

"Sorry," he mumbled. He was off and running before he heard her reply.

Sweat stung his eyes. Maybe tears too, he thought. He remembered crying on the drive to the store as he swerved around the sharp turns of the dark road, pushing the car until he was flying at 80 MPH, Red Hot Chili Peppers pumping through the speakers.

He thought of calling Grace, in case she'd woken up in the commotion. Was Hank awake, too, asking for his daddy? Maybe he should head back?

No, he told himself. This mission was more important.

He was nearing the back of the store, only a few more aisles left. Beach toys, no. Scooters and bike helmets, no. Board games, no.

He was there. An aisle of pinkness. Even the boxes that held the erect Barbie dolls were pink. The plastic pretend baby carriages and tubs, all pink. It was a little girl's fantasy. An aisle sprayed with Pepto-Bismol. There were dolls that talked and walked and pissed and moved their squat arms and legs and closed their eyes when you laid them on their backs. The motion-activated dolls sprang to life, and as he rushed past, he left a wave of mechanical giggles in his wake.

And there it was, at least twelve feet of pink and violet and silver and gold polyester, iridescent tulle and sequins that caught the fluorescent light and dazzled. Princess dress after princess dress, what his Hank had coveted for months. Maybe longer. Who knew how long Hank's princess-dress dream had percolated inside the boy's perfect little heart?

There were tiaras, some sprouting pink mesh fountains, like a bride's wedding veil. There were even tiny pink rubber shoes with miniature heels. *Princess* in curlicued cursive. On tee shirts. On the bodices of the dresses. On purses and glitter-adorned makeup kits.

He tore through the dresses, letting one after another fall, the hangers clicking against the floor. Which one would make Hank happiest? Which one would be good enough? Enough to forgive Rip for that afternoon, the way he'd scoured Hank's face with his rough fingertips to wipe away the makeup? Which would forgive him for wanting another child, one who might feel more like his own?

Rip was standing in a pile of pink pouf and puff when he found it. A gown in size XXL. Pink satin bodice and shimmery skirt. A pair of matching shoes with little heels and a tiara were part of the set—$16.99. He gave the outfit a hug, inhaling the tang of the flame-retardant chemicals, and he was off and running again.

He threw the dress on the checkout line conveyor belt and leaned over, hands on his upper thighs, coughing as he caught his breath.

The belt whirred to life.

"Just the dress, sir?" asked the checkout girl in the baggy red tee shirt.

She looked down at him with flat uninterested eyes and snapped her gum.

She had been a little girl once, Rip thought. She had been filled with dreams of pink gowns and glass slippers and sparkling tiaras.

"Just the dress," he said.

knock wood

Nicole

Something bad really *was* happening, Nicole thought.

Not just bad, the worst.

"What the fuck do you mean I can't go in there?" Allie shouted, as the rotating lights streaked the silvery white dunes red, blue, red, blue. "Dash!" Allie screamed toward the black woods. "Dash!"

Nicole had her arm wrapped around Allie's shoulders—to comfort her, but also to keep her locked in the little huddle on the beach—Allie, Nicole, Josh, Michael, and the two town police officers standing at (guarding, it seemed to Nicole) the entrance to the state park. The cops had said, politely, that they'd *appreciate* it if Allie didn't go in the woods. When Allie had raged at this—Nicole had seen saliva spray from her mouth as she shouted—the cops had apologized. There was a country charm in their *yes, ma'am* and *no, ma'am* and *sorry, ma'am*, Nicole thought. They had explained that two lost people would stretch their resources thin.

There was a team of state police on their way, the cops said. The search and rescue team was bringing canines. The thought of the drooling, barking dogs lunging on leashes sent a shiver of queasy fear through Nicole's stomach.

One cop had introduced himself as Officer Morrello—a young guy who couldn't be more than twenty-five. A spray of zits dotted his chin. He turned to Nicole and Josh, and asked, "Is the boy her son?" As if Allie weren't there. Or as if she couldn't be trusted.

"Um, yes." Nicole said. "Of course he's her son. His other mother," she began, then stopped, worrying it would confuse things. Hadn't she seen that on an *ER* episode years ago—a boy refused medical care because his biological mother wasn't there to give permission?

"Yes, he's my son," Allie said, pointing to the woods, the veins in her arm tense cords. "I *know* he is in there. Please, just go. Or let me go. We can't just stand here!"

"Ma'am, I know it is hard"—the second cop stepped forward and spoke slowly in a nasally Island accent—"but the search team will be here soon. They are on their way. They will get in there and find your boy. We cannot let you go in there, ma'am."

"Stop calling me that!" Allie yelled.

Michael spoke for the first time. "Hey, man. I was a registered lifeguard. Maybe I can search the shore." Nicole caught the antiseptic smell of hard alcohol on his breath and almost gagged. She realized she hadn't eaten since lunch and felt hungover from the Xanax she'd taken on an empty stomach.

"Sir," Officer Morello said. "You'd help us best by staying right here for now."

"Gotcha," Michael said, and stepped back, half falling to sit on the shelf of a rock.

Jesus, Nicole thought, he was wasted. And where was Tiffany? And Rip? At least Tenzin and Susanna, and hopefully Grace, were with the kids. Nicole thought of Wyatt's being tucked into bed again by Tenzin's warm hands, then she imagined Dash, barefoot and in thin nightclothes, shivering in the shadowy woods.

"Okay," Allie said loudly, "Can we focus here? What are you *doing* to find Dash? Why are we just standing here?"

"The rangers will be here any minute, ma'am. For now, we need to ask you some questions. To get vital info that will help *us* help the search team once they arrive. Okay?"

"Yes," Allie said, "Yes, please. Ask me."

Nicole tightened her grip around Allie's trembling shoulders. She felt Allie resist, then melt into her arm. The wind picked up, and the cordgrass shivered, the whisper of the stalks a shushing that momentarily drowned out the hum of the cop car's engine. Nicole and her brother had called the grass sea-hay as kids, and had used it for make-believe magic wands.

"We need to talk about anything you might have seen during the day," the second cop continued. "Anyone—a car, maybe—that seemed unusual. On the road or on the public beach." He—O'DONNELL the pin on his uniform read—looked at Nicole, and asked, "You live here, right?"

"No," she said, and it was difficult to speak at first.

O'Donnell was heavy-cheeked, clean-shaven, but she could see the red-brown stubble in the glow of the headlights. Officers Morello and O'Donnell—they sounded like fake names. Like they were characters on some cop show.

Josh finished for her, "My wife's parents live here. Over there." He pointed to the beach, to the houses that sat side by side behind the stacks of black boulders, still wet from the departing tide. "In the third house. We visit often. But I don't know much about this area. I'm sorry. We're from the city. All of us. But Nicole grew up here."

Josh looked down at her. The cop followed his eyes and took a step closer to her. So close that she thought of running away, up the beach, hiding inside one of the shell-and-pebble-filled crevices in the boulders, like she had as a child.

"Can *you* help me, ma'am?" Officer O'Donnell asked.

She? Help them? A spasm of doubt made her mumble, "Um?" and she felt that same net of anxiety fall over her, that which had stopped her short so often in the last few months. Can I really call the insurance company, the landlord, the washing-machine repairman—interactions that promised conflict, that demanded confidence, that made her feel like an agoraphobic freak trapped in a cage.

"This is just so unbelievable," she managed to say.

"Ma'am?" O'Donnell said, as the radio in the car squawked. The grass rippled again, a wave of motion and stalks clacking, and Nicole looked to the path, to the woods lined with trees that seemed to be drowning in the sand and whose branches were so gnarled by sea wind and salt that they reminded her—as they had when she was a child—of witches' claws.

Allie pulled out of Nicole's embrace and gripped Nicole's arm with what felt like the strength of a man. "Help them, Nicole!" Allie shouted as she shook her. "Snap the fuck out of it."

This was what Nicole needed. It felt like a cup of cold water thrown in her face. She almost turned to Allie and said thank you, but instead she looked at the cop, and said, "Well, it's a holiday, so the beach"—she pointed to the public beach, still strewn with bits of trash that reflected the headlights of the ranger vehicles—"it was busy like it always is on Labor Day weekend. There were some families, I think. And the usual couple of Hispanic—I mean, Latino men fishing. We spent most of the day on the beach right in front of the house. I just wasn't paying attention."

Allie interrupted. "But Dash ran into the woods. And I chased him. *This* is what I'm trying to tell you. He's in there! I know he is. He's pissed at me, and he went back in there!" Allie was pleading now, the tendons in her neck stretching as she rose on her toes and balled her fists at her side. Like a frustrated child ignored by the grownups, Nicole thought.

"Ma'am," O'Donnell asked, looking again at Nicole with a sympathetic frown, "did you see a car?" He paused and motioned for Morello. "What was it, Tony? Yeah. A Honda. Green. With a bike rack? We had a report of someone loitering in the parking lot over here. We made it part of the Amber Alert that went out."

"Oh my fucking God," Allie said, and fell to her knees. Her head bent forward, and when she looked up, Nicole saw that her forehead was dusted with sand. Nicole knelt next to Allie, the sand cold under her bare ankles.

"It's okay, Allie. It's going to be okay. I swear it. They'll find him."

Nicole couldn't make out what Allie was saying at first.

"Susanna will kill me. She'll take them away. She'll take them away forever."

O'Donnell looked to the dark road, then at Morello, who had ducked into the car. He coughed and leaned over, resting one hand on Allie's shoulder.

"She's right, ma'am. Listen to your friend," O'Donnell said. There was such gentle kindness in his voice. Nicole wanted to hug him, to cry into his muscled shoulder. "We'll find your son. Now, ma'am"—he paused—"Allie, where is your husband? Can we get him here to help you? To help us?"

He peered over Nicole's shoulder at Michael, now slumped on the sand half-asleep. "Is this him?"

"She doesn't have a husband," Nicole said, and she started to explain that Allie had a wife, but Allie's bitter laugh interrupted her.

The ranger dug a hole in the sand with the toe of his boot.

Nicole tried to rub Allie's back as she waved Josh over. They'd have to take Allie back to the house, convince her to take a pill to relax her, a glass of wine, something, but Allie shoved her away, and the girl-thin woman was running toward the woods, sand spraying out behind her heels, her pants a spot of pure white against the tangle of black branches.

The cop cursed under his breath. "Damn. Just what we need."

A few minutes later, the parking lot blazed with the headlights of three vans. Nicole leaned into Josh, shielding her eyes. Two vans pulled onto the beach, sand spitting out through back tires. The rear double doors swung open and what seemed like a SWAT team of men piled out, each wearing a fluorescent orange vest. Ten, twelve, maybe more—too many to count. A siren blared and Nicole jumped, reaching again for Josh's hand. His breath was hot in her ear. "It's okay," he whispered. "Be strong."

O'Donnell turned to her, and said, with triumph in his voice, "They'll take over from here, ma'am. You're in good hands."

He and Morello vanished into the headlights, and she felt a pang of loss as she called out, "Thank you!"

The strips of reflectors on the men's vests caught the cop-car strobe as O'Donnell and Morello backed up onto the parking lot. They were leaving them, Nicole thought, and now they were in a swarm of strangers, of broad shoulders, black boots, and low, grumbling voices. It was as if she and Josh were invisible. The men shook hands with each other, mumbled greetings, and she even caught the sound of a laugh thrown up in the wind. She felt small and naked, like a child in her white cotton summer clothes and bare feet.

"Excuse me," she said in the direction of a cluster of men, "Um, excuse me. The boy's mother—she went into the woods."

The back of the second van opened with a loud creak and the Labradors and German shepherds leapt onto the beach, lunging in all directions, straining against the chain-link leashes, and she flinched, backing away, almost stumbling onto the sand. Josh caught her and wrapped an arm around her waist. "I got you," he said, and as the dogs tugged at the leashes, a jangling that felt like the stuff of children's nightmares, she pressed her palms together and whispered the prayer she had said every night since she was a girl, five times in a row, sometimes with barely a breath between. *Dear God please keep us safe don't let anyone or anything bad hurt us. Dear God please keep us safe don't let anyone or anything bad hurt us. Dear God please keep us safe don't let anyone or anything bad hurt us. Dear God please keep us safe don't let anyone or anything bad hurt us. Dear God please keep us safe don't let anyone or anything bad hurt us.*

the whole nine yards

Allie

Allie ran through the woods, branches whipping against her face, thorns tearing at her calves. She made deals with God, although she wasn't sure if she believed in a damn God. She told who-the-fuck-ever that she'd do anything, everything, to bring Dash back. She'd be home for more family time instead of heading to her studio every weekend morning. She'd play Legos each and every time the boys asked her, no matter what. She'd give up smoking, she'd give up sleeping in, she'd give up her art, anything and everything, if whoever was in charge would make Dash appear right then and there. *Please.*

She ran, dewy spiderwebs tearing against her face. The roar of the sea was like an engine at her heels, chasing her as she hurtled deeper into the woods. She felt the percussive tremor of the waves splitting against the rocks at the seawall. He had to be in the woods, he had to be in the thick blackness in front of her, which was so finite, so contained, so safe, compared to the vast shifting sea. No, she couldn't think of her son in the water, his small body being tossed, hurled against the seafloor, his bluing skin torn by barnacles. He would have run to the woods—yes, yes, definitely—a pirate searching for buried treasure.

He would return to the scene of her crime, she promised herself as the cicadas filled her head with a mechanical drone, the spot where she had silenced him with her open palm after he had humiliated her by voicing what she knew to be true. She wasn't his real mother. How could she be, when there wasn't a natural fucking maternal bone in her body? She was like one of those animals who devoured their young. Like the gerbil in her third-grade classroom who had, overnight, eaten every last one of her squirming newborn gerbil babies, sending most of the children, and even Mrs. Sealander, their teacher, into tears the next morning when they arrived to find that the tiny, hairless, pink babies had vanished, as if they had never existed. But Allie hadn't cried. For some reason, she hadn't even been surprised.

The strap of one of her sandals snapped, and a twig sliced into the side of her foot. She stumbled over a root and went down, her hands sliding in front of her, her face knocking against a tree, warm blood filling her mouth.

She thought of that small patch of smooth skin at Dash's hairline. His beauty mark. Why hadn't she pulled him into her arms that afternoon, why hadn't she bent over him, her lips finding that square of hairless skin that she had always imagined would remain smooth, infantlike, even when Dash grew to be a deep-voiced, barrel-chested, hair-covered brute of a man? They should have told the boys more fairy tales, she thought, scary stories about wolves and witches and terrible things that happen to children in the woods, stories invented to make children eat their veggies, go to bed on time, not talk to strangers, and fear the woods. But Susanna had wanted to protect them, to shelter them, preserve their innocence. *You'll give them nightmares, Allie,* she'd said.

Allie screamed *Dash! Dash! Mommy's here!* and then, *please please,* begging, the sobs choking her now, along with the snot that dripped off her lip and into her mouth. She talked to him as she ran. *I'm sorry, babe,* she called into the trees, into the fog that hung like a shroud. *Mommy won't be bad again. Never. I'll be perfect. I'll be a mommy. A good mommy. I promise. Just please, please, please come out.*

She had to pee, desperately, so she stopped and yanked down her pants, hardly bothering to squat. Some of the piss dribbled down her legs, stinging the scratches and cuts on her legs, steaming in the chilly night air.

Her father had made her piss in her pants once. The day after her junior prom. She'd been one of the girls without a date, but she'd gone to the after-parties and sipped vodka-spiked fruit punch and made herself tongue-kiss Kyle Lucas. When she returned home late that night, she forgot to take her cigarettes out of her backpack.

She was watching TV the next day. A show about a teenage witch. She had seen the actress on glossy magazine covers at the supermarket and liked the blond waves that floated like wings around the actress's face. She had thought of the actress's strawberry-colored lips while touching herself at night, climaxing into her cupped hand.

On TV, the teenage witch was making a love potion. For the sandy-haired boy the witch was crushing on. But Allie pretended it was she the pretty witch dreamed of kissing.

When her father ran into the room, he was a blur that took shape and spread, melting into the room. He must have started running from the kitchen where he found the pack of Camels in her backpack. It felt like fast-forward and slow motion at the same time, and all she knew was the *thunk, thunk, thunk*, and the hollow echo of the flimsy metal broom. She didn't know how many times he brought the broom down on her because sound drifted away until it was as dull as the tick of a watch drowned in cotton. When the metal head of the broom broke, it sliced through her hand.

Then he was gone. Her arms were raised above her face, but she didn't remember bringing them there. For a moment, when there was still no pain, she noticed everything around her. The treads in the carpet where his work boots had stood. Dust streaming through the light of the lamp. Her breath wet and slow. She looked at her hand. The stretch of skin from thumb joint to wrist flapped open when she made a fist. Blood rose and dripped down her wrist and onto her jeans. With her right hand held steady, away from her body, she walked to the TV and shut it off. She picked the half-empty pack of Camels off the carpet and stuffed them into her back pocket.

She bandaged herself and changed her pee-soaked jeans, and when she found her father in the kitchen, he was weeping, his head cradled in his arms. She comforted him, told him she was okay. It was okay. She smoothed his hair with her bandaged hand and saw the blood blooming through the gauze.

Decades later, when Susanna asked her if she wanted babies, Allie said no. No way. Because when her dad had threatened to hang her by her ponytail from a nail in the wall, she had believed him. How could someone like her, who had believed her daddy could do such a thing, learn to love and be loved?

off the record

Rip

The living room was empty.

Rip checked the deck.

Deserted.

He stood looking out at the moon-dappled water, Hank's princess dress clutched to his body.

He returned to the driveway and saw the light on in the shed, the door open.

Somehow, he knew Tiffany was inside. And she was. Beautiful in her green dress.

"Oh," she said. "It's *you*. Come over here, mister. Look at the treasure I've found!"

He stepped farther into the shed.

"Shut the door!" she stage-whispered. "This is top secret."

He pulled the door shut.

"There are toys everywhere!" Tiffany said, delight in her voice.

He followed her eyes up to the shelves. There were stuffed bears and satin unicorns and a bag of soccer balls and another of toy trucks, all wrapped in thick plastic. The walls were lined with dusty paint-by-number canvases. Puppies and sunflowers and a little girl holding a basket of kittens.

"Nicole's dad must have kept every toy she ever had," Tiffany said in breathy awe. "He must have loved her so much."

She was crying. He'd never seen her cry. She looked softer to him now, like a little girl.

"Look," he said, and held up the princess dress. "For Hank."

She smiled at him through tears, shooing them away with her fingertips. "You, Daddy Rip, are the bestest daddy in the world."

Her eye makeup was smudged, ringing one eye black, and she sounded drunk. But she meant what she'd said. He believed her.

He reached out to touch her in the dimness and felt a sharp stab in his right middle finger. He'd snagged it on something jutting out from one of the sagging wooden shelves.

"Fuck," he said.

"What happened?" she asked, guiding his hand with her own up toward the overhead light—a single exposed bulb.

A tiny fishhook gleamed in his finger.

"Uh," he said, starting to feel faint, as if his body were turning inside out. He'd always had a fear of blood, which Grace had teased him about before Hank was born, telling him he was going to faint in the delivery room. He hadn't.

"Don't worry," Tiffany said calmly, "I'm an expert. 'Member? My granny was a fisherman's wife."

"No, please. Wait."

"Take a deep breath," Tiffany said, and, fluidly, pinched the fishhook, twisted it gently, and removed it from his flesh. He closed his eyes, and yellow spots danced across his lids.

When he opened his eyes, she had his finger up at her lips and the warmth of his blood was mingling with the warmth of her mouth, and she was sucking, his finger moving in and out of her blood-tinted lips, her tongue darting at the tip like a fish nipping at bait. She moaned, or at least he thought she did. "Oh God," he whispered, then her hand was in his pants, and he was lifting her so she sat on a shelf, a rough wooden plank. Her dress tore as a Disney princess music box fell to the floor, leaking slow, tinny sounds.

Together, they tugged at the straps of her dress, fingers fumbling over fingers, and he pulled her breasts free—they were *his*, the breasts of his dreams and his fantasies, so many long showers spent thinking of these breasts as he jerked off until the steam made the paint buckle on the bathroom walls, and the real things surprised him, their softness, their scent, their salty taste as his tongue reached for her nipples, so pale he couldn't tell where the nipple ended and the breast began, then she was saying something, directing—*from behind*—and he flipped her over, and pulled her dress up and kicked her feet apart—*yes!* she cried—and he slid his hand between her legs and then slid his wet fingers over his dick and he was inside her with one thrust, his belt buckle hitting the cement floor with a clang, and she was saying—*do it do it do it fuck me*—and he had a hand on her back, and the blood from his finger was spreading into the green silk like it was tissue paper, and he tasted something sweet on his tongue like sugar water, and it wasn't until he came with a spasm that knocked a piggy bank off the shelf, the painted clay shattering at his feet, that he realized he had breast milk on his lips.

once upon a time

Susanna

"Once upon a time," Levi repeated after her, his voice slow and dull with exhaustion.

The baby twisted inside her when it heard its big brother speak. Levi's head was in what little lap Susanna had left. She knew she smelled like vomit and anxious sweat and pee—she had lost control of her bladder when she'd looked out the window facing the water and seen the blue lights of the police boats sweeping the shore.

Levi didn't seem to mind the smell. He'd buried his head in her lap and asked for a *once upon a time* story.

"Shhh," Susanna hushed, wiping her nose on the back of her hand. "Shhh," praying that her stampeding pulse would relent. The baby, she thought. Don't hurt the baby.

Too much worrying not good for mommies, Tenzin had told Susanna, her palms pressed together, her eyes brimming with concern, before taking Harper, Hank, and Wyatt back to their beds. *And worrying not good for mommies' babies either.*

"Once upon a time," Susanna whispered, "there were two mommies."

"A mama and a mommy," Levi mumbled.

"Quiet, Lee. Please. You listen to the once upon a time story and make the pictures in your head." She coughed up a mouthful of phlegm and the baby kicked in protest. "Yes, a mommy *and* a mama. And two little boys. In a big white house in the country. With green shutters. And apple trees and berry bushes. Even a tree house."

"With a pirate-scope!"

"A telescope. Yes, sweetie. And a puppy. Maybe some chickens. Fresh eggs for omelets. Mama will make a garden for us, 'cause we need some spinach and chives to cook up in that omelet."

She stroked the back of Levi's neck where the skin seemed impossibly soft. Don't think of Dash's beauty mark, she told herself. That smooth patch of skin she'd kissed a hundred times since he'd been cut out of her. *Don't you think it, Susanna, don't you do that!*

"And a baby," Levi said.

She bit her lip to stop the sob from climbing out. Bit down until she felt her lip split.

"And a baby," she said. "You and Dash will be such good big brothers to your baby. You'll teach him to talk, and play cars, and build Legos . . ."

He interrupted her, "Nah, Mama. It a girl baby. Me and Dash, we want a girl baby."

Outside, a wave smacked into the deck and Susanna felt the floor tremble under her swollen feet.

"That's so sweet, baby," she said and leaned over her stomach to kiss his forehead. He tasted salty and it made her think of the sea, of Dash in the sea, his little body slammed into the sandy bottom, explosions of pebbles and a storm of bubbles, and she thought she was going to vomit and sat up too quickly, Levi's head bouncing off her lap and into her belly. The baby jerked one-two-three times. A temper tantrum, Susanna thought, and almost laughed. She'd tell Allie and Dash that when they returned. They'd like that.

"Mommy wants a baby girl too. It's funny." Levi giggled. "She says she wants to dress it up. Like a dolly."

"She did? Mommy really said that?" The baby rolled and jabbed Susanna so low, she imagined a tiny hand reaching out her cervix.

"Pink stuff," Levi said, then yawned big. "Pretty pink stuff. Girl stuff."

"Shhh," Susanna hushed again, this time for the baby. She rubbed her belly, and after one last ripple of movement, the baby—*she*, Susanna thought—quieted.

"Once upon a time," she began again, "there was a mommy and a mama, and two boys, and a baby girl, and they lived in a big white house in the country. With green shutters. And apple trees. And berry bushes. And a tree house. . . ."

castles in the air

Tiffany

Tiffany could feel him dripping out of her. Leaving her.

There was the whisper of cloth tearing. "Shit. I tore my dress. I love this fucking dress."

Rip was hunched over, breathing heavily, holding on to the shed wall.

"We have to get out of here," he said. "Where the hell is everybody?"

"Still looking, I guess," she said, ruffling his thick hair. "Don't worry. They'll find him soon. The cops are down there. There's nothing we can do."

"What?" He stood. "Find who? Hank? Is it Hank?" He gripped Tiffany's shoulders, too hard. "Tiffany, tell me what's going on."

"Hank is fine, silly," she said. "It's Dash who's gone missing. Just disappeared out of his bed while we were all downstairs. Poof! They're all down there. On the beach. With the cops. Looking."

Rip pushed past her, threw open the door, and was gone. Part of him was still dripping down her legs. All his future babies, she thought, dying as soon as they left her warm cove and hit the cold night air.

She stepped on something sharp on the driveway and when she lifted her foot, she stumbled and her hand reached for but then slid off the hood of a car, slick with dew. She lay on her back, the pebbles biting through the thin silk, and lifted her foot. A piece of broken pot. She yanked it free. Where were her shoes? Oh who cared? She was a sprite. *A Midsummer Night's Dream*. Sprites didn't wear shoes.

Tiffany stood and tra-la-la-ed up to the deck, trying to regain the feeling she'd had earlier, of being a fairy fantasy in her green silk dress. As she turned the corner, the sea wind hit her, pressing the dress tight against her body and making her nipples harden. She found a cushion speckled with black mold and carried it to the chaise lounge, where she lay, her legs open to the silver blanket of sea stretching all the way to the blinking lights of Connecticut. Just like Gatsby's light.

Oh, how hot she'd been for Jay Gatsby. Exactly her kind of guy. He came from nothing and made himself into everything, with his rainbow of silk shirts and his library of wall-to-wall books. She'd thought of him many nights her freshman year of high school as she lay on the bathroom floor (the only room in her father's double-wide with a lock), her cheek pressed into the pilled bathroom rug that stank of mildew, her breath held so her father and stepmother wouldn't hear as her knees knocked against the cold tile and her hips thrust into the hand she pressed tight over her white cotton panties and the circling wave of heat stirred inside her until it overflowed.

She had tried to tell her mother about the book, during one of their two-hour-long custodial visits, she and her mother in the one-bedroom rental near the school where her mother worked as a lunch aide. What a stupid child she'd been, she thought now, remembering how she'd started to read her mother a passage from the book, how she'd prefaced it by explaining the book was meaningful to her, the kind of sharing that pervy Mr. Jones, the state-mandated social worker, urged her to do in the visits with her mother.

"Girl," her mother had interrupted, "I don't got time for meaning. I got three jobs to work."

Tiffany's foot was pulsing now and she imagined the blood seeping out, trickling down the leg of the lounge, then across the deck floor to the drainage holes, stuffed with sand and pebbles and dried seaweed, mingling with the sea.

Look at me now, Mama. I was one of them. And now I've gone and fucked it all up. It's exhausting, Mama. The never-ending thinking and wondering. Worrying. Did so-and-so *really* have fun at the playdate? If yes, then why hadn't they texted to set up another date? Would there be birthday-party invites and a spot at the hoity-toity *mommy and me*, a step closer to the even hoitier-toitier preschool? Will I be good enough for them, Mama? Will they let me in, Mama? Will they love me?

She looked away from the star-pocked sky, let her knees fall together, and leaned over to vomit onto the deck floor.

taking the plunge
Nicole

As soon as the rangers had disappeared into the woods—like a legion of warring soldiers with their chained beasts—Nicole slipped out of Josh's arms and walked to the edge of the path. "Wait!" he had called to her, but she looked back at him and smiled, saying, "Don't worry. I know these woods," before stepping into the labyrinth of branches.

He had let her go, she thought now as she ran, leaping over tree roots. He had believed in her, and this filled her with an adrenaline-like rush, and she ran faster, her hands held out in front of her to bat away twigs and tear through spiderwebs.

Nothing bad is happening, nothing bad is happening, she chanted between panting, so that her voice bounced off the hulking trees, their branches black against the moon-bright sky. She tried not to think of the fairy tales she'd told Wyatt, the ones he begged for because they were the scariest. His favorites, once her own, were about little children lost in the woods, far from Mommy and Daddy, alone in a test of life or death. Would they choose the house made of candy, where a witch's bone-melting hot oven awaited? Would they befriend the blood-thirsty wolf on their way to Grandma's house? Or would they remember what their mothers had taught them, that there was so much to fear in the woods, that you must always be on guard, watching, waiting for danger.

These were her woods, after all. The woods of her childhood. Her summer playland. She and her brother had spent each dew-filled morning to cooling, firefly-flecked dusk in the state park's thousand acres. They were explorers searching for treasure, using her father's rusted machete to hack through the jungle, really a tangle of vines and shrubs, of bramble and bittersweet. They took turns being Indiana Jones (the other his sidekick) in pursuit of the Holy Grail, villains hot on their heels. When the sun was high, they sat in the shade of a flowering dogwood on rocks carpeted with soft green lichens. They ate pimento-and-bologna sandwiches with dirt-streaked fingers and chugged from a thermos of powdered lemonade.

They cooled off with a quick dip in the Sound, then back to the park, to lie on their stomachs at the lip of the pond and name the spring peepers and bullfrogs; the Eastern painted turtles and blue-gilled sunfish, and to claw through the mud in search of baby dragonflies, sea worms, and leeches. They turned on their backs and watched the Rough-winged swallows feed midair on dragonflies and damselflies.

At the end of every summer day, when she exited the woods, her sneakers slung over a shoulder, her bare feet sinking into soft, night-cooled sand—her body bug-bitten, thorn-torn, dirt- and sweat-streaked, and sore, Nicole had felt relief, but with relief, a loss. She had trudged up the dunes toward the warm glow of her parents' house, the scent of roasting chicken and onions in the wind, comforted by the thought that the woods would always be there. Tomorrow and the next day.

She had felt safe in those woods, she thought now as she ran along the trail. She laughed aloud, so it echoed off the canopy and sounded like the distant giggling of a child. A Great Horned called from above and she responded, just as she and her brother had many times in the gloaming of her childhood, "hoo-hoo, hooooo, hoo-hoo!" She raised her arms so that her fingers grazed the leaves as she ran. Sassafras, red maple, pepperbush, blackgum.

Nothing bad is happening, she was whispering under her ragged breath when she found Dash curled at the foot of an old elm tree. His arms were wrapped around his knees, his teeth chattering, his face moon-white. When she shined the spotlight on him, he shielded his eyes with a hand and let a keening wail loose, his head thrown back. As if he were begging the trees, the stars—her mother's angels—for aid.

"Don't worry," Nicole lied, "there's nothing to be afraid of."

Nicole stood on the seawall in her underwear and bra, her clothes in a tangled pile on the deck. The wind pinpricked her naked skin. She slipped the rubber band off her wrist, pulled it tight between two fingers, and let go, shooting it into the dark night.

She dove and the icy water stole her breath and she turned upside down and around, her arms reaching, fingers clawing, the pebbles and sand churning, stinging her skin, and she couldn't tell if she was swimming up or down.

She opened her eyes.

The blue-green light crawled along her arms. She looked up and found the surface and dug into the water above her head, following the glow that sparked at her reaching fingertips.

URBANMAMA.COM A Community and Forum for Parents

Welcome to UrbanMama, an anonymous forum where you can interact in sincere and open-minded conversation with other parents.

Speak your mind and share your thoughts about parenting, family life, marriage, relationships, and everything that makes you an urbanmama!

Sign up now!   Already a member, log in!

It's 12:00. We made it Web bot.

Posted 9/5/2010   12:01am

(7 replies)

—Welcome back to reality, sister. 12:04am

—Whatcha gonna do with all that duct tape now? 12:07am

　　—she'll save it for Dec 21, 2012 (; 12:08am

—I'll say one thing for Webbot. It made a 500-point dow drop seem not so bad. 12:09am

—you are an idiot 12:11am

—Just promise not to believe in shit like that anymore, okay? & that includes astrology. 12:12am

—I bought bottled water because of you!! Gawdamnit! 12:20am

Part 3

Sunday

to die for

Allie

Allie woke chilled, the cool sea air tickling her bare legs. She reached for the blanket and felt a rumpled sheet instead of Susanna's warm body. She bolted upright, and her head swam.

The boys were a tangle of browned skin, cartoon-covered underwear, and sleep-puffy lips. One, two little boy heads, Allie counted as Levi snored. Dash sucked his thumb. As if her manic race through the woods had been her own private nightmare. Then she looked at her legs, running her fingers over the scratches that crisscrossed her shins and calves, remembering the fierce tug of the thorny branches.

Where the hell was Susanna? Allie listened for the familiar retching. Susanna had wept so violently after Dash returned with Nicole that the postnasal drip had made her puke twice in the night. Now, Allie remembered standing in the front doorway, her legs torn and bleeding, her pants soaked with her own piss, and although she'd been breathless with relief at seeing Dash in Susanna's arms, she'd also felt a throb of defeat. Hadn't *she* been the one meant to find him, to save him? To right her wrong?

She pulled on her jeans, wincing as they slipped over her right hip, bruised from her fall in the woods.

She tiptoed down the creaking stairs, her boots in her hand.

No Susanna on the couch. No Susanna in the downstairs bathroom. No Susanna on the deck or in the garage, and Allie began to wonder, with a wave of nauseating panic, if Susanna had left her, and instead of being terrified for her partner (*your wife*), who, in that vulnerable end stage of pregnancy might be lying somewhere, even hemorrhaging, Allie realized that she was most terrified for herself.

Then she saw the white flutter on the front lawn, a ghostly movement. She walked to the picture window. Susanna, her big white tee shirt glowing an icy blue in the predawn light, stood in the middle of the lawn, her arms open, her head lifted, the bump of their child (*your child*) hidden. The rectangular window was a most perfect frame, for what Allie knew would make an exquisite shot, but then Susanna dropped to her knees as if she had fainted.

Allie was out the door. Running. The damp grass was cold under her feet, and she was slipping, falling, sliding on her side, a hot sting where her elbow dug into the pebble-dotted lawn.

"Are you okay? What's wrong?" Allie felt as if she were screaming. She crawled the few feet to Susanna, her hands and legs slick with mud and moisture. She gripped Susanna's shoulders, lifting her upper body off the grass, and shook her so her loose brown hair whipped away from her face.

Susanna wore an expression Allie had never seen before, as if she was stuck between tears and laughter. Between despair and joy.

"What the *fuck* are you doing?" Allie asked in a strangled whisper, and her voice sounded cruel. Like a voice that belonged to someone a child would run from, she thought.

Susanna flung her head back and laughed, and Allie watched her swollen belly bob, her loose breasts jiggle under the thin cotton. Susanna rolled to her back and spread her arms and legs out across the wet grass, out and in, out and in. Like a child making a snow angel, Allie thought, but Susanna looked more like one of those obscenely mad women in some period film. A woman accused of witchcraft, a peasant woman gone cuckoo after all her children perish in the bubonic plague. Oh my God, Allie thought, can things just return to normal?

"Susanna." Allie tried to stop her arms. "Baby, please. What is it?"

"What is it?" Susanna asked, as if Allie had asked a ridiculous question. Susanna pushed herself to a seated position with a groan. The front of Susanna's tee shirt, where the globe of her belly had pressed into the earth, was grass-stained and soaked.

"It's dew!" Susanna shouted.

Allie shushed her. "The others are sleeping."

"Don't you see it? And smell it?" Susanna asked, closing her eyes and pressing the tips of her fingers to her nose. "It's dew. So fresh and clean."

"So?" said Allie.

"It's all I want," Susanna said, moving into Allie's arms. "To have dew like this, all the time."

"You're crying over dew?" Allie said, into Susanna's hair.

"Please," Susanna said. "Let me have it. Our lives"—she clung tighter to Allie—"they're so . . . dewless."

do-over

Tenzin

"I want coffee!" Harper yelled. "I want coffee!"

Tenzin watched as all the mommies and daddies at the breakfast table did their best to ignore the little girl.

She had heard the other mommies talk, when Tiffany was not in the room, about how Harper was allowed sips of her mother's coffee. *What's wrong with that woman?* Nicole had said once. *I mean, she won't let her kid touch anything not organic, but she's fine with getting her hooked on caffeine?*

The mommies and daddies were doing good behavior that morning. As if they had forgiven one another for the messy hurtful things said the night before. They had just been overtired, Tenzin thought, oversunned, away from the comfort and routine of their homes for too long. Which is exactly when she had seen the children act out. Now, seated around the dining table, sharing breakfast, they were using their *pleases* and *thank-yous*. Exchanging pleasantries on the beautiful weather, about how hard it was to leave and go back to the hot and stinky city. They talked about which child's birthday was coming up and about the new school year and how the summer had flown by. Tiffany mentioned the new session of Tiff's Riffs classes starting soon and invited all to attend the free drop-in classes that coming week. Tenzin was so proud of Leigh, of the way her good employer smiled and nodded, although Tenzin was quite sure there would be no songs about trains flying to the moon in Chase's and Charlotte's future.

Tenzin could see how, despite the cheerful tone, the mommies and daddies avoided each other's eyes. Many, like Susanna's, were swollen from tears.

But they were doing their best.

She thought of the song from Chase's favorite television show, the one set in a world populated by robots and fuzzy green creatures that she couldn't quite name. *Keep trying! Keep trying! Don't give up, never give up.*

"Hey, man, can you pass the Half and Half?" Michael asked Rip, who, Tenzin was pleased to see, answered with his own smile, moving quickly to hand him the white, porcelain pitcher shaped like a cow, from whose mouth the cream flowed.

"Thanks," Michael said to Rip. "I love me some cow milk."

"You haven't gone dairy-free yet, man?" Rip asked. "And you call yourself a Brooklynite?"

Everyone at the table laughed, so Tenzin did, too, though she had not heard anything funny. No matter, Tenzin thought, at least they were laughing today. She said a quick prayer to Buddha in gratitude for the ever-powerful hand of forgiveness.

"Oh please," said Tiffany. "Michael'd drink the milk from the cow's own T-I-T-S if he could!"

The mommies and daddies laughed harder this time, even pale Susanna joining.

"Okay!" Tiffany called as she stood and clapped her hands, summoning the children's attention just as she did in music class. "Cleanup time."

Cleanup, cleanup, everybody do your share.

Tenzin sang along, and, as she looked around the room, she saw that everyone was singing. Even Allie. Even Michael.

Chase ran past Tenzin, his energy like a gust of wind. He roared at Levi. "I going to eat you up!"

When he came around again, Tenzin caught Chase in her arms, giving him one of the squeezie "sandwich hugs" his therapist had taught her. He resisted, his sharp little fingers poking into the soft flesh of her chest, but she held on and, finally, his grunts ceased, and his body relented. *Surrendered.*

"Which dinosaur are you?" Tenzin asked. "A swimming dinosaur? Or flying dinosaur?"

Chase looked at her and put on his thinking face. His eyes rolled up, and his lips pursed as he cupped his chin in one hand. "Don't know."

"You let me know when you make your decision," she said.

"Why?" Chase asked, giving her the gift where he looked into her eyes, even searching them. Yes, Tenzin thought, this boy will be good. Even without his mommy.

"Tenzin wants to be the same kind of dinosaur," she said. "So we can swim together. Or fly together. Forever after."

He wrinkled his nose in a shy smile, and said, "Tenzin," as if he were calling her a silly old thing. But it was a silly old thing he loved, she was sure of that.

"Okay," she announced, "Before we get in the car for long drive home, we do our calming-down exercise. Okay?"

She rearranged the boy's skinny legs so they were crossed.

"Crisscross applesauce," she sang, also just as the boy's therapists had taught her.

She crossed her own legs and began.

"Smell the flowers," she said, followed by a deep and slow inhale. "Come now, Chase. Do it with Tenzin. Smell the flowers."

Chase shook his head, as if there were flowers being pressed into his face.

"Just three times," Tenzin said. "Okeydokey?"

Together, while the other children raced cars, sorted shells, and flipped through the wrinkled pages of books, Tenzin and Chase sat crisscross applesauce and breathed in (smell the flowers) and exhaled out (blow out the candles). Until, Tenzin thought, they were like two monks on a mountaintop.

pure gold

Leigh

"Sweetie," Leigh called to Chase, "don't chew on Sophie the giraffe's head. 'Kay?"

Sophie was Charlotte's toy giraffe, the twenty-two-dollar organic rubber chew toy that Leigh loved to mock, joking that *no infant in Brooklyn could teethe without a Sophie!* Still, Leigh thought, hadn't she been foolish enough to buy a Sophie in the first place, and even replace it when it had been lost?

"Chase," Leigh said, and had to call him three more times before he turned to her. "No mouthing," she said firmly, but he turned away, the giraffe's head still lodged in his mouth. A short squeak escaping with every gnaw.

Leigh remembered their last visit to her parents' house, when her mother, tipsy from her afternoon whiskey sours, had said, "For goodness sake, Leigh, darling. The boy puts *everything* in his mouth. He's going to turn out to be a chain-smoker."

Leigh smoothed her eyebrow and plucked a little hair.

Just one.

Dark clouds moved in over the water, blotting the sun. Maybe a morning thunderstorm, Leigh thought. A perfect end to the weekend. She thought of the ugly threat she'd whispered into Tiffany's ear last night:

Your precious little Harper will never set foot in St. Ann's.

Just the act of repeating the threat in her mind, the memory of Tiffany's scent the night before, the sour, alcohol-tinged sweat that rose from the woman's glistening neck, was enough to make Leigh sit a bit taller, to feel a new strength. For the time had come, she knew, to take stock of what was about to happen. To her. To her children. To the unblemished name of the Lambert dynasty. She could already see her father, his eyes runny with Scotch and old age and contempt, as he stared at her through the shatterproof glass of a prison visiting room.

She was going to jail.

Charlotte would have no memory of her. And Chase's memory would be one tainted with shame, blurred by tears. Images of his mother's harried thin face on the cover of the local Brooklyn paper would brand his mind.

YUPPIE MOM PRESCHOOL THIEF IN SLAMMER.
TRUST FUND MOMMY STEALS FOR IN VITRO.

A week ago, she had found the courage to google "mother steals from school" and the search had produced story after story. Mothers in Miami, Long Island, Austin, and Atlanta had stolen from PTA funds, preschool fundraising accounts, and high-school charity events.

The finite details—the women's names, the sums they had stolen—had been a brief comfort. But that was before she had calculated the lawyer fees and accepted the possibility that her ruined reputation would eliminate the rare consulting work Brad found, and how would they ever be able to afford the cost of hiring Tenzin full time?

Tenzin would have to move into the house, Leigh thought, knowing that if there was one thing she'd make sure of, it would be this. Tenzin *would* be mother to her children when she was gone. They would sell the brownstone, cash in their stocks, hock her great-grandmother's diamonds to ensure Tenzin was there. Leigh would give Tenzin anything, pay her any salary she wanted. Chase was not safe with Brad. Brad could barely help Chase put on his shoes without losing his patience and flinging a sneaker against the wall.

She watched Chase and Levi run around the room, *Raaaaargh, we're dinosaurs! We going to eat you up!*

Chase was screeching now. *I a T. rex! Grawr! Graaawr!*

"Too loud, Chase," Leigh said.

She imagined Tenzin and Chase and Charlotte living in the brownstone. Tenzin's husband Lobsang, and their children, even Tenzin's mother, a childsized woman Leigh had seen only in photos. All living in the house Leigh had worked so hard to make beautiful. They were in the garden, lush and over-grown in the way Leigh liked it best, at the end of summer, the hydrangea in full bloom, the roses fragrant, bumblebees buzzing over the lavender. Tenzin had decorated the garden with stone Buddhas, and they peeked out from behind the ivy and the lilac trees, their eyes squinting with joy and their big bellies a promise of contentment. Charlotte had blond banana curls, and Chase was tall and handsome, his hair combed back to show the elegant slope of his forehead.

Tenzin told stories to the children. *Your mommy, my good employer.* She talked of Leigh's good heart, of her kind and gentle ways, as she had many times when comforting Leigh after she had lost her temper with Chase, after she had yelled at him, pushed him into a corner for a time-out, flung a toy at him in frustration, retreating to her room afterward, to her special leather chaise to weep alone. Tenzin found her every time and reunited her with her children, told her that *all was good.* That there was always a second chance. A do-over.

Then Tiffany was there, standing so close that Leigh knew she could reach out and touch Tiffany's tanned and sculpted leg.

"When're you guys heading back to the city?" Tiffany asked as she hovered over Leigh like a shadow, blocking her view of the rest of the room. "Should we do the aquarium tomorrow? Or the children's museum?"

As if nothing had happened. As if the return trip to Brooklyn would act as some reverse time machine, erasing the past three days.

"I'm not sure," Leigh started, prepared to make as believable a performance as possible. All she had to do was get back home, where she'd be safe. At least safe from Tiffany.

Tenzin appeared with a fussing Charlotte. Her Tibetan Mary Poppins, Leigh thought, her heroine.

"Baby Charlie wants some milky-milky!"

Tiffany sighed and said, the sadness clear in her voice, "I love you, Tenzin."

She linked her long fingers in Tenzin's short thick ones.

Leigh wanted to tear their hands apart.

Tiffany continued, "Every day I think about how I wish you could be with your family."

"Soon," Tenzin said, "but for now, I have my friends." She looked from Leigh to Tiffany and back to Leigh. "As the great Dalai Lama says, 'If I am only happy for myself, many fewer chances for happiness. If I am happy when good things happen to other people, billions more chances to be happy!'"

Chase raced past with a *grawr!*

"My Chase needs me," said Tenzin, and went to him.

"Well," Tiffany said, "shoot me a text, Leigh-Leigh. If you want to hang tomorrow? 'Kay?"

Leigh looked into Tiffany's mascara-smudged eyes.

"Okay," she said.

Tiffany pulled her into a furtive hug. "Love you," she said into Leigh's ear, then twirled away from her, to the front door, where her Orla Kiely weekender bag (a gift from Leigh) lay next to Harper's princess backpack. "Harp! Michael!" she called up the stairs. "Time to go!"

After the three of them were gone, Leigh sat on the pilled couch, nursing Charlotte, thinking of how today was the last playdate Harper and Tiffany would have with her and Chase. Harper and Tiffany would never join their Friday afternoon playgroup again. Rip and Hank might playdate with them still, because Rip liked Tiffany's boobs and drinking wine with her. But Leigh was certain the mommies were through with Tiffany after last night. Sure, they were all playing nice this morning, but Tiffany's e-mail address would not be included the next time a playgroup invite made the rounds.

Leigh caught her reflection in the tacky mirror on the wall opposite the sofa, cut into the shape of dolphins midair. There she saw Leigh the mother, the nurturer, her arms filled with new life, and she knew her choice had been worth all the terrible things lying in wait.

She stroked the inside of her Charlotte's arm, then her earlobe, the softest thing Leigh would ever feel, and the baby's eyes fluttered, her suck slowing to a perfect rhythm, three light sucks, then a stronger suck, three light, one strong, three light, one strong . . .

odd man (woman) out

Tiffany

As they drove farther west, the lush greenery was replaced by dull, brick apartment complexes and gas stations, and Tiffany had a rare pang of nostalgia for her hometown. The sea breeze and firefly-lit shore. The sound of boat horns in the night.

She knew she would find another set of mommies. There were plenty of neighborhoods in the city where the sophisticated, educated, and wealthy families clustered, sucking dry the culture of the people they replaced. If there was one thing Suzie Harcourt had taught her, it was that women were the same, no matter what class they were born into. The rich ones were just more skilled at hiding their flaws.

She had simply used up this particular Brooklyn neighborhood. Maybe they'd move over to Park Slope. Those mommies, in a neighborhood just a few subway stops away, were famous for their elevated domestic awareness. Maybe they were just the kind of motherhood companions she needed. She would find a group of women who took family life seriously. Who ate organic, who canned their own fruit and vegetables, who knit, and made their own soap and cleaning supplies from all-natural products. Mommies who weren't afraid to breast-feed their preschoolers in public but wore the distinction with pride. Mommies who, like her, were doing it all. They were mothers, creators, community organizers, domestic dynamites, and entrepreneurs.

Park Slope would be a trek for Rip. Maybe, if she moved, he and Hank would fade naturally from her life. She could still recall the taste of his tongue in her mouth the night before, and it made her nauseous.

Other memories of last night repulsed her, too: Leigh's hot breath on her neck, whispering, *Your precious little Harper will never set foot in St. Ann's.*

It didn't matter, thought Tiffany as she listened to Harper snuffle sleepily in the backseat. She would find her Harper Rose a different school to attend. A better one. There was no way in hell she was going to bend to Leigh's will and grovel for a second chance.

Tiffany had learned at an early age, around fifth grade, when the girls began to play nasty—a clique welcoming a girl, then exiling her in one day—that it was simple. Girls just want to be loved. She knew that on the übercompetitive playgrounds of yuppie Brooklyn, one can always use another mommy friend. And she had her mommy pick up lines perfected. Most of Brooklyn's brownstone neighborhoods were teeming with stay-at-home mommies who had put ambitious personal and professional lives on hold, to live what they (not she) came to see, with startling surprise, was a tedious life with little children. Chances were that a hint of weakness (*ugh, what a day*, Tiffany might say) exposed to the right person (preferably depressed) at the right moment (late in the day when they had the playground to themselves) could make even the most reserved mommy (Leigh) open up. The other mommy sighing and turning to Tiffany with a grateful smile to say, *me too.* A friendship born.

They were visual artists, CEOs, playwrights, chefs, opera singers, and attorneys. They had worked at the UN, the Stock Exchange, Columbia University, and Lincoln Center. They were power-hungry women (and a few men) who had sacrificed hard-won careers. Women who had birthed their children one right after another. They'd had to because they had waited so long to do the baby-dance, and before they knew it, they were making six-figure salaries, nearing forty years old and childless. Tiffany saw how this made mommying harder, having to take care of two or three kids under the age of four. *Wham bam, thank you, ma'am child-rearing,* she called it, relieved, and even a bit gloating about the fact that, at thirty, she was considered a young mother. She saw the glint of envy in many a mother's squint when they heard how young she was, when they realized that Tiffany could take motherhood nice and slow.

As they drove up the steep ramp that skirted the ancient and crowded Calvary Cemetery, and the Manhattan skyline loomed so suddenly, Tiffany felt anything was possible. She had time. Time to repair before she became a mother to another child. As they took the exit for Brooklyn, the city of never-ending promise vanishing in the rearview, she started to plan. She would inject her family's home with positivity. She wasn't clueless—she knew who she was. To be honest, she didn't believe that people could really change, but there was always trying.

Those women whose girlhoods had been good—or at least good enough that they hadn't run from them, she thought—they couldn't see how easy it was to remake yourself. All you needed was a bus ticket, a few hundred bucks, and someone, preferably, the right someone—Suzie Harcourt, Michael, Leigh—to need you. She knew she was better than the other mommies in at least one way. Their worst fear was that they were bad mommies. Not her. No way in hell. That was one thing she didn't have to question. She was a damn good mommy.

safe and sound

Rip

"Snacks?" Grace asked.

"Check," Rip said.

"Sippy cup?"

"Check."

She went on and on, until Rip thought he would hurl the two suitcases out the window, stuffed with Grace's outfits, and Hank's—matching white seersucker pants and jacket, clothes that Hank hadn't even worn. No wonder the kid had wanted a dress. Grace dressed Hank like he was her little doll, playing pretend when it suited her and, when bored, disappearing behind her bedroom door, the click of the lock a signal she'd had enough.

He tried to remember the feeling he'd had the night before, when he had knelt by Hank's cot and draped the pink princess dress over his sleeping son. A blanket fit for fairy-tale dreams, Rip had thought before kissing Hank's forehead.

Now, as he stood in front of the window, watching the seagulls drop claw-flailing crabs to their doom on the sea rocks, he couldn't summon that feeling. That unconditional love. Wasn't that what they called it in the parenting books, in therapy, and on TV talk shows? The all-consuming love that only a parent can have for their child? Wasn't that what he'd felt last night as he sped around the moonlit curves of the road, the mosquitoes splattering against his wind-shield, as he burst through the doors of Target and into the blinding fluorescent light, as he raced down the aisles, ripped the princess dress from the rack, and threw it on the whirring checkout conveyor belt?

"Extra pair of clothes?" Grace asked.

He hated that she still made them pack an extra pair of clothes, in case Hank puked on the drive. It had only been that one time that Hank had gotten carsick, and it had been over a year ago. He was about to say no, to explain that he thought it unnecessary, open up what he knew would be a can-of-worms debate about an extra fucking pair of children's clothes, when Grace said, "Hon? Did you hear me?"

Rip turned from the window. He sat on the twin bed, the springs complaining. He let his head fall into his hands, and the skin of his forehead felt rough, so unlike Hank's skin, as smooth as the fake satin of the boy's new dress. When had he grown old? When had he turned into a cliché? It was one thing to be the only dad in a mommy group—his male cousins ribbed him about it every Passover, and Grace's father barely looked at him, the disgust he felt for his son-in-law plain in the quick handshake that served as Rip's only interaction with the man. But to fuck one of the moms in a shack at a family event? He had turned into one of those potbellied losers in a cheesy comedy, knee-deep in a midlife crisis, his pants around his ankles, his whining about how he couldn't have the life he wanted. Boo-hoo-hoo.

Rip pressed his fingers against his eyes, and bouquets of stars bloomed. He had shown Hank this trick not long ago, and they had sat on the couch, Hank a lump of warmth in Rip's lap, each pressing his own fingers against his own eyelids, whispering *wow* and *cool,* until Grace, ranting about ophthalmologists and detached retinas, had made them stop.

The bed dipped with a squeak, and he felt Grace next to him. Then her small hand was on his back, rubbing circles into his sweat-damp shirt.

"You okay?" she asked.

Her hand was on his, and he could feel the cool metal of the ring he had given her years before Hank, before infertility, when he had proposed to her at the Jersey Shore, her head in his lap, sand in her hair. He'd found the ring in a consignment shop in the Village, and he'd been certain it was beautiful. Perfect. It wasn't until, weeks after Grace had said yes, his sister Melanie had seen the ring, and one afternoon, alone with Rip, had chuckled and asked how Grace liked it.

When he didn't get the joke, Melanie had said, "It's like tanzanite or something, Ricky. Not a *real* diamond."

He looked at the diamond tennis bracelet that seemed to glow against

Grace's bronzed skin, at the two-carats glimmering in her earlobes. All jewelry she had bought for herself.

But she'd never stopped wearing his fake diamond ring.

"Yes," he finally answered. "I'm okay."

They sat on the bed, and the kaleidoscopic shapes he'd seen with his eyes closed slowly faded. They kept holding hands as Hank played on the floor with his plastic animals. It was one of those sets Rip brought on car trips—an emergency tantrum antidote, a plastic tube that held three of each kind of animal. Small, medium, and large. Hank named them Hank, Mama, and Daddy.

The princess dress was too large. One side of the lace-trimmed collar slipped down Hank's shoulder. The skirt covered everything but the scuffed toes of Hank's sneakers. He'd have to get it shortened, Rip thought, or do it himself.

"Waah, waah. I sad," Hank said in a soft voice, as the baby elephant hid its trunk under its mother's wide belly.

"What's wrong, baby?" the medium-sized elephant asked the littlest in a mommylike falsetto, tipping its trunk.

Then Hank's face crumpled so completely, so authentically, it nearly drained Rip's breath. "I miss my mommy and daddy," the baby elephant squeaked.

"Don't worry," boomed the biggest elephant in a Papa Bear bass. "We are here. We will take care of you."

"Hug. Hug. Hug," Hank said in each of the voices, delicately tipping the elephants' trunks so they touched in three quick kisses.

Rip stood, his hip bumping the night table.

He wanted to turn to Grace, take both her hands in his, imprison her in his desperation, plead, How can we not have more children? How can you not want to freeze this time in life? These oh-so-brief sweet years when we are so adored, so loved, that all sadness relates to one thing—the absence of us!

Rip knew he would have that urge again, and again, that it might never leave him.

Fuck it, he thought. I'm good at this. At being a parent. At unconditional love. Just as Allie had told him the day before on the beach. No one—no daddy, no nanny, no mommy—could squash a tantrum as quickly as Daddy Rip. Tomorrow, he would call Ruth, their couples' therapist, and make an appointment. There was a lot to discuss, although there were also secrets he knew he would keep from Grace. Forever, if it meant keeping his family, and helping it to multiply.

He was hungry for time to pass, eager to return home, unpack the car, carry the flush-cheeked and sleeping Hank from the car to bed—one of Rip's favorite rituals. He would set up the kitchen for the next day's breakfast, two big bowls and one small for cereal, coffee in the filter, timer on, Hank's clothes unpacked, refolded, and put away, an outfit laid out for Hank to wear to his soccer class tomorrow. He would log onto TryingToConceive.com and consult with his girls. He would start researching the sperm bank Allie had told him about.

He and Allie had really bonded, he thought as he rubbed his phone in his pocket where her contact info was held, like a tiny little present.

promise the moon

Allie

That morning, after Susanna had wept over the dew, she continued to behave like a child. Sulking. Whining. Nagging Allie, while not helping her pack. As Allie stuffed clothes at random into their bags, trying to keep the peace between Dash and Levi (*no TV when we get home if you don't cut that out, no iPad if I see you hit your brother one more time*), Susanna droned on weepily about the stench of Brooklyn, about the inadequate life they were giving their children, alternating her lamenting with her usual trips to the bathroom.

Allie was sure the rest of the house could hear Susanna's pleading. She wouldn't let up: Couldn't Allie just *think* about leaving the city? Couldn't she just *entertain* the idea? Finally, when Susanna asked for what felt like the hundredth time—"Couldn't you just say *maybe*? Not yes. Just maybe?"—Allie had stuffed the rest of the boys' clothes in the suitcase, pulled her leather boots on over bare feet, and said, without looking at Susanna, "Okay! Maybe."

"Maybe?" Susanna croaked.

Allie wondered where that firecracker of a girl with her cocky little ponytail had gone.

"Maybe," Allie repeated, though she knew, and she sure as hell hoped Susanna knew, that maybe, in this case, meant never. She (*they*, she corrected) needed to go back home. Because that's what it was, she thought. Their home. Even the stench of garbage simmering in the late-summer heat, the cockroaches that skittered across the sidewalk on humid nights, the sirens and the exhaust and the dog shit that made every stroll with the boys feel like a booby-trapped obstacle course.

Allie waited until noon to leave, certain the other kids were down for their naps, a few of the parents bound to be indisposed, fallen asleep at their children's sides. She wanted to suffer as few good-byes as possible, not wanting to go through the whole mommies double-cheek kissing/waving ta-ta to each other's children routine.

Susanna started the engine and tugged the seat belt over her belly.

"You sure you're okay to drive?" Allie asked from where she sat in the back between the sleeping boys. The front seat was stuffed with the bags of produce, and the car smelled like damp earth and overripe strawberries.

"Please say maybe," Susanna said quietly. "Please?"

Allie sighed. "I already did."

"Again? Please."

"Okay," Allie said to the swollen face of the woman looking at her from the rearview mirror. A face she barely recognized. "Maybe."

Allie tugged on the sleeping boys' harnesses one more time to make sure they were secure. The boys' heads had fallen forward, their chins touching their chests at an awkward angle that looked painful. She lifted one boy's head, and then the other, her fingers gripping gently as she held their heads upright.

She would hold them like that for the rest of the trip, she told herself, even after her arms began to shake and her muscles began to burn. She would never let go.

Her fingertips rested over each boy's artery. The thrum of their even pulses became a chant. *Maybe. Maybe. Maybe. Maybe. Maybe.*

ever after

Nicole

Nicole rearranged her mother's Madame Alexander dolls for the third time. Had Marie Antoinette stood next to Little Bo Peep, with her dust-crusted curls, or had Scarlett O'Hara, in her sun-faded green gown, stood between them? Nicole had to get it right or her mother might suspect that ten adults and a gaggle of children had stayed there for the weekend. Then her mother would have questions and ask in that voice full of suspicion, the one that had always made Nicole confess, *What have you been up to, Nicole Marie?* No matter how hard she tried, she knew she'd spill over and the fear and shame would cascade over her lips and she would tell all; the Web bots and The End and her selfish lies, and her mother would admonish Nicole in her Queens-tinged sneer, *Snap out of it, Nicole. Get ahold of yourself. You're a mother now, for Chrissakes. Your children need you!*

Her mother was right, Nicole thought as she looked out the tall windows of her parents' bedroom. A storm was coming and the sea reflected the dark gray clouds above. The white-capped waves flung themselves at the seawall, a concussion that made the floor under her feet shudder. She flinched as a spray of frothy seawater smacked into the windows of the ground floor.

She heard shouting and Wyatt appeared on the deck below, his too-long brown hair bouncing, followed by Chase and Hank, all of them half-naked and squealing with glee as water leapt over the seawall.

"No," she said, her breath catching in her throat as she slammed an open hand against the thick glass. Didn't they know how dangerous it was?

She banged the heel of her hand against the window until her palm stung. The sea roared and the waves rocked against the boulders. *Dear God,* she thought, knowing there was no way they'd hear her.

She didn't sense Josh until he was just behind her, his warm breath on the back of her neck. She lowered her heels and let her arms fall at her sides in surrender. She rested her forehead against the cool glass of the window, fogged by her handprint.

"Ha," she said weakly. "You caught me. I guess some things never change."

"They're okay," Josh said. "You're okay."

"No, I'm not."

She was looking at him now and felt her eyes squinting and knew she looked mean. "You don't understand what it's like. To be so fucking scared all the time."

Josh gripped her wrists, and she imagined she heard her bones crunching. He shook her, hard enough that an earring flew from one earlobe and landed with a *ping* on her mother's lacquered dresser.

"Don't you think I'm scared, too?"

He held her wrists apart, and she thought he might lift her off the ground.

"One day," he said, "you wake up, and your kid's anxiety is giving you anxiety. But—you say fuck you to your own fears. Now, you are a grown-up."

She saw the lines around his eyes, the sagging skin under his jaw. She smelled beer on his breath.

He pulled her into his arms.

"I'm sorry," he whispered.

"No," she murmured back. "Don't say sorry."

She would try harder to be a better wife and mother, she thought as she unfolded herself from his arms.

She asked him (sweetly, she hoped) to go get Wyatt dressed.

She had just a few more things to tidy up here, she promised, and she would join them downstairs.

"It's time to go home," she said.

Nicole lit her last joint and stood in front of the windows, which were thick with gray-veined storm clouds. She watched the children down below on the deck, the muscles under their browned skin tensing as they anticipated the waves.

She was waiting, too. What for, she did not know.

It was true, what the experienced mothers at her tea party–themed baby shower, almost four years ago, had forewarned, with what, at the time, had seemed like kindheartedness. And just a dash of sarcasm.

Life will never be the same, they told her.

Now, in her own life after children, she wondered if there wasn't a hint of something spiteful hiding behind those mothers' chuckles. Her aunts, her older cousins, all of whom had birthed children, and who had brought her gifts of bottle warmers and onesies and diaper genies, who had oohed and aahed at unwrapped gifts with gasps that had seemed like nostalgic longing, but, Nicole knew now, were more the satisfied sighs of retribution. They were the toothless stepmothers and aging queens of fairy tales, envious of the virginal princess's beauty. *It's your turn, sweetie.*

Nicole had brushed off their warnings (*Sleep now, while you still can!*) with a complacent smile, as if their prophecies were the hyperbole of old women, as if they were just remembering motherhood wrong. As her body had swelled with Wyatt, she'd created a dream collage of motherhood, pasted together with snippets from the natural birthing class she and Josh joined, the parenting books she read, the mother characters who had populated the movies and television shows she'd consumed in the last two decades. It was all the maternal material she had to learn from, after all. She hadn't known any young mothers. Her aunts and older cousins were spread out across the East Coast. She saw them and their babies once a year at Christmas dinner. She'd never seen a baby latch on to its mother's glistening nipple. Or projectile vomit. Or have its fingernails clipped. She knew nothing of the how-to of little children. Thirty-one when Wyatt was born, she had been the youngest mother she knew, the first of her friends to give birth into a world populated with ambitious women, for whom career was priority, a choice bolstered by their knowledge of the if-all-else-fails backup of fertility treatment. All you had to do was look around at the many sets of twins, and even triplets, whose SUV-like strollers crowded the sidewalks, and you felt certain that practically anyone could have a baby at any time if they wanted one.

Those women at Nicole's baby shower had been telling the truth. She knew that now. How had she been such a fool? Why hadn't she been able to imagine the coming challenge? The foresight would have helped her prepare, maybe lessened the shock that was their first night home with Wyatt, when the baby cried hour after hour, despite the fresh diaper, the full bottle, the offered breast, the perfect swaddling technique, the shushing, rocking, and lullabies. She had listened to him cry while she stood in the hot shower, blood dripping down her thighs, blood that would drip out of her for six weeks after the birth. She remembered wishing she could stay in the bathroom, that she could lock herself in there. Forever.

After three sleepless nights, she'd been delirious, and had said to Josh, as if it were a new revelation, "We can't do this!"

"We don't have a choice, Nic," Josh had said. "We can't return him."

It was a story they now told to their friends, most parents to little children, chuckling at their naïveté over a bottle of wine, on a night they'd booked a babysitter. They could look back on the terror they had felt (this tiny little life in *their* hands) and laugh because there had been so much to love since that first night. The warm doughy smell of Wyatt's newborn scalp. His first belly laugh. The satisfied flutter of his lashes as her milk let down ten seconds after he latched on to her breast. The way he lifted his chin and closed his eyes when she buckled his scooter helmet, an invitation for a kiss she could not resist. The first time he had looked at her, and said, "You my best friend, Mama."

There were the nights she had watched him fall asleep, his eyelids like a shade slowly drawn. When he slipped into slumber, his breath deepening, diminishing, she tortured herself with the thought that he was gone forever—all for that moment of ecstasy when she thought, *no!* he was still with her, and they had so many years ahead. They—the new life that was their little family—had just begun.

Before had become a powerful word. One that needed no explanation when you were talking to another parent to a child under five. In life *after* children, Nicole often felt as if she were a character in a story; sometimes fraught with urgent meaning (fevers, falls, first steps), where time sped by, so fleeting that it made her crave for more life, for a hundred years even. Mostly, the story slogged along in monotonous tedium (diaper rashes, runny noses, potty-training purgatory).

Four years ago, she had woken groggy and sore, three layers of her body sliced open during the last-minute Caesarean that had interrupted Wyatt's birth. She rose as if still dreaming, into a new story, one that came prepopulated. She hadn't chosen these mommies and daddies. They were just the players that came with Wyatt. She had spent hours and hours with them only because they shared the story, which was a comedy, and occasionally, a tragedy. A story about loving little children.

What fools we are, she thought, to love something so brief, so fragile, as life. And especially that handful of sweet, little-children years. For all their complaining, Nicole knew that every mommy and daddy chided themselves each time they took these years for granted. It might be the best time of their lives. What else was there, after this? Freedom, *sure*. But for what? For ambition? For career? To grow old? To scrapbook, to join a book club, or garden or journal or renovate? Was that what she was waiting for?

Nicole knew there would be no more Friday afternoon playgroups. Excuses would be made. Lingering fevers, pediatrician appointments, nap-scheduling conflicts. *The* end hadn't come after all, but another had, and she felt certain she was to blame.

Epilogue

Three Weeks Later

lucky break

Rip

HANKSDADDY76 <u>BIG NEWS</u>! I'm starting the TWO-WEEK-WAIT! Anyone else?? Could use buddies to chat with to get through this brutal wait! How early have people started feeling symptoms? How soon can implantation start?

It's been 4+ years since I had a baby. I'm rusty, girls!

Me: 36
My Wife: 35
Son: Henry (aka Hank the Tank) DOB 8/3/2006 (IVF #3)
TTC #2 since December 2009
Diagnosis: Sperm mobility

HOPEFUL80 OMG!!
That is the best news EVER, HANKSDADDY76!!!!!! ♥ ♥
No one deserves to be a daddy more than you!
How many days 'til you can take a preg test?
Fingers crossed that you get a BIG FAT +++++++++++++++++++++

Me: 28 (Polycystic Ovary Syndrome)
Dear Hubby: 30 (Normal Swimmers)
Married: August 2007
2 Fur Babies (Brandy & Bailey)
TTC #1 since Nov. 2008
Miscarriage 8/13/10 6w1d (ectopic) Looking more and more like IVF in 2012 . . .

MAMA2ANGELS   I'll pray for sticky beans for you, HANKSDADDY76.
Put your trust in the hands of God! 👼
Blessings to you and your wife. Bet your little guy is excited to be a
big brother (God willing!)

Me: 39
Husband: 42
👼 June 2005—mc @ 6 weeks
👼 July 2007—mc @ 8 weeks
👼 March 2010—mc @ 9.5 weeks
On the TTC journey as of January 2005

HANKSDADDY76   Ladies! What would I do without you?
Re: MAMA2ANGELS—thanks for the prayers. I need them!

Things are a little complicated these days.
But all is good! I might have a bundle of joy on the way.
Let's just say a VERY good friend may turn out to be the surrogate
mama of my dreams.

Let's hope that evil witch doesn't show up. 🧙

Me: 36
My Wife: 35
Son: Henry (aka Hank the Tank) DOB 8/3/2006 (IVF #3)
TTC #2 since December 2009
Diagnosis: Sperm mobility

XCITED_2BA_MOMMY   Hot damn! Daddy has a bun in the oven.
Spill the beans on this mysterious mama, buddy!! 🖤 🖤 🖤

Me: 32
Fiance: 38
Daughter: Mackenzie DOB 5/22/07
TTC #2 since December 2009
Diagnosis: Unexplained infertility
Member of "Clomid Chicks"

HANKSDADDY76   Re: XCITED_2BA_MOMMY—All in good time!
10 minus 2 days and counting . . . More soon . . .

In the meantime, say it with me, ladies: *STICKY BABY DUST!*
STICKY BABY DUST!

----

acknowledgments

Endless gratitude to my ideal readers, the two women who believed in and accepted my complicated characters with open arms: Maria Massie, my brilliant agent, who made everything possible; and Elizabeth Beier, my literary fairy godmother, and the most charming and enthusiastic of editors, for her relentless optimism, boundless vocabulary, warmth, wit, and genius.

Caeli Wolfson Widger—my constant reader and my literary kindred spirit—you made this novel sing with your generous, and always spot-on, edits. Heather Aimee O'Neill, thank you, dear friend, for luring me back into writing.

To everyone at St. Martin's Press—you are as fabulous as the building that houses you, and the most hardworking and patient team an author can ask for, especially Michelle Richter, whose honesty and humor kept me grounded. Stephanie Hargadon, Angelique Giammarino, Anya Lichenstein, and Dori Weintraub—I owe you a lifetime of hand-delivered cupcakes.

Thank you to *Cutting Teeth*'s earliest readers, whose generosity and kind words reminded me why I write: Emma Straub, Megan Abbott, Karen Thompson Walker, Therese Anne Fowler, Joyce Johnson, Michele Filgate, Deborah Copaken Kogan, and Bret Anthony Johnston.

Twelve years worth of gratitude to the two thousand five hundred students and instructors who have passed through the Sackett Street Writers' Workshop since 2002, and a very special thank-you to my own students. I am grateful for every workshop around my kitchen table with the talented and compassionate writers who helped me believe, with a religious fervor, that anything is possible.

I owe much of my motivation in finishing *Cutting Teeth* to the incredible community of writers in NYC. Thank you to all the reading series, bookstores, festivals, conferences, and literary organizations that hosted me in the last three years. Reading my work aloud revved my engine each and every time, and kept me bashing on.

Thank you to Scott Adkins and Jennifer Cody Epstein of the Brooklyn

Writers Space, my home away from home, and 24/7 quiet haven; to Book-Court for making me feel like family and giving the Sackett Street Writers' community a beautiful place to thrive; and to WORD bookstore for the kind of support a debut novelist can only dream of.

Thank you to my teachers: Harvey Grossinger, the very first to believe in my writing; Ethan Canin, Frank Conroy, Jo Haxton, Chris Offutt, and Marilynne Robinson, who saw a glimpse of the writer I could be and gave me the confidence I needed to find her.

Sam Chang, Connie Brothers, Deb West, Jan Lacina Zenisek, and everyone at the Iowa Writers' Workshop, thank you for the greatest gift a writer can ask for—the time to write and the permission to believe in myself.

Thank you to my family and friends who never quit believing in me, even when I worked so hard to convince them to, especially Karen and Howie Feinstein, Matt Mahurin, Lisa Desimini, Aimee Phan, Lena Kaminsky, Amy Shearn, and Penina Roth.

To the two women who have cared for my children with selfless dedication, I am forever grateful: Anna Bauman, without whom this book would never have been written, and Samten Choden, who gave me the peace of mind to return to writing.

Thank you to all my children's teachers, and especially to Shahna Paul, who taught me to be a better parent in a difficult time.

To my mother, the strongest person I know and the first to teach me how to tell a story; and my father, a survivor, an artist, who can put his hands into the hearth without a single burn. To my brother, my constant companion and a wonderful father.

Mille grazie to all the Fierros, who gave me a rich history of stories to tell, and to all the women who came before me on both sides of my family, strong, smart, creative, but without the time and privilege to tell their stories. I write for you.

To my children, Luca and Cecilia, thank you. Before you, the only true love I knew was that which I experienced in books. Loving you has made me twice the writer. I missed you all those hours I spent writing this book.

Justin, my best friend and partner of sixteen years, thank you for saving me. Again and again.

To all of *Cutting Teeth*'s readers, thank you. You've made my dream come true. You complete this book.